THE BLACK FANTASTIC

The Black Fantastic

20
AFROFUTURIST
STORIES

Edited by andré m. carrington

LIBRARY OF AMERICA

Printed in the United States of America

Contents

Introduction

andré m. carrington

In my 2016 book *Speculative Blackness*, I described the tendency of Black people to entertain counterfactual histories, to believe in ghosts, to take pleasure in seeing ourselves represented in the future, and to sympathize with the fictitious predicaments of androids, aliens, and fantastic Others as "the speculative fiction of Blackness." I made an effort to name what superstitious and allegorical notions mean to Black people because, on a certain level, I've always thought these patterns of belief are just as influential as the backdrop of actual historical developments against which our lives play out.

To understand just one of the ways that speculative thought manifests itself in Black people's lives, take the ghost example. Now, Black people are not especially credulous. We're discerning and even inclined to be skeptical; after all, when you believe in things that you don't understand, then you suffer. But there are places—especially in the American South, where many of our ancestors first landed—that for many Black people seem literally and inescapably haunted, even in the light of day. Such places are houses not just of memory but of memory that cannot be contained, and that will not rest. For Black southerners who are receptive to them, the spirits of these ancestors are still with us, as what Kathleen Brogan calls "agents of both cultural memory and cultural renewal."[1] Their unsettled presence "collapses time and position, allowing southerners to be both the ghost and the haunted, existing in a unique space of simultaneity."[2] It may seem foolish to heed spirits, but more foolish still, in certain situations, not to listen for them.

A good number of contemporary Black artists and critics, including some in this collection, make larger-than-life claims about the ways in which various speculative practices can induce states of consciousness that scramble or upend ordinary understandings of time. This sense of historical displacement can accompany the experience of religious ecstasy, but it can also occur as a result of consistent attention to the precariousness of the present. Being overexposed to the knowledge that your experiences today and tomorrow are largely contingent on events unfolding outside of your own lifetime can make you feel helpless and adrift: rocked back and forth by the tides of history instead of involved in conscious movement with or against its flow. As often as we may chide our peers for their lack of specific historical knowledge, being Black means relying on the *tacit* knowledge that if things had worked out differently in 1619 or 1877 or 1968, the world we inhabit today might be unrecognizable.

What matters is that the determinations history has made are final—for you. And yet the desire to be free of the oppressive weight of these determinations is a strong motivation for creativity. Jayna Brown, exploring the avant-garde Afrofuturist experiments of Sun Ra and his collaborators, calls attention to their defiant, utopian ways of being-in-the-moment: for Ra, time has "officially ended," and for his vocalist June Tyson, "it's after the end of the world."[3] The sense that history is finished with us often induces a profound pessimism, because it reminds us that alternative ways of being have been and continue to be foreclosed in everyday life. Speculative fiction and the speculative arts more generally offer not just escapist diversion but real ways out of history's constrictions, and our own.

The circumstances we negotiate on a daily basis—circumstances that inform where we live, how we earn a living, what we wear, what music we prefer—are all vestiges of a deeper reality that we experience collectively, even if we can't always see it. Moving through the world with reliable intuitions attuned to the way things work steels people for survival. Good survival instincts might save you when the hazards of living are always waiting, concealed. But what if "the way things work" describes a game stacked against us? What happens when ordinary coping mechanisms and survival tools are simply insufficient? As Ashon Crawley points out in his discussion of Black Pentecostal music, any technology "can be used as outlined in user manuals or can be used otherwise to create otherwise moods, otherwise meanings."[4] In tandem with our sensitivity to the way things are, we make another technology of the spirit essential to our survival: an active, searching, "otherwise" insight into the way things *aren't*.

While Black people have to deal constantly with the repercussions of long-standing historical realities, we also confront the specters of antiblackness, all the time. The notion that Black people feel less pain is fiction. The notion that we inherit less intelligence from our ancestors than people from other backgrounds inherit from theirs is fiction. But these pervasive beliefs persist. The diminished life chances we experience are relics of social systems that we overthrew legally and politically generations ago. They're revenants we can't put to rest. Along with the past we can't keep behind us, and equally disturbing, are the phantoms from the future that tell us how things are destined to play out simply because antiblackness fears or expects it. The constraints on our potential are also terminators, that way, dispatched to fulfill some fantasies and forestall others by killing off possibilities in the present.

Other people's imaginations make us out to be paradoxes and anachronisms. Seeing other people's dreams take flight while your own are tethered to the ground is dispiriting. Everybody wants to experiment, to test the rules, to find out for themselves, but Black people don't get to discover and grow under antiblack conditions. If you deviate too far from reality's demands, things can get out of hand, fast. The same is true for departures from the laws of physics or the limits of biology: try to defy them and things may get difficult for you. We are told that we have to "face reality" and make a living, that creative play doesn't pay, that it involves taking chances we don't have. As Octavia E. Butler once recounted, growing up in a family that remembered "hungry, jobless, desperate times" taught her that "even loathsome work that was secure was better than writing, which they regarded"—rightly, she says—"as a form of gambling."[5] We're led by one hand into the belief that we can never escape the hold that reality has on us while the pernicious unreality of antiblack dogma holds us back with the other hand. This is the way, in societies and institutions that power extracted from our labors has built, that antiblackness conspires to hold us back while fulfilling its own wishes.

When the sight of Nichelle Nichols as Uhura sent young Whoopi Goldberg running to the television in the late 1960s, it wasn't simply because she was on a starship. It was because she wasn't a maid. She didn't *need* to live and work in space. She was there because she wanted to be—and she belonged. To imagine oneself as Chief Communications Officer aboard the *Enterprise*—or perhaps to imagine oneself as an author, writing because one wants to, and claiming one's place in the noble enterprise of the arts? Neither role is what the avatars of antiblackness, come to terminate aspiration, would call a "Black job"—and yet here again is Octavia Butler, sometimes described as "the mother of Black science fiction," in her private notebooks of 1988:

> This is my life. I write bestselling novels. My novels go onto the bestseller lists on or shortly after publication.

My novels *each* travel *up* to the *top* of the *bestseller* lists
and they *reach* the *top* and they *stay on top* for months
(at least two). Each of my novels does this. *So be it! See
to it!* I will find the way to do this. So be it! See to it! My
books will be read by millions of people![6]

Butler's vocational daydreams have an almost childlike, wish-
fulfilling air to them. They also more or less came true, even
beyond her great expectations (and so much in Butler's work
seems uncannily prophetic): she *is* read by millions, and is likely
to continue to be read by millions, long after most best sellers
have found their way to the remainder bin. Black creativity allows
us to reclaim the power of such wish fulfillment for ourselves: to
conceive of spaces in which we are free to experiment, to choose
to engage in occupations and to cultivate peers never intended
for us, and to carry ourselves, in our lives or in our work, like we
can do whatever we set our minds to—and then, maybe, do it. At
some point every writer in this book is likely to have looked forward—unrealistically, wishfully, it may be—to their own extraor-
dinary accomplishments. Some may still be wishing.

The main value of Black speculative fiction today isn't that it
brings Blackness to places that are especially antiblack, though
it is worth noting for the record that SF genres and fandoms
have a long and well-documented history of old-fashioned racism and exclusion, about which see, for starters, Butler's 1980
essay "Lost Races of Science Fiction," or Samuel R. Delany's "Racism and Science Fiction," the latter collected in Sheree Renée
Thomas's groundbreaking first *Dark Matter* anthology (2000),
which helped to reveal the fact that Black people have actually
been writing speculative fiction for centuries.[7] Rather, it's that it
demonstrates and exemplifies yet another flourishing of Black
creativity, extending our thinking, feeling, "otherwise" presence
into the world.

Challenging the boundaries between fictions of the real and fictions of what might be is light work, it may be, for a people who were never meant to express themselves in the first place. In Rhonda Frederick's words, the different modes of writing Black people take up express "a complex black subjectivity that lives—can live—in ways that [were] not intended to exist."[8] But there is a city of refuge in the space between what the rules of reality demand and what they make impossible. Black authors are continuing to write that space into existence in the twenty-first century. By claiming possibilities for Black life that are not readily available in the stories that have been handed down to us, they are reminding us that we have the power to define ourselves and redefine our worlds.

The freedom to harness the imagination that Black creatives put into practice is as fundamental a right as breathing. On the shoulders of generations of stargazers, inventors, and literary visionaries, today's Black SF writers are carrying on a tradition with deep, far-reaching roots. That heritage has made every story in this collection a reminder of Black people's respect for the power of the word. As Delany once said, "every time we sit down to write a new text, we become involved, however blindly, in transforming the language into what it will be in the future."[9] The subject of the writing is ultimately the word. And the legacy of the word is always the future.

The Black Fantastic: 20 Afrofuturist Stories gathers the brilliantly unreal words of some of the best of these future-oriented, otherwise-minded worldbuilders of our present moment—and it is one of the real joys of the present, for readers and critics, that irresistible new talents are emerging so often that it can be hard to keep up. For every writer who's here, there are others who could easily have been included instead, and who are worth reading too: we're in the middle of a time of creative ferment that hasn't yet been fully recognized or acknowledged, let alone fully described and sorted through. Our aim has been to explore this ferment—among U.S. Black authors of the twenty-first century, most of them writing in the last ten years or so—and to convey its dynamic and transformative energies. We've cast a wide net—generically, thematically, and formally—and have sought out unique voices, some from the mainstream, SF-oriented magazines and presses that one might expect to see represented in an anthology of contemporary speculative fiction, but others from beyond that system too, who have published mainly with alternative, literary, or Black-owned small presses, or in one-off special anthologies. At least one writer here is active in a local Afrofuturist collective, which helped to crowdfund his first book; two stories are appearing in print here for the first time, having circulated before now only online.

Ekow Eshun's *In the Black Fantastic*, an expansive, illustrated catalogue accompanying a recent exhibition of contemporary Black artists from across the globe, arranges visual examples in "audacious juxtapositions . . . to show the connections that can be made across art forms and time, conjuring the speculative, freeform spirit of the 'Black fantastic.'"[10] I'd like to claim the aptness of that curatorial program for the stories in this collection, too. They reflect the stupendous range of contemporary Black speculative writing, one that includes feminist ecofiction, the crowd-pleasing tall tale, queer and postapocalyptic horror, hard SF, lyrical fantasy, metafictional coming-of-age and protest narratives, variously magical, conjured, or fractured realisms, and much more. It's a range that surely transcends any expected or predetermined association between genre or theme and racial identity. And yet as diverse and sometimes idiosyncratic as these writers are, they are more together than the sum of their parts, and address each other in unexpected ways.

For some, to borrow Rhonda Frederick's characterization,

"fantastical blackness is a tool for . . . activism, the 'making real' that derives from the 'making up.'"[11] The heroine of the dystopian future depicted in Justina Ireland's "Calendar Girls," to mention one such timely or politically engaged story, powerfully addresses those who are fighting, right now, for reproductive freedom. Violet Allen's "The Venus Effect," to cite another, tries out a whole series of promising would-be narratives, flitting from genre to genre to virtuoso effect, but officer-involved shootings keep interrupting, over and over again: Why even bother with fantastic fiction when Black lives in the real world don't appear to matter? N. K. Jemisin's "The Ones Who Stay and Fight" revisits Ursula K. Le Guin's famous story "The Ones Who Walk Away from Omelas": To how much can one turn a blind eye for the sake of the greater good? Can utopian principles survive in a citizenry that tolerates a host of cruelties? Tochi Onyebuchi's "Habibi" asks us to consider the humanity of two men in solitary confinement, one in California and one in Gaza, their suffering and their subjectivities fantastically entwined: Don't Palestinian lives matter? Don't the lives of the incarcerated? Onyebuchi's is one of several stories in *The Black Fantastic* that register and reflect on the centrality of prisons to the lives of a sizable and disproportionately Black minority of Americans: involuntary confinement, violent policing, and state surveillance are all indelibly real here, albeit in a variety of fantastical settings.

Music and comedy suffuse *The Black Fantastic* too. Beware their guile, because artists working in these modes are as prone to use them in the interest of satire as they are to indulge in escapism. The progenitors of Afrofuturism in these forms, Sun Ra and George Schuyler, were both tricksters. They have a successor in Dawolu Jabari Anderson, whose dramatic sketch "Sanford and Sun" plays up the dissonance between the cosmic horizons of the free jazz ensemble and the homespun genius of the Redd Foxx sitcom. Jennifer Brissett's "A Song for You," featuring an artificial intelligence devoted to mourning, recalls Anne McCaffrey's *The Ship Who Sang* in its depiction of a more-than-human future. In "Bludgeon," by Thaddeus Howze, aliens play a clever game on the reader by subjecting the human race to a contest with longer odds than they expect.

In these dystopian times, it is no wonder that much of the fantastic writing in this collection veers toward horror—but it's never merely gratuitous, feeding a generic appetite for the shocking and the gory. As Jordan Peele's groundbreaking film *Get Out* (2017) and his equally groundbreaking anthology *Out There Screaming* (2023) amply show, Black horror just hits different. Alaya Dawn Johnson's gorgeously decadent vampire story "A Guide to the Fruits of Hawai'i" beguiles and entices us into a world that increasingly recalls a palimpsest of history's real atrocity sites. Craig Laurance Gidney's similarly gorgeous and beguiling "Spyder Threads" takes a Lovecraftian tour of the ballroom drag scene, with what may or may not be a happy ending. Tara Campbell's enigmatic, sensuous account of the growth of "The Orb" may or may not count as a horror story, depending on how you feel about other people and the fate of the Anthropocene.

The stories in this collection come from well-known authors with long careers and many accolades as well as from surprising newcomers. There is a novella, *We Travel the Spaceways* by Victor LaValle, in which a highly unlikely, pyromaniacal couple manages to save the world. There is also the briefest of encounters with an unmistakably earthly animal, in Nalo Hopkinson's "Herbal," which lasts just long enough to instill wonder. Phenderson Djèlí Clark's "The Secret Lives of the Nine Negro Teeth of George Washington," a compact tour-de-force, simultaneously reveals and magically reclaims the barbaric plantation world of a founding father. Stories by Nana Kwame Adjei-Brenyah and Rion Amilcar Scott explore the mythical forces at play in some of the everyday dramas and strivings of Black life, in a hospital and a small-town barbershop. Among them, these authors have won virtually every prize conferred in the genre fiction community: the Hugo, Nebula, Locus, Shirley Jackson, Bram Stoker, Tiptree/Otherwise, and World Fantasy Awards. They are standard-bearers, but they are also pacesetters. Learn their names in the hopes of seeing them again, because the best is yet to come.

1. Kathleen Brogan, *Cultural Haunting: Ghosts and Ethnicity in Recent American Literature* (University of Virginia Press, 1998), 12. Cited in Kinitra Brooks, "Speculative Sankofarration: Haunting Black Women in Contemporary Horror Fiction," *Obsidian* 42, nos. 1–2 (2016): 240.

2. Kinitra Brooks, "Haints, Hollers, and Hoodoo," *Southern Cultures* 29, no. 4 (2023): 2–7.

3. Jayna Brown, *Black Utopias: Speculative Life and the Music of Other Worlds* (Duke, 2017), 8.

4. Ashon T. Crawley, *Blackpentecostal Breath: The Aesthetics of Possibility* (Fordham, 2017), 255.

5. Octavia E. Butler, OEB 2390, Questions and Answers: Questionnaire for *Negro History Bulletin*, 1978. Octavia E. Butler Papers, The Huntington Library, San Marino, CA.

6. Octavia E. Butler, Commonplace Book, 1988. Octavia E. Butler Papers, The Huntington Library, San Marino, CA.

7. Octavia E. Butler, "Lost Races of Science Fiction," *Transmission* 1, no. 1 (Summer 1980): 16–18; Samuel R. Delany, "Racism and Science Fiction," *New York Review of Science Fiction*, August 1998; Sheree R. Thomas, *Dark Matter: A Century of Speculative Fiction from the African Diaspora* (Warner Books, 2000).

8. Rhonda Frederick, *Evidence of Things Not Seen: Fantastical Blackness in Genre Fictions* (Rutgers, 2022), xiii.

9. Samuel R. Delany, "The Loft Interview," *Occasional Views, Volume 1: "More About Writing" and Other Essays* (Wesleyan, 2021), 222.

10. Ekow Eshun, *In the Black Fantastic* (MIT, 2022), 4.

11. Frederick, *Evidence of Things Not Seen*, 7.

THE BLACK FANTASTIC

NALO HOPKINSON

Herbal

That first noise must have come from the powerful kick. It crashed like the sound of cannon shot. A second bang followed, painfully, stupefyingly loud; then a concussion of air from the direction of the front door as it collapsed inward. Jenny didn't even have time to react. She sat up straight on her couch, that was all. The elephant was in the living room almost immediately. Jenny went wordlessly still in fright and disbelief. She lived on the fifteenth floor.

The elephant took a step forward. One of its massive feet slammed casually through the housing of the television, which, unprotesting, broke apart into shards of plastic, tangles of colored wires and nubbins of shiny metal. So much for the evening news.

The elephant filled the close living room of Jenny's tiny apartment. Plaster crumbled from the walls where it had squeezed through her brief hallway. Its haunches knocked three rows of books and a vase down from her bookshelf. The vase shattered when it hit the floor.

The elephant's head brushed the ceiling, threatening the light fixture. It crowded the tree trunks of its two legs nearest her up against the couch. Fearing for her toes—well, her feet, really— Jenny yanked her own feet up onto the couch, then stood right up on the seat. It was only the merest advantage of height, but it was something. She couldn't call for help. The phone was in the bedroom, on the other side of the elephant.

The animal smelled. Its wrinkly, gray-brown hide gave off a pungent tang of mammalian sweat. Its skin looked ashy, dry. Ludicrously, Jenny found herself thinking of how it might feel to tenderly rub bucketsful of lotion into its cracked surface, to feel the hide plump and soften from her care.

Elephants were hairier than she'd thought. Black, straight bristles, thick as needles, sprung here and there from the leathery skin.

The elephant reached out with its trunk and sniffed the potted plant flourishing on its stand by the window—a large big-leaf thyme bush, fat and green from drinking in the sun. Fascinated, Jenny watched the elephant curl its trunk around the base of the bush and pluck it out of its pot. The pot thudded to the carpet, but didn't break. It rolled over onto its side and vomited dirt. The elephant lifted the plant to its mouth. Jenny closed her eyes and flinched at the rootspray of soil as the animal devoured her houseplant, chewing ruminatively.

She couldn't help it; didn't want to. She reached out a hand —so small, compared!—and touched the elephant. Just one touch, so brief, but it set off an avalanche of juddering flesh. A fingertipped pod of gristle with two holes in it snaked over to her, slammed into her chest and shoved her away; the elephant's trunk. Jenny felt her back collide with the wall. Nowhere to go. She remained standing, very still.

A new smell pulled her eyes toward its source. The elephant had raised its tail and was depositing firm brown lumps of manure onto her carpet. She could see spiky threads of straw woven into each globule. The pong of rotted, fermented grass itched inside her nose, made her cough. Outraged, hardly knowing what she did, she leapt forward and slapped the elephant, hard, on its large, round rump. The vast animal trumpeted, and, leading with its shoulder, took two running steps through the rest of her living room. It stuck briefly in the open doorway on the other side. Then more plaster crumbled, and it popped out onto her brief balcony. With an astonishing agility, the pachyderm clambered out over the cement wall of the balcony. "No!" Jenny shouted, jumping down off the couch, but it was no use. Ponderous as a walrus diving from an ice floe, the elephant flung itself over the low wall. Jenny rushed to the door.

The elephant hovered in the air, and paddled until it was facing her. It looked at her a moment, executed a slow backwards flip with a half turn, then trundled off, wading comfortably through the aether as though it swam in water.

The last thing she saw of the beast, in the crowding dark of evening, was the oddly graceful bulk of its blimp body, growing smaller, as it floated towards the horizon.

Jenny's knees gave way. She felt her bum hit floor. A hot tear rolled down her cheek. She looked around at the mess: the scattered textbooks for the course she was glumly, doggedly failing; the crushed vase in a color she'd never liked, a grudging gift from an aunt who'd never liked her; the destroyed television with its thousand channels of candied nothing. She wrinkled her nose at the smell of elephant dung, then stood again. She fetched broom and dustpan from the kitchen and started to clean up.

A month later she passed the web design course, just barely, and sold the textbooks. She felt lighter when she exchanged them for crisp bills of money. At the pharmacy, she used most of the money to buy all the lotion they had, the type for the driest skin. After he'd helped her repair her walls, her father had given her another big-leaf thyme cutting, which, sitting in its jar of water, had quickly sprouted a healthy tangle of roots. She'd told him once about the elephant. He'd raised one articulate brow, then said nothing more.

Jenny lugged the tubs of skin lotion home, then went to the

hardware store. With the remaining money she bought a bag of soil. Back home again, she transferred the cutting into a new pot that her dad had given her. She put it on the balcony, where it could enjoy the two remaining months of summer. The plant grew quickly, and huge.

She got hired to maintain the question-and-answer page for the local natural history museum. The work was interesting enough, and sometimes people asked about the habits of elephants. Jenny would pore over the curators' answers before putting them up on the web page. It must have been an Indian elephant; an African one would never have fit through her doorway. For the rest of the summer, every evening when she got home, she would go out onto the balcony, taking a container of the skin lotion with her. She would brush her hands amongst the leaves of the plant, gently bruising them. The pungent smell of the herb would waft its beckoning call out on the evening air, and Jenny would lean against the balcony railing for an hour or so, lotion in hand, hopefully scanning the darkening sky.

All That Touches the Air

W hen I was ten, I saw a man named Menley brought out to the Ocean of Starve. Thirty of us colonials gathered around, sweating in our envirosuits under the cerulean sky, while bailiffs flashed radio signals into the Ocean. Soon enough the silvery Vosth fog swarmed up and we watched the bailiffs take off Menley's suit, helmet first. They worked down his body until every inch of his skin was exposed.

Every. Last. Inch.

Menley was mad. Colonist's dementia. Born on Earth, he was one of the unlucky six-point-three percent who set down outside the solar system in strange atmospheres, gravities, rates of orbit and rotation, and just snapped because everything was almost like Earth, but wasn't quite right. In his dementia, he'd defecated somewhere public; uncouth of him, but it wouldn't have got him thrown to the Ocean except that the governors were fed up with limited resources and strict colonial bylaws and Earth's *fuck off on your own* attitude, and Menley crapping on the communal lawns was the last insult they could take. He was nobody, here on Predonia. He was a madman. No one would miss him.

The fog crawled out of the water and over his body, colonizing his pores, permeating bone and tissue, bleeding off his ability to yell or fight back.

He was on his side in a convulsion before the Vosth parasites took his motor functions and stood his body up. They turned around and staggered into the Ocean of Starve, and it was eight years before I saw Menley again.

Before that, when I was sixteen, I was studying hydroponics and genetic selection. In the heat of the greenhouse, everyone could notice that I wore long clothing, high collars, gloves. I'd just passed the civics tests and become a voting adult, and that meant dressing in another envirosuit and going out to the Ocean again. The auditor sat me down in a comm booth and the Vosth swarmed into its speakers. The voice they synthesized was tinny and inhuman.

We tell our history of this colony, they said. *You came past the shell of atmosphere. We were at that time the dominant species. You made your colonies in the open air. We harvested the utility of your bodies, but you proved sentience and sapience and an understanding was formed.*

You would keep your colony to lands prescribed for you. You would make shells against our atmosphere. You would accept our law.

All that touches the air belongs to us.

What touches the air is ours.

Endria was a prodigy. She passed her civics tests at thirteen. She was also stupid.

After two years in hydroponics, I graduated to waste reclamation, specialty in chemical-accelerated blackwater decomposition. No one wanted the job, so the compensation was great—and it came with a hazard suit. I used to take a sterile shower in the waste facility and walk to my room in my suit, past the airlock that led to the open air. That's where I caught Endria.

Emancipated adults weren't beholden to curfew, so she was out unsupervised. She was also opening the door without an envirosuit on.

I ran up to stop her and pulled her hand from the control panel. "Hey!"

She wrenched her hand away. No thanks there. "What are you doing?"

"What are *you* doing?" I asked back. "You're endangering the colony! I should report you."

"Is it my civic or personal responsibility to leave people out there when they're trying to get in?"

I looked through the porthole to see what she was talking about. I had no peripheral vision in the suit, so I hadn't seen anyone in the airlock. But Endria was right: Someone was trying to get in.

Menley was trying to get in.

He looked the same: Silvery skin, dead expression, eyes and muscles moving like the Vosth could work out how each part of his face functioned but couldn't put it all together. I jumped back. I thought I could feel Vosth crawling inside my envirosuit.

"He's not allowed in," I said. "I'm contacting Security Response."

"Why isn't he?"

Of all the idiotic questions. "He's been taken over by the Vosth!"

"And we maintain a civil, reciprocal policy toward them," Endria said. "We're allowed in their territory without notification, so they should be allowed in ours."

Besides the Vosth, there was nothing I hated more than someone who'd just come out of a civics test. "Unless we take them over when they wander in, it's not reciprocal," I said. Vosth-Menley put his hand against the porthole; his silver fingers squished against the composite. I stepped back. "You know it all; who gets notified if an infested colonist tries to walk into the habitat?"

Her face screwed up. I guess that wasn't on her exam.

"I'll find out," she said, turning on her heel. "Don't create an interspecies incident while I'm gone."

She flounced away.

I turned back to the porthole, where Vosth-Menley had smooshed his nose up against the composite as well. I knocked my helmet against the door.

"Leave," I told him. Them. It.

He stared, dead eyes unblinking, then slouched away.

I didn't sleep that night. My brain played old-Earth zombie flicks whenever I closed my eyes, staffed by silver monstrosities instead of rotting corpses. Endria thought I'd create an interspecies incident; I thought about how many people would be trapped without e-suits if a Vosth infestation broke out. How many people would be screaming and convulsing and then just staggering around with dead silver eyes, soft hands pressing into portholes, skin teeming with parasites ready to crawl into anyone they saw.

I talked to the governor on duty the next day, who confirmed that the colony would "strongly prefer" if the Vosth weren't allowed to walk around in naked fleshsuits inside the habitat. She even sent out a public memo.

Three days later, Endria came to give me crap about it. The way she walked into my lab, she looked like someone took one of the governors, shrunk them, and reworked their face to fit that impish craze back in the '20s. She even had a datapad, and a button-up tunic under her hygienic jacket. "I'm not going to enjoy this, am I?" I asked.

"I came to interview you about civil law and the Vosth," she said. "It's for a primary certification in government apprenticeship. I'm going to be a governor by the time I'm sixteen."

I stared at her.

"It's part of a civics certification, so I can make you answer," she added.

Wonderful. "After these titrations," I told her.

Endria went to one of the counters and boosted herself onto it, dropped her datapad beside her, and reached into a pocket to pull out something colorful and probably fragrant and nutrient-scarce. "That's okay. We can make small talk while you're working. I know titration isn't demanding on the linguistic portions of your brain."

Excepting the Vosth, there was nothing I hated more than people who thought they knew more about my work than I did.

"Sit quietly," I said. "I'll be with you shortly."

To my surprise, she actually sat quietly.

To my annoyance, that lasted through a total of one titration and a half.

"I'm going to interview you about the sentence passed on Ken Menley in colony record zero-zero-zero-three-zero-four," she said. "According to my research, you were the youngest person there, as well as the only person there to meet Menley again. You have a unique perspective on Vosth-human interactions. After the incident a few nights ago I thought it would be a good idea to focus my paper on them."

"My perspective," I started to say, but thought better of calling the Vosth names usually reserved for human excrement. They were shit, they were horrifying, they were waiting out there to crawl inside us, and if Endria was going to be a governor by age sixteen she'd probably have the authority to rehabilitate me by sixteen and a half. I didn't want her thinking I needed my opinions revised. "I have no perspective. I don't deal with them."

Endria rolled the candy around in her mouth. "I don't think any of my friends are friends with you," she said. "Isn't it weird to go past two degrees of separation?"

"Wouldn't know," I said. My primary degrees of separation were limited to my supervisor and the quartermaster I requisitioned e-suits from. I wouldn't call either of them friends.

Endria kicked her heels, tilting her head so far her ear rested on her shoulder. "Everyone thinks you're a creep because you never take that e-suit off."

"That's nice," I said.

"Are you afraid of the Vosth?" Endria asked. She said it like that was unreasonable.

"I have a healthy skepticism that they're good neighbors," I said.

"And that's why you wear an e-suit?"

"No," I said, "that's why I'm active in colonial politics and took the civics track with an emphasis on interspecies diplomacy." I set down the beaker I was working with. For irony.

Endria sucked on her teeth, then gave me a smile I couldn't read. "You could go into Vosth research. It's a promising new area of scientific inquiry."

I pushed the beaker aside. "What new area? We've been here for a generation. Bureaucracy is slow, but it's not that slow."

"It's a hard science, not sociological," she said. "We couldn't do that before. I don't know much about it, but there's all sorts of government appropriations earmarked for it. Don't you read the public accounting?"

I turned to look at her. She was kicking her heels against the table.

"You should go into Vosth research, and you should use your experience with Menley to open up a line of inquiry. It's probably xenobiology or something, but it might be fertile ground for new discoveries. Then you could be the colony's expert on the Vosth. Interspecies relations are an important part of this colony. That's why I'm writing a paper on them for my civics certification."

"I'm not getting this titration done, am I?"

Endria smiled, and said the words most feared by common citizens interacting with civil law. "This will only take a minute."

It wasn't against the law to go outside the compound, and some people liked the sunlight. Some people—daredevils and risk-takers—even enjoyed the fresh air. As for me, I passed the front door every time I got off work and always felt like I was walking along the edge of a cliff. I'd tried taking different routes but that made it worse somehow, like if I didn't keep my eye on it, the air-lock would blow out and let these seething waves of silver flow in and I wouldn't know until I got back to my shower or had to switch out my suit for cleaning. Or I'd be opening my faceplate for dinner and feel something else on my lips, and there would be the Vosth, crawling inside. I had trouble eating if I didn't walk past the airlock to make sure it was closed.

Yeah, Menley made that worse.

I started staring at the airlock, expecting to see his face squashed up against it. Maybe he was just outside, seconds away from getting some idiot like Endria to let him in. People walked past me, and I could hear them talking in low tones while I watched the airlock, like maybe I'd gone into an absence seizure and they should get someone to haul me away. And then they could have me investigated for colonist's dementia despite the fact that I'd been born here. And they could take me out to the Ocean of Starve ...

After two nights I realized if I didn't step outside to make sure the Vosth weren't coming with a swarm, I was heading for a par-anoid fugue.

Actually walking out took two more nights because I couldn't stand to open the airlock myself. I finally saw a couple strolling out as I passed, e-suited hand in e-suited hand, and I fell in behind them.

The airlock and the outside were the only places I could be anonymous in my e-suit. The couple didn't even cross to the other side of the enclosure as it cycled the air and opened the outer door.

The grass was teal-green. I hear it's less blue on Earth, and the sky is less green, but I was just glad neither one was silver. The sunlight was strong and golden, the clouds were mercifully white, and there wasn't a trace of fog to be seen. So that was good. For the moment.

The Ocean of Starve was a good ten-minute hike away, and I didn't want to get near it. I walked around the habitat instead, eyeing the horizon in the Ocean's direction. I'd made it about a half-kilometer around the periphery when I caught a flash of silver out of the corner of my eye and jumped, ready for it to be a trick of the light or a metal component on the eggshell exterior of the dome.

No. It was Menley.

I screamed.

The scream instinct isn't one of evolution's better moves. Actually, it's a terrible idea. The instant sound left my mouth Menley turned and dragged himself toward me. I considered running, but I had this image of tripping, and either losing a boot or ripping a hole in my e-suit.

Menley staggered up and stared at me. I took a step back. Menley turned his head like he wasn't sure which eye got a better view, and I stepped back again.

After about a minute of this, I said, "You really want inside the compound, don't you?"

The Vosth opened Menley's mouth. His nostrils flared. I guess they were doing something like they did to the speakers in the audience booth—vibrating the equipment. The voice, if you wanted to call it that, was quiet and reedy. *We are the Vosth.*

"I know that," I said, and took another step back from them. Him. Vosth-Menley.

You will let us inside? he asked, with an artificial rise to his voice. I guess the Vosth had to telegraph their questions. Maybe they weren't used to asking.

"No," I told him.

He shifted his weight forward and ignored my answer. *The Vosth are allowed inside your partition shell?*

"Look what you do to people," I said. "No, you're not allowed inside."

This is natural, they said, and I had no idea if that was supposed to be an argument or agreement.

"What?"

Take off your suit, Vosth-Menley said.

"Hell no."

The air creates a pleasurable sensation on human skin.

"And the Vosth create a pleasant infestation?"

We will promise not to take you.

If they had to tell me, I wasn't trusting them. "Why do you want me to?"

Do you want to? the Vosth asked.

I checked the seal on my suit.

Take off your suit, Vosth-Menley said again.

"I'm going home now," I answered, and ran for the compound door.

Endria was in the canteen, sitting on a table, watching a slow-wave newsfeed from Earth and nibbling on a finger sandwich, and I was annoyed to run into her there. I was also annoyed that it took me that long to run into her, after trying to run into her in the library, the courthouse auditorium, the promenade and my lab.

Endria just annoyed me.

I dodged a few people on their rest hours and walked up to her table, putting my hands down on it. I hadn't sterilized them after being outside and was technically breaching a bylaw or two, but that didn't occur to me. I guess I was lucky Endria didn't perform a civilian arrest.

"One," I said, "I don't want anything to do with the Vosth in a lab, or outside of one, and two, in no more than thirty seconds, explain Vosth legal rights outside the colony compound."

Endria jumped, kicking over the chair her feet were resting on, and looking agape at me in the middle of a bite of sandwich. Sweet schadenfreude: The first word out of her mouth was the none-too-smart: "Uh."

Of course, she regrouped quickly.

"First of all, the Vosth don't believe in civil or social law," she said. "Just natural law. So the treaty we have isn't really a treaty, just them explaining what they do so we had the option not to let them. We don't have legal recourse. It's like that inside the colony, too—we can adjust the air system to filter them out and kill them, so they know we're in charge in here and don't try to come inside. Except for Menley, but that's weird, and that's why I'm doing a paper. Did you find anything out?"

I ignored that. "And he doesn't act like the other—how many other infested colonists are there?"

She shrugged. "A lot. Like, more than forty. A few of them were killed by panicked colonists, though. We don't know much about them. In the last hundred records, Menley's the only—"

"*Vosth-Menley*," I corrected.

Endria rolled her eyes. "Yeah, that. Whatever. *Vosth-Menley* is the only one to make contact with us. There's actually this theory that the rest are off building a civilization now that the Vosth have opposable thumbs. Even if it's only, like, eighty opposable thumbs."

The base of my neck itched. Fortunately, years in an envirosuit let me ignore that. "We lost forty colonists to the Vosth?"

"Oh, yeah!" she said. "And more when everyone panicked and there were riots and we thought there was going to be a war. That's why so many Earth-shipped embryos were matured so fast. In fact, our colony has the highest per-capita percentage of in-vitro citizens. We've got sixty-three percent."

"I'm one of them," I said.

"I've got parents," Endria responded.

I managed not to strangle her. "So there's no law?"

"Not really," Endria said. "But there's a lot of unwritten stuff and assumed stuff. Like we just assume that if we wear e-suits out they won't think they own the e-suits even though they touch the air, and we assume that if they did come in the compound they'd be nice." She shot me a sharp look. "But I don't think that's an issue now, since you squealed to the governors."

"Yeah, thanks." I did not *squeal*. Endria just didn't see what was wrong with having a sentient invasive disease wandering around your colony. "I'm going to go now."

"I still want to complete our interview!" Endria said. "I think you have opinion data you're holding back!"

"Later," I said, gave a little wave, and headed off.

On the way out of the canteen I ran into one of the auxiliary governors, who pulled me aside and gave my envirosuit the usual look of disdain. "Citizen," she said, "I need a thumbprint verification to confirm that your complaint to the colony council was resolved to your satisfaction. Your complaint about the infested colonist."

I looked to the hall leading in the direction of the outside doors. "Right now?"

"It will only take a moment."

I looked to the vents, and then back at Endria.

I hated thumbprint confirmations.

Quickly, I unsealed one glove, pulled my hand out, and pressed my thumb into the datapad sensor. The air drew little fingers along my palm, tested my wrist seal, tickled the back of my hand. "Thank you, citizen," the auxiliary said, and wandered off.

I tucked my exposed hand under my other arm and hurried back toward my room to sterilize hand and glove and put my suit back together.

I went outside again. I don't know why. Specialized insanity, maybe.

Actually, no. This was like those people on Mulciber who'd go outside in their hazard suits even though the Mulciber colony was on a patch of stable ground that didn't extend much beyond the habitat, and they always ran the risk of falling into a magma chamber or having a glob of superheated rock smash their face-plate in. Some people find something terrifying and then just have to go out to stare it in the face. Another one of evolution's less-than-brilliant moves.

Vosth-Menley was stretching his stolen muscles by the shore of the Starve. I could see the muscles moving under his skin. He laced his fingers together and pulled his hands above his head. He planted his feet and bent at the waist so far that his forehead almost touched the ground. I couldn't do any of that.

I went through the usual colony-prescribed exercises every morning. The envirosuit pinched and chafed, but like hell I was going to show off my body any longer than I had to. Vosth-Menley didn't have that problem. The Vosth could walk around naked, for all they cared, if they had a body to *be* naked.

The Vosth noticed me and Vosth-Menley turned around. He clomped his way over, and I tried not to back away.

The air is temperate at this time, at these coordinates, Vosth-Menley said.

I looked over the turbid water. It caught the turquoise of the sky and reflected slate, underlaid with silver. "Why do you call this the Ocean of Starve?"

Vosth-Menley turned back to the Ocean. His gaze ran over the surface, eyes moving in separate directions, and his mouth slacked open.

Our genetic structure was encoded in a meteorite, he said. *We impacted this world long ago and altered the ecosystem. We adapted to rely on the heat of free volcanic activity, which was not this world's stable state. When the world cooled our rate of starvation exceeded our rate of adaptation. Here, underwater vents provided heat to sustain our adaptation until we could survive.*

My stomach turned. "Why do you take people over?"

Your bodies are warm and comfortable.

"Even though we proved sapience to you," I said.

Vosth-Menley didn't answer.

"What would you do if I took off my envirosuit?"

You would feel the air, Vosth-Menley said, like I wouldn't notice that he hadn't answered the question.

"I know that. What would *you* do? You, the Vosth?"

You would feel the gentle sun warming your skin.

I backed away. Nothing was stopping him from lunging and tearing off my suit. Not if what Endria said was true: that it was the law of the wild out here. Why didn't he? "You don't see anything wrong with that."

I wished he would blink. Maybe gesture. Tapdance. Anything. *You have been reacting to us with fear.*

The conversation was an exercise in stating the useless and obvious. "I don't want to end up like Menley," I said. "Can't you understand that? Would you want that to happen to you?"

We are the dominant species, the Vosth said. *We would not be taken over.*

"Empathy," I muttered. I wasn't expecting him to hear it. "Learn it."

We are not averse to learning, the Vosth said. *Do you engage in demonstration?*

Demonstration? Empathy? I shook my head. "You don't get what I'm saying."

Would we be better if we understood? he asked, and stumbled forward with sudden intensity.

I jumped back, ready to fight him off, ready to run.

We want to understand.

[Can the Vosth change?] was the first thing I wrote to Endria when I sat down at my terminal. I don't know why I kept asking her things. Maybe despite the fact that she was five years my junior and a pain in the rectum she was still less annoying than the diplomatic auditors. Maybe because she was the only person who didn't look at me like they might have to call Security Response if I walked up. I didn't really talk to anyone on my off hours.

She never wrote me back. Instead, she showed up at my door. "You're going to have to be a little more specific."

"Hello, Endria," I said as I let her in. "Nice of you to stop by. You couldn't have just written that out?"

She huffed. "You have a pretty nice room, you know that? The quarters I can get if I want to move out of our family's allotment are all little closets."

"Get a job," I said. "Look, when you said the Vosth—"

"Don't you ever take that suit off?" she interrupted. "I mean, we're inside about five different air filtration systems and an airlock or two."

I ran a hand around the collar of my envirosuit. "I like having it on."

"How do you eat?"

"I open it to eat." And shower, and piss, and I took it off to change into other suits and have the ones I'd been wearing cleaned. I just didn't enjoy it. "Can you reason with the Vosth?"

Endria shook her head. "More specific."

"Do they change their behavior?" I asked.

Endria wandered over to my couch and sat down, giving me a disparaging look. "*Nice* specifics. They adapt, if that's what you mean. Didn't you listen at your initiation? They came to this planet and couldn't survive here so they adapted. Some people think that's why we can negotiate with them at all."

I didn't follow. "What does that have to do with negotiation?"

"Well, it's all theoretical," she said, and tried to fish something out of her teeth with her pinky.

"Endria. Negotiation. Adaptation. What?"

"They *adapt*," she said. "They fell out of the sky and almost died here and then they adapted and they became the dominant species. Then we landed, which is way better than falling, and we have all this technology they don't have, and they can't just read our minds, even if they take us over, so wouldn't you negotiate for that? To stay the dominant species? I think they want to be more like us."

Would we be better if we understood, the Vosth had asked. "They said they took over colonists because our bodies were comfortable," I said.

Endria shrugged. "Maybe being dominant is comfortable for them."

I ran a hand over my helmet. "Charming."

"I mean, letting them be dominant sure isn't comfortable for you."

I glared. "What, it's comfortable for you?"

"They're not that bad," Endria said. "I mean, they're not territorial or anything. They just do their thing. When I'm a governor, I want to see if we can work together."

"Yeah. Us and the body-snatchers."

Endria tilted her head at me. "You know, I think it would be kinda neat, sharing your body with the Vosth. I mean, if it wasn't a permanent thing. I bet you'd get all sorts of new perspectives."

I gaped. I don't think Endria saw my expression through the helmet, but it was disturbing enough that she didn't share it. "It *is* a permanent thing! And you don't share—you don't get control. They take you over and you just die. There's probably nothing *left* of you. Or if there is, you're just stuck in your head, screaming."

"And that's why you're asking if the Vosth can change?" Endria asked.

"I'm asking because—" I started, and then couldn't finish that sentence.

Endria smiled. It was a nasty sort of hah-I-knew-it smile. "See?" she said, hopping off the couch and heading for the door. "You *are* interested in Vosth research."

Twenty minutes later someone knocked on my door. I opened it, thinking it was Endria back to irritate me. No. In the corridor outside my room stood a wide-faced, high-collared balding man, with an expression like he'd been eating ascorbic acid and a badge on his lapel reading DIPLOMATIC AUDITOR in big bold letters.

He'd even brought a datapad.

"This is a notice, citizen," he said. "You're not authorized to engage in diplomatic action with the Vosth."

"I'm not engaging in diplomatic action," I said, shuffling through possible excuses. It'd be easier if I had any idea what I *was* doing. "I'm . . . engaging in research."

He didn't look convinced.

"Civil research," I said, picking up a pen from my desk and wagging it at him like he should know better. "Helping Endria with her civics certification. Didn't she fill out the right forms to make me one of her resources?"

There were no forms, as far as I knew. Still, if there were, I could probably shuffle off the responsibility onto Endria, and if there weren't, the sourface in front of me would probably go and draft some up to mollify himself. Either way, I was off the hook for a moment.

He marked something down on his datapad. "I'm going to check into this," he warned.

At which point he'd argue his case against Endria. Poor bastards, both of them.

"Expect further communication from a member of the governing commission," he warned. Satisfied with that threat, he turned and went away.

For about a day, I decided work was safer. If I kept to the restricted-access parts of the waste reclamation facility I could cut down on Endria sightings, and I could work long hours. Surely the governors wouldn't work late just to harass me.

It wasn't a long-term solution. Still, I thought it'd be longer-term than one work shift.

I got back to my room and my terminal was blinking, and when I sat down it triggered an automatic callback and put me on standby for two minutes. Now, in theory automatic callbacks were only for high-priority colony business, which, considering I'd seen my supervisor not ten minutes ago and I wasn't involved in anything important in governance, I expected to mean that Endria wanted something and they took civics certification courses way more seriously than I'd thought. I went to get a drink while it was trying to connect.

And I came back to a line of text on an encrypted channel, coming from the office of the Prime Governor.

Most of my water ended up on my boots.

[Sorry I'm doing this over text,] she wrote. [I just wanted an official record of our conversation.]

When a governor wants an official record of your conversation, you're fucked.

[What can I do for you?] I typed back.

[Someone stopped by to talk to you,] she went on, the lines

spooling out over the screen in real-time. [About your not being authorized to engage in diplomatic action.]

I had expected that to be defused, not to escalate. Escalating up to the Prime Governor had been right out. [I still believe that I wasn't engaging in diplomatic—] I started, but she typed right over it.

[How would you like authorization?]

That hadn't been on the list of possibilities, either.

[I'm sorry?] I typed. What I almost typed, and might have typed if I didn't value my civil liberties, was *I recycle shit for a living. My skillset is not what you're looking for.*

[You may be aware that we're pioneering a new focus of study into the Vosth,] the Governor typed.

Vosth research. I wondered if Endria had recommended me upward. [Yes, ma'am,] I wrote.

[We now believe that we can reverse the effects of Vosth colonization of a human host.]

I looked at my water. I looked at my boots. After a moment, I typed [Ma'am?] and got up for another glass. I needed it.

I came back to a paragraph explaining [You've been in contact with one of the infested colonists. We'd like you to bring him back to the compound for experimentation.]

Okay. So long as I was just being asked to harvest test subjects. [You want to cure Menley?]

[We believe it unlikely that human consciousness would survive anywhere on the order of years,] she typed back, and my stomach twisted like it had talking to Menley. [This would be a proof of concept which could be applied to the more recently infected.]

And Menley wasn't someone who'd be welcomed back into the colony, I read between the lines. I should've asked Endria who had sat on the council that decided Menley's sentence. Was this particular Prime Governor serving, back then? Why did I never remember these things? Why did I never think to ask?

[So, you would extract the Vosth,] I started, and was going to write *leaving a corpse*?, maybe hoping that we'd at least get a breathing body. She interrupted me again.

[The Vosth parasite organisms would not be extracted. They would die.]

My mouth was dry, but the idea of drinking water made me nauseous. It was like anyone or anything in Menley's body was fair game for anyone.

[I want to be clear with you,] she said. Dammit. She could have just lied like they did in every dramatic work I'd ever read. Then, if the truth ever came out, I could be horrified but still secure in the knowledge that there was no way I could have known. No. I just got told to kidnap someone so the scientists could kill him. I wasn't even saving anyone. Well, maybe in the future, *if* anyone got infested again.

Anyone the governors felt like curing, anyway.

Then she had to go and make it worse.

[We would not be in violation of any treaties or rules of conduct,] she wrote. [If we can develop a cure for or immunity to Vosth infestation, the de facto arrangement in place between our colony and the Vosth will be rendered null, and the restrictions imposed on our activities on the planet will become obsolete.]

I wished Endria was there. She could interpret this. [Isn't this an act of war?]

[We're confident that the Vosth will regard an unwarranted act of aggression as an expression of natural law,] the Governor explained.

That didn't make me feel better, and I think it translated to *yes*. [I thought it was understood that things like that wouldn't happen.]

[It was understood that the dominant species could, at any time, exercise their natural rights,] the Governor explained. [Perhaps it's time they learned that they aren't the dominant species anymore.]

We believe the ambient temperature to be pleasant for human senses today, Vosth-Menley told me when I got to the Ocean of Starve. I was beginning to wonder whether his reassurances were predation or a mountain of culture skew.

"What is your obsession with me feeling the air?" I asked him. Them. The Vosth.

You would be safe, Vosth-Menley insisted.

I should have asked Endria if the Vosth could lie. I should have kept a running list of things I needed to ask. "Listen," I said.

We would like to understand, Vosth-Menley said again.

I read a lot of Earth lit. I'd never seen a butterfly, but I knew the metaphor of kids who'd pull off their wings. Looking at Menley, I wondered if the Vosth were like children, oblivious to their own cruelty. "What would you do if someone could take you over?"

Our biology is not comparable to yours, Vosth-Menley said.

Bad hypothetical. "What would you do if someone tried to kill you?"

It is our perception of reality that species attempt to prolong their own existence, he said.

"Yeah." I was having trouble following my own conversation. "Look, you're a dominant species, and we're supposed to have a reciprocal relationship, but you take people over and—look." I'd gone past talking myself in circles and was talking myself in scatterplots.

The back of my neck itched, and I couldn't ignore it.

"What if I *do* want to take off my suit?" I asked, and then scatterplotted, "Do you have any reason to lie to me?"

The Vosth considered. *Yes.*

Oh. Okay. Great.

Our present actions are concurrent with a different directive, he added. *There is reason to establish honesty.*

Nothing was stopping him from attacking. He could have torn off my suit or helmet by now. Even if it was a risk, and it *was* a risk, and even if I had a phobia the size of the meteorite the Vosth had ridden in . . .

I'd seen how many Vosth had swarmed over Menley's whole body, and how long it had taken him to stop twitching. If it was just a few of them, I might be able to run back to the compound. Then, if the governors really had a cure, they could cure me. And I'd feel fine about tricking the Vosth into being test subjects if they'd tricked me into being a host. That's what I told myself. I didn't feel fine about anything.

I brought my gloves to the catch on my helmet.

Two minutes later I was still standing like that, with the catch still sealed, and Vosth-Menley was still staring.

"You could come back to the compound with me," I said. "The governors would love to see you."

We are curious as to the conditions of your constructed habitat, Vosth-Menley said.

Yeah, I thought, *but are you coming back as a plague bearer or an experiment?*

I squeezed my eyes shut, and pried my helmet off.

I'd lost way too many referents.

The outside air closed around my face with too many smells I couldn't identify or describe, other than "nothing like sterile air" and "nothing like my room or my shower." Every nerve on my head and neck screamed for broadcast time, registering the temperature of the air, the little breezes through the hairs on my nape, the warmth of direct sunlight. My heart was racing. I was breathing way too fast and even with my eyes shut I was overloaded on stimuli.

I waded my way through. It took time, but amidst the slog of what I was feeling, I eventually noticed something I wasn't: Anything identifiable as Vosth infestation.

I opened my eyes.

Vosth-Menley was standing just where he had been, watching just as he had been. And I was breathing, with my skin touching the outside air.

Touching the air. That which touched the air belonged to the Vosth. I wasn't belonging to the Vosth.

I looked toward the Ocean. Its silver underlayer was still there, calm beneath the surface.

I took a breath. I tasted the outside world, the gas balance, the smell of vegetation working its way from my nostrils to the back of my throat. This was a Vosth world, unless the governors made it a human world, and I wasn't sure how to feel about that. Looking back to Vosth-Menley, I didn't know how he'd feel about it either.

"You came from beyond the shell of atmosphere," I said. "Like we did, right?"

Vosth-Menley said, *Our genetic predecessors came to this world on a meteorite.*

"And you adapted, right?" I almost ran a hand over my helmet, but stopped before I touched my hair. I hadn't sterilized my gloves. Never mind that my head wasn't in a sterile environment anymore either. "Do you understand that we adapt?"

It is our perception of reality that living organisms adapt, he said.

That was a yes. Maybe. "Look, we don't have to fight for dominance, do we?" I spread my hands. "Like, if you go off and reinvent technology now that you have hands to build things with, you don't need to come back here and threaten us. We can have an equilibrium."

His eyes were as dead as usual. I had no idea what understanding on a Vosth colonist would look like.

"We'd both be better."

We are not averse to an equilibrium, Vosth-Menley said.

I swallowed. "Then you've gotta go now." Then, when I thought he didn't understand, "The governors are adapting a way to cure you. To kill you. Making us the dominant species. Look, I'm . . . telling you what will happen, and I'm giving you the option not to let us do it."

Vosth-Menley watched me for a moment. Then he turned, and walked back toward the Ocean of Starve.

Interspecies incident, said a little voice at the corner of my mind. It sounded like Endria. Sterile or not, I sealed my helmet back onto my e-suit and walked back toward the colony at double-time.

That night I filed a report saying that I'd invited Vosth-Menley back, but he'd declined for reasons I couldn't make sense of. Communications barrier. I thought of telling the Prime Governor that she should have sent a diplomatic auditor, but didn't.

I didn't hear anything until the next day when a survey buggy came back in, and its driver hopped down and said that something strange happened at the Ocean of Starve. Far from being its usual murky silver, it was perfectly clear and reflecting the sky. He said it to a governor, but news spread fast. It came to me via Endria as I was walking out of my lab.

"The only thing that would cause that would be a mass migration of the Vosth, but that's not something we've seen in their behavior before now!" She glared at me like I might know something, which, of course, I did.

A diplomatic auditor came by later to take a complete transcript of my last interaction with Vosth-Menley. I left most of it out.

Survey buggies kept going out. People walked down to the Ocean shore. Auditors flashed radio signals out of the communications booth, but no one answered. The Vosth had vanished, and that was all anyone could tell.

I stopped wearing my envirosuit.

The first day, stepping out of my door, I felt lightbodied, lightheaded, not entirely there. I felt like I'd walked out of my shower without getting dressed. I had to force myself to go forward instead of back, back to grab my envirosuit, to make myself decent.

I walked into the hall where every moment was the sensory overload of air on my skin, where my arms and legs felt loose, where everyone could see the expressions on my face. That was as frightening as the Vosth. I'd just left behind the environmental advantage I'd had since I was ten.

But I was adapting.

Bludgeon

As luck would have it, mankind's first official interaction with an alien species (that was not covered up success-fully by the government) was with the warlords of Hurumpharump. If you sound like you are clearing your throat when you are saying it, you are saying it right; when in doubt, cough and add more phlegm.

When their mighty spaceships, fifty miles wide, appeared above every major city on Earth, humanity wet its collective pants and waited for the end. For ten days, they hovered there. I hate to admit it, but we did not behave very well. There was the requisite gnashing of teeth, weeping, some self-flagellation amongst the Catholics who were forced to admit that perhaps we had not been made in His image after all. Seeing how these aliens had been able to do something we could not, perhaps He was made in their image.

Wholesale looting, riots, destruction of government property were everywhere until martial law had been declared nearly all over the world. Most governments cracked down on their popula-tions until quiet streets were the order of the day. People went out to shop for food and supplies and quickly returned home. Stock markets all over the planet went offline, for fear of catastrophic collapse during this time of crisis. But nothing happened.

After two weeks of seeing the alien ships hovering there, people went back to work and tried to ignore them. Once people had resumed their normal lives, as normal as one's life could be with a fifty-mile-wide alien spaceship hovering above one's city, the alien ships simply disappeared. All but one. The ship over New York did not leave.

News reports of the disappearance of the other alien craft caused jubilation in some, trepidation in others. Most assumed the end of the world was nigh and we had been found wanting. Scientists madly searched the sky for any trace of the aliens and nothing could be discovered.

The next morning after the other ships left, a bright beam, brighter than any light on Earth except for the sun itself, speared down to Earth, illuminating a five-mile circle of all-encompassing radiance. Humans within the beam stopped moving, and only those at the fringe of the beam could see what was happening within.

The aliens floated slowly and majestically to the surface of the planet and began to create a space filled with decidedly non-terrestrial plants. Many of them moved, swaying to an unheard music, tentacles whipping about, and occasionally squirting a strange and noxious fluid that dissolved anything it came in contact with. Several humans who were frozen nearby disintegrated in a pink mist as they exploded from contact with the plant's venom.

The military watched from the fringe of the light barrier after several of their missiles failed to penetrate it and fell to Earth, unmoving but still quite active. After destroying several blocks of Manhattan with cruise missiles that fell far short of the target, the Navy resorted to 20 mm guns. They, too, flew unerringly to the target until they reached the barrier; then they promptly exploded, scattering shrapnel on everyone outside of the light shield. Dozens of people were unfortunately killed.

The president decided that he would tell the military to stand down before they killed any more New Yorkers by trying a nuclear strike next. Since the military could not destroy the aliens, they were forced to watch and record. Cameras were pointed into the field only to find out, once they were turned on, they did not record anything inside it.

Then artists were given binoculars and told to paint, draw, create images of the aliens as detailed as possible. Each artist did his best to create an image as true to the aliens as he could. When the military later compared all of their drawings, each one was as different as could be. Not a single image resembled any of the creatures, and none of the images resembled each other. None of the artists thought this was strange or out of place.

What most people saw were suits of armor that seemed to be made of a metal that absorbed light. They were matte black in appearance, and only small lights could be made out on the fronts and backs of the suits. Each suit carried a staff-like object that seemed to function as a multi-tool. They could destroy matter or recreate matter with the same tool.

Unable to record effectively, the military was forced to use trained observers to try and remember every possible detail. They would find out a few days later that most of those observers would remember a picnic or birthday party or some other event they enjoyed, and would not be able to be convinced otherwise. They were not reporting anything useful to their commanding officers. It took two days for the alien table, chairs, exotic plants, and force field generators to be ready.

The President of the United States sat in his office and talked to me, an anthropologist by trade, about what I thought the aliens wanted. I was about to answer that question when there was a flash of light, and we were both transported, along with two Secret Service agents, to the center of the alien conference area. Seconds later, every leader of every major population group on the planet began to appear, rapidly filling the entire space the aliens had created.

Food appeared as mysteriously as we did, and I decided to sit down and eat one of the apples, golden in color, from the table. It was the most amazing thing I had ever eaten. The Secret Service agents shook their heads while I tasted the apple. I assume they thought I was taking a considerable risk, but I did not think so. If they wanted to kill us, they did not have to teleport us here to do it. They could have just as easily destroyed us in transit, or teleported a bomb to our office. Besides, the president was a cheapskate; he did not even spring for a lunch before our meeting. I was starving.

I offered the president a bite, but he looked incredulously at me, so I kept eating. Once everyone had settled down, the alien plants moved up behind us and stood quietly.

"People and leaders of Earth: We are the Warlords of Hurumpharump, and we are here to conquer your planet. In an effort to be civilized, we have sent away our fleet and left a single vessel over your major metropolis, New York. This was done to let you know that we do not consider you a threat in any way, and it would be best for all of us if your people surrender peacefully and become servants to our House."

The alien voice did not appear to emanate from any particular alien. They had all stopped moving once the speaking took place and stood quietly in their black battle suits. Did I mention they were nearly fifteen feet tall? From a distance, without something to scale them against, it was quite a shock to be seeing the terrifying image of an extraterrestrial you had to actually look up to, one with ideas of conquest. The alien voice continued.

"As our servants, you will enjoy lives of productive work rather than going to offices and shuffling piles of paper from copier to closet. Why bother pretending to be working on financial derivatives

when you know you would rather be working in the fields, produc-
ing Triliaifid for our armies? Once you learn how to train them and
control them, you will be excellent Triliaifid harvesters. We do not
expect to lose more than fifty percent of your entire species in the
first year. As you grow more experienced, that number will diminish
significantly, and by year five, your population will begin to stabilize
and return to positive numbers."

All of the faces around the table looked shocked and unbeliev-
ing at what they were hearing. Fifty percent of the population in
a single year? The cheap president, President Walter Fox, stood
up and adjusted his tie before speaking. "Walter Fox, Republi-
can, President of the United States, the most powerful nation on
Earth. I greet you in the name of our gathered coalition of friends
from all over the globe."

His voice seemed to carry to everyone sitting around the
courtyard, and several weak smiles returned to faces, as his
familiar voice and oratory speech patterns returned order to the
world. For a moment, even my head had stopped spinning, and I
was beginning to feel hopeful. Some kind of resolution would be
reached.

"We are aware of who you are, President Fox. Please sit down.
Your species lacks the proper ability to resist us, and by the standards of the Galactic Treaties of Confederation, your world now
belongs to us by right of Conquest."

By right of Conquest. Hmmm. I had an idea. But I remember
my mother saying better to beg for forgiveness than to ask for
permission. I stood up, adjusted my tie and horn-rimmed glasses,
and proceeded to make a statement that would affect the lives
of billions. No pressure. "Excuse me, great Warlords of Hurumpharump." I have an ear for language, so I added the proper juicy
inflection; this, unfortunately, left the president seated next
to me in need of a handkerchief. "Masters of the Triliaifid and

possible rulers of Earth, I would ask if there are any rules of conflict or engagement that might stipulate how combat between our species should be fought?"

The Hurumpharump turned toward each other and then walked away from their positions behind the table to huddle together. The president looked up at me after wiping his jacket, but before he could speak, the Hurumpharump answered.

"The Codex of War says we have the option of engaging in any contest we deem an effective display of strength. We have studied your planet for weeks and determined your military effectiveness cannot prevent us from dominating your world."

"Surely, such an advanced species would not consider it civilized to simply destroy a species without offering them a sporting chance to engage in a form of combat where true prowess could be determined."

They huddled again.

"Continue your proposal."

"I propose we engage in a physical contest where technology is not a factor, allowing us both to see the other and relate as equals. If you are going to dominate us, it would be better if we knew that no matter the circumstances, you would be superior to us. Otherwise, as a species, we will simply rebel and rebel again."

"This is reasonable. Name your contest."

Looking out over the area, I realized we were in a park with a recreation center nearby. Then the idea struck me, and I knew in my gut it was the right choice.

"*Baseball.* The contest is nine innings of baseball."

"Are you out of your mind, Doctor? Did you agree to risk the entire human race on a game of baseball?"

"I don't see the problem, Mr. President. The Hurumpharump agreed to play and would not wear their battle-armors. They only required a month to learn to play the game. They were certain their physical superiority would be enough to learn to play well enough to beat us. Frankly, it seemed better than depending on the military to win a contest with them. We can't even take a picture of them unless they want us to. Were you really depending on the military to win? Mr. President, I understand the risks, but at least this way we get one shot at not becoming a harvesting world of Triliaifid spores where half the human race dies on the job."

"How do you know they will keep their word?"

"President Fox, your politician is showing again. These are not politicians; they are warriors. They do not lie to an enemy if they do not have to. These creatures are beings of honor. I may not know much about them, but I do know this: they will keep their word. They never had to give it in the first place, so it must have value to their culture."

As I left the office, I turned to the president to say, "I trust you will keep your political interests out of your negotiations, sir. If they discover you might tell a lie, they may be inclined to kill you when they discover it. I would go with open honest discourse whenever you deal with them. I know you are a politician, so it might be a stretch for you. Do your best."

"Where will you be, Doctor, in case I need you?"

"With them, of course."

The Hurumpharump had a few conditions. They would be given access to a trainer or coach well versed in the game. As a matter of fact, they wanted the best the Earth had to offer. In addition, they wanted us to put up a stake to ensure we would give them the best training possible. They decided we would surrender every major league baseball player over the age of eighteen as collateral.

The only team that would be exempt would be the team they would play against. If that team won, they would be allowed to retain their lives. If they lost, their lives were forfeit, and the Hurumpharump would rule the Earth for one thousand Earth years or five hundred birth cycles of the Triliaifid, whichever came first. Occasionally, a particularly fecund planet might alter their cycle, allowing them to reproduce even faster than normal. This has a slight effect on the handler's population, but the benefits outweighed the risk.

Coach David Reynolds, who at the time was the coach of the World Series Champions, the San Francisco Giants, was chosen to represent the Hurumpharump team. Earth's all-star team would be helmed by the coach of the New York Mets, Nevil Maynard. The all-stars were chosen from teams all over the Earth, and for the next thirty days, they would be training harder than ever. The game would be held in Yankee Stadium in New York and simulcast all over the world, in real time.

The Hurumpharump desired to train in Florida, because without their suits, they preferred the heat and humidity. Fortunately for them (and I guess for us), it was summer in New York, so it was likely to be hot and humid during the game, which was to be held August 30.

To reduce issues of coordination, every baseball player on Earth was teleported to the light field, and the all-stars were chosen from their number. Once a team was chosen—nine players, nine alternates, and three pitchers—the team was teleported to a secure location to begin their practice. They would be fed, trained, and cared for, but would not be allowed to see or interact with anyone until the game.

Coach Reynolds and myself as well as a team of seven alternative trainers would also be on hand to assist the Hurumpharump during their development. Once we gave them the specifications for a baseball field, the physical dimensions of the stadium were recreated on their ship seconds before we arrived on it, as I was told.

It was Yankee Stadium in every way (except there was no gum under the seats and no one hawking and spilling beer on me while I watched). When the Hurumpharump teleported us all to their field, they opened their suits of armor by running their hands down an invisible seam in the front and the suit peeled away, showing a semi-organic, semi-machine based device/organism. Oh, I wanted to be able to take a picture, but I satisfied myself with attempting to memorize everything and hoped they would allow me to take my memories home with me. We were told that once everything had been established, this field would be transported to an area in Florida temporarily so they could enjoy the heat and humidity there.

When their suits opened, the smell was horrible, almost as if something had crawled into their suits and died. They were pastel colored, and no two possessed exactly the same hues, shades, or color patterns. Some shared certain color characteristics, but I could not be sure what the riot of colors meant. Each Hurumpharump possessed excellent muscle tone and a shimmering scale-like skin. Their eyes were large and had multicolored iris-like fields, super-responsive pupils, and double eyelids, both an inner and an outer one.

Their bodies were bilaterally similar and relatively evenly proportioned. Without their suits, they were still six to seven feet tall, and all had very well developed teeth. Judging from the size of their craniums, they had a very good brain-to-body ratio, slightly better than ours, so they are at least as intelligent as we are. I would only know more if I had the option to observe their brains in action. I would have to enjoy what I learned without the benefit of hands-on study at this time.

Once out of their suits, they were immediately rubbed with an unguent of some kind by what appeared to be servants of another species. The servants were some sort of insectovoids. They moved swiftly, scraping away the ichor that came from within their suits and generously slathering on this much better smelling agent. Even without their armor, the Hurumpharump still maintained an unmistakable aura of power.

With their physical aptitude, they were naturals for the game of baseball. With two noted exceptions. When we first introduced them to the bat, they were very excited. They had no directly equivalent word, and the best they could do was "bludgeon," and we let it go for the sake of expediency. This excitement was one of the first showings of any emotional state other than what would appear to be boredom. They took the bat, passed it around, hefted it, marveled at its weight, swung it a few times, and nodded approvingly.

I had to ask. "What are you all so happy about?"

He (I think it was a he, they all looked the same and accepted the pronoun without comment) waved the bludgeon in the air and said, "Finally a weapon; we were unsure about this idea until now. Will we all be issued a bludgeon, or will we have to share it during the struggle for dominance?" At that point, the other Hurumpharump made noises I equate with chimpanzees and dominance activity as they crowded around the bat wielder.

"No, no. While it is true, you will be using the, uh, bludgeon, you will not be using it on the other team. You will be using it to strike the ball." Puzzled looks followed. At this time, we began to show them videos of the game, and they were fascinated and intrigued. We left them alone with dozens of recordings for three days. When we were allowed to return, they had already separated into training teams and had begun attempting to play.

This brings me to the second issue: pitching. The Hurumpharump, while physically powerful, seemed to have an inherent issue with their throwing skills. They could throw reasonably well; that wasn't the problem. It was an issue of degree. Those that could throw accurately and with some degree of precision were not very powerful. Those who were powerful could only deliver a very general degree of precision. While the coach was unhappy to discover this weakness, he had seen it in players before and continued to push them to overcome it. The Hurumpharump refused to use gloves and did not seem hindered by the sting of the ball in any way. We offered to show them how to use them, but they did not seem to understand the point.

With this disability in mind, the inaccurate throwers became outfielders, and the accurate became pitchers and infielders, inelegant, but necessary. Overcoming their disappointment at not getting to club anyone during the course of the game, the Hurumpharump became excellent players despite their throwing handicap. And they would be quite a surprise to our human team in one other amazing attribute.

We did not communicate often with the human team, but reports said they were in good spirits and confident of their ability to win easily. I read those reports with trepidation, and hoped they would not be overconfident.

When the day of the game arrived, the Hurumpharump teleported both teams to the real Yankee Stadium, and the stadium was filled with spectators, who were allowed to enter at will. The stadium was packed with humans, wearing all kinds of baseball paraphernalia, cheering their respective heroes on. Food was passed out, drinks were dispensed, and no money changed hands.

I think it was decided if the end of the world was coming, everyone should be full and perhaps a bit intoxicated. The president and his contingent, as well as those world leaders who had not returned home, had an entire box area to themselves, and they were adjacent to the insectovoid servants of the Hurumpharump, of which there were forty or so who appeared for the game. Before the game started, the insectovoids came out to the field and groomed the Hurumpharump and provided them with uniforms with numbers. After slathering them with the unguent, the players were dressed, and they awaited the National Anthem.

We were surprised to find out that a Hurumpharump wanted to sing the National Anthem, in English, no less. It was evident he had practiced for some time, because he sang without the translator we were so used to hearing. His accent was thick but passable, and he did not embarrass himself as much as many celebrities had in the past. The song resonated with the audience, and at the end, they cheered his efforts and applauded mightily. He looked puzzled and turned to me. I made the sign of approval I had seen them show each other, and he appeared to be satisfied and returned to the dugout.

"Play ball!" the umpire shouted to herald in the most important game in human existence.

The Hurumpharump started the inning, and the first pitch was a fastball, low and outside. The Hurumpharump Number 13 seemed to be a statue until a split second before the ball crossed the plate. Then his bat was a blur of motion. It moved so fast no one could even see it. The ball disappeared in a cloud of dust as it flew down the right field line and disappeared out of the field, continuing out of the stadium. The only words spoken were, "Take your bases, sir." And the score was one–zip. The Hurumpharump repeated this for fifteen home runs before their side was retired. After the fourth or fifth run, the stadium was as quiet as the grave. Humanity breathed a sigh of relief when the inning ended.

When the first human came to bat, a Darrell Mayers from the Philadelphia Phillies, the crowd went wild, and I found myself caught up in the infectious energy. He tapped his shoes, smiled, pointed out into right field, and stood over the plate. The pitcher watched the signs from the catcher, shook two off and then nodded. His pitch was a fastball at a whopping seventy-seven miles per hour, respectable from a Hurumpharump but nothing compared to what Mayers was used to hitting. He drove it from the stadium as if it had been lobbed underhand. And the game was on.

Nine innings later, the game was remarkable for several reasons. It was the highest scoring baseball game in history, not because it wasn't played well. Each team did remarkably well once they adapted to the style of play of the other. When the ball was kept in the stadium, there was some of the best baseball anyone had ever seen. Spectacular plays, incredible throws, steals. I forgot to mention how fast the Hurumpharump were stealing bases; baseball had never looked so good. In the beginning, the crowd gave no love to the Hurumpharump, but by the fifth inning, after a spectacular triple play against the humans to retire the side, the crowd cheered the sheer beauty of the game. And soon, both teams were being cheered and for just a moment, all were able to forget the fate of the world hung in the balance. During the seventh inning stretch, people got up for a moment and walked, but no one left. Even the sportscasters were excited.

The Hurumpharump added three runs to their total as their turn at bat ended, with a score of 157–154. It was possible for humanity to win, and Coach Reynolds called a time out to change his pitcher. At this time, President Fox chose to come out to address the crowd. He had to pass the Hurumpharump dugout. The insectovoids had also emerged to apply their healing unguent to the team and were bustling about the dugout as the president and his security detail passed by. President Fox shoved his way past one of the insectovoids and continued on.

The roar of the crowd was deafening, and the president had to yell to be heard. "Gentlemen, I have never been as proud of this game as I am today. I want it to be known, no matter what happens, you have been exceptional. But I want to take this moment to remind you, the fate of our species lies in your hands. You are a team comprising the finest our world has to offer. I want you to do your absolute best in this final inning."

Coach Reynolds finished out on the mound, and the president and his team rushed back to their box. The insectovoids returned a few moments later, and the game reconvened. The new pitcher was a Hurumpharump, Number 6, who had been held in reserve until now. I remembered why. He was one of the few who had been able to pitch with both control and power. Coach Reynolds had been true to his word. He would do whatever it took to win. It did not matter to the crowd, though; they were cheering manically as he took the mound.

Bu Tao of China came to the plate, and after having innings of easy hits, was surprised at the speed and power of Number 6's pitches. Stepping into a more controlled crouch, he concentrated and got a chip into left field and made it to first. Number 6 was unaffected and took the next batter in three swings. One out. The next batter was a giant from the Dominican Republic, Fernando Ayala, easily one of the best hitters in the world. The stadium quieted down after the easy out of the last batter.

The first pitch was a rocket and was outside. The second was a curve and inside. Ayala swung on the next pitch and missed, 2 and 1. Ayala grinned, and the Hurumpharump showed its teeth in challenge. The next pitch was perfect, and Ayala swung and broke his bat for a double. The outfielder, Number 12, who rushed it, had a cannon for an arm. He made the throw to home to keep Bu Tao from scoring. Men on second and third, one out.

Music blared, the crowd sang, people cheered, even the insectovoids, who until the very last few innings had sat impassively, seemed agitated, their antenna waving and their second pair of hands drumming out a strange cadence in counterpoint to the music, complementary and rhythmically pleasing. No game had ever caught the attention, the crowds, the adulation, that this game had.

David Matthews, number 42 of the Mets, came to bat; Hurum-pharump Number 6 had been briefed on the team and knew he was the best hitter with the sharpest eye. So he walked him, counting on their superior infield to make the double play against the next far weaker hitter.

Matthews took his base, visibly angered. Number 6 showed no emotion as he awaited the next batter. The next batter was from the Netherlands, number 14, Dave Rajier. He was a good fielder and chosen because of his skill in the outfield. He was a decent hitter, batting .273, but no one wanted him to be hitting right now. Too much was at stake. Rajier came to the plate, tipped his hat to the crowd, and stood ready. He exuded confidence. The crowd went wild.

The two, Rajier and Number 6, filled the count, three balls and two strikes, each working his skills, and the battle came down to their indomitable wills. The next pitch would decide it. Number 6 turned the catcher down four times before deciding. Rajier squinted, gripped, and swung hard. There was solid contact, and the ball flew high into left field. Number 11, a Hurumpharump known for his leaping ability, tracked it and ran toward the wall. He leaped and everyone held their breath. The ball was just shy of his fingers by about an inch. The same inch would have been successfully covered by a glove, had he been using one. Grand slam home run! The humans had won the game.

People cheered, music played, and everyone roared as the game came to an end. Both teams seemed exceptionally excited and ran out onto the field to hug and congratulate each other. I approached a Hurumpharump, who in his excitement, hugged me closely, and I squeaked so that he might let me go. He was powerful but gentle, and placed me back on the ground.

The cheering continued for some time, and then a pleasant chime sounded and all of the stadium music subsided. *"People of Earth, when we first agreed to engage in this challenge, we were certain we would be able to win. Our generations of battle experience and breeding made us believe the outcome was never in doubt. But instead, your people have proven to be resilient warriors and impeccable instructors, who taught with honor and patience. They gave completely to our players guidance in all aspects of the game, and as a result, their performance was exemplary, wouldn't all agree?"*

The crowd roared with enthusiasm, forgetting any sense of decorum, giddy with the win.

"It gives us great pleasure to announce we will not be using your planet as a breeding ground for the Triliaifid. We have found your species to be more developed in some ways than our own. We will instead consult with your world on more of these 'games' as you call them. On our worlds, all contests end in death, so this is a novel concept for us. In return, we shall spare your world and help guide you into the galaxy as a member of the Confederation. We will, of course, be removing weapons from your world to ensure that you do not destroy yourselves before we can experience all of your games. Your games will become the currency with which you will buy your way into the galactic community."

President Fox, finding his way to a microphone, was incensed. "Who are you to come to our planet and dictate our defense policy or any other state policy? The United States is a sovereign nation...."

"Enough, President Fox." The president was teleported in a flash of light to the center of the stadium surrounded by the Triliaifid and Hurumpharump in black armor. "You are no longer in a position to dictate anything on this planet. Your second in command, Vice President Davis, will be assuming control of your United States. You will be tried and likely found guilty of assaulting a higher life form in the performance of its duties."

"What do you mean? I don't remember assaulting anyone." In response, a holographic image suddenly showed the president shoving his way past the insectovoid grooming a Hurum-pharump.

"And? They are just servants. Who cares about servants?"

"Your crime, Mr. President, is the lack of manners and respect due any life form. You and your entire family line will be punished and directed to tend Triliaifid at our next training facility. You will be returned at the end of a ten year sentence, should you and yours survive."

The insectovoids turned and waved, and the Hurumpharump in battle armor escorted the former president into the beam. Number 6 turned to me and placed his hand on my shoulder, already aware of my next question. *They are not the servants. We are.*

A Guide to the Fruits of Hawai'i

K ey's favorite time of day is sunset, her least is sunrise. It should be the opposite, but every time she watches that bright red disk sinking into the water beneath Mauna Kea her heart bends like a wishbone, and she thinks, *He's awake now.*

Key is thirty-four. She is old for a human woman without any children. She has kept herself alive by being useful in other ways. For the past four years, Key has been the overseer of the Mauna Kea Grade Orange blood facility.

Is it a concentration camp if the inmates are well fed? If their beds are comfortable? If they are given an hour and a half of rigorous boxercise and yoga each morning in the recreational field?

It doesn't have to be Honouliuli to be wrong.

When she's called in to deal with Jeb's body—bloody, not drained, in a feeding room—yoga doesn't make him any less dead.

Key helps vampires run a concentration camp for humans.

Key is a different kind of monster.

Key's favorite food is umeboshi. Salty and tart and bright red, with that pit in the center to beware. She loves it in rice balls, the kind her Japanese grandmother made when she was little. She loves it by itself, the way she ate it at fifteen, after Obachan died. She hasn't had umeboshi in eighteen years, but sometimes she thinks that when she dies she'll taste one again.

This morning she eats the same thing she eats every meal: a nutritious brick patty, precisely five inches square and two inches deep, colored puce. Her raw scrubbed hands still have a pink tinge of Jeb's blood in the cuticles. She stares at them while she sips the accompanying beverage, which is orange. She can't remember if it ever resembled the fruit.

She eats this because that is what every human eats in the Mauna Kea facility. Because the patty is easy to manufacture and soft enough to eat with plastic spoons. Key hasn't seen a fork in years, a knife in more than a decade. The vampires maintain tight control over all items with the potential to draw blood. Yet humans are tool-making creatures, and their desires, even nihilistic ones, have a creative power that no vampire has the imagination or agility to anticipate. How else to explain the shiv, handcrafted over secret months from the wood cover and glue-matted pages of *A Guide to the Fruits of Hawai'i*, the book that Jeb used to read in the hours after his feeding sessions, sometimes aloud, to whatever humans would listen? He took the only thing that gave him pleasure in the world, destroyed it—or recreated it—and slit his veins with it. Mr. Charles questioned her particularly; he knew that she and Jeb used to talk sometimes. Had she *known* that the *boy* was like this? He gestured with pallid hands at the splatter of arterial pulses from jaggedly slit wrists: oxidized brown, inedible, mocking.

No, she said, of course not, Mr. Charles. I report any suspected cases of self-waste immediately.

She reports any suspected cases. And so, for the weeks she has watched Jeb hardly eating across the mess hall, noticed how he staggered from the feeding rooms, recognized the frigid rebuff in his responses to her questions, she has very carefully refused to suspect.

Today, just before dawn, she choked on the fruits of her indifference. He slit his wrists and femoral arteries. He smeared the blood over his face and buttocks and genitals, and he waited to die before the vampire technician could arrive to drain him.

Not many humans self-waste. Most think about it, but Key never has, not since the invasion of the Big Island. Unlike other humans, she has someone she's waiting for. The one she loves, the one she prays will reward her patience. During her years as overseer, Key has successfully stopped three acts of self-waste. She has failed twice. Jeb is different; Mr. Charles sensed it somehow, but vampires can only read human minds through human blood. Mr. Charles hasn't drunk from Key in years. And what could he learn, even if he did? He can't drink thoughts she has spent most of her life refusing to have.

Mr. Charles calls her to the main office the next night, between feeding shifts. She is terrified, like she always is, of what they might do. She is thinking of Jeb and wondering how Mr. Charles has taken the loss of an investment. She is wondering how fast she will die in the work camp on Lanai.

But Mr. Charles has an offer, not a death sentence.

"You know . . . of the facility on Oahu? Grade Gold?"

"Yes," Key says. Just that, because she learned early not to betray herself to them unnecessarily, and the man at Grade Gold has always been her greatest betrayer.

No, not a man, Key tells herself for the hundredth, the thousandth time. *He is one of them.*

Mr. Charles sits in a hanging chair shaped like an egg with plush red velvet cushions. He wears a black suit with steel gray pinstripes, sharply tailored. The cuffs are high and his feet are bare, white as talcum powder and long and bony like spiny fish. His veins are prominent and round and milky blue. Mr. Charles is vain about his feet.

He does not sit up to speak to Key. She can hardly see his face behind the shadow cast by the overhanging top of the egg. All vampires speak deliberately, but Mr. Charles drags out his tones until you feel you might tip over from waiting on the next syllable. It goes up and down like a calliope—

". . . what do you *say* to heading down there and *sort*ing the matter . . . out?"

"I'm sorry, Mr. Charles," she says carefully, because she has lost the thread of his monologue. "What matter?"

He explains: a Grade Gold human girl has killed herself. It is a disaster that outshadows the loss of Jeb.

"You would not believe the expense taken to keep those humans Grade Gold standard."

"What would I do?"

"Take it in hand, *of* course. It seems our small . . . Grade Orange operation has gotten some notice. Tetsuo asked for you . . . particularly."

"Tetsuo?" She hasn't said the name out loud in years. Her voice catches on the second syllable.

"*Mr.* Tetsuo," Mr. Charles says, and waves a hand at her. He holds a sheet of paper, the same shade as his skin. "He wrote you a *letter*."

Key can't move, doesn't reach out to take it, and so it flutters to the black marble floor a few feet away from Mr. Charles's egg.

He leans forward. "I think . . . I remember something . . . you and Tetsuo . . ."

"He recommended my promotion here," Key says, after a moment. It seems the safest phrasing. Mr. Charles would have remembered this eventually; vampires are slow, but inexorable.

The diffuse light from the paper lanterns catches the bottom half of his face, highlighting the deep cleft in his chin. It twitches in faint surprise. "You *were* his pet?"

Key winces. She remembers the years she spent at his side during and after the wars, catching scraps in his wake, despised by every human who saw her there. She waited for him to see how much she had sacrificed and give her the only reward that could matter after what she'd done. Instead he had her shunt removed and sent her to Grade Orange. She has not seen or heard from him in four years. His pet, yes, that's as good a name as any—but he never drank from her. Not once.

Mr. Charles's lips, just a shade of white darker than his skin, open like a hole in a cloud. "And he wants you back. How do you *feel?*"

Terrified. Awestruck. Confused. "Grateful," she says.

The hole smiles. "Grateful! How interesting. Come here, girl. I believe I shall *have* a *taste.*"

She grabs the letter with shaking fingers and folds it inside a pocket of her red uniform. She stands in front of Mr. Charles.

"Well?" he says.

She hasn't had a shunt in years, though she can still feel its ridged scar in the crook of her arm. Without it, feeding from her is messy, violent. Traditional, Mr. Charles might say. Her fingers hurt as she unzips the collar. Her muscles feel sore, the bones in her spine arthritic and old as she bows her head, leans closer to Mr. Charles. She waits for him to bare his fangs, to pierce her vein, to suck her blood.

He takes more than he should. He drinks until her fingers and toes twinge, until her neck throbs, until the red velvet of his seat fades to gray. When he finishes, he leaves her blood on his mouth.

"I forgive . . . you for the boy," he says.

Jeb cut his own arteries, left his good blood all over the floor. Mr. Charles abhors waste above all else.

Mr. Charles will explain the situation. I wish you to come. If you do well, I have been authorized to offer you the highest reward.

The following night, Key takes a boat to Oahu. Vampires don't like water, but they will cross it anyway—the sea has become a status symbol among them, an indication of strength. Hawai'i is still a resort destination, though most of its residents only go out at night. Grade Gold is the most expensive, most luxurious resort of them all.

Tetsuo travels between the islands often. Key saw him do it a dozen times during the war. She remembers one night, his face lit by the moon and the yellow lamps on the deck—the wide cheekbones, thick eyebrows, sharp widow's peak, all frozen in the perfection of a nineteen-year-old boy. Pale beneath the olive tones of his skin, he bares his fangs when the waves lurch beneath him.

"What does it feel like?" she asks him.

"Like frozen worms in my veins," he says, after a full, long minute of silence. Then he checks the guns and tells her to wait below, the humans are coming. She can't see anything, but Tetsuo can smell them like chum in the water. The Japanese have held out the longest, and the vampires of Hawai'i lead the assault against them.

Two nights later, in his quarters in the bunker at the base of Mauna Kea, Tetsuo brings back a sheet of paper, written in Japanese. The only characters she recognizes are "shi" and "ta"—"death" and "field." It looks like some kind of list.

"What is this?" she asks.

"Recent admissions to the Lanai human residential facility."

She looks up at him, devoted with terror. "My mother?" Her father died in the first offensive on the Big Island, a hero of the resistance. He never knew how his daughter had chosen to survive.

"Here," Tetsuo says, and runs a cold finger down the list without death. "Jen Isokawa."

"Alive?" She has been looking for her mother since the wars began. Tetsuo knows this, but she didn't know he was searching, too. She feels swollen with this indication of his regard.

"She's listed as a caretaker. They're treated well. You could . . ." He sits beside her on the bed that only she uses. His pause lapses into a stop. He strokes her hair absentmindedly; if she had a tail, it would beat his legs. She is seventeen and she is sure he will reward her soon.

"Tetsuo," she says, "you could drink from me, if you want. I've had a shunt for nearly a year. The others use it. I'd rather feed you."

Sometimes she has to repeat herself three times before he seems to hear her. This, she has said at least ten. But she is safe here in his bunker, on the bed he brought in for her, with his lukewarm body pressed against her warm one. Vampires do not have sex with humans; they feed. But if he doesn't want her that way, what else can she offer him?

"I've had you tested. You're fertile. If you bear three children you won't need a shunt and the residential facilities will care for you for the rest of your mortality. You can live with your mother. I will make sure you're safe."

She presses her face against his shoulder. "Don't make me leave."

"You wanted to see your mother."

Her mother had spent the weeks before the invasion in church, praying for God to intercede against the abominations. Better that she die than see Key like this.

"Only to know what happened to her," Key whispers. "Won't you feed from me, Tetsuo? I want to feel closer to you. I want you to know how much I love you."

A long pause. Then, "I don't need to taste you to know how you feel."

Tetsuo meets her on shore.

Just like that, she is seventeen again.

"You look older," he says. Slowly, but with less affectation than Mr. Charles.

This is true; so inevitable she doesn't understand why he even bothers to say so. Is he surprised? Finally, she nods. The buoyed dock rocks beneath them—he makes no attempt to move, though the two vampires with him grip the denuded skin of their own elbows with pale fingers. They flare and retract their fangs.

"You are drained," he says. He does not mean this metaphorically.

She nods again, realizes further explanation is called for. "Mr. Charles," she says, her voice a painful rasp. This embarrasses her, though Tetsuo would never notice.

He nods, sharp and curt. She thinks he is angry, though perhaps no one else could read him as clearly. She knows that face, frozen in the countenance of a boy dead before the Second World War. A boy dead fifty years before she was born.

He is old enough to remember Pearl Harbor, the detention camps, the years when Maui's forests still had native birds. But she has never dared ask him about his human life.

"And what did Charles explain?"

"He said someone killed herself at Grade Gold."

Tetsuo flares his fangs. She flinches, which surprises her. She used to flush at the sight of his fangs, her blood pounding red just beneath the soft surface of her skin.

"I've been given dispensation," he says, and rests one finger against the hollow at the base of her throat.

She's learned a great deal about the rigid traditions that

restrict vampire life since she first met Tetsuo. She understands why her teenage fantasies of morally liberated vampirism were improbable, if not impossible. For each human they bring over, vampires need a special dispensation that they only receive once or twice every decade. *The highest reward.* If Tetsuo has gotten a dispensation, then her first thought when she read his letter was correct. He didn't mean retirement. He didn't mean a peaceful life in some remote farm on the islands. He meant death. Un-death.

After all these years, Tetsuo means to turn her into a vampire.

The trouble at Grade Gold started with a dead girl. Penelope cut her own throat five days ago (with a real knife, the kind they allow Grade Gold humans for cutting food). Her ghost haunts the eyes of those she left behind. One human resident in particular, with hair dyed the color of tea and blue lipstick to match the bruises under her red eyes, takes one look at Key and starts to scream.

Key glances at Tetsuo, but he has forgotten her. He stares at the girl as if he could burn her to ashes on the plush green carpet. The five others in the room look away, but Key can't tell if it's in embarrassment or fear. The luxury surrounding them chokes her. There's a bowl of fruit on a coffee table. Real fruit—fuzzy brown kiwis, mottled red-green mangos, dozens of tangerines. She takes an involuntary step forward and the girl's scream gets louder before cutting off with an abrupt squawk. Her labored breaths are the only sound in the room.

"This is a joke," the girl says. There's spittle on her blue lips. "What hole did you dig her out of?"

"Go to your room, Rachel," Tetsuo says.

Rachel flicks back her hair and rubs angrily under one eye. "What are you now, Daddy Vampire? You think you can just, what? Replace her? With this broke-down fogey look-alike?"

"She is not—"

"Yeah? What is she?"

They are both silent, doubt and grief and fury scuttling between them like beetles in search of a meal. Tetsuo and the girl stare at each other with such deep familiarity that Key feels forgotten, alone—almost ashamed of the dreams that have kept her alive for a decade. They have never felt so hopeless, or so false.

"Her name is Key," Tetsuo says, in something like defeat. He turns away, though he makes no move to leave. "She will be your new caretaker."

"Key?" the girl says. "What kind of a name is that?"

Key doesn't answer for a long time, thinking of all the ways she could respond. Of Obachan Akiko and the affectionate nickname of lazy summers spent hiking in the mountains or pounding mochi in the kitchen. Of her half-Japanese mother and Hawai'ian father, of the ways history and identity and circumstance can shape a girl into half a woman, until someone—*not a man*—comes with a hundred thousand others like him and destroys anything that might have once had meaning. So she finds meaning in him. Who else was there?

And this girl, whose sneer reveals her bucked front teeth, has as much chance of understanding that world as Key does of understanding this one. Fresh fruit on the table. No uniforms. And a perfect, glittering shunt of plastic and metal nestled in the crook of her left arm.

"Mine," Key answers the girl.

Rachel spits; Tetsuo turns his head, just a little, as though he can only bear to see Key from the corner of his eye.

"You're nothing like her," she says.

"Like who?"

But the girl storms from the room, leaving her chief vampire without a dismissal. Key now understands this will not be punished. It's another one—a boy, with the same florid beauty as the girl but far less belligerence—who answers her.

"You look like Penelope," he says, tugging on a long lock of his asymmetrically cut black hair. "Just older."

When Tetsuo leaves the room, it's Key who cannot follow.

Key remembers sixteen. Her obachan is dead and her mother has moved to an apartment in Hilo and it's just Key and her father in that old, quiet house at the end of the road. The vampires have annexed San Diego, and Okinawa is besieged, but life doesn't feel very different in the mountains of the Big Island.

It is raining in the woods behind her house. Her father has told her to study, but all she's done since her mother left is read Mishima's *Sea of Fertility* novels. She sits on the porch, wondering if it's better to kill herself or wait for them to come, and just as she thinks she ought to have the courage to die, something rattles in the shed. A rat, she thinks.

But it's not a rat she sees when she pulls open the door on its rusty hinges. It's a man, crouched between a stack of old appliance boxes and the rusted fender of the Buick her father always meant to fix one day. His hair is wet and slicked back, his white shirt is damp and ripped from shoulder to navel. The skin beneath it is pale as a corpse; bloodless, though the edges of a deep wound are still visible.

"They've already come?" Her voice breaks on a whisper. She wanted to finish *The Decay of the Angel*. She wanted to see her mother once more.

"Shut the door," he says, crouching in shadow, away from the bar of light streaming through the narrow opening.

"Don't kill me."

"We are equally at each other's mercy."

She likes the way he speaks. No one told her they could sound so proper. So human. Is there a monster in her shed, or is he something else?

"Why shouldn't I open it all the way?"

He is brave, whatever else. He takes his long hands from in front of his face and stands, a flower blooming after rain. He is beautiful, though she will not mark that until later. Now, she only notices the steady, patient way he regards her. *I could move faster than you*, his eyes say. *I could kill you first.*

She thinks of Mishima and says, "I'm not afraid of death."

Only when the words leave her mouth does she realize how deeply she has lied. Does he know? Her hands would shake if it weren't for their grip on the handle.

"I promise," he says. "I will save you, when the rest of us come."

What is it worth, a monster's promise?

She steps inside and shuts out the light.

There are nineteen residents of Grade Gold; the twentieth is buried beneath the kukui tree in the communal garden. The thought of rotting in earth revolts Key. She prefers the bright, fierce heat of a crematorium fire, like the one that consumed Jeb the night before she left Mauna Kea. The ashes fly in the wind, into the ocean and up in the trees, where they lodge in bird nests and caterpillar silk and mud puddles after a storm. The return of flesh to the earth should be fast and final, not the slow mortification of worms and bacteria and carbon gases.

Tetsuo instructs her to keep close watch on unit three. "Rachel isn't very . . . steady right now," he says, as though unaware of the understatement.

The remaining nineteen residents are divided into four units, five kids in each but one, living together in sprawling ranch houses connected by walkways and gardens. There are walls, of course, but you have to climb a tree to see them. The kids at Grade Gold have more freedom than any human she's ever encountered since the war, but they're as bound to this paradise as she was to her mountain.

The vampires who come here stay in a high glass tower right by the beach. During the day, the black-tinted windows gleam like lasers. At night, the vampires come down to feed. There is a fifth house in the residential village, one reserved for clients and their meals. Tetsuo orchestrates these encounters, planning each interaction in fine detail: this human with that performance for this distinguished client. Key has grown used to thinking of her fellow humans as food, but now she is forced to reconcile that indelible fact with another, stranger veneer. The vampires who pay so dearly for Grade Gold humans don't merely want to feed from a shunt. They want to be entertained, talked to, cajoled. The boy who explained about Key's uncanny resemblance juggles torches. Twin girls from unit three play guitar and sing songs by the Carpenters. Even Rachel, dressed in a gaudy purple mermaid dress with matching streaks in her hair, keeps up a one-way, laughing conversation with a vampire who seems too astonished—or too slow—to reply.

Key has never seen anything like this before. She thought that most vampires regarded humans as walking sacks of food. What pleasure could be derived from speaking with your meal first? From seeing it sing or dance? When she first went with Tetsuo, the other vampires talked about human emotions as if they were flavors of ice cream. But at Grade Orange she grew accustomed to more basic parameters: were the humans fed, were they fertile, did they sleep? Here, she must approve outfits; she must manage dietary preferences and erratic tempers and a dozen other details all crucial to keeping the kids Grade Gold standard. Their former caretaker has been shipped to the work camps, which leaves Key in sole charge of the operation. At least until Tetsuo decides how he will use his dispensation.

Key's thoughts skitter away from the possibility.

"I didn't know vampires liked music," she says, late in the evening, when some of the kids sprawl, exhausted, across couches and cushions. A girl no older than fifteen opens her eyes but hardly moves when a vampire in a gold suit lifts her arm for a nip. Key and Tetsuo are seated together at the far end of the main room, in the bay windows that overlook a cliff and the ocean.

"It's as interesting to us as any other human pastime."

"Does music have a taste?"

His wide mouth stretches at the edges; she recognizes it as a smile. "Music has some utility, given the right circumstances."

She doesn't quite understand him. The air is redolent with the sweat of human teenagers and the muggy, salty air that blows through the open doors and windows. Her eye catches on a half-eaten strawberry dropped carelessly on the carpet a few feet away. It was harvested too soon, a white, tasteless core surrounded by hard, red flesh.

She thinks there is nothing of "right" in these circumstances, and their utility is, at its bottom, merely that of parasite and host.

"The music enhances the—our—flavor?"

Tetsuo stares at her for a long time, long enough for him to take at least three of his shallow, erratically spaced breaths. To look at him is to taste copper and sea on her tongue; to wait for him is to hear the wind slide down a mountainside an hour before dawn.

It has been four years since she last saw him. She thought he had forgotten her, and now he speaks to her as if all those years haven't passed, as though the vampires hadn't long since won the war and turned the world to their slow, long-burning purpose.

"Emotions change your flavor," he says. "And food. And sex. And pleasure."

And love? she wonders, but Tetsuo has never drunk from her.

"Then why not treat all of us like you do the ones here? Why have con—Mauna Kea?"

She expects him to catch her slip, but his attention is focused on something beyond her right shoulder. She turns to look, and sees nothing but the hall and a closed feeding room door.

"Three years," he says, quietly. He doesn't look at her. She doesn't understand what he means, so she waits. "It takes three years for the complexity to fade. For the vitality of young blood to turn muddy and clogged with silt. Even among the new crops, only a few individuals are Gold standard. For three years, they produce the finest blood ever tasted, filled with regrets and ecstasy and dreams. And then . . ."

"Grade Orange?" Key asks, her voice dry and rasping. Had Tetsuo always talked of humans like this? With such little regard for their selfhood? Had she been too young to understand, or have the years of harvesting humans hardened him?

"If we have not burned too much out. Living at high elevation helps prolong your utility, but sometimes all that's left is Lanai and the work camps."

She remembers her terror before her final interview with Mr. Charles, her conviction that Jeb's death would prompt him to discard his uselessly old overseer to the work camps.

A boy from one of the other houses staggers to the one she recognizes from unit two and sprawls in his lap. Unit-two boy startles awake, smiles, and bends over to kiss the first. A pair of female vampires kneel in front of them and press their fangs with thick pink tongues.

"Touch him," one says, pointing to the boy from unit two. "Make him cry."

The boy from unit two doesn't even pause for breath; he reaches for the other boy's cock and squeezes. And as they both groan with something that makes Key feel like a voyeur, made helpless by her own desire, the pair of vampires pull the boys apart and dive for their respective shunts. The room goes quiet but for soft

A GUIDE TO THE FRUITS OF HAWAI'I   73

gurgles, like two minnows in a tide pool. Then a pair of clicks as
the boys' shunts turn gray, forcing the vampires to stop feeding.

"Lovely, divine," the vampires say a few minutes later, when
they pass on their way out. "We always appreciate the sexual
displays."

The boys curl against each other, eyes shut. They breathe like
old men: hard, through constricted tubes.

"Does that happen often?" she asks.

"This Grade Gold is known for its sexual flavors. My humans
pick partners they enjoy."

Vampires might not have sex, but they crave its flavor. Will she,
when she crosses to their side? Will she look at those two boys
and command them to fuck each other just so she can taste?

"Do you ever care?" she says, her voice barely a whisper. "About
what you've done to us?"

He looks away from her. Before she can blink he has crossed
to the one closed feeding room door and wrenched it open. A
thump of something thrown against a wall. A snarl, as human as
a snake's hiss.

"Leave, Gregory!" Tetsuo says. A vampire Key recognizes from
earlier in the night stumbles into the main room. He rubs his jaw,
though the torn and mangled skin there has already begun to
knit together.

"She is mine to have. I paid—"

"Not enough to kill her."

"I'll complain to the council," the vampire says. "You've been
losing support. And everyone knows how *patiently* Charles has
waited in his aerie."

She should be scared, but his words make her think of Jeb, of
failures and consequences, and of the one human she has not
seen for hours. She stands and sprints past both vampires to
where Rachel lies insensate on a bed.

Her shunt has turned the opaque gray meant to prevent vampires from feeding humans to death. But the client has bitten her neck instead.

"Tell them whatever you wish, and I will tell them you circumvented the shunt of a fully-tapped human. We have our rules for a reason. You are no longer welcome here."

Rachel's pulse is soft, but steady. She stirs and moans beneath Key's hands. The relief is crushing; she wants to cradle the girl in her arms until she wakes. She wants to protect her so her blood will never have to smear the walls of a feeding room, so that Key will be able to say that at least she saved one.

Rachel's eyes flutter open, land with a butterfly's gentleness on Key's face.

"Pen," she says, "I told you. It makes them . . . they *eat* me."

Key doesn't understand, but she doesn't mind. She presses her hand to Rachel's warm forehead and sings lullabies her grandmother liked until Rachel falls back to sleep.

"How is she?" It is Tetsuo, come into the room after the client has finally left.

"Drained," Key says, as dispassionately as he. "She'll be fine in a few days."

"Key."

"Yes?"

She won't look at him.

"I do, you know."

She knows. "Then why support it?"

"You'll understand when your time comes."

She looks back down at Rachel, and all she can see are bruises blooming purple on her upper arms, blood dried brown on her neck. She looks like a human being: infinitely precious, fragile. Like prey.

Five days later, Key sits in the garden in the shade of the kukui tree. She has reports to file on the last week's feedings, but the papers sit untouched beside her. The boy from unit two and his boyfriend are tending the tomatoes, and Key slowly peels the skin from her fourth kiwi. The first time she bit into one she cried, but the boys pretended not to notice. She is getting better with practice. Her hands still tremble and her misted eyes refract rainbows in the hard noon sunlight. She is learning to be human again.

Rachel sleeps on the ground beside her, curled on the packed dirt of Penelope's grave with her back against the tree trunk and her arms wrapped tightly around her belly. She's spent most of the last five days sleeping, and Key thinks she has mostly recovered. She's been eating voraciously, foods in wild combinations at all times of day and night. Key is glad. Without the distracting, angry makeup, Rachel's face looks vulnerable and haunted. Jeb had that look in the months before his death. He would sit quietly in the mess hall and stare at the food brick as though he had forgotten how to eat. Jeb had transferred to Mauna Kea within a week of Key becoming overseer. He liked watching the lights of the airplanes at night and he kept two books with him: *The Blind Watchmaker* and *A Guide to the Fruits of Hawai'i*. She talked to him about the latter—had he ever tasted breadfruit or kiwi or cherimoya? None, he said, in a voice so small and soft it sounded inversely proportional to his size. Only a peach, a canned peach, when he was four or five years old. Vampires don't waste fruit on Grade Orange humans.

The covers of both books were worn, the spines cracked, the pages yellowed and brittle at the edges. Why keep a book about fruit you had never tasted and never would eat? Why read at all, when they frowned upon literacy in humans and often banned books outright? She never asked him. Mr. Charles had seen their conversation, though she doubted he had heard it, and requested that she refrain from speaking unnecessarily to the *har*vest.

So when Jeb stared at her across the table with eyes like a snuffed candle, she turned away, she forced her patty into her mouth, she chewed, she reached for her orange drink.

His favorite book became his means of self-destruction. She let him do it. She doesn't know if she feels guilty for not having stopped him, or for being in the position to stop him in the first place. Not two weeks later she rests beneath a kukui tree, the flesh of a fruit she had never expected to taste again turning to green pulp between her teeth. She reaches for another one because she knows how little she deserves this.

But the skin of the fruit at the bottom of the bowl is too soft and fleshy for a kiwi. She pulls it into the light and drops it.

"Are you okay?" It's the boy from unit two—Kaipo. He kneels down and picks up the cherimoya.

"What?" she says, and struggles to control her breathing. She has to appear normal, in control. She's supposed to be their care-taker. But the boy just seems concerned, not judgmental. Rachel rolls onto her back and opens her eyes.

"You screamed," Rachel says, sleep-fogged and accusatory. "You woke me up."

"Who put this in the bowl?" Kaipo asks. "These things are poi-sonous! They grow on that tree down the hill, but you can't eat them."

Key takes the haunted fruit from him, holding it carefully so as not to bruise it further. "Who told you that?" she asks.

Rachel leans forward, so her chin rests on the edge of Key's lounge chair and the tips of her purple-streaked hair touch Key's thigh. "Tetsuo," she says. "What, did he lie?"

Key shakes her head slowly. "He probably only half-remembered. It's a cherimoya. The flesh is delicious, but the seeds are poisonous."

Rachel's eyes follow her hands. "Like, killing you poisonous?" she asks.

Key thinks back to her father's lessons. "Maybe if you eat them all or grind them up. The tree bark can paralyze your heart and lungs."

Kaipo whistles, and they all watch intently when she wedges her finger under the skin and splits it in half. The white, fleshy pulp looks stark, even a little disquieting against the scaly green exterior. She plucks out the hard, brown seeds and tosses them to the ground. Only then does she pull out a chunk of flesh and put it in her mouth.

Like strawberries and banana pudding and pineapple. Like the summer after Obachan died, when a box of them came to the house as a condolence gift.

"You look like you're fellating it," Rachel says. Key opens her eyes and swallows abruptly.

Kaipo pushes his tongue against his lips. "Can I try it, Key?" he asks, very politely. Did the vampires teach him that politeness? Did vampires teach Rachel a word like *fellate*, perhaps while instructing her to do it with a hopefully willing human partner?

"Do you guys know how to use condoms?" She has decided to ask Tetsuo to supply them. This last week has made it clear that "sexual flavors" are all too frequently on the menu at Grade Gold.

Kaipo looks at Rachel; Rachel shakes her head. "What's a condom?" he asks.

It's so easy to forget how little of the world they know. "You use it during sex, to stop you from catching diseases," she says carefully. "Or getting pregnant."

Rachel laughs and stuffs the rest of the flesh into her wide mouth. Even a cherimoya can't fill her hollows. "Great, even more vampire sex," she says, her hatred clearer than her garbled words. "They never made Pen do it."

"They didn't?" Key asks.

Juice dribbles down her chin. "You know, Tetsuo's dispensation? Before she killed herself, she was his pick. Everyone knew it. That's why they left her alone."

Key feels light-headed. "But if she was his choice . . . why would she kill herself?"

"She didn't want to be a vampire," Kaipo says softly.

"She wanted a *baby*, like bringing a new food sack into the world is a good idea. But they wouldn't let her have sex and they wanted to make her one of them, so—now she's gone. But why he'd bring *you* here, when *any* of us would be a better choice—"

"Rachel, just shut up. Please." Kaipo takes her by the shoulder.

Rachel shrugs him off. "What? Like she can do anything."

"If she becomes one of *them*—"

"I wouldn't hurt you," Key says, too quickly. Rachel masks her pain with cruelty, but it is palpable. Key can't imagine any version of herself that would add to that.

Kaipo and Rachel stare at her. "But," Kaipo says, "that's what vampires do."

"I would eat you," Rachel says, and flops back under the tree. "I would make you cry and your tears would taste sweeter than a cherimoya."

"I will be back in four days," Tetsuo tells her, late the next night. "There is one feeding scheduled. I hope you will be ready when I return."

"For the . . . reward?" she asks, stumbling over an appropriate euphemism. Their words for it are polysyllabic spikes: transmutation, transformation, metamorphosis. All vampires were once human, and immortal doesn't mean invulnerable. Some die each year, and so their ranks must be replenished with the flesh of worthy, willing humans.

He places a hand on her shoulder. It feels as chill and inert as a piece of damp wood. She thinks she must be dreaming.

"I have wanted this for a long time, Key," he says to her—like a stranger, like the person who knows her the best in the world.

"Why now?"

"Our thoughts can be . . . slow, sometimes. You will see. Orderly, but sometimes too orderly to see patterns clearly. I thought of you, but did not know it until Penelope died."

Penelope, who looked just like Key. Penelope, who would have been his pick. She shivers and steps away from his hand. "Did you love her?"

She can't believe that she is asking this question. She can't believe that he is offering her the dreams she would have murdered for ten, even five years ago.

"I loved that she made me think of you," he says, "when you were young and beautiful."

"It's been eighteen years, Tetsuo."

He looks over her shoulder. "You haven't lost much," he says. "I'm not too late. You'll see."

He is waiting for a response. She forces herself to nod. She wants to close her eyes and cover her mouth, keep all her love for him inside where it can be safe, because if she loses it, there will be nothing left but a girl in the rain who should have opened the door.

He looks like an alien when he smiles. He looks like nothing she could ever know when he walks down the hall, past the open door and the girl who has been watching them this whole time.

Rachel is young and beautiful, Key thinks, and Penelope is dead.

Key's sixth feeding at Grade Gold is contained, quiet and without incident. The gazes of the clients slide over her as she greets them at the door of the feeding house, but she is used to that. To a vampire, a human without a shunt is like a book without pages: a useless absurdity. She has assigned all of unit one and a pair from unit four to the gathering. Seven humans for five vampires is a luxurious ratio—probably more than they paid for, but she's happy to let that be Tetsuo's problem. She shudders to remember how Rachel's blood soaked into the collar of her blouse when she lifted the girl from the bed. She has seen dozens of overdrained humans, including some who died from it, but what happened to Rachel feels worse. She doesn't understand why, but is overwhelmed by tenderness for her.

A half hour before the clients are supposed to leave, Kaipo sprints through the front door, flushed and panting so hard he has to pause half a minute to catch his breath.

"Rachel," he manages, while humans and vampires alike pause to look.

She stands up. "What did she do?"

"I'm not sure . . . she was shaking and screaming, waking everyone up, yelling about Penelope and Tetsuo and then she started vomiting."

"The clients have another half hour," she whispers. "I can't leave until then."

Kaipo tugs on the long lock of glossy black hair that he has blunt-cut over his left eye. "I'm scared for her, Key," he says. "She won't listen to anyone else."

She will blame herself if any of the kids here tonight die, and she will blame herself if something happens to Rachel. Her hands make the decision for her: she reaches for Kaipo's left arm. He lets her take it reflexively, and doesn't flinch when she lifts his shunt. She looks for and finds the small electrical chip that controls the inflow and outflow of blood and other fluids. She taps the Morse-like code, and Kaipo watches with his mouth open as the glittering plastic polymer changes from clear to gray. As though he's already been tapped out.

"I'm not supposed to show you that," she says, and smiles until she remembers Tetsuo and what he might think. "Stay here. Make sure nothing happens. I'll be back as soon as I can."

She stays only long enough to see his agreement, and then

she's flying out the back door, through the garden, down the left-hand path that leads to unit two.

Rachel is on her hands and knees in the middle of the walkway. The other three kids in unit two watch her silently from the doorway, but Rachel is alone as she vomits in the grass.

"You!" Rachel says when she sees Key, and starts to cough.

Rachel looks like a war is being fought inside of her, as if the battlefield is her lungs and the hollows of her cheeks and the muscles of her neck. She trembles and can hardly raise her head.

"Go away!" Rachel screams, but she's not looking at Key, she's looking down at the ground.

"Rachel, what's happened?" Key doesn't get too close. Rachel's fury frightens her; she doesn't understand this kind of rage. Rachel raises her shaking hands and starts hitting herself, pounding her chest and rib cage and stomach with violence made even more frightening by her weakness. Key kneels in front of her, grabs both of the girl's tiny, bruised wrists and holds them away from her body. Her vomit smells of sour bile and the sickly-sweet of some half-digested fruit. A suspicion nibbles at Key, and so she looks to the left, where Rachel has vomited.

Dozens and dozens of black seeds, half crushed. And a slime of green the precise shade of a cherimoya skin.

"Oh, God, Rachel . . . why would you . . ."

"You don't deserve him! He can make it go away and he won't! Who are you? A fogey, an ugly fogey, an ugly usurping fogey and she's gone and he is a dick, he is a screaming howler monkey and I hate him . . ."

Rachel collapses against Key's chest, her hands beating helplessly at the ground. Key takes her up and rocks her back and forth, crying while she thinks of how close she came to repeating the mistakes of Jeb. But she can still save Rachel. She can still be human.

Tetsuo returns three days later with a guest.

She has never seen Mr. Charles wear shoes before, and he walks in them with the mincing confusion of a young girl forced to wear zori for a formal occasion. She bows her head when she sees him, hoping to hide her fear. Has he come to take her back to Mauna Kea? The thought of returning to those antiseptic feeding rooms and tasteless brick patties makes her hands shake. It makes her wonder if she would not be better off taking Penelope's way out rather than seeing the place where Jeb killed himself again.

But even as she thinks it, she knows she won't, any more than she would have eighteen years ago. She's too much a coward and she's too brave. If Mr. Charles asks her to go back she will say yes.

Rain on a mountainside and sexless, sweet touches with a man the same temperature as wet wood. Lanai City, overrun. Then Waimea, then Honoka'a. Then Hilo, where her mother had been living. For a year, until Tetsuo found that record of her existence in a work camp, Key fantasized about her mother escaping on a boat to an atoll, living in a group of refugee humans who survived the apocalypse.

Everything Tetsuo asked of her, she did. She loved him from the moment they saved each other's lives. She has always said yes.

"*Key!*" Mr. Charles says to her, as though she is a friend he has run into unexpectedly. "I have some*thing*... you might *just* want."

"Yes, Mr. Charles?" she says.

The three of them are alone in the feeding house. Mr. Charles collapses dramatically against one of the divans and kicks off his tight patent-leather shoes as if they are barnacles. He wears no socks.

"There," he says, and waves his hand at the door. "*In* the bag."

Tetsuo nods and so she walks back. The bag is black canvas, unmarked. Inside, there's a book. She recognizes it immediately, though she only saw it once. *The Blind Watchmaker*. There is a note on the cover. The handwriting is large and uneven and painstaking, that of someone familiar with words but unaccustomed to writing them down. She notes painfully that he writes his "a" the same way as a typeset font, with the half-c above the main body and a careful serif at the end.

> Dear Overseer Ki,
> I would like you to have this. I have loved it very much and you are the only one who ever seemed to care. I am angry but
> I don't blame you. You're just too good at living.
> Jeb

She takes the bag and leaves both vampires without requesting permission. Mr. Charles's laugh follows her out the door.

Blood on the walls, on the floor, all over his body.

I am angry but. You're just too good at living. She has always said yes.

She is too much of a coward and she is too brave.

She watches the sunset the next evening from the hill in the garden, her back against the cherimoya tree. She feels the sun's death like she always has, with quiet joy. Awareness floods her: the musk of wet grass crushed beneath her bare toes, salt-spray and algae blowing from the ocean, the love she has clung to so fiercely since she was a girl, lost and alone. Everything she has ever loved is bound in that sunset, the red-and-violet orb that could kill him as it sinks into the ocean.

Her favorite time of day is sunset, but it is not night. She has never quite been able to fit inside his darkness, no matter how hard she tried. She has been too good at living, but perhaps it's not too late to change.

She can't take the path of Penelope or Jeb, but that has never been the only way. She remembers stories that reached Grade Orange from the work camps, half-whispered reports of humans who sat at their assembly lines and refused to lift their hands. Harvesters who drained gasoline from their combine engines and waited for the vampires to find them. If every human refused to cooperate, vampire society would crumble in a week. Still, she has no illusions about this third path sparking a revolution. This is simply all she can do: sit under the cherimoya tree and refuse. They will kill her, but she will have chosen to be human.

The sun descends. She falls asleep against the tree and dreams of the girl who never was, the one who opened the door. In her dreams, the sun burns her skin and her obachan tells her how proud she is while they pick strawberries in the garden. She eats an umeboshi that tastes of blood and salt, and when she swallows, the flavors swarm out of her throat, bubbling into her neck and jaw and ears. Flavors become emotions become thoughts; peace in the nape of her neck, obligation in her back molars, and hope just behind her eyes, bitter as a watermelon rind.

She opens them and sees Tetsuo on his knees before her. Blood smears his mouth. She does not know what to think when he kisses her, except that she can't even feel the pinprick pain where his teeth broke her skin. He has never fed from her before. They have never kissed before. She feels like she is floating, but nothing else.

The blood is gone when he sits back. As though she imagined it.

"You should not have left like that yesterday," he says. "Charles can make this harder than I'd like."

"Why is he here?" she asks. She breathes shallowly.

"He will take over Grade Gold once your transmutation is finished."

"That's why you brought me here, isn't it? It had nothing to do with the kids."

He shrugs. "Regulations. So Charles couldn't refuse."

"And where will you go?"

"They want to send me to the mainland. Texas. To supervise the installation of a new Grade Gold facility near Austin."

She leans closer to him, and now she can see it: regret, and shame that he should be feeling so. "I'm sorry," she says.

"I have lived seventy years on these islands. I have an eternity to come back to them. So will you, Key. I have permission to bring you with me."

Everything that sixteen-year-old had ever dreamed. She can still feel the pull of him, of her desire for an eternity together, away from the hell her life has become. Her transmutation would be complete. Truly a monster, the regrets for her past actions would fall away like waves against a seawall.

With a fumbling hand, she picks a cherimoya from the ground beside her. "Do you remember what these taste like?"

She has never asked him about his human life. For a moment, he seems genuinely confused. "You don't understand. Taste to us is vastly more complex. Joy, dissatisfaction, confusion, humility— *those* are flavors. A custard apple?" He laughs. "It's sweet, right?"

Joy, dissatisfaction, loss, grief, she tastes all that just looking at him.

"Why didn't you ever feed from me before?"

"Because I promised. When we first met."

And as she stares at him, sick with loss and certainty, Rachel walks up behind him. She is holding a kitchen knife, the blade pointed toward her stomach.

"Charles knows," she says.

"How?" Tetsuo says. He stands, but Key can't coordinate her muscles enough for the effort. He must have drained a lot of blood.

"I told him," Rachel says. "So now you don't have a choice. You will transmute me and you will get rid of this fucking fetus or I will kill myself and you'll be blamed for losing *two* Grade Gold humans."

Rachel's wrists are still bruised from where Key had to hold her several nights ago. Her eyes are sunken, her skin sallow. *This fucking fetus.*

She wasn't trying to kill herself with the cherimoya seeds. She was trying to abort a pregnancy.

"The baby is still alive after all that?" Key says, surprisingly indifferent to the glittering metal in Rachel's unsteady hands. Does Rachel know how easily Tetsuo could disarm her? What advantage does she think she has? But then she looks back in the girl's eyes and realizes: none.

Rachel is young and desperate and she doesn't want to be eaten by the monsters anymore.

"Not again, Rachel," Tetsuo says. "I *can't* do what you want. A vampire can only transmute someone he's never fed from before."

Rachel gasps. Key flops against her tree. She hadn't known that, either. The knife trembles in Rachel's grip so violently that Tetsuo takes it from her, achingly gentle as he pries her fingers from the hilt.

"*That's* why you never drank from her? And I killed her anyway? Stupid fucking Penelope. She could have been forever, and now there's just this dumb fogey in her place. She thought you cared about her."

"Caring is a strange thing, for a vampire," Key says.

Rachel spits in her direction but it falls short. The moonlight is especially bright tonight; Key can see everything from the grass to the tips of Rachel's ears, flushed sunset pink.

"Tetsuo," Key says, "why can't I move?"

But they ignore her.

"Maybe Charles will do it if I tell him you're really the one who killed Penelope."

"Charles? I'm sure he knows exactly what you did."

"I didn't *mean* to kill her!" Rachel screams. "Penelope was going to tell about the baby. She was crazy about babies, it didn't make any sense, and you had *picked her* and she wanted to destroy my life . . . I was so angry, I just wanted to hurt her, but I didn't realize . . ."

"Rachel, I've tried to give you a chance, but I'm not allowed to get rid of it for you." Tetsuo's voice is as worn out as a leathery orange.

"I'll die before I go to one of those mommy farms, Tetsuo. I'll die and take my baby with me."

"Then you will have to do it yourself."

She gasps. "You'll really leave me here?"

"I've made my choice."

Rachel looks down at Key, radiating a withering contempt that does nothing to blunt Key's pity. "If you had picked Penelope, I would have understood. Penelope was beautiful and smart. She's the only one who ever made it through half of that fat Shakespeare book in unit four. She could sing. Her breasts were perfect. But *her*? She's not a choice. She's nothing at all."

The silence between them is strained. It's as if Key isn't there at all. And soon, she thinks, she won't be.

"I've made my choice," Key says.

"*Your* choice?" they say in unison.

When she finds the will to stand, it's as though her limbs are hardly there at all, as though she is swimming in midair. For the first time, she understands that something is wrong.

Key floats for a long time. Eventually, she falls. Tetsuo catches her.

"What does it feel like?" Key asks. "The transmutation?"

Tetsuo takes the starlight in his hands. He feeds it to her through a glass shunt growing from a living branch. The tree's name is Rachel. The tree is very sad. Sadness is delicious.

"You already know," he says.

You will understand: he said this to her when she was human.
I wouldn't hurt you: she said this to a girl who—a girl—she drinks.

"I meant to refuse."

"I made a promise."

She sees him for a moment crouched in the back of her father's shed, huddled away from the dangerous bar of light that stretches across the floor. She sees herself, terrified of death and so unsure. *Open the door*, she tells that girl, too late. *Let in the light.*

DAWOLU JABARI ANDERSON

Sanford and Sun

SCENE 1

Lamont and Rollo with their three visiting guests from out of town walk through the door.

Pause for audience applause.

LAMONT: Sistas, that was one baaaaad show!

ROLLO: Told you, Jack, three celestial bodies in perfect alignment with each other: the sun, the moon, and q star.

LAMONT: Right on!

Lamont and Rollo give each other congratulatory fives.

Mild laughter.

CHINA: Thank you, bruthas. Like we said before, "It's our invitation for you to be of our space world."

LAMONT: But dig, you all say you're not professional dancers, but what you're doing is just as good as any dance choreography I've ever seen.

ETHIOPIA: Thanks for the compliment, but think of it as *kata* in *karate*. They are choreographed movements, dance movements, but the actual application is for self-defense. Well, we're stellar cartographers. My profession is astrobiology. China and Jette are stellar astrophysicists. The application of our fieldwork becomes choreographed configurations. So they are dance moves in the sense that kata employs a series of dance moves but more specifically they are ancient ceremonial movements charting the constellations or star chart rituals.

JETTE: These rituals unlock inner space chambers, unlocking us from conformity, so later for the stars and bars, dig? We salvage the stars as we liberate sistas and bruthas from their cultural bars.

Applause.

CHINA: Basically, it breaks you out of your House Negro training. [*laughter*]

ROLLO: Yeah, what if your audience is all white?

ETHIOPIA: Then we break'm out of their house Anglo training. [*laughter*]

ROLLO: Star chart rituals, that's solid.

ETHIOPIA: Dig, brutha, you have to internalize the stars and planets. *SPI* stands for *Stars and Planets Internal*. Take that *spi* and place it at the beginning of *ritual*, 'cause everything we do is spiritual. The spiritual obtainment is through the performance of ritual. To perform a ritual is to internalize patterns and cycles of celestial bodies that unlock our inner space.

LAMONT: So why not do these rituals anytime? Why only do it to music?

ETHIOPIA: Our sun emits vibrations just as the other billions of stars do. We are a billion-year-old species made of stardust. If the sun's composition is vibratory, then so are we. The sun rises in the east, so we face east.

LAMONT: That's some heavy stuff. How 'bout we chart some constellations as I place some vibrations in rotation? [*laughter*]

JETTE: We call nights like this Saturn.

LAMONT: Saturn?

JETTE: Dig. It's a Saturday night for the records to turn! [*laughter*]

LAMONT: Right on! Look here, this is not exactly the Taj Mahal when it comes to space but, Rollo, if you help me slide this couch over we can have a bit more "get down" space.

FRED, *walking out the kitchen, eating crackers*: Yeah, but it's my Taj Mahal, and if any of my treasures end up in Rollo's pocket, Ali Baba is going to find himself a thief short. [*applause and laughter*]

LAMONT: Awww, Pop, what are you doing here?

FRED: I got home early.

LAMONT: I can see that! I mean, I thought you were going to catch the late feature with Grady.

FRED: We did, son. It started off real good. *The Wolfman Meets the Creature from the Black Lagoon* [*laughter*]—it was supposed to be the scariest movie of the year, but I couldn't make myself stay and finish it.

LAMONT: Don't tell me it was too scary for Fright Film Fanatic Fred.

FRED: No, that's just it, son. See, I've become immune to all kinds of fear after years of overexposure to your Aunt Esther's radioactive face [*laughter*]—so we left early.

LAMONT: Look, Pop, we're trying to get educated by some heavy sistas. You can't go over to Grady's place to watch TV or something?

FRED: The picture on Grady's TV roll too much.

LAMONT: What? You were just over there yesterday watching the baseball game.

FRED: Yeah, but the picture rolled so much, we couldn't tell if Dock Ellis was trying to pitch the ball or bowl it. [*laughter*]

LAMONT: Ha ha. Very funny.

FRED: Look here, why don't you introduce me to your lovely friends?

LAMONT, *reluctantly*: Sistas, this is my father. Pop this is China, Jette, and Ethiopia.

FRED: That's Fred G. Sanford.

CHINA: It's a pleasure to meet you, Mr. Sanford.

ETHIOPIA: I detect some heavy wit in this house.

FRED: Oh, that'll be the "wit" I had in the leftovers.

ETHIOPIA: Leftovers?

FRED: Yeah, salt bacon wit' collards, oxtails wit' mash potatoes, and fried okra wit' hog snout. [*laughter*]

LAMONT, *with a smirk*: Pop.

FRED: I know, I know. I'm only kidding. It's good to meet you, ladies.

LAMONT: Say, Pop, they're here to perform with the jazz musician Sun Ra at the Watts Towers. China, Jette, and Ethiopia are all a part of his Arkestra.

FRED: Arkestra?

LAMONT: Yeah. Dig, Pop, an ark and an orchestra as one. Music that takes people high up to the outer reaches of new gardens.

FRED: I don't think it's the music that's getting them high. It's probably something growing in those new gardens. [*laughter*] Sun Raw might be *Sun Rotten*. [*laughter*]

JETTE: No, Mr. Sanford. It's *Sun Ra*. It's part of our heritage. Ra is the sun god in African Egyptian culture. Surely you know of the pyramids and the ancient Egyptian mummies.

FRED: All I know is the ghetto and the ancient Watts auntie named Aunt Esther. [*laughter*]

LAMONT: Would you stop it? Just stop it! You're hopeless. You always have to go and make fun of things you don't understand. You don't know anything about African culture.

FRED: Are you kiddin'? I'm the one that tried to get you to watch the late night picture the other night on Africa.

LAMONT: *The African Queen* starring Humphrey Bogart does not count, Pop. [*laughter*]

JETTE: Mr. Sanford, why don't you come down to our show tomorrow and check it out for yourself?

ETHIOPIA: Yeah, that's a great idea.

LAMONT: Ohhh no! That's a bad idea.

FRED, *with a pitiful frown*: Maybe my son is right. An old man like me with a bad heart condition would just get in the way.

ETHIOPIA: Lamont, this is your father. Mr. Sanford, we are giving you a personal invitation. Come on, Lamont, it's only right.

LAMONT: I can dig it, but my father's nature is to sabotage everything. He can't stand to see anything go right. Even when he drives he only makes left turns. [*laughter*]

JETTE: Lamont, everybody is invited to the space ways—

FRED: Yeah, Dummy, "the space ways." [*laughter*]

JETTE: And everybody is an instrument in this vast cosmos—

FRED: That's right, "cosmos." [*light laughter*]

JETTE: And each of us have a part to play in it.

FRED: Everybody's an instrument with a part to play, you big dummy. [*laughter*]

LAMONT: With all the hot air you blow, you're perfect for the woodwind section. [*laughter*]

FRED, *holding up his fists*: How would you like a "do" and a "re" across the lips by "mi," leaving you to B flat? [*laughter*]

CHINA: On the outside you two may appear to be disharmonious but in actuality you all are rhythmically in sync. A little fine-tuning is all that's needed.

FRED: That's why I always sing when coordinating the office space. [*Lamont rolls his eyes.*] [*laughter*] It brings peace in the home.

CHINA: Mr. Sanford, you can sing?

FRED: Like a bird.

LAMONT: Yeah, a strangled one. [*laughter*] [*Fred scowls.*]

CHINA: Why don't you sing something for us, Mr. Sanford! [*Jette and Ethiopia concur.*]

FRED: All right, then. [*Gestures to Lamont.*] Back up, dummy.

If I didn't care
more than words can say
If I didn't care
would I feel this way.

Laughter and applause; commercial break.

FRED: You know, I think I would like to meet Solar Rays.

LAMONT: That's "Sun Ra"! [*laughter*]

ETHIOPIA: Right on, Mr. Sanford! I know you two will hit it off. Look, it's getting late and we have to get back to our group.

ROLLO: I'll take you sistas back.

China, Ethiopia, and Jette each give Fred a peck on the cheek.

JETTE: So we'll be seeing you tomorrow, Mr. Sanford?

FRED, *smiling*: I'll be there.

CHINA: The show starts around five. Bye, Mr. Sanford.

FRED, *waves to them*: Bye-bye, girls.

The five o'clock whistle didn't blow.
The whistle is broke and whadda'ya know?
If somebody don't find out what's wrong
Oh my pop'll be workin' all night long.

Applause.

Fred closes the door while Lamont looks at him in disapproval.

FRED, *singing*: Oh, who's gonna fix the whistle? Won't somebody fix the whistle?

Fred finishes his cracker, pushes out a weak whistle, blows cracker bits on Lamont.

LAMONT: You better not mess this up, that's all I got to say. Is there anything here to eat? I'm starving.

FRED: Just some leftovers I was warming up before you came.

LAMONT, *opening a pot on the stove top*: Wheeeew! What is that in the pot? It smells horrible!

FRED: I told you it was leftovers.

LAMONT: We didn't have this last night. We had collards, beef roast, and dinner rolls.

FRED: Yeah, but the night before that we had neck bones, cornbread, string beans, and sweet potatoes, and before that we had smothered pork chops, black-eyed peas, oxtails, and Rice-A-Roni.

LAMONT: So?

FRED: So, leftovers. [*laughter*]

LAMONT: You mean to tell me you mixed together all the food from this entire week?

FRED: Yeah. I call it "sweet smothered black-ox collards and string beef-o-Roni chops." [*laughter*]

LAMONT: Yeah, and if you eat that you're going to be "graveyard-dirt smothered Fred-o-Roni." [*laughter*] You're impossible. I'm going out to eat something that has one name to it.

FRED: Good. More for me. [*laughter*]

SCENE 2

Fred walks down the stairs; Lamont looks in the mirror, putting on cologne.

LAMONT, *admiring himself and his dashiki*: Ha! When you got it, you got it.

FRED: And by the smell of it, you should be quarantined before someone else gets it. [*laughter*] What's that stuff you stinking the whole house up with?

LAMONT: Well, for your information, it's what's happening. It's a new cologne all the uptown dudes are wearing.

FRED: More like uptown fumigators. [*laughter*] Why you getting ready to leave so early anyway?

LAMONT: Rollo and I are going to help out with stage setup. You might as well head up there with us since you're going to be going there anyway.

FRED, *rubbing his stomach*: I got a bit of stomachache from last night's meal. I'll have to pass.

LAMONT: You mean pass out. I can't believe you pulled a stupid stunt like that. You have one foot in the grave and the other foot on a banana peel. [*laughter*] Pop, our bodies aren't made for eating pig, long ones or short ones. That's why we think like slaves, 'cause we still eat and live like slaves.

FRED: Well, I ain't no slave. I like to eat good food.

LAMONT: Pig snout, oxtails, pork chops? That's slave food. How are you ever going to vibrate on a spiritual frequency?

FRED: I don't want to vibrate on spiritual frequencies. That's why I always stay home for Super Bowl Sunday and watch it on VHF frequencies. [*laughter*]

LAMONT: Dig yourself, Pop. I'm talking frequencies of consciousness, not television. I'm talking transcendental experiences. Talking to you is like talking to a rusty bucket of sand.

FRED, *holding up a fist*: Watch your mouth or you'll be having a hands-in-dental experience. [*laughter*]

LAMONT: Never mind. I'm through with this conversation.

FRED, *looking bewildered*: What's that?

LAMONT: Forget about it. You'll only have some smart remark to make.

FRED: No I won't. I think it's perfectly normal to walk around in a Zulu picnic blanket. [*laughter*]

LAMONT, *looking fed up*: You only show how ignorant you are of the dashiki.

FRED: Die chic? Not in that. You'd be dying ugly. [*laughter*]

LAMONT: I give up.

There's a knock at the door.

LAMONT: That must be Rollo. [*opening the door*] Hey, Rollo.

ROLLO: What's happenin', Lamont? You ready?

LAMONT: Yeah, step in. Let me run upstairs and get my jacket.

ROLLO: What's happenin', Pops? What's the word?

FRED: The word was *abracadabra*, but you still here. So I have to figure out a new one. [*laughter*]

ROLLO: Aw, Pops. Man, you cold.

FRED: If I stand next to your jewelry I'm not. [*laughter*]

ROLLO: You got it all wrong, Jack. This ain't stolen. I paid for this. Cold hard cash.

FRED: You mean you'll pay for it in cold hard time. [*laughter*]

ROLLO: Aw, Pops. Every time I come around you always got some gag.

FRED: And you always got someone tied up and gagged, you crook. [*laughter*]

Rollo waves his hand dismissively.

LAMONT: All right, I'm ready. Let's split.

ROLLO: Solid.

LAMONT: Later, Pops.

ROLLO, *teasingly*: Later, Pops.

FRED, *mumbling, biting lip, clenching fist*: I'll later you, you ol'—

As Fred almost makes it to the couch, there's a knock at the door again; he goes and opens the door.

GRADY, *walking in*: Hey, Fred. I just saw Larry and Rothko walking off.

Laughter.

FRED: That's Lamont and Rollo.

GRADY: Oh yeah.

FRED: Come on in, Grady.

Both have a seat; Fred groans a bit.

GRADY: What's wrong with you Fred? You look like you half dead.

FRED: I think I got some stomach trouble from last night's supper. It could be the big one. The big one might be trying to sneak up on me from my stomach this time. [*laughter*]

GRADY: You don't have a bad stiffness in your back, do you?

FRED: Yeah, right between my shoulder blades.

GRADY: Do you feel a slight shortness in breath when you bend over?

FRED, *worriedly*: Yeah. Yeah, I do.

Grady slowly shakes his head.

FRED, *worried*: What? What is it, Grady?

GRADY: You remember that cousin of mine that was in real estate?

FRED: Yeah, yeah.

GRADY: Well, you have the same symptoms he had. He went to see one of those doctors that cure all your ailments with natural herbs, plants, and stuff.

Grady sits shaking his head as Fred waits for him to continue.

FRED: Well don't just sit there like a dummy. What combinations of plants did he take for it?

GRADY: A funeral wreath. [*laughter*] Now he's beneath the real estate. [*laughter*]

FRED: Grady, you're supposed to be my friend. Whatchu go and say something depressing like that for?

GRADY: I'm sorry, Fred, I wasn't thinking.

FRED: Why don't you go find someone else to depress. They ought to call you "Gray Cloud" Grady.

GRADY: I'm sorry, Fred. I was just trying to help. But you can't keep on eating like that. It'll kill you. They say more people die from their food-related sickness than homicides.

FRED: That's the same stuff Lamont always saying. You all don't know what you're talking about. "Cut out the pork, cut out the cigarettes, cut out the wine." How's someone going to look eating healthy their whole life, then on their deathbed they die of nothing? [*laughter*]

GRADY: You do have a point, Fred. I had another cousin that cut out all pork and wine from his diet. He was perfectly healthy. He ate nothing but vegetables, and, wouldn't you know it, it turned out vegetables took him to his grave.

FRED: See, that's my point exactly.

GRADY: Yeah, one day he was crossing the street and got hit by a produce truck. [*laughter*] [*Fred scowls at Grady.*] Well, I have to get going. See ya, Fred.

FRED: All right. See ya, Grady.

*Fred walks Grady to the door; on his way back to the couch, he
sees a Sun Ra album Lamont left on a counter.*

FRED: One of Lamont's albums. Hmmm [*reading the title,* Sun Ra:
Nuits de la Fondation Maeght], Sun Ra: Nutes de la fondashun
. . . mate? [*light laughter*] Let me see what this sounds like.
[*Fred places disk on the record player. The music begins to
pulsate.*] I guess it wouldn't hurt to kick my feet up a bit. Well, I
guess it wouldn't hurt to take a little nap so I can be well rested
for the show. [*Fred drifts off to sleep.*]

Hours later, a knocking at the door.

FRED, *slowly waking up*: All right, all right, I'm coming.

*Fred opens the door and a person with a huge ibis head mask of
the Egyptian god Thoth walks in.*

FRED, *backing up clenching his chest*: Oh, no! [*laughter*] Ohhhh! It's
Rodan! [*roaring laughter*] He finished eating Tokyo, Japan, now
he wants Watts, California! [*laughter*] Oh, Elizabeth! Elizabeth,
I'm coming to join you, honey! This time Polly wanna nigga!
[*laughter*]

*Sun Ra steps through the door dressed in elaborate ancient
ceremonial garb.*

SUN RA: Mr. Sanford? [*pause for applause*] Mr. Sanford, are you all
right?

FRED, *coming out of shock*: Ohhhhh. Huh? What?

SUN RA, *coming to Fred's aid*: Are you all right, Mr. Sanford?

FRED, *looking up and down at Sun Ra's clothing*: Am I all right? A black Liberace and Yul Brynner in a Big Bird mask are standing in my living room. Do I look all right? [*laughter*] Who are you?

SUN RA, *spreading his arms*: I—am Sun Ra.

FRED, *scanning Sun Ra from head to toe*: You. Are. Sun Ra?

SUN RA: I apologize if I startled you.

FRED: The way you're dressed, you'd startle Monty Hall. [*laughter*]

SUN RA, *shaking his head in amusement*: These space suits are signature clothes worn by your great ancestors both on Earth and on Saturn.

FRED: And all this time I thought junkies were only on Earth. [*laughter*]

SUN RA: Mr. Sanford, all catalysts at one time or another were criticized for their eccentric ideas.

FRED: Well, those cattle lists probably had the wrong type of cattle. [*laughter*] They probably started off like you trying to herd bird people instead of cows. [*laughter*]

SUN RA, *chuckling*: You don't understand, Mr. Sanford. I'm just going to have to show you. As the ambassador of the intergalactic federation, please accompany me on a journey to the diamonds in the sky. [*He gestures*]

FRED, *grabbing his baseball bat*: You see this Louisville slugger?

It's known for its batting average on the diamond on the ground. [*Roaring laughter*] If you don't—

A strange pulsating sound coming from outside interrupts.

FRED: What's that sound?

SUN RA: Those are the natural minors of vibro-ion accelerator engines.

FRED, *going to the door*: Engines?

Fred looks out the door and sees a spaceship.

FRED, *clutching his chest again*: What [*gulping*] is that?

SUN RA: I told you, Mr. Sanford, I'm an ambassador from the intergalactic federation of outer space.

SUN RA, *singing*:

> *Hereby*
> *our invitation*
> *we do invite you*
> *be of my space world.*

FRED, *falling into a hypnotic state as Sun Ra's entourage escorts him into the ship*: Be of your space world?

SUN RA: Rhythmic equations . . .

FRED: Rhythmic equations . . .

SUN RA: Enlightenment is my tomorrow...

FRED: Enlightenment is my tomorrow...

SUN RA: Has no plane of sorrow...

FRED: Has no plane of sorrow...

SUN RA: Be of my space world.

FRED: Be of my space world.

SCENE 3

FRED: Where am I? What is this place?

SUN RA: You are riding sacred sounds, the sounds of enlightenment by way of strange mathematics and rhythmic equations.

FRED: Sounds of what-ment? Wh-what you mean, "riding sounds of enlightenment"? [*laughter*]

SUN RA: You are flying in a spacecraft propelled by the depths of wisdom upon vibratory star patterns. Enlightenment enables us to defy the oppressive weight of ignorance.

FRED: You mean we're in the air?

SUN RA: We're in space.

FRED: Put! Me! Down! [*laughter*]

SUN RA: Down, Mr. Sanford? In the vastness of space, down is relative. It's only when earth lies beneath your feet that "up and down" has any significance.

FRED: Oooh! [*Fred stumbles back clutching his chest.*] Oh no! This is the biggest one yet! You hear that, Elizabeth? I'm with a junky from Jupiter and I don't know if I'm coming to join you, honey! I can't tell which way is up! Oooh! [*laughter*]

SUN RA: You are perfectly safe, Mr. Sanford. Everything is as it should be.

FRED: Listen, are you for real?

SUN RA: I'm not real, I'm just like you. You don't exist in your society. If you did, your people would not be seeking equal rights.

FRED: Oh, yeah? Try driving through Beverly Hills at night and see if you don't exist to the police. [*laughter*] You'll end up being nonexistent. [*laughter*]

SUN RA: That's just my point, Mr. Sanford. See, your existence is that insignificant. If you were real, you'd have some status amongst the nations of the world. So we're both myths. I do not come to you as reality. I come to you as myth because that's what black people are: myths.

FRED: This is all crazy. It has to be a dream. That's it, I'm dreaming. It was that food I had last night. That has to be it.

SUN RA: I came from a dream that the black man dreamt long ago. I'm actually a presence sent to you by your ancestors.

I understand why this is difficult for you to comprehend. Your entire life you have been veiled from the fiery truth of enlightenment. You believe the extent of your existence is the role of an ex-slave, an Afro-American. But what were you before that?

FRED: A bald-headed African? [*laughter*]

SUN RA, *smiling with amusement*: Please try to stay focused, brother Sanford. You see, you have both an outer space and an inner space to explore. One should never exceed the other. Inner development prepares you spiritually, while external works help society. When you abandon either, you suffer the consequences of subjugation. This is why you become dependent and beg for jobs from the system. This is why you beg them for rights.

FRED: We don't beg. We deserve those rights.

SUN RA: To deserve means you are "worthy of." Whoever determines you to be worthy of something wields the power to administer judgment. You have to define your own worth, not empower someone else to decide that. Coltrane determined his worth. Garvey determined his worth. You've only made a partial journey from the inner space of the womb to the outer space or outcasts of society. Your new inner space is the inner city. Control that and explore the outer world beyond your country.

FRED: Couldn't you tell me that without showing up as the ghost of Kwanzaa past? [*laughter*]

SUN RA: You had to obtain this through vibrations, through rhythmic equations. You are an instrument, brother Sanford, and I treat everybody as such. We all have a part to play in this vast Arkestra.

The engine changes frequencies.

FRED: What was that noise?

SUN RA: Not noise, music. Look out the porthole. We've arrived at the Black Sanctuary. As soon as we land we can go to the gardens to nourish our spirits.

FRED: Just so we're clear about things. When you say "nourish our spirits" in this garden, are you talking about picking and eating or rollin' and tokin'? [*laughter*]

SUN RA, *laughing*: Picking and eating, Mr. Sanford. Knowledge expands through the rigorous discipline of science, not through mind-altering stimulants. We haven't time for that. The intellect is sacred, and in our tradition we guard it.

FRED: Yeah, well, in our tradition if you're caught with that you will end up being guarded while doing time. [*laughter and applause*]

As Sun Ra and Fred nourish their spirits, rollicking frenzied polyrhythms are heard.

FRED: What's that knocking sound, that beating going on in my head?

SUN RA: Inner percussion, Mr. Sanford. Vibrations are in you. Bare the tones of life. Be a baritone. The sharps and the flats, the ups and downs. Electrify!

FRED and SUN RA, *singing*:

> *The sound of joy is enlightenment*
> *The space fire truth is enlightenment*
> *Space fire*
> *sometimes it's music*
> *strange mathematic*
> *s'rhythmic equations*
> *The sound of thought is enlightenment*
> *the magic light of tomorrow*
> *Backwards*
> *out of the sadness*
> *forward and onward*
> *others of gladness*
> *Enlightenment is my tomorrow*
> *it has no planes of sorrow*
> *Hereby,*
> *my invitation*
> *I do invite you*
> *be of my space world*
> *This song is sound of enlightenment*
> *the fiery truth of enlightenment*
> *vibrations*
> *sent from the space world*
> *is of the cosmic*
> *starring dimensions*
> *Enlightenment is my tomorrow*
> *it has no planes of sorrow*

Hereby
my invitation
I do invite you
be of my space world
Hereby
my invitation
I do invite you
be of my space world.

FRED, *singing in his sleep*: Hereby our invitation, we do invite you—

SUN RA, *touching Fred on his shoulder*: Mr. Sanford. Mr. Sanford.

FRED, *coming out of sleep*: Huh? What? Who? [*Seeing Sun Ra standing above him, he gives a hard swallow.*]

SUN RA, *touching Fred on his shoulder*: Mr. Sanford, you were singing to the record in your sleep. I cut it off.

FRED: You. How did we get back so fast? Where's Lamont?

SUN RA: Back from where, Mr. Sanford? And Lamont, China, Jette, and Ethiopia are following right behind. He told me to come on inside the house and meet you. I was knocking at the door. You didn't really answer, you just started singing.

FRED: So it was all just a dream?

SUN RA: I suppose so. We missed you at the show so when our set was over, I insisted on still meeting you.

FRED: So you don't want me to take you to my leader or anything? Even though he's kind of tied up with some tapes. [*laughter and applause*]

SUN RA, *light laugh*: No, Mr. Sanford, I don't need to see your leader.

Lamont walks in the door with China, Jette, Ethiopia, and Rollo.

CHINA: Oh, hey, Mr. Sanford. I see you two have met.

SUN RA: Yeah, but I think I gave him a bit of a fright at first.

LAMONT: Let me guess: my pops had one of his routine heart attacks? [*laughter*]

FRED: As a matter of fact, no. It's just that Sun Ra had these two giant birds, and we all got on this space— Oh, forget it. It was just a dream anyway.

FINAL SCENE

Fred and Lamont are sitting as Fred relaxes, finishing a drink.

LAMONT: Well, Pop, it was good having Sun Ra at the house.

FRED: Yes it was, son.

LAMONT: Oh, yeah, almost forgot: Sun Ra told me to tell you that perhaps someday we can ride rhythmic equations and all meet up at the Black Sanctuary. [*Fred spits out his drink.*]

He said you would understand what he was talking about.
[*laughter*]

FRED, *swallowing, his hand to his chest*: Black Sanctuary?

Fred looks at Lamont in shock and Lamont gestures confusion.

Credit music comes in.

JENNIFER MARIE BRISSETT

A Song for You

The ripples carried the head further up the river. Gently it drifted, impeded here and there by the side of some stone, only to be pushed along again by the rush of the flow. It finally found a resting place on the shore where the water ran quiet into a brown muddy clay. By the appearance of the stem, it was clear that it had been ripped away from some handsome body. The eyes remained peacefully closed, though, as if it were a young man only lightly asleep. What seemed like blood streamed from its veins and a kind of flesh dragged from its neck. There, if one was careful to look, were the remains of some circuitry, a line or two of wire, and a glowing diode still blinking lime green.

Little Maya, a child of no more than six or seven, played her weeping willow game nearby, a pastime of imaginings that allowed her to run and hide among the trees and rocks scattered across her father's land. She curved her back to imitate the low-hanging branches lining the river and swayed her body as if by the breeze. Then she envisioned herself large and able to lift root and trunk to stomp about and replant herself elsewhere. Her mother had long ago given up on the idea that her child would ever remain clean throughout the day. Into the wash her dress would go as soon as Maya returned home, as well as Maya herself into the bath for a long scrub. But for now it was all adventure and discovery. And such a discovery she would make this day.

She heard singing by the river and ran to the edge and there she found the head pushed up into the mud.

"Hello," Maya said.

The head opened its eyes and stared back at the little girl standing above it and replied, "Hello."

"Where's your body?" Maya asked, lifting her arms to the sky as if the answer could be found there.

"I don't suppose I have one anymore," the head answered.

"Oh, I'm sorry."

"Thank you," it said. "It's not your fault."

Then she poked gently at its nose with her index finger. The eyes moved slightly and fluttered.

"May I move you away from the water? You don't look that comfortable there."

"Yes, I would quite appreciate that."

And so Maya gently lifted the head into the front part of her skirt and carried it to a dry place in the woods where soft pine needles blanketed the ground. She lay the head softly near a stone and positioned it upright to face her. Its mouth moved, opening wide into the shape of an "O," giving it a surprised look, then stretched into a smile then a frown then back into an expressionless line.

"What happened to your body?" Maya asked as she sat down in front of it.

"That is a long story."

"Tell me. I like stories."

The head stared at her with a countenance the child would see again when she became older on the face of her own mother who while dying wanted to speak her last words. The head remained silent for a long moment and said, "Perhaps, it is time."

Maya folded her legs and readied herself to listen.

My existence began in an organic soup of protein and integrated circuitry chips, swirling to form a harmony of life and machine. I remember hanging in my gestation sack, lined up in a room full of others doing the same, when I heard sound for the first time. A single drip. I, of course, had no idea what it was. So I looked all around, for I had been able to see for many days by this time, but sound … sound was new.

I heard it again. One single drip. After some considerable time I finally located the source. A faucet that had not been entirely closed produced rhythmic pearls of water that fell delicately into a silver sink. Pa-lunk … Pa-lunk … Pa-lunk …

I listened for hours, maybe days, inventing in my mind alternate reflections to the constant pattern of the eventual pa-lunk of the drips and the momentary pauses between each falling dot. I didn't know it then, but I eventually learned that this rhythm and the empty silences that followed were my first exposure to music.

In the time of the selection, when our personality programming is installed and our final circuitry patterns are set, we are asked what designation we would prefer. I chose acoustic engineer, to the surprise of the technician. It was so specific, he said, and asked if I was sure because most chose more general professions and became specified over time. I told him that I was sure. He looked at me with a question still resting on his lips, shrugged, then wrote down my request.

I was eventually assigned to a small ship called the Calliope that had a regular manifest of about fifteen people and was stationed just above our planet's second moon. I performed routine maintenance and carried out support tasks for the crew. No one was unkind to me on the ship, but no one was kind either. I was a tool to them, a thing. Which I was, I know. Only I wished that they would talk to me. I was perfectly capable of carrying a conversation and was interested in their thoughts. But none of them ever did until Eura came on board.

Eura was my friend, or at least I'd like to think so. She was the only one on the ship that spoke to me like a person. She said that it helped her while away the time and that she thought that I was funny. She said it was my innocence that made her laugh. And I liked the sound of her laugh.

One day I discovered that we had a rodent living loose within the walls, chewing on the lines. I had to replace several faulty harmonic relays because of it. Eura and I attempted for hours to track down the culprit when it occurred to me to use a harmonic to lull the creature out. There was a family of frequencies I was developing that I thought might work. I emitted the waves through my oral cavity and to my surprise the creature emerged and lay before me as if in a trance.

Eura struggled to contain her laughter—and as I said before, I liked the sound of her laugh—and begged me not to harm the creature as I put it into a container. I reminded her that my programming included a directive to bring no harm to any living thing, this creature included. She nodded and smiled and patted me on the shoulder. It was the first time she had physically touched me. So for her, I cared for the rodent for the remainder of my time on the Calliope.

If it wasn't for Eura I would never have known a war might be coming. She told me a war would be bad because the enemy was strong and many. And worse, our technology was no match for theirs. I should have guessed something was happening from looking out the window. Where there had been only a few ships weeks before, now a multitude scattered about like dry rice on a plate. It felt as if it were possible to walk straight to the surface of the moon only by walking across their hulls. Eura told me that she was sure things would calm down, but I could tell from the inflection of her voice that she didn't believe her own words.

The child yawned widely and a dimness had fallen on the woods. Behind the trees the light of the sun oranged as if the forest had been set afire. So the head suggested that maybe it was time for her to go home. Maya nodded in agreement and vowed to return. She walked home covered in fresh dirt, as her mother had expected, spinning tales of a talking head she found in the river. Her mother put her child to bed wondering how it could be that she had given birth to one with such an imagination.

Maya returned the next day as promised to find the head exactly where she had left it only covered with leaves and pine needles because of the night wind. She carefully removed the debris and caressed its forehead with her open palm. It was cold to the touch. Then she wiped its cheek with the edge of her skirt.

"Please tell me more of your story," she asked, and the head replied that it would.

When we finished fixing the damaged lines, Eura asked me to sing for her. I didn't understand what she meant and told her so. The sounds that I had emitted, Eura said, were beautiful. I told her that they were only basic harmonics. She insisted that it was music and asked me to do it again at mealtime.

So that night, after the crew had finished consuming their protein rations, I played a series of acoustic waves from my subprocessor for them. I designed a composition by sampling some harmonics to mimic rain patterns, the drips of falling water. The crew remained remarkably still after I completed my piece. I didn't know what to make of it. Then I saw that one or two of them were weeping. They clapped their hands to my relief and many of them told me that what I had played was good.

Our evenings went on like this for many long days and months. After their meal, I would play a new song for them. I began to also add lyrics. I found a long-dead language in the ship's database that I was sure no one onboard would understand and composed songs with it. Many of the songs were about Eura and how beautiful she was, how kind and wonderful. I wanted to tell her without really telling her. I didn't want to embarrass her.

"Because you loved her," Maya interrupted.

"Yes, I suppose I did," the head answered.

In time, the peace we had come to know came to an end. I never understood the conflict. It all seemed so senseless to me and still does to this day. Fire and smoke filled the decks during the fighting. Many sections of the ship were exposed to open space as large irreparable holes ripped open in the hull. We struggled hard to keep the ship in one piece. And we lost many crew members. Eventually it came down to defending our homeworld on the ground; the enemy was that close. The capital had to be defended so we were ordered to the surface. What was left of my crew and I dug in behind trench lines along a border surrounding our main headquarters. They would fight hand to hand if necessary. I supported them by bringing them food and medical supplies.

Eura remained beautiful even covered in dirt and blood. I stayed with her, protecting her as best I could. The days were dark and the nights lit with flames of yellow and the thunder of explosions. We all knew that it was only a matter of time before the end.

It was hard on Eura, seeing her people die all around her, some of them dragged away screaming by an enemy rumored to keep lairs where they experimented on our people and maybe feasted on their flesh. I didn't fear death because I've never really been alive, but I could see that Eura was afraid.

She talked of what she thought it would be like to not exist anymore. She suggested sometimes that she believed death to be a black nothingness. Other times she spoke of a place where it would be warm and light and she would see her friends and family again.

When she was most afraid she would ask me to sing for her and I would, keeping my voice soft so as not to reveal our position. Then she would fold herself into my arms as if I were a real man and fall asleep and I would hold her. I know that I am not a man. I am only made to look like one. Yet these were the times that I regretted it most.

I returned from one of my regular trips to collect supplies to find that the trench had been attacked and my Eura was gone. I looked everywhere for her. If they had killed her, I would have found some of her remains. The faces of the survivors told me that our enemy had taken her.

Determined to find Eura, I searched for days through the rubble and the mud until I found a lair made of some biogenetic material, a kind of secreted resin alien to this world. It formed a cave-like structure buried far down into the soil. I went inside, climbing deep, deep below the surface, down and down and down. It smelled rank with the flesh of my people. The bodies of the dead and dying lay piled to one side. I watched quietly for a while as the aliens diligently took them, one by one, to a platform to wrap them in a dark material and string them throughout the lair. The dead hung from the ceilings and walls like shadows.

The enemy moved only slightly as I entered. I think they recognized me as an artificial life form and were curious and unafraid. I located Eura. I touched her face and felt that she was still warm. She opened her eyes. They were glassy white.

"Follow me," I told her. She stood unsteadily at first and then she walked behind me as if in a daze. I hurried to guide her towards the exit. The enemy moved in. I said that I had no quarrel with them, that I was not human, that I meant them no harm and that I only wanted the girl. They didn't seem to understand and continued to surround us. It occurred to me then to sing. I don't know why, but it did.

I sang a song that I had composed for Eura that I had never sung before. I improvised harmonics that I could not repeat even now. It was a song that said how I truly felt about her and I sang as if all of creation was at stake, because for me it was. When I finished, they were still. It was as if they were weeping.

While they remained motionless, Eura and I began our ascent out of the lair. I climbed and climbed, hearing her echoing footsteps

*behind me. I continued until I saw the light of the opening. I turned
around to say we were almost out but nobody was there. I would
have sworn that she was right behind me. But Eura was gone.*

*Just as I had learned to play music, I learned to hate. I killed
every creature I could get my hands on for days and days. I needed
no rest. I needed no sleep. I needed no comfort. I only needed to kill.
I fought not for my people, not for the war, but for Eura and, yes, for
myself. When the enemy finally caught me they were not as merciful
as they had been before. They ripped me apart, tearing off my arms
and legs and torso and leaving only my head, as you see here, and
threw me into the waters. I floated for I don't know how many years,
drifting buoyant along the seaways and rivers until I finally made
my way here to this place where I tell this tale to you.*

Maya was silent. So the head sang a song for her soft and low.
After the song ended she said, "Maybe my father can get a new
body for you."

The head considered this and said, "No, I would not like that.
But thank you. You are kind. Though, there is something that you
can do for me."

"What?" Maya asked.

"Please, reach inside of me to where the wires still connect and
pull them out."

Maya shook her head and cried, "No! That would make you
dead."

"Yes, it would be as if I were dead. But remember, I was never
truly alive."

"Don't ask me to."

"Please, this endless existence is too much for me, the memories too hard. Please," it said, "be my friend and do this for me."

"No!" Maya stood up. "I won't."

And she covered the head with leaves and dirt and stomped
away.

From then on Maya avoided the area of the woods where

the head lay and played her games elsewhere. Occasionally she would hear its singing voice, so beautiful and clear over the whispers of the wind. She closed her ears to it and tried not to listen. The backyard of friends who lived a walking distance away became her new playground. To her mother's relief, Maya left behind her solitary imagined world but she also found the suddenness of it curious. When questioned Maya never really explained why. She only said that she liked her new friends better which seemed to satisfy the subject well enough.

Yet Maya became more melancholy as she grew up. Bouts with a grieving sadness plagued her teenaged years. She occasionally found herself staring off into the distance, lost in her thoughts, feeling deep pangs of guilt for something she forgot to remember. As the years passed she was almost able to tell herself that the head was only a game that she had played, something silly best left in childhood. Maya eventually grew into young adulthood, remembering the head as only a dream.

Her education and familial status allowed her to enter into the service division where she quickly rose in rank to become a leader in artifact recovery. Every day on her job she helped to examine and catalog a variety of objects found in various locations that helped to advance her theories that an intelligent indigenous life form inhabited their world long before its colonization. The finest examples of her discoveries remained on display in the district museum of antiquities. She loved her profession and became well known and respected in the field of ancient indigenous studies. In many ways, the dream she believed she had of a singing head inspired her work. She was away at the capital to deliver a paper when she received the message that her mother had fallen ill.

Maya returned home to care for her dying mother. She spent her days alone watching the strong woman who had raised her wither away. Wiping her mother's forehead with a damp cloth reminded her of the game of the singing head in the woods behind the house. She wondered how real the memory was or if it was only the imagination of a child. But in her heart, she knew the truth.

So she made her way out to the place where she used to play. The land had changed so little since her childhood. There, under leaves and dirt and debris lay the head, just as she had left it all those years ago.

"So, you have returned," it said with no hint of malice.

"Yes," Maya said and sat down before it.

"You've grown."

"A little," she replied.

"Have you thought about what I asked of you?"

"Not really," Maya said. Then thought for a moment and said, "I still would rather not."

Then she cried. She cried for her mother. She cried for the head. And she cried for her own guilt. The head watched and said nothing. It had long ago let go of hatred and anger. When all her tears were spent, the head sang for Maya a composition it had been working on for all those years waiting for her to return as it somehow knew eventually she would.

When the song was done Maya looked down and said, "My mother will soon be making her journey to the ancestor lair. It's how we bury our dead and dying." Then she looked up and said, "I'm sure they meant no disrespect to your friend."

The head closed its eyes and a fluid seeped from its synthetic ocular glands.

"Thank you for telling me that," it said, and after a pause, "Will you help me now?"

Maya nodded yes, wiping her face with the back of her sleeve.

Then, with shaking hands, she reached into the head through its neck, passed the substance that was so much like blood and the synthetic organic solids of its flesh, felt around for the wires, and pulled. The head screamed in beautiful harmonic agony, which made Maya stop. Its eyes pleaded for her to continue and so she did. She pulled and pulled until the connecting wires let loose and fell away into her hand. Then its eyes slowly closed and the head seemed peaceful, as though it had only fallen into a very light sleep.

SOFIA SAMATAR

Tender

I am a tender. I tend the St. Benedict Radioactive Materials Containment Center. I perceive the outside world through treated glass. My immediate surroundings are barren but comfortable. I can order anything I like, necessity or luxury, from the Federal Sustainability Program. The items I order are delivered by truck and placed in a transfer box that decontaminates everything that enters it, including the air. The purpose of this system is not to protect me from contamination by the outside world, but to protect the world from me.

St. Benedict's is meant to be a temporary facility, a place to hold materials destined for deep, permanent burial, but the fears of the public make it so hard to create permanent facilities that no one knows how long this place will be necessary. My job is to monitor the levels of toxicity in and around the containment vault and submit reports to the Sustainability Program. "I used to be very unhappy," I wrote recently to the psych team, "but now I am happy because I have meaningful work." As usual, the psych team gave me an excellent evaluation. I am considered a model employee.

I went through six evaluations before I was accepted as a tender. They had to make sure I wasn't, as they put it, "actively suicidal."

"We know you've been through a tough time," one doctor told me frankly. Later, when I was accepted, she thanked me for my "sacrifice."

I am equipped with sensors, implanted under the skin up and down my back, which enable me to detect changes in toxicity levels the instant they occur. I can feel the degree of these changes, where they are located, and whether they require observation or action. It's like a sixth sense: not at all painful, and far more efficient than collecting and interpreting data. I know, however, that most people find the idea of implantation distasteful. *They've turned you into a cyborg!* wrote my best friend, the one I privately call my hurt friend, the one who still visits me.

So? I wrote back. I reminded her that the earth beneath our feet, the soil we consider the body of nature itself, is composed of air, water, minerals, and organic matter. Earth, the Mother, is also a cyborg. I added: *To tell you the truth, I find it comforting to know how poisonous everything is. I am perfectly attuned to what is good and bad. I always know the right thing to do. Yes, my sensors are strange, but they have given me something akin to a moral compass.*

In my twenty-acre glass enclosure, in my beautiful little house, in my bedroom softened by quilts and golden lamps, I read about the dawn of the nuclear age. I am moved by the young physicists, their bravery, their zeal. The delicate, somehow childish cranium of Niels Bohr. Enrico Fermi's bright melancholy gaze. Glenn Seaborg, awarded a Nobel Prize for his role in discovering plutonium, said: "I was a 28-year-old kid and I didn't stop to ruminate about it." This devil-may-care attitude seems to characterize many scientists and lies perhaps at the heart of all human advancement. Newton sticking a bodkin into his eye to investigate perception. The doctors Donald Blacklock and Saul Adler injecting themselves with chimpanzee blood.

My reading light beams gently across the desert. Insects are drawn to it but frustrated by the barrier of the glass. I fear no human intruder: my hermitage is surrounded in all directions by signs bearing the skull and crossbones.

The history of nuclear physics is a grand romance. It has everything: passion, triumph, betrayal. Those of us who work as tenders have been left holding the baby, so to speak. The half-life of plutonium-239 is 24,100 years.

Once upon a time, the story goes, some young men discovered an element. They soon realized it could produce an almost infinite amount of energy. The possibilities appeared endless, the future dazzling. There was only one problem: the element was toxic.

Once upon a time, goes another version, two young people fell in love. This love produced an almost infinite amount of energy. The possibilities appeared endless, the future dazzling. There was only one problem: one of the people was toxic.

My hurt friend visits me once a month. She used to arrive in a van driven by an assistant, but now she drives herself in a specially equipped car. She is able to walk from the car to my glass wall without a cane. "Progress!" she says wryly. She does not believe in progress.

We used to argue regularly about this, as I worked in an energy lab and believed I saw progress every day. My hurt friend was a dancer. "Don't you see yourself improving?" I asked her. "Aren't you a better dancer now than you were last year?" We were seated in a crowded restaurant and I admit I glanced at my phone to check the time. I only had twenty minutes for lunch. If the food didn't come soon I'd have to take it to go. When I looked up my friend was gazing unseeingly into the crowd, tapping her finger against her lip. "No," she said slowly. "I'm not a better dancer in any meaningful way. I think there might be something wrong with your question." I remember thinking how detached and ethereal she was, but that was nothing compared to what followed, after her injury, when she became nearly transparent.

But let us return to the story of the Toxic Lover. She was completely unaware that she was toxic. She supposed, rather, that she was beautiful, talented, and kind, destined to succeed in all aspects of life. Nothing around her contradicted these convictions. Moving from triumph to triumph, she soon had an excellent job at an energy lab, a handsome and devoted husband (the envy of all her friends), a charming small daughter, and a home overlooking a lake. Positive adjectives clashed about her constantly: it was like living inside a wind-chime. At work, she was responsible for bringing plutonium left over from the arms race into use as a source of energy. When the material proved too unstable and the project failed, she quickly recovered her footing and turned to the creation of containment centers. Her team produced small green stickers to show their commitment to the earth. Her daughter stuck the stickers all over the doors of her car. "I'm proud of you," her husband said. The woman practiced yoga, photographed the lake, and for some reason destroyed her life.

She lied. She stopped for drinks alone on the way home from work. She made secret trips to museums outside the city. She imagined herself in love with a coworker—a perfect, transcendent love, too pure for touch—and conducted an affair by text message. She felt that she was sixteen years old. The worst songs on the radio made her want to dance and also to sob with happiness. At night she did both of these things, soundlessly, in her darkened living room, while drinking the beer she kept under the kitchen sink.

All of these activities seemed quite harmless, like a vacation.

They made the woman's world bigger and more mysterious. Anything might still happen! When she walked around the yard with her child, she never felt—as her best friend put it—"trapped."

A banal story, really. Of course her husband discovered everything. He was devastated, especially by the texts to the phantom lover. The woman cried and promised to reform. Incredibly, despite all her gifts, her intelligence, and her remorse, she was unable to do so.

Progress!

The German chemist Martin Klaproth discovered uranium in 1789 while studying a material called pitchblende. It was the year of the storming of the Bastille. *Liberté, égalité, fraternité.* A century later, in 1898, Marie Curie obtained radium and polonium, also from pitchblende. Today, Curie's notebooks are considered too dangerous to touch, but radioactive isotopes are used in smoke detectors, in agriculture, in medicine. During the Great Depression, lovely green glass colored with uranium grew so cheap they handed it out free at the movies.

The possibilities. Endless.

The "Radium Girls" poisoned themselves while painting watch dials with luminescent paint at the United Radium Factory. Unaware that the paint was toxic, they licked their paintbrushes to give them a fine point for outlining the tiny numbers and lines. Later, the women's bones decayed to a kind of moth-eaten lace. Their teeth fell out. As factory workers, when they wanted a bit of fun, the Radium Girls had painted their nails and even their teeth with the beautiful, ghastly, phosphorescent, futuristic poison.

Sometimes I turn my attention to my own body. I can feel that I am becoming increasingly toxic. Will I ever start to glow like the

Radium Girls? One of them, according to her lawyer, was luminous all down her back, almost to the waist.

I write by accident: *almost to the waste.*

But why panic? There's no going back. We are exposed to radiation every day. Our sun bathes us in ultraviolet light. All of us share in the toxicity that, thanks to us, characterizes our lifeworld.

I have seen photographs of the plutonium pellets in the vault, in their bare cell at the bottom of the containment center. They bask in their own lurid glow. Radiant.

All of us are toxic, I write to my hurt friend, *but some of us are more toxic than others.*

From her apartment in the city, my hurt friend replies: *Haha.* She tells me that she is reading Attar's *Conference of the Birds*. My friend is a great reader of spiritual and philosophical texts, which she passes on to me when she's finished with them. She is working on a new dance inspired by Attar. *That's great!* I write. My friend has not worked on a dance since her injury. *The dance is all in the fingers*, she writes. As if she has forgotten she doesn't believe in progress, she adds: *It will be my best work.*

There was a time when I would not have missed this chance to tease my friend on the subject of progress, but that was before I developed my current sensitivity, before I was able to feel the fragility of the earth, of the air, before I became a person who lies on the ground and weeps. I write simply: *I can't wait.* When I visited my hurt friend in the hospital, she looked like a broken, greenish piece of glass. It was thought she would never walk again.

Overwhelmed by life, she had walked out of her dance studio and gracefully, deliberately into the path of a car.

Later she would say to me: *Don't you dare.*

In the hospital, my friend explained that she had been feeling "trapped." This feeling had grown in her invisibly, like radiation sickness. It was a relief, she told me, to have it out in the open. It was certainly visible there in her hospital bed. It was all over her skin, it blazed from her eyes. She was aglow with pain. I was shocked I had never seen it before—but, as I have already said, I was not very sensitive in those days.

The cheap green glass of the thirties, I recall, is known as "depression glass."

How strange that my friend and I, who have always considered ourselves almost polar opposites, ever since we were promising teenagers of entirely different talents, have after all wound up with such similar fates! Like me, my hurt friend has had to switch careers. She now works from home, composing advertising blurbs. She tells me that the new dance she is making causes her immense pain. She quotes Attar: *Love loves the difficult things.*

The woman's husband: *You want everything to be easy.*

The woman lied and lied. Each lie, even a tiny one, seemed to open an alternate universe. At the lake with her child, she'd stare at a leaf or discarded candy wrapper. She had to keep reminding herself not to let the child fall into the water.

What is the half-life of a lie? Each one produced a chain reaction, an almost infinite amount of energy. The possibilities appeared endless, the future terrifying. Eventually, things reached critical mass.

The woman's husband hauled all the family suitcases into the living room. "Get out," he said. He whispered because the child was sleeping.

Isidor Isaac Rabi, who witnessed the first atomic bomb test explosion: "It blasted; it pounced; it bored its way into you."

The woman walked out of the house. She walked down the street. She came to a busy road. As she walked through the traffic, she thought of her hurt friend. Wind and horn blasts whipped her, but she emerged on the other side. When she told her friend, who was still in the hospital, her friend snarled: "Don't you dare."

The woman went to a hotel. She sat in the dark. Somewhere in the room, an animal kept making a small sound.

Rabi again: "It was a vision which was seen with more than the eye. It was seen to last forever."

There are certain things I miss, though I cannot bear to think of most of them. Occasionally I can bear to remember the voice of the loon. The loon has two calls. One of them, someone once told me, sounds like "the laughter of a hysterical woman." The other, the same person explained, is "the saddest sound in the world." In films set in the jungle, which call for exotic noises, the voice of the loon is often inserted, incorrectly of course, recognizable to anyone who knows.

Sometimes I feel like that. A voice inserted in the wrong place. A hysterical woman. Loony. Saddest in the world.

My huge glass cage, stranded in the middle of the wilderness, is, at least, an excellent place for screaming.

My hurt friend has a theory that tenders are the new priests, in charge of the soul of the world. The supreme irony of this.

J. Robert Oppenheimer: "The physicists have known sin; and this is a knowledge which they cannot lose."

Still, though I cannot think of myself as a priest, I am at least a hermit. A steward. I sit with the earth as if at the bedside of a sick friend. I am so tender now, I feel the earth's pain all through my body. Often I lie down, pressing my cheek to the dust, and weep. I no longer feel, or even comprehend, the desire for another world, that passion which produces both marvels and monsters, both poisons and cures. Like the woman in this story, I understand that there is no other world. There is only the one we have made.

Abba Moses: "Sit in your cell and your cell will teach you."

A child runs up to the glass. She stops a safe distance away and holds up a picture of blue and pink clouds. What does this picture reflect? It might be an afternoon's reading, a spoonful of ice cream, an argument with the world at the moment of sleep. The woman behind the glass is cut off from the complicated daily movements that make up the world whose surface is this picture. The paper is wilted from the child's sweat, which is made of water, sugar, salts, ammonia, and other elements, including copper, iron, and lead.

The child's perspiration is perhaps slightly toxic. The woman doesn't investigate; she cannot bear to sense the child's body. The child mouths "I love you." Her eyes are veiled. This is a routine visit to her mother; afterward, she gets to go to the pool.

The woman's hurt friend smiles from behind the glass. Before she takes the child away for the promised visit to the pool, she performs a few slow, achingly beautiful gestures with her hands. She puts the child's picture into the transfer box along with a book.

The book is *Aurora* by Jacob Boehme, the sixteenth-century shoemaker who perceived the structure of divinity in the light on a pewter dish. Of *Aurora*, the deacon Gregorius Richter wrote: "There are as many blasphemies in this shoemaker's book as there are lines; it smells of shoemaker's pitch and filthy blacking."

"Behold," wrote Boehme, "there is a *gall* in man's body, which is poison, and man cannot live without this gall; for the gall maketh the *astral spirits* moveable, joyous, triumphing or laughing, for it is the source of joy."

Before I was a tender, I loved snow. I loved rainy windows that made my neighborhood look like a European city. I used to cut pictures of supermodels out of magazines and paste them in notebooks, arranged according to color. There were blue scenes that made me think of overnight journeys by train and yellow scenes that made me think of medieval bridges. Often I'd buy thrift store clothes and put them on without washing them, so that I could both feel and smell like someone else.

KIINI IBURA SALAAM

The Malady of Need

He would have looked at you like he knew all your truths. You would have wanted to unearth the secrets you saw buried in his eyes. You'd have caught his glance and your dick would have gone stiff. You would have imagined him licking your chest, your ankles, his own perfect lips.

You would have traded a week's worth of protein to get your work detail changed, to shatter the barriers between you, to ride with him only a breath away. Had you any gods you would have thanked them for the nutters who were always trying to escape. Even as your shackled hands were pulled tight over your head, you would have felt love for lockdown. When the lights cut, you would have eased yourself forward, slipping around the others, easing your tether forward as you moved into his orbit.

He would have whipped around when you stood behind him, then shushed you when you tried to explain. He would have brushed against you and you would have swayed with him, surprised to feel the tug of want stirring in your loins. When the shuttle lights blinked back on, he would have sighed before forcing blankness back into his face. You would have been left with tremors, tiny spasms whispering your need.

You would have begun to starve yourself. You would go without to nourish him. You would bring him only the best of your rations—long grasshoppers roasted crunchy, thick red caterpillars, the ones with the sweet meat. It would be the only time you would have been able to touch him—in the few seconds after your hands had been released from the shackles. You would have smiled as he slipped your food into his zip suit. It would have pleased you to think of objects you had handled resting against his skin.

He would have been thick. With pounds of flesh that could cushion all your hates and angers. You would have lost hours slack-jawed, staring into space, fantasizing about the press of his flesh.

He would have started to make demands. He would have wanted you to mark yourself, to draw blood. He would have wanted to see the scabs, the thin lines that prove how much you want him. You would have begun to enjoy it. It would have felt electric to think of him as you severed your skin. As you bled, you would have imagined him, alone in his bunk, his fingers doing the work your dick had been dying to do.

Your thoughts of him would have become incessant. You would have been thinking about him when they came for you in the night. You would have been desperate to cling to your thoughts of him as they shackled you to the rack. You would have strained to remember the contours of his mouth as they plunged the tubes into your back. You would have tried to re-create his scent as the machine began to whir. They would have begun to drain your blood, as you were imagining yourself slipping inside him. Then the pain would have overwhelmed you. You would have gone slack as everything around you melted away.

He would have known. As soon as he had seen you, he would have known that they had come for you. You would have wanted to stare at him, to drink in the vision of him to feed your sanity, but you would not have been able to bear it. You would have lowered your head so he could not see the mania in your eyes.

You would not have known how he did it, but you would have

known that he had found a way to force the shuttle to screech to a stop. As the shackles went slack and the voices of the others rose around you, he would have come. He would have freed your wrists and touched his tongue to yours. You would have fought it. You would have tried to remember where you were. But he would not have relented.

He would have dragged your buried sobs to the surface. You would have lost yourself under the press of his lips. He would have made visions flash in your mind. Touching him, you would have remembered what the sky looked like, the taste of fresh fruit, the feel of water on your skin.

You would have wanted to stop. You would not have wanted to be this naked, this disarmed. You would have lost yourself in the slickness of his body, in the work, in the friction. The itch of the compound would have dissipated against your will. The burn of the electric wristbands would have faded. You would have straddled him and pummeled him with frantic thrusts. As if you wanted to devour him. As if you wanted to re-create him, then spit him out reborn.

When the shuttle jerked back into motion, you would not have been able to look at him. Slipping your wrists back into the shackles felt like insanity, like suicide. As you worked, his scent would have gnawed at your nostrils. You would have felt as if his dark waters were rising over your body, as if you were drowning in him.

In the morning, you will erase him from existence. You will let the day's drudgery make a meal of your heart. You will withdraw. You will lock away all softness, all surrender. When the malady comes, you will clench the corners of your lips. You will go tense as it straddles your shoulders and chokes you with your own need. You will roll over and stroke your hardness. You will come in silence, consumed by dread.

The Venus Effect

This is 2015. A party on a westside roof, just before midnight. Some Mia or Mina is throwing it, the white girl with the jean jacket and the headband and the two-bumps-of-molly grin, flitting from friend circle to friend circle, laughing loudly and refilling any empty cup in her eyeline from a bottomless jug of sangria, Maenad Sicagi. There are three kegs, a table of wines and liquor, cake and nachos inside. It is a good party, and the surrounding night is beautiful, warm and soft and speckled with stars. A phone is hooked up to a portable sound system, and the speakers are kicking out rapture. It is 2009 again, the last year that music was any good, preserved in digital amber and reanimated via computer magic.

Apollo boogies on the margins, between the edge of the party and the edge of the roof, surrounded by revelers but basically alone. Naomi is on the other side of the crowd, grinding against her new boyfriend, Marcus, a musclebound meat-man stuffed into a spectacularly tacky T-shirt. Apollo finds this an entirely unappealing sight. That she and Apollo once shared an intimate relationship has nothing to do with this judgment. Not at all.

Speaking merely as an observer, a man with a love of Beauty and Dance in his heart, Apollo judges their performance unconvincing. It is the worst sort of kitsch. The meat-man against whom Naomi vibrates has no rhythm, no soul; he is as unfunky as the bad guys on Parliament-Funkadelic albums. He stutters from side to side with little regard for the twos and fours, and the occasional thrusts of his crotch are little more than burlesque, without the slightest suggestion of genuine eroticism. He is doing it just to do it. Pure kitsch. Appalling. Naomi is doing a better job, undulating her buttocks with a certain aplomb, a captivating bootyliciousness that might stir jiggly bedroom memories in the heart of the lay observer. But still. *We know that the tail must wag the dog, for the horse is drawn by the cart; But the Devil whoops, as he whooped of old, "It's pretty, but is it Art?"*

Apollo cannot bear to watch this any longer. He desperately wants to point the terribleness of this scene out to someone, to say, "Hey, look at them. They look like dumbs. Are they not dumbs?" But Naomi was always the person to whom he pointed these sorts of things out. That's why they got along, at least in the beginning, a shared appreciation for the twin pleasures of pointing at a fool and laughing at a fool. Without her, he is vestigial, useless, alone.

He turns away from the ghastly scene, just in time to notice a young woman dancing nearby. She is alone, like him, and she is, unlike him, utterly, utterly turnt. Look at her, spinning like a politician, bouncing like a bad check, bopping to the beat like the beat is all there is. She is not a talented dancer by any stretch of the imagination, and her gracelessness is unable to keep up with her abandon. She is embraced of the moment, full with the spirit, completely ungenerous with fucks and possibly bordering on the near side of alcohol poisoning. Just look at her. Apollo, in a state of terrible cliché, is unable to take his eyes off her.

There is a problem, however.

Her heels, while fabulous, were not made for rocking so hard. They are beautiful shoes, certainly, vibrant and sleek, canary yellow, bold as love. Perhaps they are a bit too matchy-matchy with regard to the rest of her outfit, the canary-yellow dress and the canary-yellow necklace and the canary-yellow bow atop her head, but the matchy-matchy look is good for people who are forces of nature, invoking four-color heroism and supernatural panache. Yet however lovely and amazing and charming and expensive these shoes might be, they cannot be everything.

The center cannot hold; things fall apart.

Her left heel snaps. Her balance is lost. Her momentum and her tipsiness send her stumbling, and no one is paying enough attention to catch her. The building is not so high up that a fall would definitely kill her, but death could be very easily found on the sidewalk below. Apollo rushes forward, reaches out to grab her, but he is too late. She goes over the edge. Apollo cannot look away. She falls for what feels like forever.

And then, she stops. She doesn't hit the ground. She just stops and hangs in the air. Apollo stares frozen, on the one hand relieved not to witness a death, on the other hand filled with ontological dread as his understanding of the laws of gravitation unravel before his eyes, on a third hypothetical hand filled with wonder and awe at this flagrant violation of consensus reality. The young woman looks up at Apollo with her face stuck in a frightened grimace as she slowly, slowly descends, like a feather in the breeze. She takes off as soon as she hits the ground, stumble-running as fast as one can on non-functional shoes.

Apollo does not know what has just happened, but he knows that he wants to know. He does not say goodbye to the hostess or his friends or Naomi. He just ghosts, flying down the ladder and down the hall and down the stairs and out the door. He can just make out a blur in the direction she ran off, and he chases after it.

There is a man in a police uniform standing at the corner. Apollo does not see him in the darkness, does not know that he is running toward him. The man in the police uniform draws his weapon and yells for Apollo to stop. Inertia and confusion do not allow Apollo to stop quickly enough. Fearing for his life, the man in the police uniform pulls the trigger of his weapon several times, and the bullets strike Apollo in his chest, doing critical damage to his heart and lungs. He flops to the ground. He is dead now.

Uh, what? That was not supposed to happen. Apollo was supposed to chase the girl alien, then have some romantically-charged adventures fighting evil aliens, then at the end she was going to go back to her home planet and it was going to be sad. Who was that guy? That's weird, right? That's not supposed to happen, right? Dudes aren't supposed to just pop off and end stories out of nowhere.

I guess to be fair, brother was running around in the middle of the night, acting a fool. That's just asking for trouble. He was a pretty unlikeable protagonist, anyway, a petty, horny, pretentious idiot with an almost palpable stink of author surrogacy on him. I think there was a Kipling quote in there. Who's that for? You don't want to read some lame indie romance bullshit, right? Sadboy meets manic pixie dream alien? I'm already bored. Let's start over. This time, we'll go classic. We'll have a real hero you can look up to, and cool action-adventure shit will go down. You ready? Here we go.

APOLLO ROCKET VS. THE SPACE BARONS FROM BEYOND PLUTO

There are fifteen seconds left on the clock, and the green jerseys have possession. The score is 99–98, green jerseys. The red jerseys have been plagued by injuries, infighting, and unfortunate calls on the part of the ref, who, despite his profession's reputed impartiality, is clearly a supporter of the green jerseys. The green jerseys themselves are playing as though this is the very last time they will ever play a basketball game. They are tall and white and aggressively Midwestern, and this gives them something to prove. Sketch in your mind the Boston Celtics of another time. Picture the Washington Generals on one of the rare, rumored nights when they were actually able to defeat their perennial adversaries, mortal men who somehow found themselves snatching victory from the god-clowns of Harlem.

Fourteen.

One of the green jerseys is preparing to throw the ball toward the hoop. If the ball were to go into the hoop, the green jerseys would have two points added to their score, and it would become impossible for the red jerseys to throw enough balls into the other hoop before time runs out. The green jerseys are already preparing for their win, running over in their minds talking points for their post-game interviews, making sure the sports drink dispenser is full and ready to be poured upon the coach, and wondering how the word "champions" might feel on their lips.

Eleven.

But this will not happen. Apollo is in position. He reaches out with his mighty arm and strips the ball from the green jersey before he can throw it.

Ten.

Apollo runs as fast as he can with the ball, so fast that every atom of his body feels as if it is igniting. He looks for an open teammate, for he is no ball hog, our Apollo, but there are no teammates to be found between himself and the hoop. So he runs alone. He is lightning. There are green jersey players in his way, but he spins and jukes around them before they can react, as if they are sloths suspended in aspic. Do his feet even touch the floor? Is it the shoes?

He's on fire.

Three.

He leaps high into the air and dunks the ball so hard that the backboard shatters into a thousand glittering shards of victory. The buzzer goes off just as he hits the ground. The final score is 100–99, red jerseys. Apollo Triumphant is leapt upon by his teammates. Hugs and pats on the back are distributed freely and with great relish. The crowd erupts into wild celebration. *Apollo, Apollo*, they chant.

Patrick, the captain of the opposing team, approaches Apollo as confetti falls from above. There is a sour look on the man's face, an expression of constipated rage at its most pure. He balls his fingers into a fist and raises it level with Apollo's midsection. It rears back and trembles as an arrow notched in a bow, ready to be fired.

"Good job, bro," he says.

"You too," says Apollo.

They bump fists. It is so dope.

A small child limps onto the basketball court. He smiles so hard that it must be painful for his face. Apollo kneels and gives him a high-five, then a low-five, then a deep hug.

"You did it, Apollo," says the child.

"No. We did it," says Apollo. "They'll never be able to demolish the youth center now."

"My new mommy and daddy said they could never have adopted me without your help."

Apollo puts a finger to his own lips. "Shhhhh."

"I love you, Apollo," says the child, its face wet with tears. "You're the best man alive."

Apollo drives home with his trophy and game ball in the back seat of his sports car, a candy apple convertible that gleams like justice. He blasts ~~Rick Ross~~ a positive, socially conscious rap song about working hard and pulling up one's pants on his stereo. The road is his tonight. There are no other cars to be seen, no other people for miles. For all his successes as balla par excellence, Apollo still appreciates the beauty and quiet of the country.

Suddenly, a sonorous roar pours out from the edge of the sky, so powerful that it shakes the car. Before Apollo can react, a yellow-silver-blue ball of fire shoots across the sky and explodes on the horizon, for a moment blotting out the darkness with pure white light before retreating into smoke and darkness. Apollo ~~jams his foot on the pedal~~ proceeds in the direction of the mysterious explosion while obeying all traffic laws and keeping his vehicle within the legal speed limits.

"~~Holy shit~~ Golly," he says.

Apollo finds a field strewn with flaming debris, shattered crystals, and shards of brightly colored metals. He hops out of his car to take a closer look. Based on his astro-engineering courses, which he gets top marks in, he surmises that these materials could have only come from some kind of spaceship. He is fascinated, to say the least.

He hears movement from under a sheet of opaque glass. He pushes it away and sees that there is a woman lying prone underneath. At least, Apollo thinks she is a woman. She is shaped like a woman, but her skin is blue, and she has gills, and she has a second mouth on her forehead. Woman or not, she is beautiful, with delicate, alien features and C-cup breasts.

"Oh my God," says Apollo. He kneels down next to the alien woman and cradles her in his arms. "Are you okay?"

She sputters. ". . . Listen . . . ship . . . crashed . . . There isn't much . . . time . . . You must stop . . . Lord Tklox . . . He is coming to . . . answer the . . . Omega Question . . . He will stop at nothing . . . please . . . stop him . . . Save . . . civilization . . . Leave me . . ."

Apollo notices a growing purple stain on the woman's diaphanous yellow robes. Based on his Theoretical Xenobiology class, he hypothesizes that this is blood. He shakes his head at her, unwilling to accept the false choice she has presented him with. "I'll do whatever I can to stop him, but first I have to help you."

She reaches up to gently stroke his hand with her three-fingered hand. "... So kind ... I ... chose well ..."

With his incredible basketballer's strength, it is nothing for Apollo to lift the woman. He may as well be carrying a large sack of feathers. He places her in the passenger seat of his car and gets back on the road lickety split.

"You'll be okay. I just need some supplies."

He stops at the nearest gas station. He races around inside to get what he needs: bandages, ice, sports drink, needle, thread, protein bar. With these items in hand, he rushes towards the register, which is next to the exit. He is stopped by a man in a police uniform. The man in the police uniform asks him about his car.

"It's mine," Apollo says.

The man in the police uniform does not believe Apollo.

"You have to come help me! There's a woman in trouble!"

The man in the police uniform does not believe Apollo and is concerned that he is shouting.

"~~This is ridiculous!~~ Sorry sir. I am sure you are just doing your job. Let me show you my ID and insurance information so we can clear all of this up," says Apollo.

Apollo goes to fish his wallet from his pocket. His naked hostility, volatile tone, and the act of reaching for what very well could be a weapon are clear signs of aggressive intent, and the man in the police uniform has no choice but to withdraw his own weapon and fire several shots. Apollo is struck first in the stomach, then the shoulder. He does not immediately die. Instead, he spends several moments on the floor of the convenience store, struggling to breathe as his consciousness fades into nothing. Then, he dies.

What the fuck is happening? Seriously. Where is this dude coming from? I haven't written that many stories, but I really don't think that's how these things are supposed to go. The way I was taught, you establish character and setting, introduce conflict, develop themes, then end on an emotional climax. That's it. Nobody said anything about killers popping up out of nowhere. Not in this genre, anyway.

So hear me out. I think we may be dealing with some kind of metafictional entity, a living concept, an ideo-linguistic infection. I don't know how he got in here, but he should be easy enough to deal with. I think we just need to reason with him. He's probably a nice guy. Just doing his job, trying to keep the story safe. He was probably genuinely afraid that Apollo was reaching for a gun. You never know with people these days. Life is scary.

Besides, that story wasn't working either. That Apollo was a big phony, totally unbelievable. Guys like that went out of style with Flash Gordon and bell-bottoms. It's not just about liking the pro-tagonist. You have to be able to relate to them, right? I think that's how it works. That's what everybody says, anyway. To be honest, I don't really get the whole "relatability" thing. Isn't the point of reading to subsume one's own experience for the experience of another, to crawl out of one's body and into a stranger's thoughts? Why would you want to read about someone just like you? Sto-ries are windows, not mirrors. Everybody's human. Shouldn't that make them relatable enough? I don't know. I don't have a lot of experience with this kind of thing. I thought smoking was a weird thing to do, too, but then I tried smoking and was addicted forever. Maybe I've just never come across a good mirror.

So let's do a child. Everybody loves children, and everybody was one. Plus, it's really easy to make them super-relatable. Just throw some social anxiety disorder and a pair of glasses on some little fucking weirdo and boom: You got a movie deal. It'll be a coming-of-age hero's journey sort of thing, adolescence viewed through a gossamer haze of nostalgia.

BULLY BRAWL: AN APOLLO KIDD ADVENTURE

This is 1995. A group of young people sit on the stoop of a decaying brownstone just off the L. The topic is television. Some show or another. Who can remember? Broadcast television in the year 1995 is terrible all around, hugs and catchphrases and phantasmal laughter suspended in analog fuzz. Is *Full House* on in 1995? Is Urkel? They don't know how bad they have it. Naomi leads the conversation. A skinny, toothy girl with a voice like a preacher. You can almost hear the organ chords rumbling in your chest whenever she opens her mouth. She jokes about what she would do if her own hypothetical future husband were to comically declare himself the man of the house, with the punchlines mainly revolving around the speed and vigor with which she would slap the black off him. She is sort of funny, but only because the television shows she is describing are not.

Apollo does not make any jokes. He is sort of funny himself (people laugh at him, at least), but he does not know how to make funny words happen. He is mostly quiet, only chiming in with the factual, offering airtimes and channels and dropping the names of actors when they get stuck on the tips of tongues. Six or seven of them are gathered, and Apollo believes himself to definitely be the or-seventh. He is wearing a T-shirt with a superhero on it. Not Superman. Superman gear can be forgiven as a harmless eccentricity if you're otherwise down. But Apollo's rocking some kind of deep-cut clown in a neon gimp suit on his chest. Remember, this is 1995, and this man is thirteen years old. Unforgivable. He's not just the or-seventh, he is the physical manifestation of all the or-seventhness that has ever existed in the world.

The new girl is sitting next to him. She might have been the or-seventh were she not new. Check that sweater. Yellow? Polyester? Sequin pineapples? In this heat? Worse than unforgivable. But who knows what lies under it? A butterfly? A swan? Any and

all manner of transformative symbology could be hiding, waiting, growing. There's still hope for her. She may be four-eyed and
flat-butted and double-handed and generally Oreoish, but there
is hope. She can at least drop into the conversation sometimes,
in the empty spaces after the punchlines. She has that power.
For instance, after Naomi does a long routine on what she would
do if she ever found a wallet lying on the sidewalk like on TV (in
brief: cop that shit), the new girl says something about losing her
own money and getting punished harshly by her mother. It is
not a funny thing to say, but memories of belts and switches and
tears are still fresh in their adolescent minds, and it is comforting
to laugh it out. Apollo laughs the hardest, and he does not know
why.

The sun is gone. Just a little light left. The new girl can't go
home alone. Not in the almost-dark. This is 1995, not 1948. Apollo
volunteers to walk with her.

"He like you," says Marcus, Naomi's not-quite-but-basically-
boyfriend, by way of explaining why Apollo is the best one for the
job.

Apollo denies this so fervently that he has to go through with
it, lest she think he truly hates her. The walk is quiet for the first
few blocks. Apollo is not a big talker, and the new girl has been
here for two weeks, and no one, except maybe the ultragregarious
Naomi, has had a real conversation with her. Still, Apollo finds
himself feeling strangely comfortable. Maybe it is the sweater.
Perhaps the fact that it should be embarrassing her is preventing
him from being embarrassed himself. Perhaps it is the sartorial
equivalent of imagining one's audience naked. Perhaps she's just
sort of great.

Apollo stops short just before they reach the corner. He holds
out his arm so that the girl will stop, too. There's danger up ahead.
A gang of street toughs. Six of them. One of those multicultural,
gender-integrated '90s gangs, a Benetton ad with knives. Red

jackets, gold sneakers. One of them has a boombox. KRS-ONE maybe? Early KRS-ONE. Stuff about listening to people's guns as they shoot you with them. Their victim is an old, gray-haired man. His hands are up. There is a briefcase at his feet. The gangsters taunt him stereotypically.

"Give us ya money, pops!"

"Don't make me cut you!"

"Nice and easy!"

"Don't be a hero!"

"I need to regulate!"

Apollo takes a slow step back. He means for Shayla to step with him, but she does not. He pulls on her arm, but she is still. She has a look on her face like she wants to fight motherfuckers. This is the most frightening expression that can appear on a human face.

"We have to go," he says.

"No," she says. "We have to help him."

"C'mon."

He pulls on her arm again, hard this time, but she slips his grasp. She runs at the gang, leaps into the air, and tackles the nearest one. The gangsters are surprised at first, to see this little girl brazenly attacking one of their own, but they quickly pull her off him and throw her to the ground.

"What's your malfunction?!" one of them screeches.

The girl stands and pulls out, seemingly from nowhere, a fantastic-looking ~~gun~~ object that in no way resembles a gun or any other real-life weapon. "Stand down, jerks."

"Oh dag! She got a ~~gun~~ object that in no way resembles a gun or any other real-life weapon! Kick rocks, guys!"

The gangsters run off into the night. Apollo runs over to the girl.

"What's going on? What's that thing?"

"Don't worry about it. Forget you saw anything," says the girl.

"Exactly," says the old man. He begins to laugh, first a low, soft chuckle, then an increasingly maniacal cackle that echos in the night. "You have fallen for my trap, Princess Amarillia! I knew you could not resist helping a stranger in need."

The girl gasps. "Lord Tklox!"

"What?" says Apollo.

Smiling, the old man reaches up and grabs his face, pulling it off to reveal pale skin, elegant features, and hair the color of starlight. His body begins to bulge and swell as he grows larger, eventually doubling in height. He laughs as a shining sword appears in his hands.

"Run!" shouts the girl.

"What is happening?!"

"No time to explain. Take this." She hands him her fantastic-looking ~~gun~~ object that in no way resembles a gun or any other real-life weapon. "I'll hold him off with my Venusian jiu-jitsu. Just go! Don't stop. Please. Don't stop. Just run. Don't let him get you like he got the others."

The girl takes a martial arts stance and nods. Apollo does not need further explanations. He runs in the opposite direction. He runs as fast as he can, until his lungs burn and he cannot feel his legs. Stopping to catch his breath, he holds the ~~gun~~ object that in no way resembles a gun or any other real-life weapon up to the light. He does not even know how to use it, how it could possibly help him in this strange battle.

So wrapped up in thought, Apollo does not even see the man in the police uniform. He does not hear him telling him to drop his weapon. He only hears the gun go bang. Later, his body is found by his mother, who cries and cries and cries.

Did you ever read "Lost in the Funhouse"? I just re-read it as research on solving metafictional problems. Not super helpful. We get it; fiction is made up. Cool story, bro. But you know the flashback to the kids playing Niggers and Masters? Is that a real thing? Or is it just a sadomasochistic parody of Cowboys and Indians? I can't find any information on it online, but I'm sure somebody somewhere has played it. If something as cruel as Cowboys and Indians exists, why not Niggers and Masters? There is no way a game like that is only theoretical. It's too rich, too delicious. The role of Master is an obvious power fantasy, presenting one with the authority to command and punish as an adult might, without any of the responsibility. The role of Nigger is just a different kind of power fantasy, power expressed as counterfactual. In playing the Nigger, one can experience subjugation on one's own terms. There is no real danger, no real pain. You can leave at any time, go home and watch cartoons and forget about it. Or you can indulge fully, giving oneself up to the game, allowing oneself to experience a beautiful simulacrum of suffering. It is perfect pretend. There are probably worse ways of spending a suburban afternoon, and there is something slightly sublime about it, baby's first ego death. Sure, it's profoundly offensive, but who's going to stop you? But whatever. I'm probably reading too much into it. It's probably a made-up, postmodern joke. When I was a kid, we just played Cops and Robbers, and it was fine.

Anyway, that was a digression. I admit that it's difficult to defend the actions of certain uniformed narrative devices, but I'm sure there were good reasons for them. After all, there were gangsters with actual knives in that one, and Apollo was holding something that maybe sort of looked like a weapon in the dark. How are we supposed to tell the good ones from the bad ones? Can you tell the difference? I don't think so. Besides, this was to be expected. Children's literature is sad as fuck. It's all about dead moms and dead dogs and cancer and loneliness. You can't expect everyone to come out alive from that. But you know what isn't sad? Fucking superheroes.

GO GO JUSTICE GANG! FT. APOLLO YOUNG

Oh no.

Downtown Clash City has been beset by a hypnagogic Leviathan, a terrifying kludge of symbology and violence, an impossible horror from beyond the ontological wasteland. Citizens flee, police stand by impotently, soldiers fire from tanks and helicopters without success, their bullets finding no purchase, their fear finding no relief.

It is a bubblegum machine gone horribly, horribly awry, a clear plastic sphere with a red body and a bellhopian cap, except there is a tree growing inside it, and also it is several hundred feet tall. The tree is maybe a willow or a dying spruce or something like that. It is definitely a sad tree, the kind of tree that grows on the edges of graveyards in children's books or in the tattoos of young people with too many feelings, when not growing on the inside of giant animated bubblegum machines.

It trudges along Washington Avenue on its root system, which emerges from the slot where the bubblegum ought to come out, and inflicts hazardous onomatopoesis upon people and property alike with its terrible branches.

Bang. Crack. Boom. Splat. Crunch.

Splat is the worst of them, if you think about the implications.

Various material reminders of American imperialist power under late capitalism, the bank and the television station and the army surplus store, are made naught but memory and masonry in its wake. The ground shakes like butts in music videos, and buildings fall like teenagers in love. Destruction. Carnage. Rage. Can nothing be done to stop this creature? Can the city be saved from certain destruction?

Yes!

Already, Apollo Young, a.k.a. Black Justice, is on his way to the Justice Gang Headquarters. Even as his fellow citizens panic, he keeps a cool head as he drives his Justice Vehicle headlong into danger. When his wrist communicator begins to buzz and play the Justice Gang theme song, he pulls over to the curb, in full accordance with the law.

"Black Justice! Come in! This is Red Justice!" says the wrist communicator.

"I read you, Patrick! What's the haps?!"

"The city is in danger! We need your help! To defeat this evil, We, the Justice Gang, need to combine our powers to form White Justice!"

"Yes. Only White Justice can save the city this time!"

"Also, can you please pick up Pink Justice? She is grounded from driving because she went to the mall instead of babysitting her little brother."

"What an airhead!"

"I know. But she is also a valuable member of the Justice Gang. Only when Pink Justice, Blue Justice, Black Justice, and Mauve Justice combine with me, the leader, Red Justice, can our ultimate power, White Justice, be formed!"

"As I know."

"Yes. All thanks to Princess Amarillia, who gave us our prismatic justice powers in order to prevent the evil Lord Tklox from answering the Omega Question and destroying civilization!"

"Righteous!"

"Just as white light is composed of all colors of light, so White Justice will be formed from our multicultural, gender-inclusive commitment to Good and Right."

"Okay! Bye."

Apollo hangs up and gets back on the road. He picks up Pink Justice on the way. She is a stereotypical valley girl, but that is okay, since the Justice Gang accepts all types of people, as long as they love justice, are between fifteen and seventeen, and present as heterosexual. They ride together in silence, as they are the two members of the Justice Gang least likely to be paired up for storylines, owing to the potentially provocative implications of a black man and a white woman interacting together, even platonically.

"Do you ever think that we're just going in circles?" asks Pink Justice, staring idly out the window.

"What do you mean?" asks Apollo.

"A monster appears, we kill it, another monster appears, we kill it again. We feel good about getting the bad guy in the moment, but it just keeps happening. Week after week, it's the same thing. Another monster. More dead people. We never actually fight *evil*. We just kill monsters. Evil is always still there."

"But what about justice?"

"What is justice? People are dying. I just don't know what we're fighting for sometimes, why we keep fighting. It's the same every time. It's just tiring, I guess."

"I think we have to fight. Even if nobody gets saved, we are better for having done it. Maybe the world isn't better, but it's different, and I think that difference is beautiful."

"Like, for sure!" says Pink Justice.

A police car flashes its lights at Apollo. He pulls over. The man in the police uniform walks to the passenger side and asks Pink Justice if she is okay.

"I'm fine. There's no problem," she says.

The man in the police uniform tells Pink Justice that he can help her if something is wrong.

"Everything is fine. Nothing is wrong."

The man in the police uniform tells Apollo to get out of the car.

"~~What is this about? What's your probable cause?~~ Yes sir, officer," says Apollo, getting out of the car.

The man in the police uniform slams Apollo into the side of

the car and pats him down. Pink Justice gets out and begins to yell that they have done nothing wrong, that he has to let them go. This obviously agitates the man in the police uniform.

Apollo's wrist communicator goes off, and without thinking, he moves to answer it. The man in the police uniform tackles him to the ground, sits on his chest, and begins to hit him with a flashlight. Apollo's windpipe is blocked. It continues to be blocked for a long time. He dies.

Come on. Really? That one was really good. The white guy was in charge and everything! This sucks. I'm trying to do something here. The point of adventure fiction is to connect moral idealism with the human experience. The good guys fight the bad guys, just as we struggle against the infelicities of the material world. That's the point of heroes. They journey into the wilderness, struggle against the unknown, and make liminal spaces safe for the people. That's how it works, from Hercules to Captain Kirk. It's really hard to create ontological safety when people keep dying all the time. Barth was right; literature is exhausting.

So I guess Apollo shouldn't have been in a car with a white lady? That's scary, I guess. He didn't do anything, but he was probably no angel. He was a teen. Teens get into all kinds of shit. When I was in school, I knew so, so many kids who shoplifted and smoked drugs. They were mostly white, but still. Teens are shitty. The man in the police uniform probably had good intentions. Like, he wanted to make sure the girl wasn't being kidnapped or anything. Why else would they be together? I still think he only wants to keep people safe, especially potentially vulnerable people.

I've fucking got it. This is 2016, right? Sisters are doing it for themselves. Why not a lady-protagonist? Women are empathetic and non-threatening and totally cool. Everyone is chill with ladies. That's why phone robots all have feminine voices. True story. Why would you just kill a woman for no reason? She's not going to hurt you. This time, no one is going to hurt anybody.

APOLLONIA WILLIAMS-CARTER
AND THE VENUS SANCTION

Naomi walks into Apollonia's private office just before 5:00. It is a cramped and dingy room, lit by a single fluorescent bulb and smelling strongly of mildew. Without greeting or warning, she drops a thick, yellow binder down on Apollonia's desk.

"Read this," she says.

The binder is marked A.M.A.R.I.L.L.I.A. Project. It is filled with photographs, exotic diagrams, and pages and pages of exhaustively researched reports. Apollonia proceeds slowly, taking in each and every fact printed on the pages, running them over in her mind and allowing them to settle. She feels a sinking sensation in her stomach as she journeys deeper and deeper into the text.

"Dear God," she whispers. "Can this be true?"

"Yes," says Naomi.

"This is absolutely disgusting. How could they do something like this? How could they sell us out to aliens?"

"They don't care about our world. Not anymore."

"What can we do?"

"I don't know. That's why I brought this to you."

Apollonia opens one of her drawers, retrieving two shot glasses and a bottle of whiskey. She pours a double and pushes it toward Naomi.

"Have some. It will calm your nerves."

Naomi throws the glass to the ground, shattering it.

"This is no time to drink! We've got to do something!"

Apollonia takes her shot. "We can't do anything if we can't keep our cool."

"You want me to be cool? The department will have my head if they even know I am talking to you."

"My head's on the line, too. I might be a vice-president here, but they'd kill me as quickly as a break-room cockroach."

"So what do we do? I came to you because I have the utmost respect for your work with the company."

"We go to the press. It might cost us our lives, but at least the truth will be out there."

"Should we try to rescue the girl?"

"No. First, we get the truth out. I'll handle this. Delete any digital copies of these files and meet me tonight at the Port Royale."

"Fine."

"Remember. Anyone you know could be one of them. Use caution."

Naomi nods and exits.

Apollonia takes another double shot of whiskey as she continues to read the binder. How could this happen? She had never trusted the powers that be, but how could they be doing this? How could they be killing people with impunity? The notes on the files indicate that it is in the name of safety and the greater good, but whose safety are they really talking about? Man or monster?

Apollonia leaves at 7:00, as she does every evening. She hides the pages of the binder in her purse. She puts on a cheerful face, smiling at coworkers and greeting the support staff as she passes. She takes the elevator down from her floor to the lobby, then the stairs to the parking garage. She makes sure no one is following her as she walks down the corridors of the unlit parking garage, turning her head every few moments to get a full view of her surroundings. She sees her car and breathes a sigh of relief. She is almost out.

"Hey there."

She turns to see a young man in a suit. He is at least six feet tall and aggressively muscled. He smiles brightly and broadly at Apollonia, as if trying to hide something.

"Hello Patrick," she says.

"Where ya headed in such a hurry?"

"Just going home."

"Home, huh? I remember home."

He laughs. She joins him.

"Long hours, huh? I feel for you."

He sticks out his finger at her purse. She clutches it closer.

"Hey. Is that new? I think my girlfriend pointed that purse out at the store. I'm sure it was that one."

"I've had this thing forever."

"Do you mind if I see it? I just want to know if it's well made."

Apollonia swallows. "I'd really prefer it if you didn't."

The smile leaves his face, and his eyes begin to narrow. Apollonia takes a step back. She has been trained in self-defense, but this man has at least one hundred pounds on her and also might be an alien. She begins to slowly, subtly shift into a combat stance. If she times it right, she might be able to stun him long enough for her to escape. She just has to find the right moment. She waits. And waits. And waits.

Finally, he chuckles. "You're right. That was a weird question. I haven't been getting enough sleep lately. Sorry. I'll see you later."

Apollonia gets into her car. On the way to the Port Royale, she is pulled over by the man in the police uniform. While patting her down for drugs, he slips his fingers into her underwear. She tries to pull his hands away, prompting him to use force to stop her from resisting arrest. Her head is slammed many times against the sidewalk. She dies.

She. Didn't. Do. Anything. And even if she did do something, killing is not the answer. That's it. I'm not playing anymore. I can quit at any time. No one can stop me. Look, I'll do it now. Boom. I just quit for two days. Boom. That was two weeks. Boom. Now I have to change all the dates to 2016. What's the point of writing this thing? What's the point of writing anything? I just wanted to tell a cool story. That's it. No murders. No deaths. Remember? It was just a love story.

I once read that people get more into love stories and poems in times of political strife and violence. What better way to assert meaning in the face of meaninglessness than by celebrating the connection between human beings? Our relationship with the state, the culture, the world, these are just petals in the winds compared to the love that flows between us. Fuck politics. I set out to do a love story, so I'm doing a love story. Plus, I've got a plan. So far, the Apollos have all died while messing around outside. The solution isn't relatability at all. It's so much simpler than that: transit. It doesn't matter if the guy can't sympathize with Apollo if he can't find him. There are tons of great stories set in one place. I'll just do one of those.

APOLLO RIGHT AND THE ARCHITECTURAL-ORGANIC WORMHOLE

Apollo and Naomi sit alone on the couch by the window, the dusty brown one held together with tape and band-aids, quiet, listening to the rain and the night, watching the play of wind and glow on the raindrops outside, refracted lamplight and neon diffusing into glitter in the dark. His head rests on her lap, which is soft and warm and comfortingly "lap-like," which is to say that it possesses the qualities of the Platonic lap in quantities nearing excess, qualities which are difficult to articulate, neotenous comforts and chthonic ecstasies of a sublime/cliché nature, intimacy rendered in thigh meat and belly warmth. Her left hand is on his shoulder, just so, and her right is on his chest, and he takes note of the sensation of her fingers as his chest expands and contracts, and it is pleasant. He takes a breath, sweet and slow. There is a little sadness, because this moment will wilt and wither like all moments, and he does not want it to, more than anything.

"Remember this," he says.

"What?"

"I would like it if you would remember this. Tonight. Or at least this part."

"Why wouldn't I remember tonight?"

"You never remember any of the good parts."

"You say that."

"It's true. You only remember the bad parts. The before and after. Anxiety and regret. Never the moment."

"Who says this is a good part?"

"That's a cutting remark."

"I just think we have different definitions of the good and bad when it comes to certain things."

"So this is a bad part?"

"I didn't say that."

"Which is it, then?"

"It's good to see you."

"You know what my favorite memory of us is?"

"Leon."

"I'm sure you don't remember it."

"Don't."

"It's not weird or anything. One time I came over to your place, and you smiled that smile you have—not the usual one, the good one—and you gave me a hug. Just a long, deep hug, like you were just really happy to see me. Genuinely happy. Not angry or annoyed at all. Just cruisin', y'know. Just cruisin'. We made out afterwards, and maybe had sex? I don't remember that super great."

"The fact that you don't see anything weird about that is why we had to break up."

"Whatever, lady."

The door flies open. The man in the police uniform shouts for everyone to get down. A flashbang grenade is thrown inside. Apollo pushes Naomi away but is unable to get away. He suffers critical burns to his head and chest. After being denied medical treatment on the scene, he dies weeks later in the hospital from opportunistic infections. Ironically, the man in the police uniform was actually meant to go to the next apartment over, where a minor marijuana dealer lives.

They didn't even get to the cool part. There was going to be a living wormhole in the closet, and all kinds of space shit was going to come out, and in the process of dealing with it they were going to rekindle their love. It was going to be awesome. We can't even have love stories anymore? What do we have if we can't have love stories?

Okay. Now I'm thinking that the issue is with the milieu. 2015 is a weird time. Shit is going down. It's politicizing this story. I'm not into it. What we need is a rip-roaring space adventure in the far future. That'll be cool. All this shit will be sorted out by then, and we can all focus on what really matters: space shit.

APOLLO _____ VS. THE VITA-RAY MIRACLE

The crystal spires of New Virtua throw tangles of intersecting rainbows onto the silver-lined streets below, such that a Citizen going about his daily duties cannot help but be enmeshed in a transpicuous net of light and color. A Good Citizen knows that this is Good, that beauty is a gift of Science, and he wears his smile the way men of lesser worlds might wear a coat and hat to ward off the cold damp of an unregulated atmosphere.

Lord Tklox is not a Good Citizen, and he rarely smiles at all. On those occasions when he does experience something akin to happiness (when his plans are coming to fruition, when he imagines the bloody corpses of his enemies, when he thinks of new ways to crush the Good Citizens of New Virtua under his foot), his smile is not so much worn as wielded, as one might wield the glowing spiral of a raymatic cannon.

"Soon, my vita-ray projector will be complete, and all New Virtua will tremble as I unleash the Omega Question!" he exclaims to no one, alone in his subterranean laboratory two thousand miles below the surface.

Cackling to himself, Lord Tklox waits in his lair for those who would challenge his incredible genius.

He waits.

He keeps waiting.

Lord Tklox coughs, perhaps getting the attention of any heroes listening on nearby crime-detecting audioscopes. "First New Virtua, then the universe! All will be destroyed by the radical subjectivity of the Omega Question!"

Waiting continues to happen.

More waiting.

Still more.

Uh, I guess nobody comes. Everybody dies, I guess.

So I checked, and it turns out there are no black people in the far future. That's my bad. I really didn't do my research on that one. I don't know where we end up going. Maybe we all just cram into the Parliament-Funkadelic discography at some point between *Star Trek* and *Foundation*? Whatever. That's an issue for tomorrow. Today, we've got bigger problems.

It's time we faced this head on. Borges teaches us that every story is a labyrinth, and within every labyrinth is a minotaur. I've been trying to avoid the minotaur, but instead I need to slay it. I have my sword, and I know where the monster lurks. It is time to blaxploit this problem.

APOLLO JONES IN: THE FINAL SHOWDOWN

Who's the plainclothes police detective who leaves all
the criminals dejected?
[Apollo!]
Who stops crime in the nick of time and dazzles the
ladies with feminine rhymes?
[Apollo!]
Can you dig it?

Apollo's cruiser screeches to a halt at the entrance to the abandoned warehouse. He leaps out the door and pulls his gun, a custom gold Beretta with his name engraved on the handle.

"Hot gazpacho!" he says. "This is it."

Patrick pops out of the passenger seat. "We've got him now."

They have been chasing their suspect for weeks now, some
sicko responsible for a string of murders. In a surprising third
act twist, they discovered that the one responsible is one of their
own, a bad apple who gets his kicks from harming the innocent.

"We've got him pinned down inside," says Apollo.

"He won't escape this time."

"Let's do this, brother."

They skip the middle part of the story, since that has been
where we've been getting into trouble. They rush right to the end,
where the man in the police uniform is waiting for them.

"Congratulations on solving my riddles, gentlemen. I'm im-
pressed."

"You're going down, punk," says Apollo.

"Yeah!" says Patrick.

"I doubt that very much."

The man in the police uniform pulls his weapon and fires three
shots, all hitting Apollo in the torso. He crumples to the ground.
Patrick aims his own weapon, but the man in the police uniform

is able to quickly shoot him in the shoulder, sending Patrick's pistol to the ground.

"You thought you could defeat me so easily? How foolish. We're not so different, you and I. You wanted a story about good aliens and bad aliens? Well, so did I."

"How's this for foolish?" says Apollo, pulling up his shirt to reveal he was wearing a bulletproof vest all along. Then, he unloads a clip from his legendary golden Beretta at him. The man in the police uniform falls to the ground, bleeding.

Patrick clutches his shoulder. "We got him."

"We're not quite done yet," says Apollo.

He walks over to the body of the man in the police uniform. He tugs on the man's face, pulling it off completely. It is the face of Lord Tklox.

"This was his plan all along," says Apollo. "By murdering all those innocent people, he was turning us against each other, thereby making it easier for his invasion plans to succeed. All he had left to do was answer the Omega Question and boom, no more civilization. Good thing we stopped him in time."

"I knew it," says Patrick. "He was never one of us. He was just a bad guy the whole time. It is in no way necessary for me to consider the ideological mechanisms by which my community and society determine who benefits from and participates in civil society, thus freeing me from cognitive dissonance stemming from the ethical compromises that maintain my lifestyle."

"Hot gazpacho!" says Apollo.

They share a manly handshake like Schwarzenegger and Carl Weathers in *Predator*. It is so dope.

"I'll go call dispatch," says Patrick. "Tell them that we won't be needing backup. Or that we will be needing backup to get the body and investigate the scene? I don't really know how this works. The movie usually ends at this point."

Patrick leaves, and Apollo guards the body. Suddenly, the

warehouse door bursts open. Seeing him standing over the dead body, a man in a police uniform yells for Apollo to drop his weapon. Apollo shouts that he is a cop and moves to gingerly put his golden gun on the ground, but he is too slow. Bulletproof vests do not cover the head. He is very, very dead.

I wasn't trying to do apologetics for him. Before, I mean. I wasn't saying it's okay to kill people because they aren't perfect or do things that are vaguely threatening. I was just trying to find some meaning, the moral of the story. All I ever wanted to do was write a good story. But murder is inherently meaningless. The experience of living is a creative act, the personal construction of meaning for the individual, and death is the final return to meaninglessness. Thus, the act of killing is the ultimate abnegation of the human experience, a submission to the chaos and violence of the natural world. To kill, we must either admit the futility of our own life or deny the significance of the victim's.

This isn't right.

It's not supposed to happen like this.

Why does this keep happening?

It's the same story every time. Again and again and again.

I can't fight the man in the police uniform. He's real, and I'm an authorial construct, just words on a page, pure pretend. But you know who isn't pretend? You. We have to save Apollo. We're both responsible for him. We created him together. Death of the Author, you know? It's just you and me now. I've got one last trick. I didn't mention this in the interest of pace and narrative cohesion, but I lifted the Omega Question off Lord Tklox before he died. I don't have the answer, but I know the question. You've got to go in. I can keep the man in the police uniform at bay as long as I can, but you have to save Apollo. We're going full Morrison.

Engage second-person present.

God forgive us.

You wake up. It is still dark out. You reach out to take hold of your spouse. Your fingers intertwine, and it is difficult to tell where you stop and they begin. You love them so much. After a kiss and a cuddle, you get out of bed. You go to the bathroom and perform your morning toilette. When you are finished, you go to the kitchen and help your spouse with breakfast for the kids.

They give you a hug when they see you. You hug back, and you never want to let go. They are getting so big now, and you do everything you can to be a good parent to them. You know they love you, but you also want to make sure they have the best life possible.

You work hard every single day to make that happen. Your boss is hard on you, but he's a good guy, and you know you can rely on him when it counts. You trust all your coworkers with your life. You have to. There's no other option in your line of work.

After some paperwork, you and your partner go out on patrol. You've lived in this neighborhood your entire life. Everything about it is great, the food, the sights, the people. There are a few bad elements, but it's your job to stop them and keep everybody safe.

It's mostly nickel and dime stuff today, citations and warnings. The grocery store reports a shoplifter. An older woman reports some kids loitering near her house. Your partner notices a man urinating on the street while you're driving past. That kind of thing.

As you are on your way back to the station, you notice a man walking alone on the sidewalk. It's late, and it doesn't look like this is his part of town. His head is held down, like he's trying to hide his face from you. This is suspicious. Your partner says he recognizes him, that he fits the description of a mugger who has been plaguing the area for weeks. You pull up to him. Ask him what he is doing. He doesn't give you a straight answer. You ask him for some identification. He refuses to give it to you. You don't want to arrest this guy for nothing, but he's not giving you much choice.

Suddenly, his hand moves towards a bulge in his pocket. It's a gun. You know it's a gun. You draw your weapon. You just want to scare him, show him that you're serious, stop him from drawing on you. But is he even scared? Is that fear on his face or rage? How can you even tell? He's bigger than you, and he is angry, and he probably has a gun. You do not know this person. You cannot imagine what is going through his mind. You have seen this scenario a million times before in movies and TV shows.

You might die.

You might die.

You might die.

The Omega Question is activated:

Who matters?

P H E N D E R S O N   D J È L Í   C L A R K

The Secret Lives of the Nine Negro Teeth of George Washington

"By Cash pd Negroes for 9 Teeth on Acct of Dr. Lemoire"
—Lund Washington, Mount Vernon plantation, Account Book
dated 1784.

The first Negro tooth purchased for George Washington came from a blacksmith, who died that very year at Mount Vernon of the flux. The art of the blacksmith had been in his blood—passed down from ancestral spirits who had come seeking their descendants across the sea. Back in what the elder slaves called Africy, he had heard, blacksmiths were revered men who drew iron from the earth and worked it with fire and magic: crafting spears so wondrous they could pierce the sky and swords with beauty enough to rend mountains. Here, in this Colony of Virginia, he had been set to shape crueler things: collars to fasten about bowed necks, shackles to ensnare tired limbs, and muzzles to silence men like beasts. But blacksmiths know the secret language of iron, and he beseeched his creations to bind the spirits of their wielders—as surely as they bound flesh. For the blacksmith understood what masters had chosen to forget: when you make a man or woman a slave you enslave yourself in turn. And the souls of those who made thralls of others would never know rest—in this life, or the next.

When he wore that tooth, George Washington complained of hearing the heavy fall of a hammer on an anvil day and night. He ordered all iron making stopped at Mount Vernon. But the sound of the blacksmith's hammer rang out in his head all the same.

The second Negro tooth belonging to George Washington came from a slave from the Kingdom of Ibani, what the English with their inarticulate tongues call Bonny Land, and (much to his annoyance) hence him, a Bonny man. The Bonny man journeyed from Africa on a ship called the *Jesus*, which, as he understood, was named for an ancient sorcerer who defied death. Unlike the other slaves bound on that ship who came from the hinterlands beyond his kingdom, he knew the fate that awaited him—though he would never know what law or sacred edict he had broken that sent him to this fate. He found himself in that fetid hull chained beside a merman, with scales that sparkled like green jewels and eyes as round as black coins. The Bonny man had seen mermen before out among the waves, and stories said some of them swam into rivers to find wives among local fisher women. But he hadn't known the whites made slaves of them too. As he would later learn, mermen were prized by thaumaturgically inclined aristo-crats who dressed them in fine livery to display to guests; most, however, were destined for Spanish holdings, where they were forced to dive for giant pearls off the shores of New Granada. The two survived the horrors of the passage by relying on each other. The Bonny man shared tales of his kingdom, of his wife and chil-dren and family, forever lost. The merman in turn told of his under-water home, of its queen and many curiosities. He also taught the Bonny man a song: a plea to old and terrible things that dwelled in the deep, dark, hidden parts of the sea—great beings with gap-ing mouths that opened up whirlpools or tentacles that could drag ships beneath the depths. They would one day rise to wreak vengeance, he promised, for all those who had been chained to suffer in these floating coffins. The Bonny man never saw the merman after they made land on the English isle of Barbados. But he carried the song with him, as far as the Colony of Virginia, and on the Mount Vernon plantation, he sang it as he looked across fields of wheat to an ocean he couldn't see—and waited.

When George Washington wore the Bonny man's tooth, he found himself humming an unknown song, that sounded (strange to his thinking) like the tongue of the savage mermen. And in the dark hidden parts of the sea, old and terrible things stirred.

The third Negro tooth of George Washington was bought from a slave who later ran from Mount Vernon, of which an account was posted in the *Virginia Gazette* in 1785:

> *Advertisement: Runaway from the plantation of the Subscriber, in Fairfax County, some Time in October last, on All-Hallows Eve, a Mulatto Fellow, 5 Feet 8 Inches high of Tawney Complexion named Tom, about 25 Years of Age, missing a front tooth. He is sensible for a Slave and self-taught in foul necromancy. He lived for some Years previous as a servant at a school of learned sorcery near Williamsburg, and was removed on Account of inciting the dead slaves there to rise up in insurrection. It is supposed he returned to the school to raise up a young Negro Wench, named Anne, a former servant who died of the pox and was buried on the campus grounds, his Sister. He sold away a tooth and with that small money was able to purchase a spell used to call upon powers potent on All-Hallows Eve to spirit themselves away to parts now unknown. Whoever will secure the said Tom, living, and*

*Anne, dead, so that they be delivered to the plantation
of the Subscriber in Fairfax County aforesaid, shall have
Twenty Shillings Reward, besides what the Law allows.*

To George Washington's frustration, Tom's tooth frequently fell out of his dentures, no matter how he tried to secure it. Most bizarre of all, he would find it often in the unlikeliest of places—as if the vexsome thing was deliberately concealing itself. Then one day the tooth was gone altogether, never to be seen again.

George Washington's fourth Negro tooth was from a woman named Henrietta. (Contrary to widespread belief, there is no difference of significance between the dentition of men and women—as any trained dentist, odontomancer, or the Fay folk, who require human teeth as currency, will well attest.) Henrietta's father had been John Indian, whose father had been a Yamassee warrior captured and sold into bondage in Virginia. Her mother's mother had come to the mainland from Jamaica, sold away for taking part in Queen Nanny's War. As slaves, both were reputed to be unruly and impossible to control. Henrietta inherited that defiant blood, and more than one owner learned the hard way she wasn't to be trifled with. After holding down and whipping her last mistress soundly, she was sold to work fields at Mount Vernon—because, as her former master advertised, strong legs and a broad back weren't to be wasted. Henrietta often dreamed of her grandparents. She often dreamed she was her grandparents. Sometimes she was a Yamassee warrior, charging a fort with flintlock musket drawn, eyes fixed on the soldier she intended to kill—as from the ramparts English mages hurled volleys of emerald fireballs that could melt through iron. Other times she was a young woman, barely fifteen, who chanted Asante war songs as she drove a long sabre, the blade blazing bright with obeah, into the belly of a slave master (this one had been a pallid blood drinker) and watched as he blackened and crumbled away to ash.

When George Washington wore Henrietta's tooth he sometimes woke screaming from night terrors. He told Martha they were memories from the war, and would never speak of the faces he saw coming for him in those dreams: a fierce Indian man with long black hair and death in his eyes, and a laughing slave girl with a curiously innocent face, who plunged scorching steel into his belly.

The fifth Negro tooth belonging to George Washington came by unexplained means from a conjure man who was not listed among Mount Vernon's slaves. He had been born before independence, in what was then the Province of New Jersey, and learned his trade from his mother—a root woman of some renown (among local slaves at any rate), having been brought to the region from the southern territories of New France. The conjure man used his magics mostly in the treatment of maladies affecting his fellow bondsmen, of the mundane or paranormal varieties. He had been one of the tens of thousands of slaves during the war who answered the call put out by the Earl of Dunmore, Royal Governor of Virginia in November 1775:

> *And I hereby declare all indentured servants, Negroes,*
> *hedge witches and wizards, occultists, lycanthropes,*
> *giants, non-cannibal ogres and any sentient magical*
> *creatures or others (appertaining to Rebels) free and*
> *relieved of supernatural sanction that are able and*
> *willing to bear Arms, they joining His MAJESTY'S Troops*
> *as soon as may be, for the more speedily reducing this*
> *Colony to a proper Sense of their Duty, to His MAJESTY'S*
> *Crown and Dignity. This edict excludes Daemonic beasts*
> *who should not take said proclamation as a summons*

who, in doing so, will be exorcized from His MAJESTY'S realm with all deliberate speed.

The conjure man was first put in the service of Hessian mercenaries, to care for their frightening midnight black steeds that breathed flames and with hooves of fire. Following, he'd been set to performing menial domestic spells for Scottish warlocks, treated no better there than a servant. It was fortune (aided by some skillful stone casting) that placed him in Colonel Tye's regiment. Like the conjure man, Tye had been a slave in New Jersey who fled to the British, working his way to becoming a respected guerilla commander. Tye led the infamous Black Brigade—a motley crew of fugitive slaves, outlaw juju men, and even a Spanish mulata werewolf—who worked alongside the elite Queen's Rangers. Aided by the conjure man's gris-gris, the Black Brigade carried out raids on militiamen: launching attacks on their homes, destroying their weapons, stealing supplies, burning spells and striking fear into the hearts of patriots. The conjure man's brightest moment had come the day he captured his own master and bound him in the same shackles he'd once been forced to wear. The Brigade stirred such hysteria that the patriot governor of New Jersey declared martial law, putting up protective wards around the province—and General George Washington himself was forced to send his best mage hunters against them. In a running skirmish with those patriot huntsmen, Tye was fatally struck by a cursed ball from a long rifle—cutting through his gris-gris. The conjure man stood guard over his fallen commander, performing a final rite that would disallow their enemies from reanimating the man or binding his soul. Of the five mage hunters he killed three, but was felled in the attempt. With his final breath, he whispered his own curse on any that would desecrate his corpse.

One of the surviving mage hunters pulled the conjure man's

teeth as a souvenir of the battle, and a few days hence tumbled to land awkwardly from his horse and broke his neck. The tooth passed to a second man, who choked to death on an improbably lodged bit of turtle soup in his windpipe. And, so it went, bringing dire misfortune to each of its owners. The conjure man's tooth has now, by some twist of fate, made its way to Mount Vernon and into George Washington's collection. He has not worn it, yet.

The sixth Negro tooth of George Washington belonged to a slave who had tumbled here from another world. The startled English sorcerer who witnessed this remarkable event had been set to deliver a speech on conjurations at the Royal Society of London for Improving Supernatural Knowledge. Alas, before the sorcerer could tell the world of his discovery, he was quietly killed by agents of the Second Royal African Company, working in a rare alliance with their Dutch rivals. As they saw it, if Negroes could simply be pulled out of thin air the lucrative trade in human cargo that made such mercantilists wealthy could be irrevocably harmed. The conjured Negro, however, was allowed to live—bundled up and shipped from London to a Virginia slave market. Good property, after all, was not to be wasted. She ended up at Mount Vernon, and was given the name Esther. The other slaves, however, called her Solomon—on account of her wisdom.

Solomon claimed not to know anything about magic, which didn't exist in her native home. But how could that be, the other slaves wondered, when she could mix together powders to cure their sicknesses better than any physician; when she could make predictions of the weather that always came true; when she could construct all manner of wondrous contraptions from the simplest of objects? Even the plantation manager claimed she was "a Negro of curious intellect," and listened to her suggestions on crop rotations and field systems. The slaves well knew the many agricultural reforms at Mount Vernon, for which their master took credit, were actually Solomon's genius. They often asked why she didn't use her remarkable wit to get hired out and make money? Certainly, that'd be enough to buy her freedom.

Solomon always shook her head, saying that though she was from another land, she felt tied to them by "the consanguinity of bondage." She would work to free them all, or, falling short of that, at the least bring some measure of ease to their lives. But at night, after she'd finished her mysterious "experiments" (which she kept secret from all) she could be found gazing up at the stars, and it was hard not to see the longing held deep in her eyes. When George Washington wore Solomon's tooth, he dreamed of a place of golden spires and colorful glass domes, where Negroes flew through the sky on metal wings like birds and sprawling cities that glowed bright at night were run by machines who thought faster than men. It both awed and frightened him at once.

The seventh Negro tooth purchased for George Washington had come from a Negro from Africa who himself had once been a trader in slaves. He had not gone out with the raids or the wars between kingdoms to procure them, but had been an instrumental middleman—a translator who spoke the languages of both the coastal slavers and their European buyers. He was instrumental in keeping the enchanted rifles and rum jugs flowing and assuring his benefactors a good value for the human merchandise. It was thus ironic that his downfall came from making a bad deal. The local ruler, a distant relative to a king, felt cheated and (much to the trader's shock) announced his translator put up for sale. The English merchant gladly accepted the offer. And just like that, the trader went from a man of position to a commodity.

He went half mad of despair when they'd chained him in the hold of the slave ship. Twice he tried to rip out his throat with his fingernails, preferring death to captivity. But each time he died, he returned to life—without sign of injury. He'd jumped into the sea to drown, only to be hauled back in without a drop of water in his lungs. He'd managed to get hold of a sailor's knife, driven it into his chest, and watched in shock as his body pushed the blade out and healed the wound. It was then he understood the extent of his downfall: he had been cursed. Perhaps by the gods. Perhaps by spirits of the vengeful dead. Or by some witch or conjurer for whom he'd haggled out a good price. He would never know. But they had cursed him to suffer this turn of fate, to become what he'd made of others. And there would be no escape.

The Negro slave trader's tooth was George Washington's favorite. No matter how much he used it, the tooth showed no signs of wear. Sometimes he could have sworn he'd broken it. But when inspected, it didn't show as much as a fracture—as if it mended itself. He put that tooth to work hardest of all, and gave it not a bit of rest.

The eighth Negro tooth belonging to George Washington came from his cook, who was called Ulysses. He had become a favorite in the Mount Vernon household, known for his culinary arts and the meticulous care he gave to his kitchen. The dinners and parties held at the mansion were always catered by Ulysses, and visitors praised his skill at devising new dishes to tingle the tongue and salivate the senses. Those within the higher social circles frequented by the Washingtons familiarly called him "Uncle Lysses" and showered him with such gifts that local papers remarked: "the Negro cook had become something of a celebrated puffed-up dandy."

Ulysses took his work seriously, as much as he took his name. He used the monies gained from those gifts, as well as his habit of selling leftovers (people paid good money to sup on the Washingtons' fare), to purchase translated works by Homer. In those pages, he learned about the fascinating travels of his namesake, and was particularly taken by the figure Circe—an enchantress

famed for her vast knowledge of potions and herbs, who through
a fine feast laced with a potent elixir had turned men into swine.
Ulysses amassed other books as well: eastern texts on Chinese
herbology, banned manuscripts of Mussulman alchemy, even
rare ancient Egyptian papyri on shape-shifting.

His first tests at transmogrification had merely increased the
appetite of Washington's guests, who turned so ravenous they
relieved themselves of knife or spoon and shoveled fistfuls of food
into their mouths like beasts. A second test had set them all to
loud high-pitched squealing—which was blamed on an over-
imbibing of cherubimical spirits. Success came, at last, when
he heard some days after a summer dining party that a Virginia
plantation owner and close friend of the Washingtons had gone
missing—the very same day his wife had found a great fat spotted
hog rummaging noisily through their parlor. She had her slaves
round up the horrid beast, which was summarily butchered and
served for dinner.

Over the years, Ulysses was judicious in his selections for the
transfiguring brew: several slave owners or overseers known to
be particularly cruel; a shipping merchant from Rhode Island
whose substantial wealth came from the slave trade; a visiting
French physiognomist and naturalist who prattled on about the
inherent "lower mental capabilities" to be found among Negroes,
whose skulls he compared to "near-human creatures" such as the
apes of inner Africa and the fierce woodland goblins of Bavaria.
Then, one day in early 1797, Ulysses disappeared.

The Washingtons were upset and hunted everywhere for their
absconded cook, putting out to all who would listen the kindness
they'd shown to the ungrateful servant. He was never found, but
the Mount Vernon slaves whispered that on the day Ulysses vanished a black crow with a mischievous glint in its eye was found
standing in a pile of the man's abandoned clothes. It cawed once,
and then flapped away.

When George Washington wore the tooth of his runaway cook, it was strangely at dinner parties. Slaves would watch as he wandered into the kitchen, eyes glazed over in a seeming trance, and placed drops of some strange liquid into the food and drink of his guests. His servants never touched those leftovers. But that summer many Virginians took note of a bizarre rash of wild pigs infesting the streets and countryside of Fairfax County.

The ninth, and final, Negro tooth purchased for George Washington came from a slave woman named Emma. She had been among Mount Vernon's earliest slaves, born there just a decade after Augustine Washington had moved in with his family. Had anyone recorded Emma's life for posterity, they would have learned of a girl who came of age in the shadows of one of Virginia's most powerful families. A girl who had fast learned that she was included among the Washingtons' possessions—treasured like a chair cut from exotic Jamaican mahogany or a bit of fine Canton porcelain. A young woman who had watched the Washington children go on to attend school and learn the ways of the gentry, while she was trained to wait on their whims. They had the entire world to explore and discover. Her world was Mount Vernon, and her aspirations could grow no further than the wants and needs of her owners.

That was not to say Emma did not have her own life, for slaves learned early how to carve out spaces separate from their masters. She had befriended, loved, married, cried, fought, and found succor in a community as vibrant as the Washingtons'—perhaps even more so, if only because they understood how precious it was to live. Yet she still dreamed for more. To be unbound from this place. To live a life where she had not seen friends and family put under the lash; a life where the children she bore were not the property of others; a place where she might draw a free breath and taste its sweetness. Emma didn't know any particular sorcery. She was no root woman or conjurer, nor had she been trained like the Washington women in simple domestic enchantments. But her dreams worked their own magic. A strong and potent magic that she clung to, that grew up and blossomed inside her—where not even her owners could touch, or take it away.

When George Washington wore Emma's tooth, some of that magic worked its way into him and perhaps troubled some small bit of his soul. In July 1799, six months before he died, Washington stipulated in his will that the 123 slaves belonging to himself, among them Emma, be freed upon his wife's death. No such stipulations were made for the Negro teeth still in his possession.

The Hospital Where

"I think I will go to the hospital. My arm is paining me." My father's voice. I heard him from some shallow corner of a quiet, hateful sleep. I imagined waking up somewhere different. I opened my eyes and was not somewhere different. I had no command over this place or the people in it. And yet, for the first time in more than three weeks, I felt the mark of the Twelve-tongued God, an *X* followed by two vertical slashes, burning on my back. My muse, my power, was awake again.

"What?" I asked.

"Can you drive?" my father asked.

"Okay," I said. I got ready. My father sat on a white plastic chair in the kitchen near the microwave and the hot plate. The only ways we had to cook. Beneath his leather sandals was a thin puddle of water that had leaked, as it did every day, from the shower in the adjacent bathroom. It was a basement. Dark mold had to be attacked with bleach regularly. But it never died. I hated this place we lived in and had for a very long time. My father scooped oatmeal into a bowl.

"Arm pain can be linked to other problems," he said. I tried very carefully to tie my shoes. "Better for you to drive." This was all long before we knew of the cancer nesting in his bones.

"You'll be fine," I said.

"I know, but just in case," he finished through a mouthful of oatmeal. While I waited for him to eat, I grabbed the latest issue of a small journal of stories and poems called *Rabid Bird* and one of my notebooks. The Twelve-tongued God beckoned in the form of the heat I felt on my back, and while I waited for my father to finish his oatmeal, I tried, finally, to write. I scribbled and felt the free feeling of fire in my bones. Transported into a world where I had command and anything was possible.

"All right, let's go," my father said too quickly. I closed my notebook and followed him outside. The drive was long and tired. My father explained to me what the doctors had told him when he'd called earlier. Essentially, he was now old enough that anything could be a big deal. They told him where to go while his normal hospital underwent renovations. We crossed the bridge. There was a spot pretty close. My father got out of the car and went into the hospital. "I'll find you," I said. I straightened the car out, then fed the meter. I walked toward the entrance thinking, *Remember this: the first time you drove a parent to a hospital.*

"What are you looking for?" said a woman who I hoped knew I was already lost and scared. She stood in front of me in purple scrubs and colorful nurse-type shoes. Her brown hair was spun into something that let everyone know she was very busy and hadn't slept in a long time. The tone of her voice, spiced with the Bronx, said I was one of many inconveniences in her life.

"I'm looking for my dad; he just came through here a second ago."

"Is that all?" She tapped her clipboard with a pen. "What department?" I had no idea what department my father was looking for, so I told her the truth about that. "Well, I don't know how you don't know, but—" She was about to take great pleasure in telling me that I was in this situation due to my own incompetence and that even though she could not help me, she herself was very competent. I walked away from her before she could finish.

Down the first hallway and to the left was a room that looked like the main lobby of a hotel. At the front desk was a computer and two empty seats. A woman in a suit and badge was pacing back and forth in front of the desk.

"Hi, I'm looking for my dad," I said.

"Well, there's a whole lotta dads in this place," the security guard said.

"He probably just came by asking questions, too. Black guy. I'm sure he just came down this way."

"Check in emergency—that's where I've been sending everybody who doesn't know where the heck they're going." She paused so I could be certain she was ridiculing me. "You're gonna go down this hall, make a left the first chance you get. You'll be in radiology. Then walk straight through there and make another left, and you'll basically be there. You'll see."

"Thanks so much," I said.

Soon I was staring at a small entryway sign that read RADIOLOGY I. In the hall there was an extremely old man in a wheelchair. He groaned steadily. His white skin looked stretched and spotty. It seemed someone had forgotten him or maybe was using him to prop open the door. There were so many tubes going in and coming out of him that I couldn't imagine where they began or ended. I walked past quickly. Farther down the same hall, a black guy in a wheelchair stared in my direction with eyes so empty I thought they might suck something out of me. I made a left, then saw a pair of double doors. A lot of healthy, able-bodied people talk about how much they hate the hospital. I've said it, too, I guess.

White coats and scrubs power walked in all directions. To my right was a family of six or seven. I imagined them Italian. It seemed they were waiting on news that everyone already knew was going to be bad. They clung to one another. They pointed frustrated looks at their shoes.

"Dad," I said as I stepped through the double doors. My father looked at me, then returned to arguing with an attendant seated behind a lectern in the corner of the emergency room. "I called and was told I could meet with someone since my doctor isn't in. And now I am here, and they are telling me to wait in the emergency room. They told me to come right away." My father was speaking the way he did to a rude waiter or a careless cashier.

"I'm sorry, sir, I don't know who you called. Things are a little hectic today. Please sign the sheet," said the attendant.

"I have." My father did one of his I'm-smarter-than-you laughs. "Already signed."

"Then please wait like everybody else." It was unseemly for anyone who wasn't about to die right that second to make any kind of scene in the emergency room is what he was trying to say.

"Dad," I said. "Just wait." My father stopped and looked visibly calmer. He sat. I gripped my notebook and the journal. I felt the mark tingle on my back. "Can you call again?" I asked.

"I have already. Doctor Koppen isn't in, and now they don't know how to direct me to another doctor. Imagine!"

"I'll go back and see if I can find some kind of directory," I said. What I wanted to do was sit and reread a story called "Free Barabbas" from the latest issue of *Rabid Bird*. It was pretty good, the story. I was especially interested in it because it had won a contest I had also entered. I'd received an email saying that though they'd loved my submission, "Does Anybody Want a Kitten?" I was still a loser. My story was about a family and all the things that happened to them and their new kitten: sometimes the kitten is hiding under the new bed, sometimes the kitten is sick, other times it's not and the family just appreciates its furry innocence. At one point the kitten runs away, and the family thinks their new home will never feel the same again.

The winning story concerned a guy who, in his own roundabout way, confronts his past through a series of events in his old neighborhood. It wasn't so much what it was "about," but rather the way the narrator was so funny and so mean and, somehow, so honest, that made it an awesome story, the kind you don't forget. It also happened to be nothing like anything I could ever write.

In "Does Anybody Want a Kitten?" the kitten eventually comes back, but she's pregnant.

The sick feeling growing in my throat matched the burning on my back. It was a warning. My time was running out. The Twelve-tongued God had promised me I would make our lives better. That I could use the power it had granted me to change things. It wouldn't matter what I did if my father wasn't there to see what I'd done.

I got up. I left my father sitting in his brown coat with his hands on his lap. I hoped he wouldn't ask me where I was going. He said nothing. Through the double doors, the eyes of the Italian family jumped up at me. Their eyes held something I would normally take as a look of pity, but then and there, I'm not sure what it was.

I walked back through radiology. The black guy was still there, alone. The other man, the one strangled by tubes and age, was also still there, but now he was wearing a Mets cap. I felt certain someone was using him as a hat rack. In the front lobby, the security guard looked nervous, then tough, when I approached.

"Is there, maybe, a directory kind of person? Or someone who can help me find which department I'm supposed to be in?" I asked. I pointed to the empty chairs behind the lobby desk. "Is someone going to be sitting in one of those seats soon?"

"Not today, nobody's coming. But if you don't know the department you need, then you probably wouldn't get much help anyway."

"When people come in and are trying to figure out where to go, who do they usually speak to? My dad called and he spoke to someone who told him to come in, but now that we're here, we can't figure out where to go. He normally goes to Riverhead, but they transferred him here."

"Who did he speak to?"

"He says her name was Martha."

The security guard almost smiled. "Just Martha?"

"Yes. I'm just wondering, if we call this hospital who are the people we would speak to? Who would help us?"

"There's a lotta phones in this hospital. You're better off going to the emergency room."

The security lady adjusted her pants and made a sound. "Thanks so much," I said, and walked back the way I came.

The *XII* on my back burned. I would have to write in the emergency room.

I sat next to my father. I quickly explained that in terms of guidance this hospital was not going to help us. My father shook his head and muttered something about how this would never happen at his usual hospital. I opened my notebook. Quietly, I prayed to the Twelve-tongued God. I looked around. Across from us was someone so old they didn't really have a gender anymore and a Hispanic woman about my father's age. I noticed a puddle beneath her seat. I didn't know what the liquid was. Seeing it in the emergency room made me feel queasy. It could have been water.

"What are you writing?" my father asked. I looked up from my notebook.

"I don't know," I said. Which was the truest thing anyone had ever said. It was still new for me to write in front of my parents— or anyone. It felt like announcing I was running for some huge office as a Green Party candidate.

"Well, what is it about?" My father turned toward me and winced as he did. "You write a lot now. What do you write about?" His curiosity stunned me. I also really had no idea how to answer.

What I could never tell my father was that I'd given myself to the Twelve-tongued God. It had happened many years before.

We'd been in a house that the bank would soon want back. The nights were dark because the gas and electric company had decided enough was enough. I'd learned that many of the things I loved, the comforts that made me feel good about myself, could disappear very slowly and also suddenly. I'd learned to hate then. To hate others for having things, to hate myself for not. One day, like an angel, the Twelve-tongued God emerged from the midnight black around me, as mysterious and vital as my own breath.

"I can give you new eyes. Eyes that will work, that won't cry. I can put your hurt to use," Twelve-tongue said. "I can give you what you want." After every other word, it pulled off a mask to reveal yet another beautiful new face. Its voice sounded like every voice I'd ever heard speaking at once. "I can give you the power to be anywhere. To heal the world. To own time. To turn lies to truth. To make day into night and night into day." I nodded viciously. "You will have the power to change everything, to make the life you want."

"What do I have to do?" I asked.

"You are not yet ready," said the Twelve-tongued God, revealing a new mask, one that wore a deep frown and jubilant eyes. Then it disappeared.

I waited. After we lost the house, we spent a year cramped into a small apartment. Then we were displaced again.

The night I saw another pink eviction notice, I prayed to that mysterious being that had found me those years before. Twelve-tongue appeared again in the basement we called a home. It smiled and frowned and laughed and cried. It stood in front of me. I watched it closely. As if to impress me, it winked and where before there had been a hot plate now there was a stainless-steel oven and range. The god laughed and the hot plate was back, the range gone.

I begged on my knees for its power.

"Serve me and you will live in a different world forever."

"I'll do anything," I said. I could feel the skin on my back beginning to sear. I could smell my own burn.

"Then prove it." The Twelve-tongued God opened its mouth and reached a hand in. From its throat, it pulled out what looked like a human hand but was actually the hilt to a sharp blade, the edge growing from the hand's middle finger.

"Please," I begged. The god watched me closely; the face it wore had an insane smile and drowning eyes. It held the knife and stared at me. Then it stuck its tongue out and quickly cut it off. I watched its bleeding mouth.

"Fo eve," said the Twelve-tongued God, a new tongue growing in its mouth. "You wi ver be the same."

"Please," I begged again. The god handed me the blade. I stuck my tongue out and placed the sharp edge near my bottom teeth. I pulled up and screamed. My tongue fell, and the Twelve-tongued God reached down and snatched it before it could hit the floor.

"The pact is made," the Twelve-tongued God said, and it stuffed its own newly cut tongue into my mouth. I wish I could share what it was like to feel the new tongue weaving into my flesh. I felt the Roman twelve brand into my back. Suddenly, I could see in the dark. Day became night. I felt free.

"Thank you," I said.

"We'll see," the Twelve-tongued God said as it popped my old tongue into its mouth and chewed. Then it disappeared.

That night I wrote my first story. I saw I was chained to the new power. I had to stay with the story. Work it harder and harder until it was something greater than I could have imagined. From that day forward, I prayed to Twelve-tongue every night and every morning, asking for more tongues. For sharper tongues. When I didn't write, my brand pulsed and ached. When I wrote badly, it screamed fiery chords. But then, when I made sentences that lived, it quieted and I could feel my ability growing. Still, I craved more tongues, new worlds to live in, and more power to change the one I was in now. I loved it. It was very lonely.

A nurse called out sounds that we both understood as her attempt to pronounce our last name.

"What kind of stories do you write?" my father asked again.

"It's about a guy who's hurt, I guess," I answered.

"Oh, that could be interesting," my father said. This was the most we'd ever discussed my writing.

"I don't know," I said. Someone attempted to call our name again. My father looked at me, then got up. He left his long coat on the seat beside me. I scooped the mess of brown cloth onto my lap.

"I'll wait here," I said.

My father didn't say anything before he disappeared through the double doors.

I exhaled. I closed my notebook and sat back in the emergency-room chair. I pressed my eyes shut. I could hear the quiet chatter of the healthy and sick.

After a while, I opened my eyes. A couple came in supporting each other with interlocking elbows. I couldn't tell the afflicted from the crutch. They found a seat in the room's corner near the attendant and his lectern.

"Did you ever find your mother?" The nurse I'd seen when I'd first entered the hospital was standing in front of me. I remembered her color-splashed scrubs and shoes.

"It was my dad, but yeah," I said. The nurse smiled.

"Was it? What if it was your mother?" the nurse said. She winked once with her left eye. Then she winked again. I looked down. My father's coat was gone. In its place was a black coat with a flourish of black sequins. It smelled lightly of a fruity perfume.

"No," I said. "It's my father. It is my father I'm waiting for."

"Fine," said the nurse. The Bronx accent waned, and a voice that could be anything took its place. "At least you know that much." I was again holding a brown trench coat that smelled like talcum powder and sweat.

I stared at the Twelve-tongued God, overjoyed and afraid as usual.

"Why now?" I asked. "Why now?" I wanted to yell but didn't.

"Don't be silly," said the Twelve-tongued God. She put her stethoscope in her ears, reached over my shoulder, and pulled my shirt up. She pressed cold metal on my mark. Since I'd first gotten it, the mark had grown and evolved. Around the *XII* was a dark mural of shadow figures and words I couldn't understand. "You're the one who's neglected me; I wasn't even sure it was you." The Twelve-tongued God smoothed my shirt back down, then pinched my cheek.

"I've been trying," I said. My fists were clenched.

"Really," said the Twelve-tongued God. She reached down and unclenched my fists. "Are you really trying?"

"You have no right to—"

"I am the right to," the Twelve-tongued God said. "Aren't I the one who made you something? Or maybe you'd rather cook on a hot plate for the rest of your life?"

"No," I said. I was on the verge of tears. The Twelve-tongued God sighed deeply. I was, um . . . a burning pulled at the corners of my eyes. "It's not easy for me. I need more from you. I need more tongues. I'm not good enough yet. I want to go all the way."

"Then go all the way," the Twelve-tongued God said to me. "Make what you want to see." The Twelve-tongued God reached down and kissed me on the forehead. "Really?" said the Twelve-tongued God.

I focused. I imagined what I wanted and what should be. And as I did, I saw that actually, no, the Twelve-tongued God hadn't kissed me on the forehead. That didn't happen. Instead, she grabbed me by the face and pressed a long hard lick up my neck, stopping at my ear. It felt warm and wet, like so many good things. My *XII* glowed and pulsed. "Don't be boring," the god said as she started to leave. I wanted to ask, *When will I be a winner?* And though the thought never reached my throat, the Twelve-tongued God turned to me just before disappearing through the double doors, and said, "When you win something."

I felt the power of the Twelve-tongued God spinning in my gut, looking for a place to go. I got up, carrying my father's coat in my arms. I needed to feed the meter. I wanted to check in with my father but realized he'd left his cell phone in the jacket. I sighed. Then I remembered that there were people around me who might not see their loved ones ever again. I walked out through the double doors.

The Italian family was still there, though I could tell that since I'd seen them last they'd either heard the terrible news they'd been anticipating or that the lack of any news at all had finally broken them. One woman in the family was crying into another's chest while a younger man rubbed both of their shoulder blades. I slipped by them quickly. If there was a ticket, it would be my fault.

The old men in radiology were as forgotten as ever. I made a point of noticing the old white guy exploding with tubes and the empty-looking black man because I felt like their not giving me anything meant I was to forget them, and I did not want to forget them yet.

The security guard who took pleasure in not helping me was adjusting her belt and strolling along a tiny circle. Outside, it was alive and sunny in stark contrast to the hospital, which was bright but dead. There were people walking around everywhere. None of them had any idea that maybe my father was sick and damaged. I swapped the old ticket for a new one. Adulthood is paying the meter on time, I thought. I walked back toward the emergency room.

Inside, the security guard was now arguing with a woman in a tight suit who seemed to want to make a show of things. I was happy to see angry people.

Back in radiology, the old men were still dying. I continued to the emergency room. On the way, the colorful nurse walked by; she yawned into her clipboard then looked at a watch on her wrist. I tried and failed to make eye contact.

The Italian family was with a doctor now. They huddled around him, as if he were a quarterback explaining the face of the next down. I stood away from them. Nurses and doctors rushed around. Trying to help when, really, what could they do? From the looks of things, that's what the doctor was telling the family: he wasn't a miracle worker despite the white coat and the machines. Then, suddenly, he rose up out of the huddle and pointed at me. He said, "That young man there can end your suffering. He is putting you through this. Maybe for no reason at all. He doesn't know why, and he doesn't even have the heart to end it. He's just going to—" I pretended I didn't hear the doctor say anything and continued back into the emergency room. I felt Twelve-tongue's hand like hot oil washing over my back. I wanted to tell the family that they mattered and weren't just grim decor. I didn't know how to tell them that, so I sat down and opened my notebook and tried to direct the fear and fire I felt in my body onto the page.

I looked up from the notebook.

Another older woman was coming in with what had to be her husband. They'd been together so long they were basically twins. The same hunched backs and thick glasses and drooping, tired faces. She used a blue rolling walker. I tried to ignore the couple and think. The old lady with the walker told the woman at the information window she'd been feeling very faint for the last three days. I could see that she and her husband were pretending they didn't know the "faintness" was her soul stretching out before a great marathon.

Is the family of—I heard something like my last name over the screeching PA system and decided it must be my turn to speak with the lady at the information window.

"Hi." I told her my name and that I was the son. I smiled at the old couple. That was my way of pretending with them.

"Do you have your father's insurance information?" the woman at the window asked.

"I don't," I said. "I can go find him and get it," I added quickly. "But I'm not sure where he is, exactly."

"He should be in bed fifteen," the woman said. "Just down the hall."

"Fifteen?" I asked. "Like, he's in an actual bed?" I could no longer pretend I wasn't afraid.

"Bed fifteen," she repeated.

As I passed the Italian family, I put my notebook, the journal, and my father's coat down and did a cartwheel to show them that kind of thing was still possible. They looked up at me, unamused. Then they returned to their sorrowful hugs and mutterings. I picked my stuff back up. I found my father wearing a dotted hospital gown. He'd spent most of his life in a tie. We stared at each other for a while. There were beeping sounds everywhere. He was carving out the last of a cup of Jell-O.

"They gave you food?" I asked.

"Well," my father said. "I was hungry."

"So what's happening? I need your insurance stuff." My father asked me to find his pants, which were somewhere beneath his hospital bed. I pulled two cards from his wallet and waited for him to answer me.

"I'm still waiting for the—well, there she is now."

The colorful nurse trotted toward us in a way that made me uneasy. She rubbed the back of my neck as she walked by me.

"Is this your son?" the Twelve-tongued God said to my father.

"Yes, can't you tell by how handsome he is?"

"I can, I can," said the Twelve-tongued God. She winked at me and I saw diminished blood cells, emaciation, chemotherapy, hair loss, diapers, more chemotherapy, fading fathers and heartsick sons grabbing, grabbing with weak hands for anything. Words that tried to make something pretty out of shit. "You must be wondering what's going on?" the god continued.

"We are," my father said. He laughed weakly.

"Okay, it looks like"—the Twelve-tongued God seemed to be looking at her clipboard, but she peered over the edge—*nothing is more boring than a happy ending*, her eyes said. I stared back and tried not to flinch from the gaze of my creator. I took a deep breath.

"Your blood pressure was a little higher than we'd like, so we checked that out, but other than that, everything looks great. After you give them your information, you'll be free to go." The Twelve-tongued God smiled at my father, then looked at me with a face both bored and disgusted.

Once my father was dressed, we began to walk back to the emergency room to handle his paperwork. "I can do it," I said. "You go back; the meter's almost up."

"Okay, good idea," he said, and disappeared in the direction of radiology.

For what I hoped would be the last time, I walked by the grieving family. I stepped into their family circle. The pain in my back, the fire of the *XII*, made it difficult to walk. I spoke clearly. "Whoever you think you've lost is not lost. Go home." They looked at me like I was a static-garbled television. "Go home, whoever it is, they're alive and well."

"How?" a woman said.

"It just is. They just are. Strange miracle. And now you've real-ized the power of family bonds. Everyone wins."

"It's so unlikely," said a man, who I assume was some kind of uncle. "Feels almost cheap?" he said, grinning despite himself.

"Well, yeah," I said. "It is what it is."

The colorful nurse walked by. "Coward!" she screamed at a nearby doctor. I skipped into the emergency room. All of the bro-ken people there groaned and groaned. I made my voice big and announced to the masses, "There's been a great miracle. None of you are hurt. Go home." They looked up at me and blinked. Some smiled weakly, but none moved.

"Please be decent," the attendant hissed. He looked at me with pleading eyes.

"Please, sir," said the clerk at the window who needed my father's insurance information.

"Here you go," I said, and threw the insurance cards at her. She stared at me, and then went to pick the cards up from the floor. While she was bent over, I leaned over the threshold and punched the intercom. I spoke into it, and my voice flew all over the hospital. "You are all healed. Go home. This is the hospital where sickness ends. Everything will be fine, and you are happier than you've ever been. Leave. Everyone is good. Especially you."

"Sir," the attendant said. But I was already running toward radiology. The tube-tied old man was very, very slowly pulling himself free of the plastic. The other man was also sitting up, eyes opened and locked on me. I felt my *XII* like it was a new brand.

"That's it," I said. "Go forth and be healed. I'm trying to help you." I was happy. As happy as a sunflower in a field of other less radiant sunflowers. The man with tubes crawled to the edge of his bed, then fell flat on his face toward the tile floor. I screamed, "No." And the man, dislodged finally from all the tubes, froze in the air, a weightless icon, a displaced swimmer who waded in the open air. With great effort, he looked up at me as he floated. "This is the hospital where the affliction is flight," he said. Then he returned to the call of gravity and fell hard back down to the ground.

He did not move once he was there. The other man never took his eyes off me. "This is that place," he said.

I ran away toward the entrance. A sea of hospital-gown-wearing humans surrounded the security guard. She tried desperately to direct groaning patients back to wherever they belonged. She caught my eye and scowled as I ran by.

"Please, no running," the security guard yelled.

Outside, my father was sitting in the driver's seat. I was relieved to be a passenger. From all the entrances and exits of the hospital, hobbled, hurt people were emerging. They were mostly old, anywhere else they'd be untreatable, and still they made their way out into the sunshine. The affliction is flight, I thought with a hazy focus, the only kind I could muster with the exploding pain I felt in my back. And suddenly, just as they stepped through the threshold into the outside, the old sick bodies rose into the air and floated a few inches above the ground; there they hovered, weightless, immaculate, wearing thin hospital gowns and colorful socks. They were in the air for almost ten seconds, taking careful steps forward before they fell back to the earth. Their ankles gave out immediately. On the ground, they crawled like babies, if they moved at all. More stepped forward, flew, then fell. It kept happening. It kept happening. I turned to my father.

He stared at all the people flooding and floating out of the hospital. He shook his head and said, "What have you done?"

"It's about a hospital where people can fly," I said.

"What have you done?" he begged.

N. K. JEMISIN

The Ones Who Stay and Fight

It's the Day of Good Birds in the city of Um-Helat! The Day is a local custom, silly and random as so many local customs can be, and yet beautiful by the same token. It has little to do with birds—a fact about which locals cheerfully laugh, because that, too, is how local customs work. It is a day of fluttering and flight regardless, where pennants of brightly dyed silk plume forth from every window, and delicate drones of copperwire and featherglass—made for this day, and flown on no other!—waft and buzz on the wind. Even the monorail cars trail stylized flamingo feathers from their rooftops, although these are made of featherglass, too, since real flamingos do not fly at the speed of sound.

Um-Helat sits at the confluence of three rivers and an ocean. This places it within the migratory path of several species of butterfly and hummingbird as they travel north to south and back again. At the Day's dawning, the children of the city come forth, most wearing wings made for them by parents and kind old aunties. (Not all aunties are actually aunties, but in Um-Helat, anyone can earn auntie-hood. This is a city where numberless aspirations can be fulfilled.) Some wings are organza stitched onto school backpacks; some are quilted cotton stuffed with dried flowers and clipped to jacket shoulders. Some few have been carefully glued together from dozens of butterflies' discarded wings—but only those butterflies that died naturally, of course. Thus adorned, children who can run through the streets do so, leaping off curbs and making whooshing sounds as they pretend to fly. Those who cannot run instead ride special drones, belted and barred and double-checked for safety, which gently bounce them into the air. It's only a few feet, though it feels like the height of the sky.

But this is no awkward dystopia, where all are forced to conform. Adults who refuse to give up their childhood joys wear wings, too, though theirs tend to be more abstractly constructed. (Some are invisible.) And those who follow faiths which forbid the emulation of beasts, or those who simply do not want wings, need not wear them. They are all honored for this choice, as much as the soarers and flutterers themselves—for without contrasts, how does one appreciate the different forms that joy can take?

Oh, and there is *such* joy here, friend. Street vendors sell tiny custard-filled cakes shaped like jewel beetles, and people who've waited all year wolf them down while sucking air to cool their tongues. Artisans offer cleverly mechanized paper hummingbirds for passersby to throw; the best ones blur as they glide. As the afternoon of the Day grows long, Um-Helat's farmers arrive, invited as always to be honored alongside the city's merchants and technologers. By all three groups' efforts does the city prosper—but when aquifers and rivers dip too low, the farmers move to other lands and farm there, or change from corn-husking to rice-paddying and fishery-feeding. The management of soil and water and chemistry are intricate arts, as you know, but here they have been perfected. Here in Um-Helat there is no hunger: not among the people, and not for the migrating birds and butterflies when they dip down for a taste of savory nectar. And so farmers are particularly celebrated on the Day of Good Birds.

The parade wends through the city, farmers ducking their gazes or laughing as their fellow citizens offer salute. Here is a portly woman, waving a hat of chicken feathers that someone

has gifted her. There is a reedy man in a coverall, nervously pluck-
ing at the brooch he bears, carved and lacquered to look like a
ladybug. He has made it himself, and hopes others will think it
fine. They do!

And here! This woman, tall and strong and bare of arm, her
sleek brown scalp dotted with implanted silver studs, wearing a
fine uniform of stormcloud damask. See how she moves through
the crowd, grinning with them, helping up a child who has fallen.
She encourages their cheers and their delight, speaking to this
person in one language and that person in another. (Um-Helat is
a city of polyglots.) She reaches the front of the crowd and immediately spies the reedy man's ladybug, whereupon with delighted
eyes and smile, she makes much of it. She points, and others see
it, too, which makes the reedy man blush terribly. But there is
only kindness and genuine pleasure in the smiles, and gradually
the reedy man stands a little taller, walks with a wider stride. He
has made his fellow citizens happier, and there is no finer virtue
by the customs of this gentle, rich land.

The slanting afternoon sun stretches golden over the city,
reflected light sparkling along its mica-flecked walls and laser-
faceted embossings. A breeze blows up from the sea, tasting of
brine and minerals, so fresh that a spontaneous cheer wafts along
the crowded parade route. Young men by the waterfront, busily
stirring great vats of spiced mussels and pans of rice and peas
and shrimp, cook faster, for it is said in Um-Helat that the smell of
the sea wakes up the belly. Young women on streetcorners bring
out sitars and synthesizers and big wooden drums, the better to
get the crowd dancing the young men's way. When people stop,
too hot or thirsty to continue, there are glasses of fresh tamarind-
lime juice. Elders staff the shops that sell this, though they also
give away the juice if a person is much in need. There are always
souls needing drumbeats and tamarind, in Um-Helat.

Joyous! It is a steady joy that fills this city, easy to speak of—but ah, though I have tried, it is most difficult to describe accurately. I see the incredulity in your face! The difficulty lies partly in my lack of words, and partly in your lack of understanding, because you have never seen a place like Um-Helat, and because I am myself only an observer, not yet privileged to visit. Thus I must try harder to describe it so that you might embrace it, too.

How can I illuminate the people of Um-Helat? You have seen how they love their children, and how they honor honest, clever labor. You have perhaps noted their many elders, for I have mentioned them in passing. In Um-Helat, people live long and richly, with good health for as long as fate and choice and medicine permits. Every child knows opportunity; every parent has a life. There are some who go without housing, but they can have an apartment if they wish. Here where the spaces under bridges are swept daily and benches have light padding for comfort, they do not live badly. If these itinerant folk dwell also in delusions, they are kept from weapons or places that might do them harm; where they risk disease or injury, they are prevented—or cared for, if matters get out of hand. (We shall speak more of the caretakers soon.)

And so this is Um-Helat: a city whose inhabitants, simply, care for one another. That is a city's purpose, they believe—not merely to generate revenue or energy or products, but to shelter and nurture the people who do these things.

What have I forgotten to mention? Oh, it is the thing that will seem most fantastic to you, friend: the variety! The citizens of Um-Helat are so many and so wildly different in appearance and origin and development. People in this land come from many others, and it shows in sheen of skin and kink of hair and plumpness of lip and hip. If one wanders the streets where the workers and artisans do their work, there are slightly more people with dark skin; if one strolls the corridors of the executive tower, there are a few extra done in pale. There is history rather than malice in this, and it is still being actively, intentionally corrected—because the people of Um-Helat are not naive believers in good intentions as the solution to all ills. No, there are no worshippers of mere tolerance here, nor desperate grovelers for that grudging pittance of respect which is *diversity*. Um-Helatians are learned enough to understand what must be done to make the world better, and pragmatic enough to actually enact it.

Does that seem wrong to you? It should not. The trouble is that we have a bad habit, encouraged by those concealing ill intent, of insisting that people already suffering should be afflicted with further, unnecessary pain. This is the paradox of tolerance, the treason of free speech: we hesitate to admit that some people are just fucking evil and need to be stopped.

This is Um-Helat, after all, and not that barbaric America. This is not Omelas, a tick of a city, fat and happy with its head buried in a tortured child. My accounting of Um-Helat is an homage, true, but there's nothing for you to fear, friend.

And so how does Um-Helat exist? How can such a city possibly survive, let alone thrive? Wealthy with no poor, advanced with no war, a beautiful place where all souls know themselves beautiful . . . It cannot be, you say. Utopia? How banal. It's a fairy tale, a thought exercise. Crabs in a barrel, dog-eat-dog, oppression Olympics—it would not last, you insist. It could never be in the first place. Racism is natural, so natural that we will call it "tribalism" to insinuate that everyone does it. Sexism is natural and homophobia is natural and religious intolerance is natural and greed is natural and cruelty is natural and savagery and fear and and and . . . and. "Impossible!" you hiss, your fists slowly clenching at your sides. "How dare you. What have these people done to make you believe such lies? What are you doing to me, to suggest that it is possible? How dare you. *How dare you.*"

Oh, friend! I fear I have offended. My apologies.

Yet . . . how else can I convey Um-Helat to you, when even the thought of a happy, just society raises your ire so? Though I confess I am puzzled as to *why* you are so angry. It's almost as if you feel threatened by the very idea of equality. Almost as if some part of you needs to be angry. Needs unhappiness and injustice. But … do you?

Do you?

Do you believe, friend? Do you accept the Day of Good Birds, the city, the joy? No? Then let me tell you one more thing.

Remember the woman? So tall and brown, so handsome and bald, so loving in her honest pleasure, so fine in her stormcloud gray. She is one of many wearing the same garb, committed to the same purpose. Follow her, now, as she leaves behind the crowd and walks along the biofiber-paved side streets into the shadows. Beneath a skyscraper that floats a few meters off the ground— oh, it is perfectly safe, Um-Helat has controlled gravity for generations now—she stops. There two others await: one gethen, one male, both clad in gray damask, too. They are also bald, their studded heads a-gleam. They greet each other warmly, with hugs where those are welcomed.

They are no one special. Just some of the many people who work to ensure the happiness and prosperity of their fellow citizens. Think of them as social workers if you like; their role is no different from that of social workers anywhere. Word has come of a troubling case, and this is why they gather: to discuss it, and make a difficult decision.

There are wonders far greater than a few floating skyscrapers in Um-Helat, you see, and one of these is the ability to bridge the distances between possibilities—what we would call universes. Anyone can do it, but almost no one tries. That is because, due to a quirk of spacetime, the only world that people in Um-Helat can reach is our own. And why would anyone from this glorious place want to come anywhere near our benighted hellscape?

Again you seem offended. Ah, friend! You have no right to be.

In any case, there's little danger of travel. Even Um-Helat has not successfully found a way to reduce the tremendous energy demands of macro-scale planar transversal. Only wave particles can move from our world to theirs, and back again. Only information. Who would bother? Ah, but you forget: This is a land where no one hungers, no one is left ill, no one lives in fear, and even war is almost forgotten. In such a place, buoyed by the luxury of safety and comfort, people may seek knowledge solely for knowledge's sake.

But some knowledge is dangerous.

Um-Helat has been a worse place, after all, in its past. Not all of its peoples, so disparate in origin and custom and language, came together entirely by choice. The city had a different civilization once—one which might not have upset you so! (Poor thing. There, there.) Remnants of that time dot the land all around the city, ruined and enormous and half-broken. Here a bridge. There a great truck, on its back a rusting, curve-sided thing that ancient peoples referred to by the exotic term *missile*. In the distance: the skeletal remains of another city, once just as vast as Um-Helat, but never so lovely. Works such as these encumber all the land, no more and no less venerable to the Um-Helatians than the rest of the landscape. Indeed, every young citizen must be reminded of these things upon coming of age, and told carefully curated stories of their nature and purpose. When the young citizens learn this, it is a shock almost incomprehensible, in that they literally lack the words to comprehend such things. The languages spoken in Um-Helat were once *our* languages, yes—for this world was once our world; it was not so much parallel as *the same*, back then. You might still recognize the languages, but what would puzzle you is how they speak . . . and how they don't. Oh, some of this will be familiar to you in concept at least, like terms for gender that mean neither he nor she, and the condemnation of words meant to slur and denigrate. And yet you will puzzle over the Um-Helatians' choice to retain descriptive terms for themselves like *kinky-haired* or *fat* or *deaf.* But these are just words, friend, don't you see? Without the attached contempt, such terms have no more meaning than if horses could proudly introduce themselves as palomino or miniature or hairy-footed. Difference was never the problem in and of itself—and Um-Helatians still have differences with each other, of opinion and otherwise. Of course they do! They're people. But what shocks the young citizens of Um-Helat is the realization that, once, those differences of opinion involved differences in respect. That once, value was ascribed to some people, and not others. That once, humanity was acknowledged for some, and not others.

It's the Day of Good Birds in Um-Helat, where every soul matters, and even the idea that some might not is anathema.

This, then, is why the social workers of Um-Helat have come together: because someone has breached the barrier between worlds. A citizen of Um-Helat has listened, on equipment you would not recognize but which records minute quantum perturbations excited by signal wavelengths, to our radio. He has watched our television. He has followed our social media, played our videos, liked our selfies. We are remarkably primitive, compared to Um-Helat. Time flows the same in both worlds, but people there have not wasted themselves on crushing one another into submission, and this makes a remarkable difference. So anyone can do it—build a thing to traverse the worlds. Like building your own ham radio. Easy. Which is why there is an entire underground industry in Um-Helat—ah! crime! *now* you believe a little more—built around information gleaned from the strange alien world that is our own. Pamphlets are written and distributed. Art and whispers are traded. The forbidden is so seductive, is it not? Even here, where only things that cause harm to others are called evil. The information-gleaners know that what they do is wrong.

They know this is what destroyed the old cities. And indeed, they are horrified at what they hear through the speakers, see on the screens. They begin to perceive that ours is a world where the notion that *some people are less important than others* has been allowed to take root, and grow until it buckles and cracks the foundations of our humanity. "How could they?" the gleaners exclaim, of us. "Why would they do such things? How can they just leave those people to starve? Why do they not listen when that one complains of disrespect? What does it mean that these ones have been assaulted and no one, *no one*, cares? Who treats other people like *that*?" And yet, even amid their shock, they share the idea. The evil . . . spreads.

So the social workers of Um-Helat stand, talking now, over the body of a man. He is dead—early, unwilling, with a beautifully crafted pike jammed through his spine and heart. (The spine to make it painless. The heart to make it quick.) This is only one of the weapons carried by the social workers, and they prefer it because the pike is silent. Because there was no shot or ricochet, no crackle or sizzle, no scream, no one else will come to investigate. The disease has taken one poor victim, but it need not claim more. In this manner is the contagion contained . . . in a moment. In a moment.

Beside the man's body crouches a little girl. She's curly-haired, plump, blind, brown, tall for her age. Normally a boisterous child, she weeps now over her father's death, and her tears run hot with the injustice of it all. She heard him say, "I'm sorry." She heard the social workers show the only mercy possible. But she isn't old enough to have been warned of the consequences of breaking the law, or to understand that her father knew those consequences and accepted them—so to her, what has happened has no purpose or reason. It is a senseless, monstrous, and impossible thing, called murder.

"I'll get back at you," she says between sobs. "I'll make you die the way you made him die." This is an unthinkable thing to say. Something is very wrong here. She snarls, "How dare you. How *dare* you."

The social workers exchange looks of concern. They are contaminated themselves, of course; it's permitted, and frankly unavoidable in their line of work. Impossible to dam a flood without getting wet. (There are measures in place. The studs on their scalps—well. In our own world, those who volunteered to work in leper colonies were once venerated, and imprisoned with them.) The social workers know, therefore, that for incomprehensible reasons, this girl's father has shared the poison knowledge of our world with her. An uncontaminated citizen of Um-Helat would have asked "Why?" after the initial shock and horror, because they would expect a reason. There would *be* a reason. But this girl has already decided that the social workers are less important than her father, and therefore the reason doesn't matter. She believes that the entire city is less important than one man's selfishness. Poor child. She is nearly septic with the taint of our world.

Nearly. But then our social worker, the tall brown one who got a hundred strangers to smile at a handmade ladybug, crouches and takes the child's hand.

What? What surprises you? Did you think this would end with the cold-eyed slaughter of a child? There are other options—and this is Um-Helat, friend, where even a pitiful, diseased child matters. They will keep her in quarantine, and reach out to her for many days. If the girl accepts the hand, listens to them, they will try to explain why her father had to die. She's early for the knowledge, but something must be done, do you see? Then together they will bury him, with their own hands if they must, in the beautiful garden that they tend between caseloads. This garden holds all the Um-Helatians who broke the law. Just because they have to die as deterrence doesn't mean they can't be honored for the sacrifice.

But there is only one treatment for this toxin once it gets into the blood: fighting it. Tooth and nail, spear and claw, up close and brutal; no quarter can be given, no parole, no debate. The child must grow, and learn, and become another social worker fighting an endless war against an idea . . . but she will live, and help others, and find meaning in that. If she takes the woman's hand.

Does this work for you, at last, friend? Does the possibility of harsh enforcement add enough realism? Are you better able to accept this postcolonial utopia now that you see its bloody teeth? Ah, but they did not choose this battle, the people of Um-Helat today; their ancestors did, when they spun lies and ignored conscience in order to profit from others' pain. Their greed became a philosophy, a religion, a series of nations, all built on blood. Um-Helat has chosen to be better. But it, too, must perform blood sacrifice to keep true evil at bay.

And now we come to you, my friend. My little soldier. See what I've done? So insidious, these little thoughts, going both ways along the quantum path. Now, perhaps, you will think of Um-Helat, and wish. Now you might finally be able to envision a world where people have learned to love, as they learned in our world to hate. Perhaps you will speak of Um-Helat to others, and spread the notion farther still, like joyous birds migrating on trade winds. *It's possible.* Everyone—even the poor, even the lazy, even the undesirable—can matter. Do you see how just the idea of this provokes utter rage in some? That is the infection defending itself . . . because if enough of us believe a thing is possible, then it becomes so.

And then? Who knows. War, maybe. The fire of fever and the purging scourge. No one wants that, but is not the alternative to lie helpless, spotty and blistered and heaving, until we *all* die?

So don't walk away. The child needs you, too, don't you see?

You also have to fight for her, now that you know she exists, or walking away is meaningless. Here, here is my hand. Take it. Please.

Good. Good.

Now. Let's get to work.

ALEX SMITH

The Final Flight of the Unicorn Girl

"We grinned at sin, mostly, spiraling through black ether as a bright yellow wave, crash-landing on the roof or splashing into windows on wires, reeling off one-liners and brash talk that belied the danger of the situation. A flunky with bad breath and an ill-fitting suit would pull some kind of lever, and these hired goons—probably deadbeat fathers with no pension or former mercenaries bored and ill-adapted to civilian life or meatheads spawned from some cult or hate group they'd been kicked out of—would all come trotting out, decorated with surplus pouches and clunky artillery hanging from the taut string of their utility belts.

"We waded across floors riddled with spent shell casings and turned these goons' guns into splinters. We jacked up men in suits, crashed through the skylight in the boardrooms of these shadow corporations; we hemmed mobsters fat with the toxic nuclear steroid of the month to cement walls. Guidos jacked up on super-powered drugs and contaminants, they all flinched and fired aimlessly at our swift, gliding rainbow of dizzy confusion.

"We bounced on drug tables and kicked over artifacts illegally procured from alien worlds in alternate universes. We burned buildings down to the ground, a gleeful flick of a finger on a kerosene-soaked hallway, swept away in the backdraft, watching the flames lick at our winged footies as we blasted back into the night sky. We stood there defiantly in the streets as we razed villain enclaves or looked through high-tech binoculars from a few miles away as one after the other—these towers of oppression—fell from the lines in the sky, crumbling into a pit of ash and mold—just fragments of ideas left, just the rocks. We smiled wildly at the sight, some of us running up light posts and baying at the moon or waving flags bigger than our young bodies, bright crimson drapes of cloth swaying gently in the night breeze, emblazoned with our crests. Or some of us would let loose, wearing jetpacks and bursting out of fireworks and letting the lights entangle us in red stars and green lightning bolts and violet hearts.

"So, don't just let us die out here."

The rain is almost toxic, feels like acid is going to eat through my overcoat. I look at this boy in my arms. He's wearing a silver spandex suit; he's also wearing about seven bullets lodged in places that don't seem to make sense. He's such a lithe thing, just a ragged string, really, tattered and bleeding out in this alley behind this club, one hand holding his guts in and the other raised at an awkward angle toward my stubby face. His touch is like Popsicles on my skin.

"Don't let us die," he squeaks out. His eyes roll up in their sockets, and it seems like he disappears, like his skin tightens right there. I lower him to the ground, gently laying him on a pile of newspapers and trash. I close his eyes and promise him a proper burial, that I'd come back when it's all over and take his body out to sea or scatter his ashes over some great mountain. It's a gentle lie, I think to myself as I clutch my gun, rising to my feet.

There are searchlights overhead. It's heavy and opaque all over with the radiant stench of D.A.R.K. Patrol's heliports. I make my way up the alley, careful not to cast my shadow in their lights. It's not a lockdown, but I'm trying to keep a low profile. There are too many of them out here.

Something's going down tonight. I can feel it in my gut.

As the last heliport disappears over the bridge, their engines reduced to a safe hum, the streets seem quiet. Hollowed-out sports cars and abandoned motorcycles for blocks; storefronts boarded up and rotting, some still emanating their husky dust and ash, pieces still falling. The occasional vagrant passes by with a shopping cart or something on fire, cackling, then tossing that fiery thing into a bus, a building, or dumpster. The whirs of alarms stretch from all angles of the city and lurch down its streets. It's a sound that registers as infinitely more calming than the three seconds of silence before it.

These streets are an abyss, a coiled snake choking itself on the husks of old subway cars, billowing smoke and foul steam cascading off its prostitutes; these hustlers stay backlit by a piss-yellow glow of tech-spruced Cadillac headlights. The steady drum and thrum of bass music bursting out of shit-drenched tenements and muscle cars is an unnerving soundtrack. It's giving me a headache. I tuck further into my trench coat, the blood of the silver-clad boy slowly drying on my fingers.

What was his name? Silver Soul? I think. I can't keep all of them straight anymore. No full memories that any of them ever happened. Just bits and pieces like distorted dreams. How they'd streak the air like shooting stars. Back then you could take your child to the park at night and watch them light up, beautiful beacons. We were safe. They kept us.

Yeah, Silver Soul.

He could turn metal into light. He was Captain Starjack's sidekick. Just this wispy little sprite, flitting in and out of hyperspace. Silver would turn entire tanks into flurries of light . . . man, it was something.

On a routine outing, the two of them under attack by some nefarious, now defunct corporation—I'm going to say it was Amnodyne—was when all of this wonder, this dream life we lived traversing the stars only to come spraying back into the atmosphere aglow, anew—all crashed. Amnodyne, we'd all find out later, was somehow controlling the city—its politics, its police officers, its private and public interests. If they didn't control it outright, they owned a heavy controlling interest in it. When Amnodyne's android minions attacked a hostel, laying into a group of boy travelers, Silver Soul saw red and unleashed an array of energies that annihilated a city block. He was inconsolably angry, pulsating with the chroma of the cosmos.

I remember Captain Starjack staring blankly into a news camera at the podium the day that he announced his retirement, that they'd all be retiring, melting back into obscurity, and that some of them, the ones with the real power, would be working for a new corporation that would rise in Amnodyne's wake, take control, and lead us out of the coming darkness. They called it "D.A.R.K. Patrol."

Maximus, Killgirl, Vehenna, White Star, G-Man. They all put on business suits and became the brainwashed henchmen of an international corporation that would strangle the life out of the city it swore to protect.

Where I'm standing isn't the entrance to a club. Not really. It's a boarded-up wall wheat-pasted with wanted posters seeking the capture of Kid Lightning, Girl of Thunder, Hippy John, Coldwave, the Young Arrows Guild, Fangra, Black Bird, Silver Soul. Dead or alive. I touch the boy's face again. On the poster he's glowing, his smile looking sadder now than when that picture was taken.

Some surly young men on junk motorbikes are rolling silently up and down the block. They're waving empty beer bottles around like Molotov cocktails. They've got pig snouts sewn into their flesh with enormous rings or pins made of human bones.

The spikes on their jackets have all dulled or chipped away. They're all armed with their square guns and satchel grenades. I try to stay out of the streetlight, just duck into the blackened jamb of a nearby doorway and watch them motor on.

I run my hand, tapping gently on the wall until I find a hollow spot, and bang on it in a deliberate rhythm. Three seconds later, a small hole slides open. Two eyes glare back at me then dart around, widely surveying the surrounding street. They speak. It's a hollow, disinterested timbre. "Go to the alley."

So, another alley. There's a rusting metal door. I bang out the rhythm again, and this time the door creaks open, revealing a blackness that is almost impenetrable. I hug alongside what I think are walls, tracing my path forward with my hands until the walls move, slowly pulling away and rolling like logs down a river. They're not walls anymore. They're people, pulsating and gyrating, clamped to each other in lust. Fucking disgusting. I tear away from them, their bodies slick with sweat.

As the darkness starts to dissipate and morph into a low light, the hallway becomes imbued with a dim redness immersed in a murky underwater glow. The walls turn into glass tanks. Young men and women are swimming nude in a green soup. They are moving in and out of each other's bodies. It makes me dizzy. I finally hear a rumble of bass, a roiling, muddy sound that grows louder as I approach another door. This one is guarded by a big bear of a man. He gives me a nod. I've made it this far, I must be "cool." When he opens the door I'm left standing in Leviticus.

The club isn't massive, but its nondescript outside belies its true size. The music is a dense, thick briar of wiry, disconnected sounds, stabs of half-beats and exploding loops, and a tireless tribal drum. Then there is relentless, merciless, unending bass.

Club Leviticus, the hidden world of decadence, of release. There are bodies everywhere, covered in glitter, shimmering in refracted light. They are swinging on the house lamps; they are hugging the speakers; they are in cages; they are on platforms gyrating in waves. Most of them are young men, barely nineteen, all with a stunned, gray coldness in their eyes, which long to burn, long to find the joy and flame of the heavens again.

I'm at the bar.

"You, there!"

A cackling thing in a pink suit with dull strings of green, red, orange lights piping around the torso haphazardly. She's got a unicorn's horn protruding from her forehead, and she's carrying a ridiculously oversized bottle of malt liquor. "You there, Mr. Trenchcoat! Come to save us all!" she burps out, stumbles through the crowd, and crashes into the stool next to me. Did she pass out?

I look down. She's still moving.

"What do you want?" the bartender, a man with a large head, leathery green skin, and sawed-off horns, asks.

"Nothing." I take another glance at the flesh moving behind me, spitting their drinks back into each other's mouths, grabbing their crotches, or wrapping themselves up in cable wire. "I'm OK."

"Well, you can't sit at the bar if you're not going to order anything," the bartender yells over the music, slamming his huge mitts on the counter.

"Hey, Chang," a voice calls from the other end of the bar. "Relax. He's with me."

A young man with his face buried in a drink gives me a light nod. Chang turns around in a huff.

The kid, however, just sits there silently through what I perceive to be about two songs. I've got nowhere to be tonight but here. So I sit, too. I finally break and glance over in his direction. The long locks on his head drape over his deep cavern of a face. I can't make out any of his other features, but I lean toward him, and ask, "Are you Coldwave?"

"Ha." He snorts. "Coldwave. Haven't heard that one in awhile."

There's another bout of silence from him, then: "Yeah. Yeah, haven't heard that one in awhile, man. What brings you here?"

The boy pulls a flask tucked into his pants, dumps one of the shot glasses in front of him, pours some, and slides it over to me. One sip and my head spins. It feels like I'm watching a really bad home movie on a failing VHS player: my vision is blurry and distorted, and the whole scene warbles in and out of focus. I try to adjust my eyes in the mirror, but all I can see is a young boy running roughshod through a mansion. He's wearing a cape and twirling a staff that seems five feet longer than his body. His exuberance is astonishing as he leaps through the air, over couches, sliding down the length of a dinner table and crashing into bookshelves. A hapless staff of maids and butlers cower at the display.

"Scout." A voice, stern and meaty, so clear in my head. The young boy turns around, and a sadness creeps over him. "What is this?"

The man is a square-jawed titan, his chest barreling out of a black Kevlar vest rife with bullet holes and ripped and gashed at the seams. His face is lined with fresh cuts and drying blood. Strangely, he looks a lot like me. He's holding a tattered notebook. He begins to read:

"'Scouts log 22. Today, after patrol, I went to Unicorn Boy's secret, secret Secret Lair. We played video games and talked about our adventures. He has a voice like a thousand gamelans chiming in a soft, sweet rain. So, like, anyway, in the middle of us talking about our battle scars, he took off his shirt to show me one of his, and I touched it, right above his navel, and traced my hand down ...'

"Jesus, I can't even read the rest of this out loud."

The man that looks like a younger, brasher, thinner me stands there, his arms folded.

"You disgust me," he says to the boy. "I want you out of this house by the morning."

He turns away, and the boy sinks to his knees, his long staff falling gracelessly by his side, rolling out into the middle of the floor. The boy cries and cries.

". . . don't know anything, man. In fact, I'm not even sure how you got in here—how you even heard about this place—but it's not safe for you here."

Coldwave has been talking for a few minutes. I used to be so astute, my every thought trained on my surroundings. Now I'm 40 pounds heavier with a slumped back, and I'm wearing a trench coat in a seedy nightclub filled with a bunch of mutants and alien freaks, tomboy acrobats and junior assassins with glowing teeth. I've missed out on the drunk ramblings of a desperate teenager who could turn mountains into water vapor.

"See, this is where it all went wrong." Coldwave bangs his glass on the counter. "We got too powerful, man. We always were more powerful than the supers. They couldn't handle it. We were just a buncha rags, just some punks with Day-Glo underwear and pink spandex with our pathetic, little wish powers that we couldn't control.

"But the day Silver exploded, man, that's when it all changed. We started using science to . . . to . . . to fuel our imagination, right? To get good at using our little joke powers. We started transforming the world, man.

"Sun Runner, who could fucking talk to the sun, ha ha, right? Well, dude figured out how to turn his gift into solar energy, man, and powered all those villages in Africa. Or that dude, Shells from Detroit, who could create those little force fields? Well, he figured out how to use that shit to grow these little bubbles in all the brains of them corrupt politicians, nearly brought the city to its knees.

"Some of us wanted to make a difference, man! And look what they did, used the supers to take us down, stopped returning our phone calls. Now G-Man is working for the pigs in Washington. They forgot where they fucking came from!"

Coldwave downs another, bangs his glass. Chang grunts, then fills it. Another silence.

"So. What are you looking for, anyway, old man? Are you an ex-super trying to relive his sick fantasies all over again, huh? That get you off, old man? You wanna fuck one of us in your big, stupid mansion out there in the 'burbs?"

I want to retch at the thought. "No," I tell him, reaching into my coat. He flinches, braces himself. I pull out a piece of paper. "I don't know why, but I need to find this person."

I put the paper on the counter, and Coldwave's eyes beam. He crackles alive, his formerly sullen face now bursting with a ray of hope.

"But that's . . . so you're . . ."

A body is tossed into the glass behind Chang. It's the bouncer. He's covered in glass, writhing in pain, lacerated and bloody. The place erupts in startled screams as the unwelcomed hint of danger becomes real. The pig-nosed thugs from the street are inside the club, and they are gunning everyone down. Shards of wood and steel fly savagely around the room.

I'm crouching under the bar, reaching up to pull Coldwave in.

"Fuck yeah!" he screams.

Coldwave slams his glass down onto the table, shattering it. The liquid inside spirals upwards. Before it hits the table, he's turned it into a hundred cold pieces of nitrogen bullets—ice that goes boom—and he's blasted two of the *Mad Max* rejects into a mirrored wall.

But there are three more of them. They have trained their square guns on him. Chang appears from behind the bar and fires an errant shotgun blast. Then his large head explodes into a bloody pulp, the bottles behind him shattering, raining glass and bad alcohol everywhere. In a flash Coldwave is consumed in concussive fire, his body puffs smoke through gaping holes. More guns go off, more bodies fall to the ground in nearly poetic waves of humanity.

Glass canisters of green soup rip open, and fleshy young men pour out of them, choking and gasping for air until they turn into husks.

It's faint, but from my hidden vantage point amid the wail of gunfire, I can hear the gunmen laughing until the table I'm hiding under disappears and their guns are trained on me.

In that split second I see the static memory of a beautiful young boy darting from window to window, running on the roof-tops. He's an orange blur twirling a staff—a majorette. He's holding it aloft, and he drops down from a tower into the crime-rich stew of the city, straight toward me, poised to strike. I hear the *click-clack* of a gun trained to fire.

"Scout." I try not to whimper. "Oh, Scout."

When the bang comes, I feel blood trickling in small drops onto my face. And another. *I'm bleeding?* I think. I pat myself, still alive. No, I'm not bleeding. I look up. One of the pig goons has been impaled by a unicorn horn.

The drunk woman, pink suit wrapped in plastic wires, is standing over me. She sinks spike after spike into the three remaining killers. They all go down in a violent heap. When the carnage is over, she wipes her horn with a discarded piece of spandex, fixes her thick dreadlocked mane of hair, and looks at me. She seems to be sobering up quite quickly. I reach up to her, but she just dents her eyebrows toward me, fuming.

"Fuck you," she mutters through gritted teeth. "Just . . . you know what? Fuck you."

The other patrons who have survived the onslaught slowly gather themselves, whimpering and cradling each other, shaken with fear. "And you know what else? Fuck THIS!" She kicks one of the bodies of the gang members. "I'm fucking Unicorn Girl! I'm fucking sick of being treated like an anomaly, like hiding in the crevices and existing only in the imagination. I touched the goddamn stars, I made these dark motherfuckers who they are. And you know what? I'm taking this shit back. So fuck you."

"Where are you going?"

She walks back toward me, through the dead bodies, and past the simpering clubgoers.

"I'll tell you where I'm going, asshole," she says to me, two inches from my face, her breath like an acidic onion on fire in a porn theater. "I'm going to walk out that hole in the door and back up to hell. I'm going to dance in a field of space locusts and swim with star dolphins. I'm going to the Nebula Zoo, to the Enchanted Goddamn Forest of the Outraged Mermen. I'm going to barter with ghost Martians at a street bazaar on the hidden moon of Jupiter. I'm going to find G-Man and Maximus and White Star, and I'm going to kick their skulls into a fucking volcano. That's where the fuck I'm going."

She looks at me with an unforgiving fierceness, then her face softens. She tilts her head to the side, and through one solitary, long tear, she touches my face. "I'm going to find Scout, you stupid, useless, bigoted fuck."

But the roof tears off of the club, an implosion like a soundless warp ripping through. Bodies are sucked up through a purple tractor beam and into the air, a rapture of dead and dying lifted into the sky. A heliport hovers ominously, its presence there like a planet's, just pumping gravity by the ton into the atmosphere.

"*Attention, Joshua Jones aka Unicorn Boy.*"

"It's Unicorn Girl, you fucking breeder!"

The swirl of wind and light is great. We are standing there like miniatures of ourselves before this machine, its dark, sprawling technology seemingly blotting out the moon. I can barely feel my legs under me.

"This is G-Man of D.A.R.K. Patrol. You are in violation of Supers Code #DP234. Please come quietly and face trial and subsequent punishment for your crimes."

Suddenly, I remember: I took Scout to a dojo on his first day under my mentorship.

"I thought we'd start on the ground level," I told him, smiling, patting him on the back. He slumped his shoulders, pouted. If he'd had his way, he'd have been turning back flips on the limos of mob bosses and drop kicking tundra barbarians his first night on patrol. I wanted to teach him discipline. What I got was a call from the sensei screaming into the phone, demanding that I pay all of his students' medical bills, repair all of his gym equipment. He barred both of us from the local martial arts community.

When I picked him up from a small village in Viet Nam after leaving him there for a year, he pouted all the way home, listening to Tibetan monks chanting in his headphones while we rode quietly in our private jet. And yeah, it made me sick to my stomach. In fact, it was all I could think about: Scout lying on a cot, wrapped up in the arms of Unicorn Boy, the two of them . . . making love on that filthy mattress in some squat somewhere downtown, lost in the gallows of their own desires.

Well, it did then, anyway. But now . . . I don't know, I'm looking at him, at her—now, Unicorn Girl, tiny fists clenched and ready, staring into the abysmal shadow of the D.A.R.K. Patrol's heliport.

I straighten my collar, smooth out the edges of my coat, try to stand erect, and I say directly into the purple light, "It's OK, G-Man. I'll take it from here." My voice is deep and resonant. It's a full, square-jawed voice like a radio announcer's. "The young lady's with me."

Unicorn Girl turns her head. "You say the dumbest shit, old man," she says to me with a cocky smile.

This is right before her face sinks back into sadness. She's drifting away from me, pulled toward the empty, black hole, lost in the tractor beam's pull, and in a blink . . . she's gone.

JUSTINA IRELAND

Calendar Girls

Alyssa posted up on her corner and watched the late-afternoon foot traffic with feigned disinterest. Friday was her busiest day. Saturday was decent, no doubt, but Friday was lit. Folks were still full of hope that they could somehow fix their busted-ass week by getting lucky. TGIF and all that shit. By Saturday most folks had a hangover and were broke. Unless you wanted a bunch of ankle biters, smashing cakes cost a lot of money. So Friday, that was Alyssa's best day.

Everyone liked to be prepared for the weekend.

Whether it was textiles, monthlies, or squish, Alyssa had it. She'd owned this corner since the Dvorah Sisters went down a couple of months back, and she'd been making bank. People in the Financial District liked to fuck, but not a single one of them wanted a baby.

Alyssa's greatest asset was that she was pretty. That made her approachable, and it had kept her business safe and booming even though she was slight and young. She wasn't like the Sisters, who'd successfully held on to their turf through brute force. Alyssa knew to give the cops their cut and to dress nicely enough that no one suspected she was anything other than some schoolgirl waiting for the uptown bus. Her hair was neat, her skin was moisturized, she smiled at strangers, and she always helped the older women on and off the bus.

A man in a pricey suit wearing a fedora paused to tie his shoe near Alyssa, dropping a hundred-dollar bill as he did so. "Textiles?" he muttered, his eyes skidding left and right.

Alyssa grinned and languidly bent over to pick up the money, the beads on the ends of her cornrows clacking together as she did so. These hedge-fund bros had no fucking chill.

"My man," she said, picking up the cash and depositing the condoms in the man's waiting palm in a single smooth move. "Don't use them all in one place."

The man gave her a single panicked glance before he scurried off. When the siren whooped, Alyssa knew why he'd been so nervous.

She'd been set up.

"Hands up!" the cops said, vaulting out of the car and drawing down on her, like she was one of those Christian terrorist cells instead of a slight teenage Black girl wearing a high school uniform.

"What's going on, Officer?" Alyssa asked, widening her eyes and holding up her hands. She'd already dropped her bag and kicked it over toward the wizened old woman on a nearby bus bench. It was only possession if they caught you holding.

She recognized the officer who grabbed her hands, spinning her around as he cuffed her. "Damn, Findley, if you wanted a bigger cut you could've just said so."

"It's out of my hands, Lyss. I'm sorry," he said, running his hands over her body in a way that was perfunctory, not perverted. She appreciated the small mercy. This wasn't her first arrest, but at least this one wouldn't leave her feeling like garbage.

He plucked her cellphone out of her sweatshirt and pocketed it, along with a couple of packs of monthlies and a handful of shiny foil textile packets.

And then she was hustled to the police car, no rights read, no identi-chip scanned. The other officer just watched her through narrow eyes as Findley put her in the back of the car. "Damned harpies," he spat.

As the car pulled away, a small Asian girl ran up to grab Alyssa's bag, taking up the spot that she had just vacated.

Alyssa couldn't help but tilt her head back and laugh.

They didn't go to the city jail or even county. Alyssa had been to both of them, and she knew what to expect. They'd book her and send her to the juvenile wing. There was a reason younger girls like her ran the corners. By the time she was an adult, her rap sheet would be expunged and she'd be taken off the streets, sent to work somewhere else for someone else, a job that looked legit, a life that was mostly hers. That was the promise, and so far the Matriarchs had kept every single one.

But now the plan was in flux. They didn't head to the county lockup; instead, they drove to the highway. And kept driving. Everything had been copacetic when Alyssa thought she knew the script, but once they started down a tree-lined drive in an unfamiliar part of town, she began to fidget.

"Hey, where we headed? Where you taking me?" Alyssa asked.

"Shut up, bitch," said the officer on the passenger side, the one she didn't know. Findley said nothing, and Alyssa couldn't see his face from where she sat behind him. When they'd thrown her into the car, they secured the handcuffs to a loop in the door, and Alyssa leaned as far to the right as she could, trying to get a glimpse of Findley's face. She knew him. She'd babysat his kids, all nine of them, and kept his wife in a ready supply of monthlies. Findley had been red-faced when he'd asked for the contraceptives, confessing that the wife had threatened to go celibate otherwise. He'd seemed less like a killer with a badge and more like a regular guy, a good guy with too many kids trying to get by in this world, like so many folks.

But he was also a cop, which meant nothing good at all.

The police car turned down a small cobblestone road that led to a guard shack. Findley pulled the car up alongside the small building. A huge Black guy with skin the color of a moonless night stepped out, his bald head glinting in the late-afternoon sunlight.

"Yeah," the man said, glancing at Alyssa in the backseat and dismissing her. There was a gun holstered under the man's suit jacket, and she wondered where the hell they were. Who needed a handgun in the middle of the fucking woods? Dude didn't exactly look like he was going after Bambi.

Fear tried to rise up, but she shoved it down. As long as she could play at being chill, everything was cool. She'd been in worse jams.

Maybe.

"Our captain sent us. She's a harpy," the cop in the passenger seat said. "Fucking baby killer."

The man from the gatehouse looked at the car once more before returning to the guard shack. He picked up a phone, a landline, and had a brief conversation before coming back.

"Sit tight a sec. I've got some troopers who are going to run down here to grab her."

"We could take her up," Findley said, a strange tone in his voice. Regret?

That wasn't good.

The other car pulled up, a fancy black town car with tinted windows. Another guy in a suit—this one white, with a head full of brown hair gelled to within an inch of its life—got out.

"You can uncuff her; we'll take it from here," he said. He wore sunglasses, but Alyssa still had the feeling that his eyes were scanning the area for potential threats. It creeped her all the way out. There was no way she wanted to stay here, in these pretty woods full of danger.

But she didn't exactly want to spend any more time with the cops, either.

Findley got out and opened the door, unlocking her cuffs. "I'm sorry," he murmured again. "I really had no choice."

"There's always a choice, even when they tell you there isn't," Alyssa answered, voice equally low. Findley made to hand her the cellphone and contraband, but she only kept her phone, pushing the textiles and monthlies back into his hands.

"Keep them. You're going to need them more than me." She threw back her shoulders and strode to the town car, refusing to show even a smidgen of fear.

Whatever fuckery was about to unfold, she would meet it with swagger.

When Alyssa was eight years old, her mother died in childbirth.

It was completely preventable, the aunties said at the funeral, their voices hushed as they cast sidelong glances at Alyssa. In another time, they said. Maybe in another place. There, Alyssa would have a mother and there might be some sadness at a lost son, but there would be a chance for more kids.

But there was no other time or place. The doctor had told Alyssa's mother that she would die if she tried to carry the child to term. The law ensured that there were few other options, not without a trip to the border and a lot of money to get a Moses to take them across. The Matriarchs might've been able to help earlier on; there were ways to keep from getting pregnant and ways to fix mistakes if you were desperate enough, but Alyssa's mother believed in the law, believed in a country built on freedom and justice. So she did the right thing, the good thing, writing to the state board for permission to end her pregnancy in light of her health and young daughter.

The men in the state capital denied the petition.

Alyssa's mother died three days later, laboring futilely in a city hospital while state senators argued over whether or not to lower the marrying age for girls from fourteen to twelve.

It was the first time Alyssa understood that being a woman was a curse.

They drove for a short while, Alyssa and the dudes with all of their firepower tucked up under expensive suit jackets. A house appeared after a turn, and it was like a terrible revelation. The building sat on sprawling grounds that were impossibly green considering the drought. The entire thing was made of bricks, and Alyssa couldn't help but think of all those people laying each piece, one on top of another, until a monstrosity of architecture had been born. She'd never seen a house so big, hadn't even considered that such a thing could exist.

At this point she was certain of two things:

1. Someone with money or power or both had paid the cops to snatch her from her corner, and
2. She was fucked in the worst kind of way.

The suited security guys gestured for her to walk up the stairs to the front door, which opened as if by magic. An Asian man wearing a gleaming white polo shirt and pressed khakis opened the door with a smile.

"Ms. Pearson, so glad to see you looking well. I'm Brian, Senator Gaines's personal assistant. Please, come in." Alyssa schooled her face to blankness, refusing to let the man see how intimidated she felt.

She was maybe mostly successful.

He stood back from the door to allow Alyssa to enter. She stepped forward, all of her bravado draining away. The foyer was opulent, marble and dark woods and paintings conspiring to make her feel insignificant. She had the momentary urge to take her shoes off or apologize for her presence, before she managed to take a deep breath. She thought of her mother, the same way she always did whenever she felt scared or small. It made her feel strong.

Angry.

"How do you know who I am?" Alyssa asked. She kept her voice neutral, picking her words carefully, the same way she did when speaking to a teacher. This was uncharted territory.

"I'll let the senator explain that to you," he said, leading Alyssa through the house and to a sitting room not far from the foyer. She'd only snatched glimpses of the rest of the mansion, and that was enough.

She didn't belong here, and the sooner she could figure out what this was about and get out, the better.

Brian offered to get Alyssa a drink, which she politely declined. Without another word he exited the room, closing the door behind him and leaving her alone.

She didn't have much time, so she pulled her phone out of her pocket and tried to text her contact within the Matriarchs. But her phone just kept on displaying her home screen, a picture of her mother from before Alyssa was born.

"No use in trying to use that. I've got this system that blocks all signals except the ones I choose. Neat gadget."

Alyssa looked up from her phone. A middle-aged white man walked into the room, his smile perfect and gleaming and utterly fake. "I'm Senator Gaines, Ms. Pearson. And can I just say it is a pleasure to meet an entrepreneur such as yourself?"

"What do you want?" Alyssa asked. Her voice was steady, as was her gaze, and she imagined her mother looking down on her with pride. After all, Senator Gaines had been instrumental in passing the law that had eventually killed her.

The senator kept his placid smile in place as he sat in a leather wing chair and indicated for Alyssa to do the same. She kept standing. He pretended not to notice.

"Ms. Pearson, I'm sorry to have interrupted your afternoon. But I'm afraid I need a woman of your considerable talents, and I didn't think you'd answer a polite invitation. Would you like a drink?"

"No," Alyssa said. Fuck no. She couldn't trust these people. They'd probably drug her and sell her into slavery in the manner of their ancestors. "Are you going to kill me?"

As soon as the words slipped out, Alyssa swore to herself. She wanted to be cool. But she was terrified, trying to figure out how to get away from Senator Gaines. He was legendary. As a state senator he'd started the Abstinence League, and as the founder of the Senate Commission on Morality he'd pushed through legislation that had severely limited everything from contraception to clothing. Once upon a time people had said he led the war against women, but that was before folks decided that they could live with his legislation. After all, hadn't he also helped bring back manufacturing and a handful of other industries?

People were willing to give up a lot in order to have a few more dollars in their pockets. It was the price they paid for freedom and the American Dream.

But that was long before Alyssa and her mom, and Senator Gaines had been in office nearly forty years. The idea that there was anything Alyssa could help him with was laughable, and the more she failed to figure his angle the more frightened she got.

"I know you're probably wondering why I brought you here. After all, pretty girls like yourself go missing all of the time, and for no good reason," the senator said with a smile. If it was meant to reassure Alyssa, it failed. "The answer is: I need you to help my girl get rid of an unfortunate complication."

"Your mistress?" Slinging contras required a certain understanding of why people needed them, and extramarital affairs weren't unusual, despite all of the Morality Laws.

"No, sorry to disappoint. My daughter is sick, and if she doesn't terminate her pregnancy she'll die."

"Sounds like she needs to file an appeal," Alyssa said.

His eyebrows twitched, but that was the only sign of emotion.

Alyssa didn't say anything else, just let the silence drag. Her answer was cold but honest. What kind of world did this man live in where he could have the police grab some random girl who sold illegal contraceptives and expect her to act as a Moses, ferrying his daughter to the Promised Land?

Jail was a much better alternative. She'd serve her time and be back on her corner by New Year's.

The senator gave Alyssa a frustrated smile. "I picked you because I know what happened to your mama," he said. His pose was still relaxed, but there was now an edge to his words. "Don't you want to make sure that doesn't happen to another woman?"

Alyssa shrugged. "I'm good."

The senator's smile faded, and a vaguely perplexed expression came over his face. It was like he'd never considered that she might say no, that maybe she worked her corner not because of some greater good but because she just liked the extra cash.

"Well, how about this: You get my daughter to the Dakotas and I'll pay you. Name your price."

Alyssa laughed. "Why me? I just sell contras. I'm all about before the fact, not after. This is a whole bunch of mess I'm not qualified for."

The senator steepled his fingers under his chin. "Which is exactly why I need you. You deal, so you already don't agree with the Morality Laws. An established Moses would compromise my daughter and is entirely unsafe. I could send her directly, but I can't take that sort of trip, and I can't send my security detail—it's too dangerous for me. So, name your price. I'll give you a car and two days to get her there."

Alyssa said nothing. How fucking stupid did he think she was?

She might be a dealer, but that didn't mean she couldn't see bullshit when she was neck deep.

The senator didn't like her indecision. "Oh, and let me be clear: If you refuse, you aren't going to prison. Those officers have already been paid off, and my security detail has been informed that you are a known terrorist that I'm trying to negotiate with. Should you refuse, Brian will return and defend me against your plot to try to assassinate a sitting senator. You really don't have a choice. Now, shall we say a hundred thousand dollars for your time and effort?"

"One fifty and you give me half now."

The senator smiled, slow and crocodile-like. "Deal."

For the first time all afternoon, Alyssa relaxed. This was exactly how things were supposed to go.

She was given a car, and a sleeping girl was gently laid across the backseat by Brian and a woman who looked to be the senator's wife. The girl was bundled in a blanket, and at one point the edge of it fell away to reveal golden skin and curly blond hair. The woman quickly covered the girl's face again before planting a kiss on her forehead. Alyssa watched it all without saying a word. After they were done, Brian handed Alyssa a card with her name on it.

"This is the account where your money will be. You can use as much of it as you want to get you to North Dakota."

"North Dakota?" Alyssa asked. Wasn't that a strange place to take a sick, pregnant girl? When the senator said *the Dakotas*, she'd thought he was just giving general directions, not an actual destination.

The man didn't even blink as he said, "Yes. The family has a compound there and a doctor waiting. You have forty-eight hours. If you aren't there we will find you. Your directions are pre-programmed into your GPS. Do not deviate from the route."

Alyssa said nothing but took the card. Then she climbed into the car and began to drive toward the highway. She passed other large houses until the landscape smoothed to farms and eventually suburban neighborhoods of identical-looking homes. The directions took her toward the highway on-ramp, where she stopped at a red light. A van pulled up next to her and Alyssa stared straight ahead.

A middle-aged woman exited the van, walked up to the driver's side door, and raised her eyebrows in question. Talking was no good, because the senator and his people were most likely listening.

Alyssa gave the woman a thumbs-up, pointing to the backseat.

The woman flashed an okay sign. Alyssa popped the locks. The woman opened the rear door and gently grabbed the girl by the shoulders. Another woman exited the van to grab feet. The two women hoisted the girl into the van, closed the doors on both vehicles, and, when the light turned green, drove away.

Alyssa got onto the on-ramp, her heart light. For the first time in a while, she smiled.

"I have a proposition for you," the woman said.

Two weeks before Alyssa was snatched off her corner by Findley and his partner, she sat in a diner and waited patiently for her pancakes. On the television in the corner was a report about the latest terrorist attack, this one carried out by a group of women's rights activists known as the Harpies. They'd bombed the factory where a male-enhancement drug was made. Alyssa thought it was funny. The government called it the worst crime in history.

She tore her gaze away from the television to the woman sitting opposite her. She had dark-brown skin and a slight smile that seemed to indicate that everything was amusing and silly. The expression immediately put Alyssa on edge. "I don't know you, lady."

The woman smiled. "I know. But you seem to like my products."

That got Alyssa's attention, and she straightened. "Who are you?"

The woman made a complicated wing gesture with her hands. She had to be a Matriarch, one of the women who organized the Calendar Girls.

Alyssa had thought it was all a bunch of bullshit. She'd become a Calendar Girl because it let her move out of foster care into her own place, not because she believed in all of the women's rights bullshit they fed her. With the money she saved, she would be able to leave the country, go somewhere women weren't expected to be married by twenty and knocked up by twenty-one. Somewhere she could get a real education, not the "smile and submit" bullshit they taught in school.

But this woman being here complicated her life, and she could see all of her dreams suddenly teetering on a precipice.

"How do I know you're legit?"

"You moved six hundred and twenty-three monthlies last month, your best month on record. You had to re-up three times."

Alarm bells clanged in Alyssa's head. "I haven't done anything wrong; I've followed all of the rules," she said, not looking up when the waitress came by to deliver her pancakes. The restaurant was where she usually picked up her stash each week, and the woman would have known that. It all felt like a trap now, the predictability of it all.

"Of course you have, my dear. You've been great at your job. And not a snitch, either. Which is why we now need you to take care of this for us."

"Okay," Alyssa said. There wasn't much else to do. You didn't talk back to the Matriarchs.

"In two weeks the police officers in your area will pick you up, seemingly without provocation. Do not fight them; do not argue.

They will take you to either the city or county jail, and from there you will be offered a deal that will be too good to be true. You will balk at first, because they will expect you to. After that you will accept it. Do you understand?"

Alyssa nodded, and the woman's polite smile stretched into a grin.

"Excellent. You're going to love Canada, by the way."

The woman got up and walked away, and Alyssa watched her go. Canada?

Why the fuck would she ever go to Canada?

Once Alyssa could, she stopped and withdrew as much money as possible on the card. It was only five thousand dollars. She got back in the car to do the same thing at another machine. By the time the card refused to keep giving her money, she'd withdrawn twenty-five thousand dollars. The daily limit.

She drove the rest of the day, stopping to sleep in rest stops along the way. Eventually she'd be able to stop, but until then it had to look like she was following the senator's plan.

At seven-thirty, her phone beeped, the first sound it had made in nearly a day. The message was just a link, and when Alyssa clicked it she laughed.

"MORAL" SENATOR'S DAUGHTER DEFECTS TO FRANCE WITH OUT-OF-WEDLOCK PREGNANCY AND DIRT ON DADDY, INCLUDING MURDER PLOT

Alyssa didn't bother reading the story. There was a picture, and she recognized the unconscious girl who'd been in the backseat. Her part in this tale was at an end.

Another text message came across with directions, and Alyssa read them quickly before turning her phone off.

She took the next exit into Minneapolis. In a crowded gas station parking lot, she dumped the car, leaving the money inside. She then made her way to a run-down mall, where she dumped her clothes and phone after a white girl in a red hoodie handed her new ones. At a kiosk in the mall she had her identi-chip wiped and reloaded with new information. Including sixty thousand dollars.

For a minute she toyed with the idea of staying. Things would change. The Matriarchs would eventually reverse the laws and restore the rights of women. Maybe she could even help with the fight, a little.

But the reality was, Alyssa didn't care. She just wanted to live her life.

So she bought a bus ticket to Toronto, one way, and for the first time in her entire life was free.

RION AMILCAR SCOTT

Shape-ups at Delilah's

The night after Jerome's brother turned up on a South-side sidewalk, bloodied and babbling in and out of consciousness, Tiny took Jerome's hand, sat him on a stool, wiped tears from his cheeks, draped a towel over his shoulders, and whispered, Relax, baby, you can't go to the hospital like that. Your brother'll wake up to that damn bird's nest on your head and fall right back into another coma. For the next two hours, Tiny sheared away Jerome's knotty beads until his head appeared smooth and black, with orderly hairs laid prone by her soft, smoothing hand. Back when they met, she'd told him she cut hair, said she was damn good, too. Jerome had nodded, smiled a bit, as if to say, *How cute*, and changed the subject. But now, the way his eyes danced in the mirror, the joy that broadened his face, it all said, *Where in the hell did a woman, a W-O-M-A-N, learn to cut like that?* She circled him as she did her work, looking at every angle of his head. She lathered up the front and went at it with a straight razor so that his hairline sat as crisp and sharp as the bevelled edge of the blade that cut it. Tiny imagined slicing her finger while sliding it across the front of his head; her imagined self then smeared the blood all over Jerome's face. After she finished and had swept the fine hairs from his shoulders and back, Jerome and Tiny collapsed onto the floor, spent, as if they had just made love for hours. On a bed of Jerome's shorn hair, they slept into the early morning.

A year to the day after Jerome's brother got out of the hospital, Jerome showed up at the only place he'd ever found comfort, on the doorstep of the woman he no longer loved and who, by agreement, no longer loved him. When Tiny opened the door that night she snorted and looked him up and down, this man she had been comfortable not seeing or speaking to for the past several months. Before she could complete her condescension, Jerome spoke: My mother is dead.

Tiny's face grew tender with sadness and disbelief. She opened her arms and called for Jerome to rest his head on the soft roundness of her chest. But he breezed by her, eyes on the floor, and crumpled onto the couch. His face was so fallen she barely recognized him; sadness so chiseled into his cheeks and his brow that Tiny couldn't imagine anything softening the rock of his face, so she sat and said nothing. She thought of how much she had loved Jerome's mother—but that wasn't the truth, simply one of those things people tell themselves when someone dies. The woman, Tiny realized, was just a proxy; it wasn't for Jerome's mother that she had once held an unshakable love but for Jerome himself. She opened her arms wide again and pulled him tightly to her body. His head nestled itself between her breasts. It felt wrong, terribly, terribly wrong. Jerome trembled in her arms. He wept and sniffled. Tiny brushed her lips against his cheeks, and then she stopped.

I'm sorry, Jerome, she said. I want to end all that pain you're carrying, but I can't do what you want me to do.

Damn it, he said. My mother just died. Is it that hard for you to break out your clippers and make me look presentable? Is your heart that full of ice for me? I got a funeral to attend. God damn it, my little brother was doing better, now I can't find him and you not trying to help me. My brother is God knows where, doing God knows what drugs, in God knows how much pain, and you can't offer me this simple kindness?

No, Tiny whispered. No. I can't.

Still, she walked into her bathroom, whispering, No, as she grabbed the clippers, the razor, the rubbing alcohol, and a towel. She draped the towel over his shoulders and, in silence, she cut his uncombed locks. They both whimpered and sniffled a bit, avoiding each other's eyes. When the tears blurred Tiny's vision, she didn't stop; instead, she let the salty drops drip onto Jerome's head as she cut from memory, her smoothing hand rubbing the tears into his scalp.

It took her double the time of her most careful cuts, four whole painful hours. When she finished, Jerome thanked her and left, wiping his cheeks. I'm crying, he said, 'cause of my mom, but also 'cause this haircut is so goddam beautiful.

Tiny nodded, hoping that Jerome would never return. After she shut the door, she sat in the hallway sobbing into the night, until she felt as useless as piles and piles and piles of dead hair.

Tiny had started cutting hair almost on a whim. She had found her father's old clippers at the bottom of a dusty box beneath the sink in a seldom used bathroom in the basement. Her father used to zug crooked lines and potholes into his three sons' hair when they were young and not yet vain. Soon her older brothers no longer allowed the maiming, so someone buried the clippers under piles of stuff. When Tiny stumbled on the clippers, she realized she had grown tired of her perm. The time had come to shave it all off and let her natural hair grow long. She'd shape it and twist it, braid it and maybe lock it, as her mother had, but whenever her hair grew she felt the urge only to trim it into what everyone called "boy styles": a faded-in Mohawk, or just a fade, or a Caesar, or a temple taper. It changed every two weeks. Soon Tiny began to choose her lovers based partly on the shape of their heads, what styles she could carve on their domes. When their heads no longer intrigued her, she would lose interest. These days, her hair grew long enough to keep in a simple ponytail, and that was how she wore it. She no longer had any interest in her own hair, just other people's.

Nearly a year to the day after Tiny watched the folds at the back of Jerome's freshly cut head bob out her door for the last time, Tiny's Hair Technology opened up, on River Way. The Great Hair Crisis was raging on with no visible end. Every single barbering Cross Riverian man somehow losing his touch, the ability to deliver even a decent shape-up. Afros had abounded within the town's borders since that moment in '05 when all the clippers and cutting hands began shaving ragged patches into heads. It had been ten years of this wilderness, this dystopia. Men with beautiful haircuts became as mythical as the glowing wolves—lit up like earthbound Canis Majors—that are said to walk the Wildlands. Sonny Beaumont, Jr., once Cross River's greatest barber, now looked like a haggard old troll; he was about forty-five years old, and resembled a wrinkled set of intertwined wires covered in the thinnest, baggiest brown flesh. There would never again be any good days for Sonny. Even decent haircuts stayed frozen in his past, and all he was capable of now were messes—carefully, carefully carved messes. His remaining customers patronized him only out of loyalty—poisoned nostalgia for the perfect cuts they'd once received—and false hope.

All those Cross Riverian Afros left one to ask, Who cursed Cross River? A shop opened up on the Northside—a decent shop—only for the owner to die of a heart attack mid-cut. The two remaining barbers opened shops of their own, and eventually murdered each other in a gunfight over customers and territory. Kimothy Beam closed his business, Mobile Cutting Unit, after his haircut van flipped during a police chase. He served three months and hung up his clippers for good when the authorities turned him loose. There was a long scroll of such mishaps: haircutting men, always men, driven from the business and, in some cases, from this world, through some misfortune. That's not going to be me, Tiny thought. The simple science of haircutting gets down into one's bones, into the soul of a person. She watched the peace settle over her customers after a good cut. They'd walk out into the world, where the noise would start again, but that moment at the end of a fresh cut—from the crack of the cape, as she removed it from a patron's shoulders, to the door—was pure, pure magic.

Tiny no longer cut her lovers' hair for free. They'd have to pay like anyone else. After Jerome, she'd loved Cameron, and then Sherita passed through her life, and then Bo and Jo, and Katrina, and De'Andre and Ron. They all fell out of love with her when they realized she wouldn't use her magic on them. And that was fine with her; it was easy for Tiny to fall out of love with them, too. Jerome seemed so long ago. She hadn't even loved him best.

In the scheme of things Tiny's Hair Technology is just a footnote, but it would be even less than that had the shop not opened during such desperate times. A shop of lady barbers? Who had ever heard of such a thing? It was Tiny and Claudine and Mariah at first; later, a whole cast of lady barbers passed through. No one expected anything but another business popping up and then shuttering within a couple of months. There had been five in three years in that location. Folks in the neighborhood had taken to calling it the Wack Spot, a dingy cardboard box of a structure tucked away at the edge of an unimpressive side street. Behind the building stood knotted trees that stayed bare no matter the season. The jutting branches resembled skeletal fingers, so the building appeared always on the verge of being snatched into an abyss. The Wack Spot was salted earth; no successful business could sprout from the ruined soil. There was the roti shop that never seemed to have any roti. Then there was Ice Screamers (later Sweet Screamers, and, as a last ditch, Sweet Creamers), a soft-serve spot run by a surly guy with an eyepatch. For the previous several months the Wack Spot had housed an adult bookstore that, much to the dismay of the surly ice-cream peddler, retained the final name of the soft-serve spot. It was common knowledge that only a witch spouting the most forbidden of spells could make the Wack Spot work, and Tiny figured she would be that witch, conjuring the pitchest black magic from the back of her spell book.

When Jerome walked into the shop, shortly after it opened, he was still tall and fine, though scruffy—he appeared to be trying to grow a beard, but had managed only wild crabgrass patches along his cheeks.

Woman, cut my hair, he said with a smirk.

Tiny spun her chair and dashed herself onto it. She loved to hear the lumpy springs whine beneath the heft of her backside.

Hello, Jerome, she said. Can I help you with something?

All this formality now?

She didn't respond, tried to make her eyes blank as if she'd never seen him before. She couldn't hide everything, though; as she glanced at him she flashed a twinkle he took for a bit of residual love.

This is boring me, he said. I just want a cut. One of your perfect little tight cuts.

Well, I'm busy now. Jerome looked about the empty shop. Mariah, Tiny said, should be here in a few. Would you like me to make an appoint—

I don't want a cut from some-damn-body named Mariah! I want you. No one makes me look as good as you do.

Tiny turned her head, reached for a magazine, and pawed

through the pages with the bored, languid movements of a cat. How's your brother? she said, finally.

Dude is doing great. Jerome smiled a little. Just great. It took Mom to die, but you should see him. Designer suit every day. This fucking little Dick Tracy hat. Looks fly on him. I'm proud of the guy. He needs a haircut, though. If you do it good to me—the haircut, I mean—I'll recommend you.

How'd you even hear I was over here?

You think niggas not gon' talk about a new shop full of lady barbers during the Hair Crisis? Now, you gonna cut me, or what?

I'm sorry, Jerome, but I have a few things to do now—

I'm trying to give your failing business some work.

Like I said, Jerome, Mariah—

You're just going to repeat your bullshit over and over, huh? I already know how you do. Thought you would have matured by now, Tiny. Wanna take the little-girl route? Gotcha. It's fine.

Jerome jutted out his lips, did a quick head nod, and watched his ex-lover as if silence could break her. Don't worry, bitch, he continued, sweeping a stack of magazines to the ground and walking out the door. You'll get yours. See you real soon.

After weeks of barber-chair emptiness and a floor sadly clean of shorn hair, Tiny arrived one morning to find a line of men—many sporting unkempt dandruff bushes—waiting outside.

I thought you opened at ten, called the first desperately uncombed man in line to a chorus of grumbles. It's nearly noon!

You guys been here since ten? Tiny asked. As she unlocked the door, the men dazed her with numbers. Six in the morning, one said, his voice trembling with a mixture of embarrassment and pride.

I been here since five-fifty-five, a man whose hair was cut into an asymmetrical field of black said. He held the hand of a boy who looked everything like a little Jackson 5 Michael Jackson except for the gopher hole shaved into the center of his head.

But . . . but, it's a school day, Tiny said.

And? the father replied. I take him out of school when he got a doctor's appointment, too.

When she finished with the first man, he strutted out to cries of admiration and even applause. His hair—once dangerously overgrown—now glittered. Tiny slapped the chair with the cape and cried, Next up!

A tall Eritrean man with curly hair and a tall—shorter than the Eritrean, but still tall—man with an oblong head scrambled for the seat. As they tussled, a short dark-skinned man with salt-and-pepper hair and the twisted but unbecoming grin of a mischievous child strolled to the barber's chair. A Ghanaian guy they called Doc pointed and laughed. Don't forget to get the booster seat for my man, he said.

Quiet, you fool, the short man replied.

You folks rowdy, Tiny said with a smile. Don't make me have to call the police to keep things quiet in here. How'd y'all even hear about my shop?

The short man grinned and pointed to the tall Eritrean.

I heard from Doc, the tall Eritrean said.

That first guy you cut today, Doc said. That loudmouth. I heard from him.

Hmm, Tiny grunted. He said someone I never even heard of told him.

All I know, the short man said, is that the Great Hair Crisis is over!

That day, Tiny cut as if possessed, head after head, each cut better than the last. She ignored the non-stop talk, the chatter about sports and politics and the proper way to beat young children.

After hours of clutching the vibrating clippers, her hand trembled. Men kept coming, though. Man after man. Each with a different story as to how he'd learned of Tiny's shop. Mariah showed up midafternoon to pick up the slack. The first man she cut approached her chair hesitantly, but when she finished he looked in the mirror and turned his head this way and that.

She better than Tiny!

Watch it! Tiny called, not taking her eyes off the head she was trimming.

As Mariah's customer walked out, a man with dark glasses and a shining silver mane stomped in. He clutched a thick Bible so old it looked as if the pages had begun to sprout hair. He held his book aloft and cried, *And De-li-lah said to Samson, Tell me, I pray thee, wherein thy great strength lieth, and wherewith thou mightest be bound to afflict thee.* That's from Judges 16:6. You men here giving away your strength, and for what? A nice haircut? Wrong is wrong is wrong is wrong in the eyes of the Lord.

Get out of my damn shop, Tiny called. Now! Get out!

Dale! the Bible man called to the customer in Tiny's chair. I'm surprised at you. Real surprised. Your wife know you in here giving away your power?

Rev. Kimothy, Dale said. I . . . I . . . I'm tired of coming into your church looking like I just stumbled in off the street.

Kimothy? Tiny asked. Kimothy Beam who had the Mobile Cutting Unit?

I found God in prison, and you must be Delilah—that's who you are.

I'll be that, Rev.

Dale stood from the chair, half of his head shaved close, the other wild and unshorn. He held a fistful of twenties in his outstretched hand. I'm sorry, Tiny, he said. Real sorry.

That's right, Rev. Kimothy said. Sorry as snake shit.

Naw, Tiny said. You sit your monkey ass down and keep your

money. You ain't telling no one Tiny did that to your head. Sit and you can rest your eternal soul in Hell, Rev. Kimothy shouted. Dale stood paralyzed, looking back and forth between his reverend and his barber, until some guys from the back of the shop made Dale's decision easier, snatching Rev. Kimothy by his arms and tossing him onto the sidewalk as he struggled and screamed, Lady barbers! Whoever heard of such a thing? The Devil, that's who! You gon' burn! You gon' burn! You gon' burn!

Even as Dale sat back down in the barber's chair, three Afroed men slipped quietly out the door.

Bunch of bitches, Mariah mumbled, staring into the sharp lines she had trimmed into her customer's head. Bunch of little pussy-ass bitches.

This has been some day, Tiny muttered into Dale's hair. Some day.

Late one night—say, nearly eleven—a man in a beautiful cream serge suit and a white panama hat came in just as Tiny finished her last head, a woman whose husband had recommended the shop. Tiny's feet ached from standing, and she could feel her eyelids hanging heavy like curtains falling over her eyes. Ordinarily she would have turned the cream-suited man away, but he had pushed through a line of protesters out front. Rev. Kimothy and his new legion of followers had grown relentless. Fighting through those fools just to get a haircut, especially at this time of night, was a level of dedication that deserved a reward, Tiny thought. She glanced at him, didn't take him in much. She yawned.

Tiny's life was now love and hatred falling on her in equal measure. Accolades and applause, followed by bricks wrapped in Bible verses sailing through her window at night. The woman stood and stared into a handheld mirror, admiring her new fade from all angles. This shit right here fine, she said. Sonny trash now. From now on, you my barberess.

The Barberess. What a title. Tiny had thought about changing the shop's name. That old name had grown stale. Barberesses, maybe. Maybe. It would look beautiful out front in red and white, Tiny thought.

Wow, you sure are deep in thought, Tiny heard a voice say. She looked up and the woman and her fade had left. The man with the cream suit took her place in the chair. He held the panama hat in his lap. It took Tiny a half second to recognize the face. It seemed to have aged since she'd last seen it. Jerome's patchy beard had turned into a choppy bush, but it was definitely him, and this realization made Tiny close her eyes for what seemed to her like a long minute or two.

You thinking about what you gon' do with all this mess, huh? he said, pointing to the unkempt pikes of locks jutting from his scalp. I never, never, ever take off this hat for any reason nowadays, unless I'm home or something. Got a new attitude, a new style, Tine. The hat allows me to conduct business without looking like a vagrant, but it's havoc on me, I tell you. Havoc. This thing itches and flakes. My bush, I mean. These amateurs around here worse than they ever been. I'm ready to give anything a try, even a woman barber who ain't you. Jerome chuckled. Mariah here? I'll wait for Mariah if you want me to.

I've seen worse on you, Tiny said, combing out the coils. The prongs of the pick made a *plink, plink, plink* music. You better give me a big tip, making me revisit your big head.

When Tiny had finished, she took a straight razor and cleaned up the sprigs from Jerome's cheeks and chin. She placed a warm, wet towel on his face. When she removed the towel, she nearly jumped back in fright. With his beard and sideburns trimmed, the smile Jerome flashed took on a sinister edge; he grinned as if he had already poisoned her and was just waiting for her to die.

How you work this magic, huh, babe?

There's that evil look again, Tiny replied. Like you the Devil come to burn me right here where I stand.

No, Jerome said. No. Of course not. I haven't gotten a proper haircut in I don't know how long. And you did something divine up there, Ms. Tiny. I just want to know what you got that them fools lack.

Tiny sighed. Look at my eyes, she said. I'm tired. I'm half 'sleep. I don't have the energy to talk to you anymore tonight.

I must be half 'sleep, too, 'cause even when you was cutting me back in the day I thought it was a fluke. I thought it was 'cause you loved me. You clearly don't love me now. You hate me, as a matter of fact, but you still the best cut around. You cut other people's hair perfectly, too. You can't be in love with all them people. How a woman cut hair like this, huh?

Men barbers got some kind of secret? Tiny said. They grip the clippers with they dicks or something?

I guess not. He chuckled again and looked down, shifted in his seat. You know, I bought this fancy suit from my brother.

How he doing?

He good, he good. He off that stuff. Not owing no thugs no money no more. He don't be off disappearing no more. He good. I helped him apply to his new job selling these things at the haberdashery. Nigga had no experience selling anything—anything legal, that is. No experience being good at selling anything. None. I helped him 'cause I couldn't lose nobody else after you and then my mother. I buy a lot of fancy suits with his discount. So do he. Getting high off your own supply is not a big deal when you selling suits, it turns out. But look, Tiny. My brother says I'm a fool for coming here.

Damn right.

You owe me, though.

How you figure?

You see that? Jerome pointed to the fools outside pacing with signs reading *Delilah! Repent!* and *Bitches Ain't Shit (at Cutting Hair)!* You don't think that mess organized itself, do you? You think Rev. Kimothy's dumb ass put all this together by himself?

You telling me you behind this mess? She scrunched her face for a second and then straightened her brow. Jerome, I knew you could be a goddam bastard, but—

Hold on, Ms. Tiny, Jerome replied. It's not even like that. I was mad at you when you turned me away, but I was still proud, so I told every nigga I know about this shop. Thought Rev. Kimothy would be interested, since he used to cut hair. Figured he'd tell his congregation, and he did. It's just that he told them to meet him out front to protest this *new Delilah.* Got to admit, though, Rev. Kimothy's dumb ass is good for business.

Is he, though? I had a full shop before he started his nonsense. Now I got a hassle of men outside my door at all hours. Tiny sucked her teeth. She looked to the floor, shaking her head. Y'all men something else, boy. Something else. I don't respect Rev. Kimothy or any of them stupid-ass niggas outside, but I can't be mad at you for their dumb shit.

Yeah ... He trailed off. But, look, you gotta tell me your secret.

Secret?

Every lady barber in here know how to do something extra special with her clippers.

You can't be this much of an idiot, Jerome. There is no secret. Secret is I get a good night's rest before I cut. Now I'm tired and don't know if I can work magic tomorrow. That's my secret. I got another secret: I'm going home. I'll come early to clean up before the day get started. I need my beauty rest.

Let me walk you, Tine.

No thanks. I'm done with you again.

Gotta be careful, sis. All those fools out here—

Tiny turned out the lights and pushed open the door. With

the black of the sky as a backdrop, and the bright bluish-white glow of the street light hovering above like a low-hanging moon, the faces of the men who rushed Tiny appeared to her as hovering, disembodied fright masks. The shouting sounded like sharp, high winds battering her eardrums. Tiny tensed and clutched her hands to her chest before she stumbled and nearly fell backward. She caught a glimpse of one of the signs. It featured an obscene drawing and read *I Like My Hair Like I Like My Junk, Raw and Uncut.* The man who held the placard had a bush that sat atop his head like a woollen black cube. His face looked grotesque and plastic. Jerome shoved the forehead of the block-headed man and snatched at Tiny's arm. He pushed his way through the protesters, who had suddenly quieted, offering no resistance, giving Tiny and her guardian space to escape into night's darkness.

When they got to her house, Tiny looked up into her protector's eyes and examined his freshly shaved face. Stray hairs dotted his cheeks and his forehead like black snowflakes. She looked away.

That was quite impressive, she said.

Well, he replied. I told you to let me walk you. You gon' to let me walk you tomorrow?

Jerome's face hovered over hers, a different sort of fright mask, fearful instead of terrifying. This time she didn't turn away. Maybe, she said.

Look, Ms. Tiny, you owe me.

I hope this isn't your corny way of trying to get a kiss or something, 'cause we too old to be speaking in riddles.

You can kiss me if you want, Jerome said. I'll take that. But what I really want is the secret. How y'all lady barbers cut like that, huh?

Tiny kissed his cheek. That's not so wrong, is it? she asked herself.

A lady barber's got to keep her secrets, she told him. What if I give away my secret and the result is you can't get no more good cuts, huh?

I'll take the chance.

There is no secret, 'Rome—how's that for a secret? She watched his eyes as they began dimming in sadness. I cut with love. That's it. Tiny said this because she assumed that was what Jerome wanted to hear. His eyes grew sadder still; they rimmed with an unbearable melancholy that she had seen before. Tiny looked down. She wanted it to stop.

Lye, she said. It's lye. Red Devil Lye. That's the secret. Makes the hair manageable. Mix in some eggs and potatoes and you got good old-fashioned conk juice. That's the shit I be spraying on your head. Makes anyone with a little skill cut with magic. Even a lady barber.

I knew I felt my head burn a little, Jerome said. I knew it. I'ma keep this secret close to my heart, Tine. Jerome blathered with joy as Tiny walked slowly into her house.

Tiny woke one morning with the urge, just a throbbing and unrelenting urge, to change the name of the barbershop to Delilah's. She hired a woman to paint a new sign, and the woman worked at it all day. Tiny hung it after the last customer left. When Jerome met her at the shop that night he took a look at the sign and said, You're such a troublemaker. This was after Claudine had left for good, unable to handle the crowds, the hatred, the men who shouted vile threats and called her bitch, as if it were the name her mother had given her. Tiny understood. She welcomed a rotating cast of women, each a better barber than the previous one. The new woman would claim Claudine's chair and then disappear after a week or so, afraid of the angry men outside. And with "Delilah's" on the front of the window, no one called her Tiny anymore. Tiny became D. As the new name took hold, she smiled

secretly, especially when Mariah bought her a black apron emblazoned with a bright-red "D."

Each morning brought a new influx of men. A madness of
men. So many men. Since there were more men than seats, the
men gladly stood. Men bursting out of the little shop, sometimes
pouring onto the sidewalk. Everywhere Tiny turned she saw men.
Men who had previously protested, once yelling, now quiet as
sheep. Sheep-men walking upright to be shorn. These men said
things like *Real men, Tiny, real men can admit when they wrong.*
But, really, it was that they'd observed other men, their friends
who were now shining, beautiful men because of their perfectly
cut heads. Tiny and Mariah and whoever took the third chair
couldn't cut fast enough to keep up with all those men.

Tiny could scarcely understand the uptick, until one day Dale
burst into the shop, his eyes wild, pupils dilated, his head covered
in a cap of soft black silk.

Them nig—uh, dudes up the hill done gone crazy!

Say, bruh, a man from the back called. I think you got on your
wife's bonnet.

Yeah, another voice called. This nigga wearing hair underwear!

You clowns laugh, Dale said. Did you know that the idiots up
the hill started putting lye in people's hair without any goddam
warning? Pardon my language, but that shi—stuff burned so bad
I ran to the damn—pardon me—Cross River and stuck my head
right in!

Dale uncovered his head; the once coarse grains of his hair
were now straight and wavy. The nig—guy, the darn barber,
Sonny, said it makes the hair easier to cut. D, you ever hear anything so stupid?

Mariah and Tiny exchanged glances as Dale took a seat to
wait.

Jerome arrived that night just as the shop was closing. Unfallen tears rested in the corners of his eyes. The shop sat empty except for Tiny and Mariah. When he walked through the door, Tiny turned and pretended to straighten the hair products on the table behind her chair.

Why is there no trust between us? he said. After all I did for you? All our walks.

Mariah swept, trying to look away from Jerome's sad, dim eyes while suppressing a smile.

Go somewhere, Tiny said. You fools believe anything.

Yeah, Mariah said. Red Devil Lye? Everyone knows we lick our razors just before every cut.

Mariah! Tiny called.

Don't mind me, Mariah said. I'm half 'sleep.

Look, Jerome, Tiny said. I don't want you in my shop no more. At all. Go. You're not different. You're not welcome. You can't seem to grow up. You're the same goddam fool I didn't want to be with anymore.

But our walks—

You can get a head start. Go on.

Jerome didn't argue or fight; he simply backed out of the shop, slowly, with a strange feline walk.

Late in the afternoon the next day, a man with a tuft of spongy and unruly hair sat in Mariah's seat and called for his hair to be cut into a high-top fade.

You want it tall, right? Mariah asked.

Yeah. But please don't do nothing weird. I almost had to knock Sonny out this morning. I caught the nigga licking his clippers like some kind of goddam animal.

Back when they were together, Jerome never found out how she'd gained the name Tiny, but another man did, over a per-

fect haircut one afternoon while Jerome was elsewhere looking the other way. The illicit haircut was something else Jerome
never found out about, and so that particular betrayal was not
even why they broke up. And why should it matter that she cut
another man's hair, huh? Why does a haircut become an intimacy simply because Tiny's a woman? Such absurdity. But then
that whispered story. Surely that was an intimacy. Or perhaps she
spoke so freely, so easily, because she knew she'd never see this
man again. This man who smiled at her when she passed him at
the bus stop. She couldn't bear his smile, because the animal atop
his head made him look defective. Every man around her during
the Great Hair Crisis had become a ruined sculpture. She felt like
a lapsed superhero, all that power she shrank from wielding, all
that responsibility she shirked day after blessed day. Let me cut
your hair, she said to the man, as an act of charity. Shortly after
that, she cut another man. And another man. They grew as indistinguishable as strands of hair in her memory. One man told the
next about Tiny. And she accepted them into her house, warning
them all that she'd cut them only once. One time and no more—
that way, she could control the flow of hair-blighted men and she
could tell herself that by seeing these men only once she wasn't
betraying Jerome.

   She cut their hair and never saw them again, and usually
during the shape-up she'd whisper the source of her name and
they'd all miss the point and ask the source of her power.

   One man, though, managed to slip in a second time. He was
a small man with a reddish Afro. He hunched as he walked and
scrunched himself into a ball as he sat. His voice sounded like
a high-pitched strain, and both times his hair had grown wild
and unkempt. Balls of white lint coiled into his curls. Tiny had to
wash his hair to soften it in order to move the clippers through
his knots. As he bent over the sink in the back of Tiny's basement with the water and lather dripping through his naps, she

told him, as she usually told the men, about her name. When I was small, she said, I was tiny. She chuckled, as she always did. The youngest and the tiniest one in the family. But that's not why they call me Tiny. I been a big girl ever since, like, fourteen, but it's like no one could see that. When someone felt disrespected, they'd say something like, *You must think you talking to Abigail or some shit?* That's me, Abigail. Abby. Disrespecting me was nothing to them, I guess. Like disrespecting a bug or something. Tiny. Inconsequential. Eventually, I told folks to stop calling me Abigail, Abby, all that shit—

Before Tiny could finish, the man looked up at her with glowing eyes and finished for her: *Told 'em to call me Tiny and no one ever asked why.* It's a beautiful story. You told me last time. He laughed as if he had carved out some sort of victory.

Last time? She looked at his head and suddenly remembered. Uh-uh. I told you my rule then, I told you when you came in the door today. One-time-only deal. Dry your head, and then you gotta go.

You can't do that to me, Abigail. He smiled wider. You can't do that to Cross River. Too many heads in crisis. Uh-uh, you gon' cut this. He snatched at her wrist. Come on, Abby. Just give me a little trim. He chuckled a mean, mean little chuckle. Make magic.

The small man let go of Tiny's wrist and sat with his back to her. Just a Caesar today, he said, so confident he was that Tiny would cut his hair with little fuss. And he was right. It was easier to start shearing his nappy kinks than to keep arguing. Her hand shook as she trimmed, though. She rushed the tricky parts she would usually have moved through with precision and care. The sooner she finished, the sooner she'd never have to see him again. Tiny cut with disgust, watching the stubborn dirt and dandruff as if they had left indelible splotches on her, forever staining her soul.

When the small man stood and looked into the mirror, he said nothing at first, and then he balled his fists.

What is this trash? he screamed. You did this on . . . You did this 'cause I wouldn't leave!

No, I—

Of course you did. This is worse than one of Sonny's cuts.

You want your money back? Tiny tried to joke, but that seemed to make the small man even more angry. It's the curse, Tiny said, still trembling in fear. The Hair Crisis, she said, it comes for every barber in Cross River eventua—

You think I'm a fool, bitch? The man snatched at Tiny's shoulders. All I wanted was a good haircut for once. Is that too . . . Tell me your secret, Abby. How come the Crisis ain't come for you, huh?

I don't have a secret, she said, shoving the man. Please leave.

The small man raised his right fist as if about to throw a punch. The gold bracelet on his wrist, the gold chain around his neck, they both jangled. Tiny raised her arms and flinched to curl away from the blow, but the small man lowered his fist with a snort and a chuckle. He tossed the towel that lay around his neck before stomping up the stairs and out of Tiny's house.

The next day, when Jerome came for his weekly cut, Tiny's hand trembled as if still trimming the small man's red bush. She could feel the heaviness of his fingers at her shoulders and her wrist.

What in the fuck is this? Jerome said, peering into the mirror.

I don't know what's wrong, Tiny lied. It's the curse.

For the rest of the week, Jerome remained sullen, only frowning at Tiny or grumbling her way. She wanted to tell him what had happened, but that would be a long story, beginning with the first man she cut behind his back.

Or perhaps it would begin with her name and how her family made it into a curse, how they made her into a small, tiny thing. She imagined him laughing at her, sneering and calling her Abigail the next time she accidentally cut jagged marks into his head. Two, three weeks of bad haircuts made Jerome into a different man. If there was a fight to be picked, he picked it like some naps.

One day after a particularly bad haircut, Jerome fingered the slanted frontier that was now his hairline as they ate Chinese food. Tiny's clippers had pushed it back so much that Jerome's forehead now looked like an eroding coastline. Tiny asked Jerome to pass her a packet of soy sauce.

Get it your damn self, Jerome barked, standing sharply from his seat. Got me out here looking like George Jefferson. I was the dude with the good haircuts! Who the fuck am I now?

He stomped out the door, hunched and scarred like the small man. Tiny watched his disappearing form with sad eyes, vowing to never cut another man's head. Tiny held firm to her promise no matter how many men knocked and cried and pleaded. She remained firm until that night Jerome returned to her doorstep several months later with tears in his eyes.

After that, she vowed to never again give up her power. To never again freely give away something as precious as a haircut.

Tiny swept the hair of her last couple of customers into woolly piles late one night. She rubbed her clippers, razors, and combs with alcohol even as she felt her eyelids forcing themselves shut. She enjoyed the solitude, though she stumbled through the shop with her eyelids low, sleep trying to ambush her. The one thing she couldn't allow herself was a seat. To sit down would be to fall asleep and make herself vulnerable to an opportunist, one of Rev. Kimothy's legion out there, always looking to catch her slipping so they could do her harm. Tiny grasped the broom again and went at some hair clumps she'd missed, and as she swept she heard the flat slap of an open palm against the window. Without looking up she waved the interloper away. The noise persisted. She slowly turned to the entranceway. Jerome stood at the window waving. A sharp pang of irritation ran through Tiny, but also relief. At least it wasn't another head to cut. At least it wasn't a protester. Any annoyance Jerome was about to cause would not end in her destruction. When she opened the door she noticed he wore that same serge suit. The same panama hat. Dirt stains now ringed the hat's brim and the jacket's wrists.

D! he exclaimed, stretching his arms out as if preparing to strangle her. D! Why is there no trust between us?

Look at my eyes, Tiny said. I'm half 'sleep.

Please, please, please, please, D, please tell me your secret.

Tiny sighed. She just wanted to sleep. This man in front of her looked so anguished that it sent sharp pains shooting through her joints.

It's piss. She dashed these words off halfheartedly, surprising even herself with the sting of her sarcasm.

Piss? You mean you pee on your clippers?

No, silly. That would be ridiculous. I soak all my clippers, my combs, everything I have . . . I leave them all to soak overnight in jars of piss.

Really? True this time?

Yep. That's my secret.

Yes, Jerome said. That makes so much more sense than all that other stuff you told me.

Does it? Tiny said, and then she sighed again. Of course it does.

Tiny looked at Jerome with sad, tired eyes. She forced a smile onto her lips. She wanted to say, *No, fool, what do you take me for?* But to point out his gullibility now would be a true act of cruelty. If only Jerome knew how to read the crooked tilt of her lips. Her face was a book he could never truly comprehend. These men, she realized, would believe anything. They preached logic and reason but followed only magic. Things would always be like this. Always and forever. As long as she lived and cut hair. Tiny felt more exhausted than she had ever felt before, like weights had attached themselves to her eyelids, her limbs, her neck, everywhere. After Jerome left, she locked the door and walked through the protest and into darkest night, never to be seen in Cross River again.

It was better this way. Perhaps Tiny sensed the horrors that hovered on the horizon. Sonny sitting alone every day in an empty shop surrounded by endless jars of his own piss. Soon would come the hair cults. The Cult of the Licked Razor. The Cult of Red Devil Lye. The Cult of Blood. The Cult of Piss.

But then there were also the Children of Delilah, the barbers, the barberesses, sprouting all over town like new growth and shining like the brightest points of light, like the finest, most luxurious hair, smoothed with a slick sheen of grease, growing faster than any havoc the Hair Crisis could cause, faster than any curse could possibly curse.

TOCHI ONYEBUCHI

Habibi

Dear Omar—

Solitary kills niggas, but it ain't gon kill me. That's facts.

After everything I been through so far, I know it ain't for me. They got me in here, but can't no kinda block hold me. I'm too big for that shit. Like, you know how shit just sometimes leaves you alone? Or, like, passes you by? I don't know how to explain it, but it's like bad shit just be missing me, bro. I'm not about to snitch or nothin, but one time the homie Victor and I—Victor's half-and-half, like half-black, half-Mexican but he ain't been jumped into no cholo gangs—we was headin back from school early on some bullshit. And I remember what day it was too, because Miss Frazey, who was always on our ass about something or something else, she took me to the side and she was like "you're gonna have to make a choice between your future and your friends" and you know how much it can mess you up to hear that when you're twelve? On the set. All I know is this gang-banging, you feel me? But Victor and I are leaving school and we on our way to the Lakewood Mall when I see some Pirus literally headin right toward us. Now, they used to go to the other school around the way, and we used to play football against them until their set started showing up to the games carrying hammers and the schools were like "we ain't tryna see no dead kids on this football field," but these Pirus

are headin straight for us. Like, we're about to get caught slip-
pin, and it's just me and Victor and these four brolic-ass Bloods
headin our way. So I figure, they bout to get the drop on us. And,
like, if you're gonna get stomped out, you can't just go down like
no bitch becuz people talk and it's gonna get around and maybe
it's gonna turn into a thing where they give you the whoop-dee-
whoop and now you gotta kill one of them and then they gotta
kill one of you and it's just a lotta cryin mamas and a lotta wakes
and, on the dead homie, I'm tired of that shit, you feel me? Like,
this gang-banging shit ages you, bro. Anyway, they're bout to get
the drop on us, and, you gotta understand, I got the rag out, yo.
I'm Cripped up, all Crenshaw everything. I can't tuck nothin. And
I left my hammer at Mac's place becuz we sometimes hang there
after school and chill in his studio while a bunch of them make
music and all that. But, get this, just when I think I'm bout to get
the whoop-dee-whoop, they walk right past us. I'm talkin, right
past us, bro. They don't even see us. Like we ain't even there. Victor notices it too, and at first we were like okay what if they're
just waitin till we alone, you know? But, nah, we catch up to the
homies at the Mall and it's on and crackin again. And at first, I
ain't know what happen and I ain't even tell the other homies, but
now I know what that was. I'm special. I'm Protected, yo. Like, I
been shot at but never shot, you feel me? 16 years here and damn
near everything's tried to kill me, but I ain't die yet. It's weird to
say at 16, but sometimes it feel like forever yo.

But that's how I know, fam. I'm special. Like, that happen and
so many other things. Like this.

I still don't know how this started or how exactly your letter
got to me here. I swear, one second I'm takin my shit, then there's
this piece of paper lyin in the dookie water and I'm so sick from
bein in solitary without hearin or seein or talkin to nobody that
I'm like "is this for real?" and I get the letter out right before I
flush, and I look at it and it's all in these letters I ain't never seen

before, like backwards cursive. And I don't know how you write like that, all the letters connected. Least, I think they're letters.

If this were happening to anybody else, they'd have all these questions. But not me. I know exactly why this is happening to me. Same reason we ain't get the whoop-dee-whoop from those Bloods. Same reason I ain't never been shot. And you gotta know this before I eat this letter and send it to you.

I'm special. They ain't gon kill me here. They can't.

Quincy—

I think I know what you speak of. That feeling that you are special. That Allah has wrapped His blanket over your shoulders. I saw it once. Outside. In Gaza. It is hard to imagine Gaza City if you have not already been there. Everything is close. We live on top of each other. There is garbage in the streets and it is tough to escape the smell even if you go all the way to the sea. And when you're young and you get to the sea, you might think you've found a moment of freedom, of peace. But there are Israeli ships in the distance—you learn to notice them from an early age—and there are people arrayed on the water to shoot you if you go too far out.

That happened to some fishermen I knew. The tide was receding and it had been a bad day for them. Everywhere they went, the fish fled. As quiet as they tried to be, as much as they'd tried to still themselves, to vanish and be like the air around them and the sea beneath them, they were always too clumsy. Their bodies would get in the way of their mission. So, frustrated, their boat kept moving further and further away from shore. Normally, it is an easy thing to keep track of. You don't need the buoys, you just learn early on, first from your parents, then from your friends who disobey and are punished, until the lesson lives in your bones. But some days, if you haven't caught the fish you need to cook to feed your family for that night and if you've had several days like this now that build up and cloud your mind and bring

fog between your ears and behind your eyes, sometimes you forget the lessons in your bones and you drift far out and you don't
even hear the gunshot.

Your friend collapses. Their legs just fold beneath them. And
a part of you is angry that they've fallen so gracelessly, because
maybe some of your supplies have now slipped into the water
and these are things that you paid very hard and dear money
for that you will now never have back. And maybe you're angry
because your friend falling the way they did threatens to capsize your boat, tossing you all overboard. And the water is clean
enough to swim in if you needed to, but then it would be easy
for the snipers to say you and the others abandoned your boat
simply to swim further out, as though that were a thing we would
ever want to do.

Your friend doesn't capsize the boat. You don't tilt over. But
you know from the way that red blossoms on their chest that
they're dead. A sniper has shot them.

But that's not what I was talking about when I said I knew
what you meant. There was one time, by a border crossing with
Israel, several of us were protesting. It is often a family affair. People bring their instruments and we have signs and, because so
many of us live together, we make the trip together.

We get to the beaches and there they are waiting for us. Soldiers. Some of them sit in armored personnel carriers and other
huge vehicles. They have put up towers from whence they can
snipe us. And soon, after a few warnings in Hebrew, they fire the
first tear gas canisters at us. And the smoke, thick and white,
swells towards us. The wind did not like us that morning and
swept the tear gas right in our direction and soon we were all
choking and crying out for milk.

It looked as though we would end our march as soon as we
began. But then wind came and whisked the tear gas away. Someone had set fires nearby, or maybe the soldiers had shot at our

electricity generators, setting them on fire, but large columns of black smoke seemed to rumble along the horizon on the beach. They made a sort of fence, as though this portion of beach were all that was left of Gaza.

And I look, as the tear gas clears away and a friend is pouring milk on my face and my eyes to stop the burning, and there, in the center of the fence, with smoke billowing around her, is my sister in her denim overalls. She's with several of her friends. All of them wear keffiyeh around their necks. And in their hands are strings of beads, and they swing them as they dance the dabke.

It is a joyful thing to watch the dabke. It is danced at weddings and other joyous occasions. It is a sort of line dance, led by one person in particular who is supposed to be like a tree but with legs that stomp into the ground like roots, and arms that wave like tree branches caught in autumn wind. There's chanting and the leader drives all of it, kicking and hopping and flaring their legs and skipping and spinning. And there is my sister, kicking and hopping and skipping and spinning, and she twirls her string of beads and leads the chanting. She is a warrior, the bravest thing I have ever seen.

Then I hear the thwip sound that rubber bullets make when they buzz by you. Sometimes they make a crackling sound when they hit rock or a thudding sound when they hit your chest or your stomach or your shoulder. But around her, all there is is thwip thwip thwip. As though she is dancing around them. As though she is dancing through them.

Do you think it ever stops? The protection? The thing that kept bullets from hitting you and that shielded her that day? Do you think a day comes when you wake up and suddenly you're no longer protected? Do you even know it? What would it feel like?

Would it feel like going to sleep, thinking that you can control what you see and hear and think in this nightmare, and hoping that you might finally wake up somewhere familiar where you are loved, somewhere filled with the sweet smell of kanafeh, somewhere busy with the voices of your siblings and your cousins, where everyone is alive and loud and happy to see you . . . then waking up to see that nothing has changed?

You are still here. In this cell. Alone. So alone that the magic of this letter, which I will eat and chew up and swallow and which I will somehow pass to you, feels hollow. Morning comes when I wake up and chastise myself for having spent so much time talking to a ghost.

Please write me back.

Even if you aren't real.

Omar—

I'm real, bro. I'm here. And whatever it is that's going on, it's real too. And if it ain't, then that means we got the same dream going on at the same time, and that's gotta be its own type of magic.

But, bro, so much of this is mental, you feel me? It's like say I'm a ballplayer in the NBA and my pops manages me and he says I'm better than everybody. You ask him, "is your son better than Steph Curry?" and Dad's like "he could be." "Is your son better than LeBron?" "Well, he could be." And you know for a fact that all those kids that play ball in college maybe 50 percent of them make it to the League, so it's all mental. Mad people got talent and can learn skills and all that, but to get to the next level, yo? You need to be gassed up. Let me find out my dad's gettin asked if I'm better than people and he's like "oh man I don't know." Get outta here, for real? You my dad and you not gonna call me the best ballplayer that ever lived? But I hope you get what I'm tryna say.

I guess what I'm tryna say is that you gotta keep your mental straight, you feel me? Becuz sometimes when that shit gets broke you can't put it back together.

I seen some shit the other day, they was walkin me out of my cell for my hour of rec time in the yard, and on the way out, we passed by this other cell in solitary and there was a bunch of guards outside this one door and they had the door open and they were talkin all quiet and whispering and you could tell they was tryna frame someone or build a lie around whatever it was that had happened. And that's when I seen the nigga foot like stickin out past the door. You can't see all his body because of the way the guards are standing, but you can see some of it, and he's lyin face-up on the floor, with his head and upper back propped up against something and there's just that shiny stickiness ALL over the floor. It come back that he slit his wrists while he was in there, and you're not supposed to be able to do that. They give you the suicide blanket for that reason, and it's not even a blanket thing, it's like this thing they just basically wrap you in and zip up to your neck. It's like nylon or something and they basically trap you in it. You can't move for shit. And they call it a suicide blanket becuz you're not supposed to be able to tear it open and make a noose like how you would normally do if you were gonna do yourself like that.

But I guess the guards thought that he was better. He looked like he could be about my age. I don't know if I ever seen him around on the outside. He coulda been from any block really. But I'm glad it wasn't me. Coulda been. He and I got the same setup. A bunk. A toilet. And a mesh window. There's a slot they slide your food in and that's how the roaches and all that get in to your cell and sometimes they make so much noise it gets hard to sleep. It don't feel like you have company, tho. The Box could be fulla bugs, but you still feel alone.

Sometimes I cry and that helps. Not loud or nothin, but real quiet. You know the type where your shoulders heave and it feels like the sadness is tryna bust right outta your body. Just like that.

Dear Quincy—

I am sorry to hear about your fellow prisoner. May his soul be blessed. May Allah guide him. Suicide is sin here. But I know many who have taken their own lives, and I do not blame them.

There was a boy in our neighborhood, Mohanned. He was a writer. He was older than me; thus, we all looked up to him as an older brother. When he wrote, you could feel the despair that moved through him and see that it was the same despair that moved through the rest of us. By the time I was 7 years old, my home had been bombed by the Israelis three times. Three times our memories had been reduced to rubble. And three times we had to rebuild. For some, it was like starting from scratch. Like the whole of your life until that moment had been wiped away and was nothing more than broken stones and metal and dust. But some of us could still recover the toys we had played with or the shoes our parents had purchased for us when we were children.

Mohanned used to write and write and write. He would shut himself up in his room for entire days, just reading and writing. We all thought he was a sort of prophet and that he simply lived differently than the rest of us. He had a direct line to Allah that the rest of us could only hope one day to have. He would post his stories on Facebook, and as soon as they went online they would get hundreds of likes that would then turn to thousands of likes. We loved him. So when his mother found him in his room, no longer breathing, it was not just she who grieved. It was all of us. Then, on the heels of that grief was fear. Because he was suffering just like the rest of us. And now we knew that what took him could take us as well.

You see it sometimes in the way that we practically throw ourselves in front of their bullets. Everybody protests, no matter your age or whether you are a man or a woman. But often you will see the young boys in the buffer zone, and if you ask them, they would say that they didn't care if they died. During the siege, we live without electricity, without running water, and without any sign that things will change. So hopelessness is logical. But we are taught to be stronger. There is always a family member or a member of someone else's family who would feel a loss too great for you to ever want to inflict on them. And we have been suffering for over 70 years, so what is another month of this sort of life?

Even if I wanted to, there is nothing for me to do it with here. We had our blankets taken away when it was announced that several of the prisoners had begun a hunger strike. They are protesting their conditions. There is nothing in our cells to regulate the temperature. The food is crawling with insects. Occasionally, we are taken out and beaten for no reason. There is no interrogation, only the beating. And we are not given prayer mats for salat. All of this because I once threw a stone at a settler's car.

But maybe I am safer in here than I am out there.

Still, I dream of the Rimal district and all of its leaves. It is like an oasis in this desert of misery. It is where the wealthy in Gaza congregate. It contains the Governor's Palace and the Presidential Palace, but it also has the school for refugees, maintained by the UN. The Gaza Mall is there. But also there is coastline. Mohanned went there often to write. Also, foreigners who came to Gaza would bring books. And we would sometimes fight over them. They were portals to different worlds. And in them you could sometimes see yourself. Even though they were rarely about Arabs, and rarely about young Arab boys like me, if I squinted, I could see in the contours of their heroes something of my shoulders and my hair and my hands and feet. If I closed my eyes, I could imagine myself as the main character. And I was a hero who did not destroy things but saved them.

You are right. We are special. Because when I hear of other prisoners, I always feel as if their loneliness is bottomless. But, because I have you, that is not the case for me. We have this gift. And you give me courage.

I think I will join the hunger strike. It is an opportunity to build something. I do not see it as destroying my body. I see it as transcending it. I am preparing myself to live on a higher level of existence. I am flower petals being whisked on a breeze ever upward. Heroes take control of their destinies.

I will be a hero.

Dear Omar—

We heroes?

I like thinkin I'm a hero, but do kids like us get to be heroes? My homie got shot like 8 times over some bullshit and he ain't stop no bullets. He still alive tho, so maybe he is. But like we just kids. We beef with other sets and stomp kids out and get stomped out and laugh and sometimes I go to Cee's house to listen to the music he makin with Mac and them but I gotta leave the hammer in a locker cuz he don't like guns in the studio and I can't forget it on the way out cuz I have to cross the way to get back to Artesia and that's Bloods over there.

There's lots of empty houses in the hood, and when I was little, we didn't think nothin of it. Maybe ghosts was in them, but couldn't be nothin scarier than what was out on the streets. Still it was fun. We was havin fun. I mean, that's Long Beach. Everybody from everywhere so really we don't do that whole "where you from, cuh?" and all that stuff. But that's the thing is like heroes gotta have origin stories, right? Like Superman is from Krypton, he some undocumented immigrant or whatever. And Batman's from Gotham. Spider-Man's from somewhere in New York or whatever. But Long Beach, do you even have history before you get to Long Beach? Our parents and grandparents, they came back from the wars way back when and it was like ownin a home was the most important thing in the world so they bought up all these houses and you get these families movin in but then the houses get foreclosed on and the government snatch them right back up and ain't nobody livin in em no more so all you got is ghosts maybe. I don't know why I'm so hung up on needin to know where heroes is from.

Maybe it has somethin to do with order, you know? Heroes are all about restorin order or bringing balance back to things. There's a bad guy who's messin everything up and the hero's gotta get rid of the bad guy, but it's like, what does a bad guy look like here?

Before I got put in solitary, there was a couple East Coast cats who wound up here (everybody's from everywhere) and they was talkin about street justice. And I ain't really know what that meant and they was talkin bout how if somebody did something wrong they'd have somethin happen to them. Everybody was talkin about some kid or another who got boo-bopped by the cops and street justice meant that "aight, you goin after the kids, you gon get got" and one of them was in here and is actually servin life becuz he capped a cop who he said had killed a little black kid and gotten away with it. And it's like, over here anybody could get it. It just happen here. Like "Oh that cop boo-bopped cuz? That's craaaazy. Oh they robbed the bank and the little girl AND her mama got boo-bopped? That's craaaazy." And you just go about your day. Street justice? They talkin bout some dude from the streets puttin all they beef to the side to go down to Florida to pop George Zimmerman. Niggas in the streets got bigger things to worry about, feel me?

But I been thinkin that when I get out, I might try to learn, you know? Cuz kids out here is smart! My ex-girlfriend's son autistic, but you give that kid a math problem? He a genius. Long division. Algebra. Three seconds, he got the whole thing figured out. And they got a Youth Program at the YMCA in Long Beach. You can learn the piano, play pool, do gymnastics stuff. Get strong and smart.

It's tough, tho, cuz you gotta ride the Blue Line to get there and niggas be gettin in trouble for not havin a ticket. That's one of the first cases I caught. Ridin the train without a ticket. Then they give you a ticket that's like $500 and I can't pay that cuz I'm 12 years old. Where I'ma get the money to pay that off? So, boom, I got a warrant. And if you already on probation on some other shit, boom, straight to jail.

How I'ma be a hero if that's part of my origin story?

But I like what you said about not bein a hero that destroyed things but a hero that saved things. That's how I be feelin these days. It's weird. I thought bein in the Box would make me more selfish, you know? Make me think more about myself and about survivin. But I seen what happened to dude across the hall and one of my first thoughts was "what could I have done to keep him from doin that," you know?

Sometimes I be hearing things and seein things that ain't there. Feelin them too. On the dead homie, I swear the other day I swear I musta transported myself to some other nigga hood I ain't never been to before. I know it wasn't no kinda memory or nothin because it was all strange and new and different.

Shoes dangling from power lines like some kinda ballet over this potholed street with cracks makin a spiderweb from one small crater to another, and they was gettin made bigger from the wheels of Camaros and Hondas and beat-to-shit Subarus, all these worndown four-doors takin kids to and from school or this local park with a green-and-orange jungle gym for a afternoon where they'll learn how to ride bicycles and where they'll fall while speeding down that hill by the parking lot and realize that the natural way to deal with pain is to cry. There was weeds poking out above freshly mowed grass where the men in tank-tops was maintainin their yards, and there was these gates of green and white and yellow, with grasshoppers playing tag, in front of two-story brown and black brick project towers where extension cords tangle and hang, pulled by gravity into a slump around their middles, between windows, and people siphoning power, sharing it, experiencing the same electricity that sparks the small satellite dishes on top of certain roofs and the bootleg cable boxes in other windows, and some other ledge was taken by an air conditioner, and it was groanin beneath the weight of this oppressive heat that just sits on your shoulders and bends your knees and soaks your shirt and makes everything too heavy. And the kids was comin out with their magnifying glasses to aim the sun on the ants scurrying out from under their badass attentions, intentions, and a crow's head is gettin all moldy in the middle of the yellow-striped street, its body lost somewhere in the weeds of a nearby hill where other kids had tossed it. Beer cans lost in the tall grass, half-eaten chicken with the meat smoldering at each end of the wing's bones.

And I swear on the dead homie that I was there. It was just for a second, but I was out. I was out of my cell.

Maybe, next time, I could take someone else with me. If I can figure out how to do it again, maybe I can take you with me.

Dear Quincy—

I am sorry it has taken me so long to respond to your latest letter. What you described sounds magical. Through your words, I could feel the heat on my chest. And I could feel the beginnings of a breeze on my face. I could smell the grass. I could hear the sizzle of electricity and the hum of the air conditioners. You say that it is difficult to imagine yourself a hero, but perhaps Allah has gifted you with abilities beyond our comprehension.

I have been seeing things too, but I don't know that it is because of any gifts.

The hunger strike has entered its second week, and everything hurts. My entire body sometimes feels as though it has been swallowed by fire. My throat is a desert as I have also refused water. There is talk of forced feeding. It is when jailers bind you to a chair and insert a tube through your nose into your throat and inject liquid nutrients so that you do not die. They say it is to protect us from ourselves, but I have heard from some of the older prisoners that it is the most painful thing a man can endure. Many have been left weeping and broken by the end of it. They say it lights your brain on fire, and the whole world explodes into whiteness. It is like dying, but there is no release.

I'm scared.

I don't know what I'll do if they come for me. I will try to pray if they ever put me in that chair, but I fear my thoughts will become too scattered for me to form the words. I fear I will already start crying before they begin.

I am sorry for how messy my writing has become. My hands have begun shaking. I don't know if it is because I am afraid or because my body is breaking down.

There is no real way for me to communicate with the others. We have our secrets, but they are all coded messages with instructions. I have not seen my family in over six months. I don't know who is alive and who is dead. I don't know who has celebrated a birthday. I don't know who has married. The world moves on outside this cell, and I feel like the only way for me to rejoin it is to die. And I'm scared. I wish that just once I could receive a message from another one of the hunger strikers that was not a set of instructions or a number for how many days we have been doing this for already. I wish I could receive from them a poem. Or a photograph.

All I have is you.

Omar—

Whatchu look like?

I'm asking because when I take you to where we're going, I want to recognize you. I don't know if I'll meet you alone or if you'll be in a crowd, and this might sound mean but I don't know if I'd really KNOW it was you. Even with all of what's been happening to us. Like, you think that with this thing we got, we'd know each other instantly, but, like, I have no picture of you. I ain't never seen you before. And before that first letter, I had no idea you even existed.

But now sometimes when I close my eyes, I try to picture you. I try to put your face together. At first, it's kinda like a Mr. Potato Head thing where the lips are too big and the nose is way too big and the eyes are kinda googly, but then it starts to come together, you know?

Here's what I picture, and you can tell me if I'm wrong.

I never met a Middle Eastern person before and I don't think I know any Palestinians, except DJ Khaled. He's a Palestinian, right?

But I picture you having this straight nose that juts forward a little bit with tiny down-facing nostrils. And your bottom lip is a little plump, but you got your lips pursed together in this straight line. And your eyebrows are bushy and curve sharp-like towards the ends. And your eyes are shaped like almonds. Like the kind Mama was always eating. And your skin is dark but not dark-dark like mine. More like when water wash up on the shore but the sand ain't dry yet. Like, dark but not dark-dark. It's the type of brown that's nice to look at. And you got this sloping jawline. It's smooth and curved. I think you're my age so you don't got no baby fat left. Maybe you hit your growth spurt. Some of the cats who play basketball around the way call it your Mango Season. Maybe that has somethin to do with the South, I don't know. But maybe you're tall. And maybe you could hoop too. When you get out, you should think about playing ball.

You ain't gotta say what you think I look like or nothin. Ur a good writer but my face too pretty for words. Haha, I'm just kiddin. I'm just a regular nigga. Regular-degular. Nothin special.

But I think that's what you might look like. It's what I think a hero might look like.

Quincy—

Do your hands have long fingers? Like those of a piano player?

I imagine you with strong hands. Your grip isn't bony, it's iron. You hold tightly to what is dear. I imagine your skin dark as seabed on the backs of your hands and your palms are the color of milky coffee, and I can now imagine every line, every crease, every crevice. Once upon a time, your knuckles were cracked, and I think they have bled often. You have broken the skin of them on many things, trying to survive. But what has grown over that broken skin is rough and safe and secure. That's what I imagine when I imagine your knuckles on my cheek. Security.

It is more difficult to see your face. I think that my sight is failing me. It took me a long time to read your last letter. The words themselves were slipping away right before my eyes. I cough now and when I cough, I can feel the blood moving in my chest. If I cough into my hands, they come back red. They have started trying to force feed us, but I have remained resilient, and I find the occasional message of support and congratulations waiting for me in my cell. I can barely lift my arms, and I have stopped trying to walk the length of my cell for exercise. My legs no longer support me. Sometimes, I feel nothing at all. I don't feel my bed beneath me, nor do I feel the heat of this cage on my forehead. Sounds come as though from far away. I sometimes hear screams, but I tell myself I am only dreaming them. If it is a lie, then let it be mine.

When I try to imagine you, I imagine your hands, but I also imagine your arms. They are thin and sinewy. Strong but light.

Running is easy for you. And your legs are the same, and I can see them kicking behind you as you dive into the water. You are an arrow fired into it.

We are just off the shore, swimming into the Mediterranean. The sun is shining so bright it turns the rippling waves into a bed of diamonds. And I see you swimming and swimming.

I hope you get this letter. My stomach has stopped working. I don't know if I can pass anything through it anymore. I think I'm dying.

I am sorry if my writing is messy. My tears are falling on the page, and I can't stop them. You told me that crying helps, so I am trying it now.

Habibi, come to Gaza some time when you are able. You will find me.

Now that you know what I look like.

Omar—

Bro, I'm not gonna lie. Your last letter had me shook. Your eyes aren't getting bad. It's just these new pencils they're making us use. They're all made out of rubber and they don't have any lead in them so that we can't hurt ourselves. You're good. ~~You gotta~~ you gotta stay. ~~I can't~~

The other day, I was waiting. Trying to see if I just needed to take a shit and get another letter from you but nothin was comin and I just kept tryin and tryin and nothin was happenin and I got so mad I couldn't eat and when they tried to bring me more food I took the tray and threw my food everywhere and started bangin the tray on the doors and on the walls and I couldn't stop. I knew what I was doing. I saw myself doing it, but I couldn't stop. It was like my old self took over. My out-there self.

That Quincy was always angry. Even when I was laughing and havin fun and all of us was hangin out at that abandoned house on Pico and one time we locked the homie in a shed and he was poundin on it for like hours and we finally let him out and we was laughing our asses off, even at that time I was angry. Then there's the Quincy that did everything he could to take care of his mama. Maybe I go to school but that don't work so maybe I slang on the corner and that don't work so you just fall into the gang-bangin and everybody already go into that angry so it ain't nothin to pop somebody or to give them the whoop-dee-whoop. Then there's the Quincy that loves reading and kinda likes writing and is tryin to get good at it but they make it so hard for a nigga to learn in here, and it's like there are all these Quincys inside me and they all tired. They all tired. And the only time they all feel glued together is when I'm readin your letters.

I don't know that I can stick it out in here if I ain't got your letters. You're saving my life, man. You can't go. I'm beggin you. Please.

I been trying to see if I can do that trick again. Where I see a place I ain't never been to before. But I haven't been able to do it since that one time. Sometimes I wonder if it was really real. Like I musta dreamt it. But it was the realest dream ever. And it wasn't no part of Cali I'd ever been to before. That's the thing. It was a new place. So I been tryin. Like, I tried it with the Rimal place you told me about. And I could almost get there but not quite. It still felt like there was this fence between me and that spot.

(Sorry, I had to take a walk. I almost ripped up what I wrote so far, but I want you to get all of this if the letter gets to you. I'm sorry. I can't keep you from doin what you need to do. You fightin your fight is inspirin me and all. But you know what too? It's like the songs say: if you love somethin, you gotta be able to let it go. I just . . . I just don't want you to die, homie. On the set, you the best thing that ever happened to me and I don't know that this coulda happened if I didn't wind up here in solitary. Someone catches me shittin out a whole piece of paper they gon take me straight to the hospital, you feel me? Haha. But you a real nigga for what you doin. That's on the set. Out there, niggas die over all sorts of petty shit and it's like we don't see the bigger things that's above us, you know? Like the homie who got asthma because his house is right by that coal plant and that's why the property value low enough for black families to buy it in the first place. And his mama and em was always tellin him to sleep with the window shut but he liked the breeze on his face so he'd always open it every night till one night he fell outta bed and couldn't breathe and they took him to the hospital and told him he had asthma. See, I wasn't thinkin bout none of that before I got in here. I was seein it. I was seein kids get jammed up over ridin trains without payin the fare then windin up behind bars over that shit and I just figured it was normal, but I wasn't seein the bigger thing hangin over it. I don't know. You opened my eyes to thinkin that kind of way. And that's why I'ma get out. That's right. I'ma get outta here. I'ma get outta the Box and I'ma beat my case and I'ma be clean on probation and I'ma make it so kids don't be gettin locked up over bullshit fare evasion and so kids don't get asthma from living to close to the coal plant and so ppl stop getting shot over bullshit. I'ma get out.)

And when I get out, I'ma find you, and we're gonna go swimmin.

And I'm gonna ask you what that last word meant. Habibi. It sounded important but it didn't translate in my brain when I read it. I hope that don't mean my powers is fading. Haha. Cuz I still gotta make it to you. And I think Gaza's a long way from Cali.

There's another reason I need to see you. And I wasn't even sure I was gonna write this, but whatever.

When you were talkin about my hands . . . I felt . . . I don't know. I felt Good. Like, Good good. Ain't nobody ever told me about my hands like that. And it ain't feel weird either. It felt right. I don't know. I just wanted you to know that.

Quincy—

Beloved. Habibi means beloved. I hope this letter gets to you in time.

Find me.

Habibi—

I'm coming.

CRAIG LAURANCE GIDNEY

Spyder Threads

The SUV was shiny black, as if it had just been waxed and polished. The windows were tinted so dark that I couldn't see through them. The license plate frames had LED lighting. I don't remember the license number, but I remember that it was all letters and it was strange. All vowels or all consonants—an unpronounceable word.

It had been following me for a while as I walked from the old theater where the Sparkle Ball would be held to the fleabag hotel where I was staying a few blocks away. Maybe it was a coincidence.

It was just me and the black van in a deserted city. I didn't see a soul out in that neighborhood of boarded-up houses, cracked sidewalks, and broken windows. It could have passed by me at any time. Instead, it crept along at a snail's pace.

I stopped in the middle of an empty block, and turned to face the van.

It was silent as it drove up to me, and stopped.

The side of the van was emblazoned with a logo. A lopsided circle of vivid purple with flakes of glitter in the dark center.

Was it an eye?

Or a mouth?

An opening?

An exit?

The color of the circle was too bright. I couldn't look at it too long. But I couldn't look away, either.

The window rolled down. A fragrance oozed out of the van, perfuming the air with bergamot and licorice.

A bony-looking brother, dark and bald in sunglasses directed his gaze at me. He said, "He would like an audience with you." His voice was deep, soft and expressionless.

"Who?" I asked.

I already knew the answer.

They called him Spyder.

His couture work was legendary.

Where he was from, even where he lived, was of much conjecture. Some said that he was from the slums of Detroit. Others said that he grew up in Watts. Oakland, D.C., and Gary, Indiana were all possibilities.

Among the more fanciful: he was the unacknowledged child of one of the great designers. One indisputable fact, though, is where and when he burst on the Ballroom Scene.

It was five years ago, at the Peacock Ball, held annually in the D.C. area. That year, it was held in the basement level ballroom of the past-its-prime Imperial, which stood in the shadow of the Capitol building, in a block full of Brutalist architecture. The Imperial was in the Beaux Arts style, solemn columns, arched windows and doors, rococo cornices, statues of Diana and Dionysus in the lobby, all covered in the soot and grime of city pollution.

The Grand Salon Ballroom had been transformed into an alien landscape. Nets with balloons hung from the ceiling. Dining room tables were terraformed with colored fabrics in tones of electric blue and emerald green. House music full of shrieking divas pulsated from speakers. Stages were set at the far end of the room, with the long tongue of a catwalk extended out into the audience.

During the last runway performance, as the audience was drifting away from their seats, an announcer said over the P.A., "We have a late addition to the show. From the House of Spyder."

The houselights were on at this moment, and the dull chatter of inebriated patrons swallowed and muffled the announcement. The music began to play, a music that was different from the high energy, pulse-pounding dance music. It was becalmed, tentative piano notes held in a suspension, in a thick jelly of sound that oozed over the crowd. A chord would play, followed by rippling that sounded like white noise.

The model who took the stage looked nothing like the other models who'd pranced and vogued down the catwalk before. The Peacock Ball was fashion-based, run by a regime of fashionistas who took their cues from *Vogue*, *Marie Claire*, and the fiefdoms of Versace and Vuitton. They had been long-limbed and lithe, like gazelles, garbed in mesh and nylon and gabardine and muslin, hooved in stiletto heels, made up to conceal and twist their genders. This model, though, was fat. No other euphemism was appropriate for him—and it was undeniably a him. The beard made sure of that.

The queens in the audience were vicious when they saw him. The words whale, hippopotamus, and hog floated about the gathering, as if it were a schoolyard.

But when the model stepped into the spotlight, a hush came over the crowd, a silencing wave, so all that was heard was the droning hum of the music. The lower part of the gown was made of wood, or so it appeared. The silver ash of birch bark, punctuated with sickle marks of the wood beneath. Rising out of the trunk of the gown were branches, which seemed to be living, as these wiry digits were bejeweled with leaves of acid green fabric.

The model's bearded face was surrounded by a nimbus of leaves and white branches.

The birch-tree model glided down the runway, graceful as a dancer. The weight of his body, and of the outfit, were nothing to him. In fact, as the gargantuan man went down the aisle, it was impossible to imagine anyone else wearing the couture outfit. This was the daily wear of a god or some mythological being.

The birch-tree god came to the end of the runway. Some say that the model bowed and at that moment, the leaves changed from green to gold through some optical illusion. Others say that a sudden wind (possibly from a backstage fan) blew and scattered the leaves over the audience.

But I was there that night.

I saw the large queen stand on the edge of the catwalk and freeze. The lights went out for a heartbeat or two. And when the houselights went up, a real birch tree somehow grew out of the ballroom floor.

The fumes in the van were so strong that my eyes watered. I asked the driver to open a window. He ignored me. He might have been a robot, or made of stone. He wore a dark suit that sparkled as if there were chips of mica embedded in the fabric.

We drove through the city, past industrial warehouses, dockyards, and seemingly empty office towers. There was a web of phone wires slicing the grey sky into ribbons. Factory smoke stacks belched out blue clouds of pollution. Maybe keeping the windows shut was the better option.

I got a headache just the same, drowning in a sea of citrus and anise aroma. The A/C was on full blast and so cold that I saw little puffs of breath.

What had made me get into the van, anyway? I must have had a death wish. After all, everyone who wore one of Spyder's threads seemed to vanish. People thought it was because of some ironclad NDAs.

I didn't think that was the reason.

Maybe it was the cold or the intensity of the reeking van, but I zoned out as we passed empty streets.

I had followed Spyder from ball to ball, coast to coast. From Chi-town to Motor City, D.C. to Philly, Newark to Watts. In empty warehouses and on theatre stages. I might have seen all of his outfits. Like the skirt he made of writhing snakes. The veil made of discarded cauls. The bustier made of finger bones. Spyder never disappointed. Each outfit was more outrageous than the last one. But I didn't follow him just because I loved his work.

I wasn't just obsessed like some stupid Yeezy or Jay-Z groupie. It was deeper than that. Can you feel me? You see, it was my dream, my aspiration, to wear a Spyder outfit. To be one of his models!

At San Francisco's Chimera Ball, the model walked on forearm crutches (apparently, he had multiple sclerosis). The corset was constructed of honeycombs, still dripping with royal jelly. The close-fitting skirt seemed to have writhing masses of honeybees. Some of them crawled on the model's crutches, leaving gold-dust pollen on them. Several attendees swore that they had been stung.

In autumn of that year, at Chicago's Chthonian Ball, the dress was seashells: conches, cowries, abalones, junonias and numerous others. The model had *ichthyosis vulgaris*, a condition that turned his skin into scales. Barnacles rested in his cornrowed hair. He embodied Oceanus himself. Many of the attendees of the Chthonian Ball, held in a shabby K-town hotel, swore they smelled the salty air of the sea and that a dampness pervaded the ballroom. The organizers were banned from using the hotel afterwards, due to the appearance of mildew on the flocked wall-paper and the outdated industrial green carpet.

Spyder's models were all outside of the beauty standard. He celebrated and elevated otherness.

The van slowed down at a gate. Behind the gate were a cluster of corrugated tin storage units. The driver rolled down the window, releasing some of the perfumed air and punched in a code in a keypad. The gate opened with a pneumatic groan, and we went forward.

"How did Spyder know that I'd be at the Sparkle Ball?" I asked.

The sparkly-bony man didn't answer. He just drove and parked the SUV in front of a unit, one that was indistinguishable from any of the others.

I was frightened. I could hear the blood pounding in my ear. I was also excited. Exhilarated, even.

The driver led me down the narrow path between two putty-colored units and unlocked a nearly invisible door.

My heart leapt up into my throat when the door opened.

I began staying after the shows, when the sets were dismantled, hoping to catch a glimpse of the elusive figure. Was he the dude decked out in Dior? The thin man in the navy Burberry coat? Was he the thick queen in a mesh shirt, lipstick, guy liner, and a diamond-encrusted grille? No, no, and no.

Then, I changed my tack. I tried cornering the models who were Spyder's creations after the shows. I could never catch up with them. Maybe they left immediately after their perfor-mances. I trawled the dressing rooms and backstage areas, find-ing them empty.

The only one I managed to speak with was after the Flower Ball, held in San Francisco. The Ball was held in an abandoned warehouse in SoMa. The dude was maybe 6'5" or even 7 feet tall. A real Watusi. Spyder had outfitted him in a pantsuit made of lady slipper orchids that seemed to grow out of his skin, as if he were some kind of living mangrove tree. I saw him hanging around backstage. I offered to buy him a drink.

We found a dive bar nearby, catering to the S&M crowd. A giant and a dwarf weren't the strangest pair in that place, if you know what I mean. We got no second looks.

I asked him, "When did you meet Spyder?" when we were sitting at the bar.

He said, "Who?"

"Quit playing."

He gave a blank stare, one that was genuinely confused. "Who da fuck is Spyder?"

I tried not to roll my eyes. "You know. The dude whose outfit you wore. The one who dressed you."

"Oh," he said. Something by Drake came on through the speakers. The model, whose name was Levi, started swaying on his stool and mouthing the words. "I don't remember anyone named Spyder," he finally said.

"Really?" I said. "I mean, who pasted those flowers on your body? That must have taken hours."

Levi glanced at me, then away, to the light show of green and purple beams that wavered over the dance floor. I saw men in black dog masks. Men in leather caps and harnesses. Men dressed like the police, or S.S. officers. It was creepy.

But not as creepy as the look that Levi gave me.

I don't quite know how to explain it. He leaned towards me, getting ready to speak to me. But then, he froze. It was like he had a mini-stroke. His face went slack, and his eyes, I swear to God, changed color. Just for a moment. Maybe even less. They went from dark brown around black irises to violet. Like Elizabeth Taylor's eyes supposedly were. Then Levi leaned back, as if nothing had happened.

I asked him about Spyder again.

He opened his mouth, about to speak. Something fell out of his mouth.

A petal, yellow with scarlet stripes, covered in a gooey, sticky substance.

I said his name.

Another cobwebbed petal fell out, followed by another. And another.

"Are you okay?"

Levi left me to go to the bathroom, roughly pushing aside the men in the bar.

I waited the length of a song before I went into the bathroom.

Levi was gone. The trough urinal, though, was full of urine, ice, and browning flower petals.

Behind the door was a set of metal stairs that went down. I couldn't see the bottom, and there were no lights. The bony-sparkly man said, "Come on. He's waiting." He held a flashlight in his hand, which he switched on. It did not illuminate anything. Then he went down the stairs, his footsteps echoing.

This was what I wanted. What I needed. I wanted to be beautiful, if only for one moment. To be bathed in the spotlight, adored by the crowd. I was unloved. Kicked out of my home at sixteen, not pretty enough or tall enough or pale enough to fit into gay culture. Queens can be vicious. I was called a midget, or Gary Coleman. But if I were outfitted in one of Spyder's threads, I could transcend my defects. Be elevated and celebrated. That was worth whatever terrible thing that happened to other models, wasn't it?

We went down and down, the flashlight's beam bouncing against cinderblock. The flights of stairs seemed to be endless, and it was dizzying. How far underground were we? It defied logic.

My eyes adjusted to the darkness to the point that the bony-sparkly man's flashlight was unneeded. He did not remove his sunglasses, for some reason.

The smell of the SUV—bergamot and licorice—drifted up. And, at last, I could see the end of this descent.

The sub-sub-sub-basement was a chamber to the right of the column of stairs. I looked up, got Escher vibes at the interlaced metal mesh that I'd just come down. Was this some forgotten bunker or nuclear fallout shelter? The stairs were a tower that tunneled upwards, leaving the surface world forever out of reach. I was tired, just thinking about going back up.

The driver gestured me to enter the chamber. I hesitated. The smell was so strong that I could almost see the haze of fumes. It was like a perfume factory on steroids.

I stepped into the chamber. Alone.

The walls of the room were concrete hung with scattered capsule-shaped light sconces. The floor I stood upon was metal grating, like you would find in an abattoir. In the center of the room was a mound of dirt that was roughly in the shape of an anthill. But it wasn't made of mounded dirt. It was made of some substance that resembled puckered flesh. A pale violet mist trickled from the hill.

I crept toward this, against my better judgment, to get a better look—

"Don't get too close," someone said. The voice came from *within* the pit.

I stepped back. Far back, almost to the chamber door.

A hand emerged from the pit. Followed by another hand. And another. And another.

Until a tall, thin man with too many appendages was up and out of the mound.

How tall was he?

How thin?

How many arms did he have? And how long were they?

I did not see a nose or mouth. Just tiny beadlike eyes that were black.

What I saw was incoherent and hard to look at. He was a blur of motion, with stick-like arms and legs, and a long thin face. He reminded me of a daddy longlegs.

"Spyder," I said. And in saying his name, his shape's frenzy stilled. He was still too tall and too thin, but he had the correct number of hands and eyes.

"I love your work," I stammer like a starstruck teenager.

"Oh, honey chile, I know. I had my eye on you for a while." His voice has a smooth, narcotic quality, aural cough syrup.

"How do you make such wondrous outfits?" I say. It sounds stupid and pedestrian. "You're better than all of the designers— Balenciaga, Lagerfeld, Gaultier . . . Did you go to Parsons, or . . ."

He laughs. His black eyes sparkle with violet glitter.

"Oh, doll," he says to me. "You are about to see how the magic is done."

In this hollow, echoing room, I find no evidence of fashion design. No mannequins, no rolls of fabric, no sewing machines.

As I undress, he speaks:

"When I was a child, I saw the most marvelous movie I'd ever seen. It was called *Mahogany*. Maybe you've heard of it. It's the story of a young department store clerk who becomes a fashion model, and eventually, a designer. The plot is basically a morality play in which the designer gets enmeshed in the decadent world of couture fashion. Not that interesting. But the displays of fabric and the shapes of clothing that could be created from them imprinted my young soul. It was a spiritual awakening. My soul had been plain white linen. The movie soaked that linen, dyed it a rich vibrant hue, and changed the composition of its fabric to a rich satiny finish.

"In the movie Diana Ross was transformed into Mahogany, a high priestess of fashion . . .

"The universe, of course, is a black and cold place. And if it cares not for humanity, what are the dreams of little sissy black boys to it? I learned this the hard way, when Mommy and Daddy kicked little old me out of their Good Christian nest."

Spyder takes my hand, and walks me up to the geyser.

"Ah, my diminutive muse, the universe *did* listen to this faggot's *cri de coeur*. It gave me access to the most marvelous thing in existence. Meet Mahogany." He gestures grandly to the puckered abyss.

He embraces me in his many, many arms, and jumps—

I am bathed in the essence of bergamot and licorice. It flows around me, licking my unloved body. Tasting and penetrating every crack and orifice.

In the grape darkness, I feel them. The industry of Spyder's arms and fingers coiling around my naked form. They cocoon me in satiny, shimmering fabric around my form in a haphazard, zigzagging way as I hang there. Every contour of my body, sans face, arms, and feet, is covered in cobwebs made of light.

The dress seems to be a living thing. It breathes, like a rising chest. It is made of feathers, thousands of them stitched together like wings. The iridescent gray of pigeons, the snow-white of doves, the technicolor scream of parakeet wings. Where the bones of the wings meet, there are eyeballs. Human eyes of blue, seagreen, earth-brown, hazel, and grey. Eyes that are speckled like eggs, and eyes that have the frost of glaucous glaze. There are also the eyes of cats, slits in pools of primrose and topaz. The eyes of birds—the hot yellow of eagles, the beadlike eyes of sparrows. The silhouette of the gown is striking; it looks like it's about to take flight. And in the searing spotlight, the eyes appear to blink.

The music that accompanies my catwalk is made of breath and wing flutters and coos.

All of the eyes are on me, and for one shining moment, I am the angel of the Sparkle Ball. I am beautiful, am Beauty itself.

When the runway walk ends, I stand in front of the spangled lavender curtain. I make a final gesture. The spotlight extinguishes.

Then, I flex my many wings, and take flight.

TARA CAMPBELL

The Orb

Every time I stir the biomass, I feel lucky to have been chosen. The stirrer is flat and smooth, made of blonde wood; the biomass is thick and smells of overripe fruit. I look down into the buttery orange swirls in the bucket, and it amazes me that just a few months ago I was helping a friend paint her new nursery walls a similar color. But before her baby arrived, I was selected, and now I'm here making history.

I walk across the dusty field to the wooden shed in our small corner of the "estate"—which is more like a compound—and press my palm to the scanner, one of the Master's few concessions to modern technology. Electricity and running water seem almost out of place here. Everything else on the compound is rustic: the big farmhouse in which he lives; the bunkhouse where the assistants sleep; a couple of small cabins, one of which is crammed with materials, the other which I claimed for myself by virtue of being the first. This was a fortunate turn of events, given that the assistants are in their twenties and I'm—not.

The air inside the shed is a sweeter, rottener version of the biomass. Although the fumes aren't harmful, the odor would overwhelm at length. I hold my breath against the stink of seaweed, the rot of fertility. The Master doesn't want us wearing masks anymore. He doesn't want the Orb to think it's unwelcome. We created it, after all.

I roll up my sleeves, then dip my hands into the bucket and slather the Orb with biomass. We aren't supposed to use gloves, for purposes of bonding. I enjoy the lushness of the substance— thick, smooth, slightly grainy—and the swell of the Orb under my palms. Its surface is silky and taut, but pliable. There's muscle under there. From time to time I feel it contract.

I start with the Orb's sides and bottom, then climb onto a stepstool to reach the very top of it. By now I can do this with- out soaking my apron and skirt. After I smooth biomass into the last bit of its skin, I keep my hand in place, waiting for another contraction. Sometimes, if I wait long enough, there's a rumble underneath my fingers. A purr.

The Orb continues to grow, to the point where even with a step- stool, we can't reach the top of it. One of the assistants suggested using a long-handled brush, but the Master insists that human touch is essential. He's ordered me to build a scaffold around the Orb so we can reach all of it. Luckily one of the assistants is a car- penter—I wouldn't know how to begin.

I've had to ask for the assistants' help so many times. I'm not their leader, per se, but the Master has developed a habit of giv- ing all the orders through me, and through some twisted alchemy of misplaced guilt, the orders become favors the assistants are doing for me, adding to my account on some imaginary ledger.

I don't get that feeling from Michael, the carpenter. He arrived with his girlfriend Sarah a month ago. Julian, however—he's been here twice as long, doing the bare minimum, and yet is jealous of anyone else the Master notices and seems to appreciate. No matter that Julian's work is sloppy, such that I have to check his batches to make sure he's mixed the biomass properly; he's still angry at those of us who are doing well. He's sure to be piqued when Michael invents some ingenious articulated system that expands along with the growth of the Orb. The Master loves this sort of thing, praises intricate inventiveness, admires the time and effort lavished on any sort of niche, analog, temporary measure.

Soon Julian, Lucy, and I will finish the new structure for the Orb. It's something of the Master's design. It looks like a Quonset hut, but we call it a hangar because he finds the former term too militaristic. Even though it will involve destruction, he reminds us, the Great Devouring is ultimately about peace.

The Orb is now over ten feet in diameter. Still in the old structure, we've expanded Michael's scaffolding as far as it will go, leaving only a small gap for us to slip through with our buckets between it and the wall. Even Julian, the tallest of us, can barely reach the top of the Orb from the scaffolding, and the rest of us must resort to slopping biomass over the last bit we can't get to. We'll have to take down the wall to get it out of the shed.

But the new hangar isn't ready yet. It doesn't sit right. We tried to follow the Master's instructions, but the frame is listing to the side, and we don't dare compound the problem by finishing it. Julian's complaining throughout has not only been demoralizing, but, as it turns out, there may be some truth to it: the blueprints were more sketches than actual plans. The Master is angry, of course, but as he says, he was wrong to expect a team of nonbuilders to interpret his design correctly.

That's why he's bringing on Hamish, a *real* builder. He's very busy, says the Master, because he's *qualified*, and he will only be here long enough to build the hangar. The Master warns us not to speak with Hamish about the project, or if we must, tell him it's art. That's what the rest of the "estate" is for, after all, this five-hundred-acre art colony with its ramshackle pavilions and gallery barns; its outdoor sculpture and scrap-metal whirligigs spiraling in the wind; its massive, rusted robot looming vast on the western horizon.

The Master has arranged for us to be in this little fenced-off area, courtesy of the absentee matron who owns the estate. She has a history of funding mysterious projects by mysterious male artists, demanding they surprise and delight her with the first viewing in exchange for absolute secrecy. Perhaps she likes the feeling of power, of creation. Perhaps she thinks it gives her an edge of danger in her dotage.

If she only knew.

Hamish is here.

The night before he arrived, Sarah complained to me that we shouldn't have extra people coming in and out, "willy-nilly." She claimed to be concerned about having an outsider so close to the project, but I suspect she's more annoyed that the Master didn't give Michael an opportunity to redesign the hut. I told her to have faith in the Master's judgment, and she didn't say anything, but I could tell by her expression she wasn't entirely satisfied.

I didn't dare admit to her that *my* main concern was losing my cabin for the new builder's lodging. Fortunately, the Master had us clear out the second cabin for his use. And when Hamish arrived, I grasped the wisdom of this decision, as he appears to be close to my age, and similarly desiring and deserving of some privacy. *Especially* someone like him, who seems the type that would draw other people toward him: strong build, muscular from work; a clever designer's mind; a welcoming smile and kind eyes. I can understand why he might need his own space to get away to.

At any rate, Sarah hardly needs to worry that Hamish will see something he shouldn't, because he and the Master spend all of their time together conferring in the farmhouse, then coming out to stare at our shamefully tilted attempt while holding up draw- ings as wide as their arms can spread. We watch from a distance, the Master's eyes warning us away. But I've caught a peek at the new drawings, which I assume are Hamish's due to their clean, straight lines. The Master's updated the hangar, adding more scaffolding and thicker walls.

I think about those drawings and marvel at how far we've come from the days of the earthen hut with a padlock and a thousand-gallon tank.

Before I arrived, the Master says, the Orb was no more than a seashell, the perfection of the infinite designer spiraling outward in the golden ratio. At first the shell was small enough to fit on the palm of his hand, and looked laughably small in its five-foot cube of fluid. Of course I would never laugh at the Orb—it was already up to my knees when I arrived—so I have to take the Master's word for its modest beginnings.

As it grew, he says, the spiraling of the shell disappeared, erased by a layer of pinkish matter accumulating on its surface. But shortly after I arrived, I was witness to a wonder: the gelatinous matter developed a subtle formation of bulges spiraling from the top to the bottom of the sphere. This sense of memory, this intelligence, convinced me that I was part of something truly life-altering, that I had been chosen to help build this new life. That the Master and I would be the architects of a new age.

Back then it was just the two of us. Every day he and I would add nutrients to the tank and take measurements—temperature, salinity, alkalinity, ammonia, nitrate, phosphate, ionic strength, viscosity, and so on. As the Orb grew, its surface morphed from a rosy ooze into something more substantive, condensing itself into something resembling the skin we know now. It hardly looked like something that would subvert the world order, but this was the stage the Master was waiting for, the indication that the Orb was ready to come out of the tank. Now was the time, he said, for a new assistant to join us.

Not "*an* assistant" but "a *new* assistant."

I told myself the twinge I felt was merely protectiveness of the project. And I was indeed wary of a new person joining our work, but the Master assured me he'd screened Lucy the same way he'd screened me: she'd found his "art project" online (another necessary concession to modernity), read deeply of his teachings, passed multiple interviews with him, agreed to travel here.

"The path to power," says the Master, "is strewn with the bodies of those who wanted to save the world. It is a golden staircase littered with the remains of those who tried—and failed—to protect vulnerable animals and ecosystems, to rescue the planet itself."

He means the victims of corporate greed: environmentalists, journalists, protestors, activists. But as far as I'm concerned, these corpses include everyone in the world, all of our bodies rotting from poisoned water and filthy air and processed food. The Orb will protect *all* of us by crushing the drills, poaching the poachers, strong-arming the strongmen, and bleeding out greedy CEOs—devouring the devourers until human beings finally have to respect the power of the earth.

This "art" is very real. When the Master speaks, he doesn't share exactly *how* it will happen, but he has his reasons for keeping that knowledge safe. He has a plan, and it's not for us to question it. Our calling is to care for the Orb. The Master will share the rest of his vision when the time comes.

The morning Lucy arrived, and the Master winched the Orb out of the water and positioned it over a bedding of damp blankets, she didn't hesitate to reach up and help guide it, dripping, to its nest.

It would need frequent feeding and watering now, said the Master. We were weaning it off the tank. Toughening it.

I volunteered for the first shift, advising Lucy to go and rest. The Master offered to show her the project notes and help her get caught up. I don't like to recall how petty I felt, noticing how he placed a hand on the small of her back as he guided her out of the hut.

But Lucy has turned out to be trustworthy. Unlike me, she moved naturally in the clothing from the start. I've yet to see her fidget with her bonnet, and she's always used the apron for its actual purpose, rather than keeping it clean like part of a costume she'd have to return later.

Knowing now how reliable she is, I don't like to recall how during those first few weeks I listened after she'd bedded down for the evening, alert for any footsteps around her bunkhouse, any stirring inside. How I watched for any deviation in the Master's path from the farmhouse to the hut protecting the Orb.

Lucy was never the problem.

Hamish has come and built and left, though I can't say I wished for the last of those things. But there would have been no way to fully shield the Orb as we transferred it, and no one uninitiated can see it yet. Michael devised a way to gently lift and transport the Orb to its new hangar. At the same time, the Master has screened and initiated a new batch of assistants, bringing us up to almost a dozen now. I'm grateful for the additional help with the Orb's care, as well as with chores around the compound—the Master has brought in chickens for eggs and cows for milk, and we've begun gardening and baking bread to minimize the necessity for contact with the outside. He says his patroness was very supportive of the investment, finding this all very mysterious and amusing; not realizing, of course, that we are also fortifying our compound to exist in the new world order we are ushering in. But this influx of people leaves me more uneasy than relieved.

I observe the new trainees stirring their buckets of biomass. The buckets are metal now, as are the stirrers, and we're all required to wear elbow-high gloves and full-body aprons, men and women alike. The Master has changed the formula. It's green now, and runnier, and smells of rosemary and vinegar.

When the biomass is ready, I lead everyone up a set of exterior steps to the rooftop, show them how to pour their buckets into the chute, explain how this chute will bathe the Orb in the nutrients it needs to grow. Tell them their contributions are much appreciated.

The new trainees, however, have never seen the Orb, let alone touched it. The Master says this physical closeness is no longer necessary because we are biologically engineered into the Orb (he once admitted to me how surprised he was that HeLa cells were so readily available, even for artistic endeavors, which allows him to describe his work this way). The Orb is already enough like us—*of* us—for the connection he wanted to create. Early touch, he says, was sufficient to activate its sense of empathy, its instinctual bond with those of us who mean it well. Like will protect like.

Now we are supposed to treat it with respect, which doesn't include touch. Anymore. At least, not for the Orb.

After the last trainee empties her bucket, I show them all how to clean the equipment and send them off on their next assignments. This is where the genders separate again, some of the women cooking and cleaning in the farmhouse with Lucy, others gardening with Sarah, the few men fixing things around the compound under Michael's guidance, Julian monitoring the Orb's development (and fuming) under my supervision. It's clear to everyone, even the Master, that he would rather have a team of his own; add to that the sting that Michael and Sarah were given permission to move into the cabin after Hamish's departure.

I walk back out to the hangar and palm the scanner to unlock it. Everyone except the Master, Julian, and I have been programmed out.

Inside, the air is fragrant. The sickly rot of the previous shed has given way to something fresh and green, a field after rain.

The Orb is still slick with a dull gleam of biomass. Still feeding. I climb the newer, bigger scaffold so I won't have to crane my neck to look up into its swelling form. I walk the catwalk around its perimeter, where only those of us who have been here since the beginning are allowed to tread.

Up close, I can hear it growing, crinkling with a tiny, wet *snick*.

Life before the Orb seems so distant now.

It's been a week since anyone has seen Julian.

The last time I saw him, I was on my way out of the hangar. I stopped—it's not that I'd done something wrong, but I didn't have a particular reason for being with the Orb just then. It was night, and I wasn't sure if he'd seen me, so I hurried around the corner out of sight.

My first thought was to just go to my cabin and forget it, but I couldn't. Julian had been stirring things up recently, disgruntled by Michael's increasing prominence, accusing the Master of being attached to certain new trainees—although, I have to admit, it does seem that the Master has taken a special interest in the new recruits.

I only got a few steps before I turned back to see what Julian was up to himself, sneaking around at night. Perhaps I was paranoid, but when I saw that he was heading toward the Master's farmhouse, I was alarmed—what if he'd seen me just then? What if he'd seen me all those other times, visiting the Orb when I wasn't supposed to?

I followed him at a distance, and by the time I reached the farmhouse, the Master had already let him inside. Standing in the shadows outside, I couldn't hear anything in particular, just muffled voices rising and falling. After several minutes, the voices got louder and footsteps pounded the floorboards. I ducked around the corner of the house, and from there I heard the front door creak open. Two sets of shoes clomped across the porch and down the front steps.

"Let me show you, Julian," I heard the Master say. "You deserve to see."

That was a week ago, and no one has seen him since.

Man is the apex predator. We all knew this before the Master told us; it's why we came. We're here to balance the scales, to create another life form that can mitigate our domination over all other life on the planet. For the good of the Earth, we're here to create something more powerful, more durable than humans and all of our technology—something to keep us in check.

The Orb shares our genetic material. It will have a deep knowledge of us, the way a stem cell "knows" how to build itself into skin or muscle, blood or bone. It will know what we need. Our weaknesses. How to kill us.

And, I believe, it will share our instinct to save itself above all other forms of life.

But it had to be done. Just like the Master tells us, other systems for mitigating human control—earthquakes, floods, disease, drought, crop infestation—were random and untargeted. Nature doesn't care who it kills, and oligarchs have the means to avoid these plagues: stockpiles of food and supplies in undisclosed locations, private planes to escape, hired guards for protection, and piles of money to keep them loyal. As long as the same corrupt figures remain in charge of manmade systems, he says, they will continue to be destructive.

But I've been thinking: what if it's not just specific people that are to blame? What if human nature is to blame? Amassing of resources leads to the fear of losing them, which leads to the amassing of more resources to prevent losing the original resources. I get that; coming here is what broke me out of that perilous cycle myself. So maybe it isn't certain individuals that need to be eliminated, but our entire flawed species that needs to be put in check. There has to be a counterpoint to our absolute power—doesn't there?

The Master believes we can teach the Orb who to target.

He and I might simply have different ideas of how wide the net needs to be.

Either way, we needed to create something more powerful than us, something we couldn't kill.

It was the only way.

Last night I saw the Orb give birth.

It was in the hangar. I was concerned for the Orb, because even these few weeks after the move, it's already beginning to outgrow its new environment. The Master says we don't have enough funding to expand the structure, so we're creating space in the other direction, excavating into the ground. Instead of starting right away, as I thought he should, the Master wasted days on additional training and an oath-taking ceremony before allowing the newest recruits to enter the hangar and see her.

The work has been slow, with pickaxes to break through concrete floors, shovels to clear away rocky dirt. I fear we're not moving quickly enough, but the Master doesn't want to upset the Orb with the noise and exhaust of more powerful tools. We've got to dig deep and wide, far enough so she won't roll in by accident, but close enough that we can gently tip her in when her new nest is complete.

I need to stop calling it "she." The Master says that's sloppy anthropomorphizing.

Last night I'd come into the hangar to massage the Orb with oil, to soothe its skin during its rapid expansion. Her—its skin is soft and fragrant, as always, but it's begun seeping a milky substance.

The Master sees it, of course, but he hasn't told us what, if any-thing, to do about it. The oils are all I can think of, and at that point it had been three days since I'd been able to apply any.

I don't have the luxury of a special blend; I just have to take what I can sneak out of the kitchen. I've been varying my sched-ule and keeping the main lights off to avoid attracting attention. Master has changed the Orb's schedule to include times when it must not be disturbed, mimicking our sleep patterns. During these times the lights are kept at a low, golden glow, to provide a comforting environment for rest. I don't think the Master believes that the Orb actually sleeps; this is merely his way of continuing its training in our ways.

I walked around the Orb, running my fingers lightly over its skin to check for lesions. I don't know if the Orb can feel pain, but her skin is so taut, I can only imagine she does—another thing that doesn't seem to concern the Master. Now we are not only discouraged from touching her: it's forbidden. I'm not sure how he imagines this tipping-in will work.

I hadn't even completed a circuit around the Orb when she began to shudder. The milky fluid rose to the surface of her skin, cresting in a cloudy, glistening slick. This time, however, the liquid didn't simply run down the sides and drip to the floor. It coalesced, growing thicker, until I spotted a bulge high up on her side—it must have begun at the very top, too far up for me to see. The bulge spiraled downward along the shuddering Orb, circumnavigating her, gathering up the milky sheen as it trav-eled. I realized that this bulge was not just covering itself in the viscous liquid, but growing itself out of it. It *was* the milk. When it reached the bottom, it rolled off the Orb onto the floor. It was now a separate, autonomous orb in itself.

The Orb's shuddering slowed, then stopped. The smaller orb, about half my height, leaned against the larger one, suckling a few deposits of milky fluid it had missed, absorbing them into itself. Then it rolled toward me.

I quickly stepped to the side and the new orb headed toward the door. For a moment I panicked, but the door was locked, and the orb couldn't reach the release bar. Somehow, I was convinced that its lack of height was all that stopped it from pressing the bar and freeing itself.

I followed the little orb as it explored the hangar, rolling across the floor until stopped by a wall, then following along that wall until the next barrier—shelving, a desk, a pile of boxes. I followed it the way one might follow a baby or a puppy, lingering at a solicitous distance as it investigated its world.

The small orb completed a circuit of the hangar before returning to its mother. I realize calling her—it—"mother" is more "sloppy anthropomorphizing," but then the Master wanted to create something close to human.

And it was very human in this: the smaller orb approached its mother once more, absorbed the last few drops of milk, then rolled itself down into the excavated hole in the floor. I ran to the edge and looked down just as the last of its body slipped into the earth.

I don't know how long I stared into the hole. Eventually I sensed a wetness between my legs and went back to the privacy of my cabin. There I found my underwear damp with a milky discharge that smelled of vinegar and rosemary.

I should tell someone. In all of his planning, the Master has never spoken of anything like this. I can't tell him, though: he'd tighten access, lock me out of the palm scanner, keep me farthest away of all because I broke the rules. I wasn't even supposed to be there.

No, I can't tell him. But it's not because I'm concerned for myself.

I'm not the one who needs protection now.

It's *her.*

I haven't been able to concentrate for days now, ever since I saw the birth. I need to tell someone—but who? They all feel like part of the Master now.

He chooses a new young man or woman every couple of weeks, lingering near them as they work, calling it mentorship. It's clear which ones are interested, how they straighten their backs and lean their heads a certain way. Smile with a certain warmth. Later, he'll bump into one of them on his stroll, invite them to the farmhouse for dinner. More than a few of the young workers have developed a fondness for solitary walks.

I'm too old to be of interest to him. He wants the young, the beautiful, the bountiful, bound to him. The Master has fierce appetites and a golden tongue, and they are all mesmerized. From the very beginning, they were invested in our project, content to be part of a larger whole—he's merely adjusted the details of the arrangement.

I'm not bitter that he's never come to me. That Hamish never noticed me. I'm past caring. This just means I have more time for my work, for the Orb.

For now, I'll scratch my misgivings into the dirt with a fingernail, whisper them into the grass for safekeeping. I'll continue to rub the Mother with oil and reassure her that—unlike Julian, who is still missing—her child will return.

I awake from a deep sleep, my underwear damp with milky discharge.

I change and rush to the hangar, expecting a birth. That's when I find the skull.

As though the Orb has been expecting me, the skull lies next to her where I would see it as soon as I entered. I cannot breathe.

One by one, the Orb lays the rest of the bones out for me, spiraling them down the milky ooze of her bulk as she did with her baby orb several days prior; first an arm bone, then a leg bone, a series of ribs, a cascade of tiny wrist and ankle bones. And last, a golden ring, an Irish design of two hands holding a crowned heart. I'd always been fond of the pattern, and had said so to Julian the first time I met him, when I shook his hand and noticed this very same ring.

I don't know what to do, and there's no time—a digging crew is due any minute. As the Orb grows, the Master has grown impatient, and the excavation work now starts before dawn.

I gather the bones in a wheelbarrow and push them out past the fence to a far corner of the estate. Part of me wants the wheel to squeak, wants to be discovered, wants the Master to be exposed, to pay for what he's done.

But then what would happen to the Orb? We designed her to be a competitor. A murderer. Despite this, no one seems to see her as a danger.

Yet.

The bones knock together with a sticky, dull *thunking* as I dump them onto the ground. As I wash out the wheelbarrow, I tell myself this is for the safety of the Orb, and the benefit of our project. With luck, some animal will carry the remains away to suck the marrow.

With luck, they'll never be seen again.

This morning we settled the Orb into the hole—her nest, as the Master calls it. The pit is large enough for the moment, but we're all aware it won't last. The Master is nevertheless relieved at the time we've gained, time for him to find the next solution. I know he doesn't want to write to his patroness for more funding—he doesn't want any outside contact at all anymore—but I'm not sure what other options he has. I know we haven't dug enough.

Soon enough the Orb will press against the sides of the pit. I wonder if it will hurt her.

Still, for the moment the Master exudes relaxation. He has solved more than one problem—one of the new trainees has been sent away. There's been no announcement, but we hear the Master's judgment in whispers, in second-hand snippets: she wasn't careful enough, and that kind of carelessness wouldn't do around the Orb.

She—the trainee—was beginning to show.

Some of us wonder in whispers who the father is, what will happen to him. But this is all theater, meant to signal innocence.

We all know nothing will happen to the father.

Another night of discharge. Another dash to the hangar.

Another baby orb is coming.

The process goes more smoothly this time; the Orb a practiced mother. This baby orb is more confident in its perambulations, traveling the room in fluid arcs. This time there is no hole for the baby to sink into—it has been taken over by the bulk of the Orb. I open the door and let the offspring out into the night.

The afterbirth comes more quickly now as well. Another skull, more bones. Another skeleton's birth.

No ring this time.

The trainee who was sent away wore no rings.

But the absence of proof is not proof.

This time I want to leave the bones. I want someone else to find them—but aside from Julian, whose palm no longer exists, the only ones with access are the Master and me.

I think about hauling the bones outside and leaving them there. I want for there to be repercussions, but on the other hand I can't bear the thought that there might not *be* any, that this might be accepted as just punishment for the carelessness the Master accused her of. That he might—would surely—be excused, even vindicated by her death.

But once again, I must consider what might happen to the Orb. I cannot betray her. We created her.

And she's a mother, after all.

As I load the bones into the wheelbarrow, I must also admit that I enjoy the power a secret creates. *I know* are two of the most powerful words on earth.

I roll the bones to the same far corner of the estate. The others have long since disappeared. I tip the new remains out onto the same spot.

Throwing away the proof of one secret is a small price to keep another.

He thinks we'll never tell. Somehow he thinks we won't even remember any of this because he has taken away all our computers, all paper and pens, all sticks. But I will remember it. It will not be forgotten, because I'm whispering it to the trees and thrumming it at bees as they buzz by. I'm writing it into the air with my fingers. At night I bend down and mumble it into the earth.

Why was he so certain the Orb would know the difference between our enemies and us?

We tried. That was the idea behind touching the Orb, letting it feel our intention. Surely, he thought, it would remember those who wanted it to thrive, and surely it would recognize that we were different from those in power who threatened it, destroyed its environment. We wanted to create a way to fight back.

Was it the Master's sudden directive against touch that was flawed, or was it the original plan? Were we doomed from the start?

All of this is to say that the Orb has disappeared. Not by some magic poof into thin air—there are signs, streaks of gelatinous matter between the seams of the walls, the cracks in the floor, the slats of the roof, as though it exploded outward in all directions, all at once.

The Master is angry at everyone, least of all himself, which is as we've all come to expect, but of course cannot say. Everyone thinks the Orb has failed, that we've lost it, that we'll have to start again. But I don't believe this is true.

Every few nights since the Orb has disappeared, a worker has gone missing. The Master accuses them of cowardice, of running away to escape his wrath. I might agree, except each time it happens, I wake with the sympathetic discharge of another birth. I've taken to lining my underwear with rags, and the spot where I twice took my wheelbarrow is now gathering bones without me. My little pile has become an altar. The Orb is preparing the earth, just as we planned.

We just don't know what for.

Michael and Sarah are packing their belongings. It's down to four of us now: the two of them, the Master, and me. Up until the moment of their departure, they ask me to come with them, but I merely wish them well as they walk the path to the main road. The chickens cluck and scratch for food in their dusty wake.

The bone altar grows.

Eggs are a fine and fitting meal, if not a bit monotonous. I've kept up a little vegetable plot of my own, and there are nuts and berries to forage. But it's all right, because there's only myself to feed—I haven't seen the Master in weeks now—and I find I'm not that hungry anyway.

Now I'm the one who goes for solitary walks, not hoping to meet the Master I initially served, but seeking the new one. Seeking *her.*

I walk and I search for her in a fragment of bone, in a viscous slick on a blade of grass, in a whiff of sweetness on a breeze. I want to place my hand on her skin and know if she still recognizes me. I want to know how many children she's delivered, if she will bear my presence in peace, or if she will consume me.

I search for her, but I also want to believe she's not searching for me, that she's looking instead for the destroyers of the earth, her enemies, her destiny.

I want to believe she would sense the cloudy wetness we still share.

But if not, if she did consider me her enemy—would I dissolve away into nothing, extruded into a pile of bones in the wilderness, never to be found or mourned by another soul? Or would I become one of them: an orb, one of *her*? One *with* her?

And still I search for her, and still am left to wonder: Will she someday circle back to find me? Will I ever know what it is to dissolve all the evils of mankind and slip away, down into the dirt, an avenging angel of the earth?

VICTOR LAVALLE

We Travel the Spaceways

1

They call me Grimace. I do not like that nickname. I mean, Ronald McDonald has those sharp red kicks, and Mayor McCheese wears a top hat and sash. Grimace is just purple and pear-shaped. And that's what these people decide to nickname me. But what can I do? If I make a fuss about it, the local store owners would just call the police; between them and me, it's easy to guess who'd get handcuffed and hauled away. So, they call me Grimace, and I have to live with it. I try to find solace in the fact that I'm a man on a mission. Top secret business. Big, big things. But before I could get to any of it, I had to try and get myself a meal.

"Change?"

The lady walked right past me, turned her head; that kind of thing used to hurt my feelings long ago, but I'd been living on these streets for the better part of a decade. You spend enough time being actively ignored, and you learn to protect yourself. Stuff your feelings in one sock, slip them down around your left ankle, they fit as snug as an ankle monitor, and believe me, I know about such things.

"Change?"

I might've said it louder that second time. Not talking to that woman again, but two men walking by, hauling hot dogs and biting into them so casually. Meanwhile I'd been trying to get myself a meal for about a century. Well, more like two days, but forty-eight hours ain't nothing to fuck with.

"Get outta here." [him; hostile]

I turned to see the deli owner, who meant to brush me off like trash kicked off the curb. It must've been because I yelled at the guys. In midtown Manhattan potential customers are a protected class. The deli owner—he's never told me his name—looked back into the store.

"It's Grimace. He came back." [him; hooting to the cashier, his wife]

I'd been lurking by Bryant Park. At lunchtime this place gets crowded. Tourists and teenagers—the former tended to be more generous than the latter. But so far I'd hardly made a quarter off these mugs. Then here comes the deli owner deciding he'd had enough. It's because I yelled at the guys. I have a problem with volume sometimes. Also, Manhattan makes you tired and then living makes it worse, and worse was how I was feeling. Also hungry. Did I mention that?

"Give me a bag of chips, and I'll never come back again." I said this to the deli owner, and he scanned me from head to toe.

"That's what you told me six days ago." [him; stating facts accurately]

"But this time I mean it."

He almost smiled. I saw his top lip quiver. But the crowds kept rushing around us. Can't make real contact with another person when you've got foot traffic interrupting the connection. The top lip settled into a sneer instead.

"Come back here one more time, and I call the cops the second I see you." [him]

The deli owner got off the sidewalk, but he remained in the doorway. Arms folded and his eyes gone flat. Back to business, so to speak. And there I was, wishing he'd just given me the chips.

A little food might've helped me think clearer. For instance, UY Scuti is the largest star in the universe. A red supergiant, 1,700 times wider than the sun. It's 5,219 light-years from here.

Sorry. Wait. What? Where was I?

Oh yes, in midtown Manhattan, fucking famished.

The deli owner waved for his wife, and she brought him a cordless phone, and he dialed for the police while he stared at me. Calling in the cavalry. I'll be honest, when New York City voted in Mayor Dinkins, a Black mayor, I swore there would be a change down here on street level. But so far I hadn't seen it. The cops still carried guns and clubs and used them at their discretion.

Nineteen ninety-one; when the cops come, Black man, you better run.

"I liked that rhyme," I said to myself as I stepped off the sidewalk and into oncoming traffic. A taxi nearly smashed me, but I'd learned to be sanguine about such things. Fuck a crosswalk. That's the motto of a true New Yorker.

Anyway, picture Grimace (I've decided to embrace the name) crossing Fortieth Street, causing a logjam of taxis and trucks, ignoring the insults pelted at him, making it to the edge of Bryant Park, to the steps that lead inside, where he finds his friends still hiding in a bush.

By *friends* I mean my garbage bag full of cans and bottles.

Laugh if you like, but this bag counted as the sum total of all I valued. Worth more than a suitcase full of nickels. I fled from the deli owner and snapped up my garbage bag, and I felt my stomach grip because I definitely could've used that bag of chips. Then I heard five words that reminded me of what really mattered.

"You have work to do."

I heard them, but the phrase was muffled. So I untied the top of my garbage bag.

"Who said that?" I asked.

"You have work to do." [Coke bottle; made of glass, all elegant design, and speaking more clearly this time]

"But I'm hungry."

"Feed your soul, not your belly." [Coke bottle; who had never known hunger pangs]

"Listen here," I told him. "I am running on empty."

"What about the bakery on Forty-Third? They throw out their bread the second it gets moldy." [Mello Yello; so smart and good in her brass-yellow brightness; a woman who remembered everything and knew I was no damn use to anyone if I was dead]

"You see that," I said. "That's *teamwork*."

Once more my volume proved a problem. For the citizens of Bryant Park, at least the ones near me, I'd been shouting again. I looked around at them, and they did their best to avoid returning the gaze.

"These people act like I'm out my damn mind," I muttered.

"You are shouting at a bag full of cans, my man." [Cherry Coke; black-and-red in those new can colors; always one to tell it to me straight]

Well I couldn't argue with that.

"Let's try the bakery on Forty-Third. But no matter what, right after that . . ." [Coke bottle; always on message]

Scientists estimate the temperature of UY Scuti is 3,365 Kelvin, but they've underestimated that number. Its actual temperature is closer to 3,500 Kelvin.

2

Nighttime was train time, and I was on one.

The E train, specifically. Hungrier than a motherfucker. The bakery had been a bust. They knew me over there too. The nickname trailed me. *Get outta here, Grimace!* I like to imagine they wouldn't have said it if I wasn't wearing the purple coat, but I know it's got more to do with my silhouette.

Anyway, the E train. Me and my bag headed out to Queens. Back to work. Last stop on the line. I took one of the two-seaters at the end of the car. My bag on the ground beside me. Boarded in Times Square, sitting upright; by the time we reached the first stop in Queens, I'd slumped over. So hungry I had no choice but to try and fall asleep. Straight up hibernation.

Meanwhile, commuters boarded one stop after the next. If they got on close to me, they skedaddled to the other end of the train. It wasn't the sight of me, but the smell. Maybe a bit of both. By now I'd taught myself to dismiss their angry glances, the way one or two threw a hand over their noses theatrically, but maybe I also fell asleep to keep from seeing them seeing me.

"You're going to miss your stop." [Dr Pepper; maroon from top to bottom; a lady who could be spicy and sweet simultaneously]

"Keep an eye out for me," I whispered. I whispered because people react worse when you shout on trains. They're trapped with you, after all.

"I'll tell you when we're there." [Coke bottle; always assuring us that she had every answer; she'd be a pain in the ass if she wasn't always right]

I let the rhythm of the train help me drift. I can't say how long it lasted, but eventually I awoke.

"If you scared, say you scared."

That wasn't me talking. And it wasn't any of my friends. New voices. Young ones. Nearby. Like right up close.

"I'm not scared of some bum ass nigga." A second voice.

Two boys. Teenagers.

My mind was awake, but my body hadn't quite caught up. Oh, sleep paralysis, my old friend, you are always fucking with me.

"Well do it then."

Now I heard a clicking noise. Once, twice. The more I tried to rush my eyes open, the slower they seemed to go. The train didn't feel like it was moving, which made me guess we'd reached the end of the line—Jamaica Station. These boys must have shown up, and I must have seemed like a fun way to pass the time.

In that moment I feared for my friends, not myself. Who was more vulnerable than them? So I kicked my left foot out just to be sure the bag still sat there. It was the first bit of body movement I was able to perform. Imagine my relief when I heard the clink and clang of the bottles and cans there inside the bag. They were still with me.

"He's waking up!"

"Then you better hurry!"

I opened my eyes, and that's when I found these two fools trying to set my ass on fire.

They would already have done it, but the boy holding the foot-long lighter didn't know how to use the technology. He couldn't get the trigger to work. Just stood over me, clicking that thing, getting more and more frustrated. This boy might've been fifteen. He looked a bit like me when I was younger. And behind him stood another one, a little older but still barely out of diapers, at least compared to me.

"You ever seen the Milky Way from the rim of a red super-giant?"

Not what they expected, to be sure. So weird it actually worked better than if I tried to play tough and trade fists. Those boys yelped like puppies, and the one holding the lighter dropped it on the floor, and they straight up *flew* out of the damn train car.

Me? I bent over and picked up the lighter. I thought it might be useful.

"Is this our stop?" I asked Coke bottle.

"Close enough." [Coke bottle; because she was empty, her voice always carried an echo, it made her sound vaguely mechanical, machinelike]

As I left the station, taking the elevator up to street level, I had to straighten my spine.

"You like the way I took that lighter?" I asked Coke bottle.

She didn't respond, but I knew I'd done well.

"It was good thinking." [Coke bottle; the closest she'd ever come to paying me a compliment]

"*Thank you*," I said as I exited the elevator. "Give a brother some positive re-in-force-ment."

It was nighttime, and she told me which way to go. I threw the bag over one shoulder—it was pretty full, but it didn't weigh much. I wondered if those kids had believed me, about seeing the universe from the rim of a star, or if it had just been a boss thing to say.

I wasn't sure if I even believed me.

3

Guy R. Brewer Boulevard is named for Guy R. Brewer, obviously. One of the first Black folks elected to political office in Queens. Came to Queens because the white Manhattan political machine wouldn't let him live. Served in the New York State Assembly for nearly a decade. His wife, Marie Brown Brewer, was the first Black woman to be elected district leader in Queens. When Mr. Brewer died, they renamed the street I was walking on in his name. Before that, it was called New York Boulevard. Brewer was better.

Anyway, I'm acting like I knew all this shit, but it's not true. Mello Yello told me about it as I marched along. I think she was bored. Guy Brewer is one big ass road, runs all the way from Jamaica, Queens, to the edge of JFK Airport. Luckily I wasn't going quite that far, or else Mello Yello might've gone into the minutia of Brewer's political platform, and I was too tired, and hungry, to listen to all that.

Guy Brewer Boulevard at night is lonely, if not quiet. Still some street traffic—buses and vans; kids in cars pumping music so loud it made my shoulders quake—but it's a commercial artery, and that meant foot traffic was at a minimum. Most of the businesses—besides gas stations and corner stores—were closed. That was better for me.

"OK. Stop." [Coke bottle; but by now you probably guessed that]

"I see," I told her. "I see."

A big, broad building, well maintained. Tan colored and architecturally sound. One half of the building was built on a slope, its ceiling made of glass. Nothing on Guy Brewer could compare to the elegance, I dare say opulence. It was like finding a pair of shined-up dress shoes in a closet full of old sneakers. Every part of the property sent the same message: "God Lives Here."

"Now how am I going to get inside this church?" I asked.

I wasn't speaking to Coke bottle or Mello Yello or Dr Pepper. There was one friend, and one friend only, who always found a way in.

"Go around the corner, there's a door with a weak lock." [Cherry Coke; no door opens without him]

So around the side I went, and sure enough I found it. Even better, it was tucked away behind some trees, so my entrance would be hidden. What a gift.

"Knock three times." [Cherry Coke; acting like I hadn't done this before]

Three strong kicks and I was in. I carried my friends through the threshold and waited there a moment. I'd been tripped up by alarms in the past. One time I lost my entire bag and had to start collecting cans and bottles again. Of course, I know the cans and bottles themselves aren't important. They're *vessels*. But aren't we all?

I counted to sixty or six hundred, I can't remember, and when the blue lights didn't flash outside, I figured my path was blessed. So in I went. Through the back offices, a bit of a maze, but I had a guide. Coke bottle walked me through, in the dark, as if she already had a map of the layout memorized. She knew exactly which office door I needed to crack. All my other friends had gone silent as could be. Not a clink or a clunk or an aluminum crinkle. This happened every time. They were holding their breath. Me too.

Finally found the pastor's office. In here, they spared no expense. If I could've sold his wooden desk, I might've paid for a six-month stay in a hotel room. I could've slept in a place with a mattress and a reliable shower, and instead this man had a fancy place to set his papers. So I rested my bag right on top.

On the walls were frames and frames of God people, I mean good people; some smiled and some stood solemn. The man that owned the desk—that owned the church, though I know he wouldn't put it that way—was in many of the photos. He looked like the kind of man who might buy you flowers if he loved you. This was a Black church and many of the faces in the photos looked a lot like mine.

"You don't have time for this." [Dr Pepper; spilling out of the bag so she could survey the room]

After Dr Pepper got some air, the whole damn crew decided to come out for a stretch. Raining from the desk to the ground. Did they make a sound? I can't say. I could only hear my own heartbeat. This happened every time too, a rise in my heart rate as I came closer to the act.

I regained my composure and set four friends on the desk. Coke bottle, Dr Pepper, Mello Yello, Cherry Coke. My pantheon. I went down on one knee before them.

"Would you stop doing that every time." [Cherry Coke]

"It's a sign of respect," I said.

"It's a waste of time." [Cherry Coke]

"And time is one thing you don't have." [Dr Pepper]

I rose again. An oblong knight in unwashed armor.

"Go downstairs now. Near the boiler room. You'll find a lawn mower." [Mello Yello; whose tone was always patient]

"You want me to drag the whole thing up here?"

"No. You won't need to do that." [Coke bottle; finally ready to be filled]

Down the stairs and on with the lights. How did Mello Yello know it would be there? And how did Cherry Coke know about the door? This is what I'm trying to say. Such things made a believer out of me.

I could still remember the very first message I'd ever heard from them; they told me where to find shelter during a snowstorm, a truck that had been abandoned along the West Side Highway; I slept in the cab, shivered the whole night, but I survived. If not for them, I would've been dead. When they began giving me missions, I felt like I owed it to them. They were more reliable than city or state government.

I found the lawn mower and unscrewed the gas cap. I tipped the mower on its side and held my old friend up to the hole.

"This is going to be messy," I told her.

"Just try not to get too much on yourself." [Coke bottle; speaking softer now, as we were alone]

I watched as the gasoline glugged down my friend's thin throat.

I climbed the stairs, carrying Coke bottle loosely so her insides wouldn't spill. When we returned to the office, all the cans had packed themselves away in my bag again. I appreciated them for doing something useful with their time.

The office had a second door, which led out to a dressing room where the preacher's robes were kept. I found an old rag, dark with shoe polish.

I slipped one end of the cloth down Coke bottle's neck and hoped I wasn't choking my friend.

Another door led out of this changing area and opened to the church itself. Moonlight fell through the angled glass ceiling, and I stopped to let it bathe me. Then I walked to the pulpit and looked out at the pews.

How many people sat here on Sundays? I tried to imagine the place so full even this enormous room would feel crowded. Five hundred? One thousand? And this wasn't the only church nearby. Five blocks away there was another, just as large. And down the block three more, less high-tone but just as earnest in their worship. What would they think of what I did tonight? Would they believe this was a hate crime? Nothing worried me more than this. That my meaning would be misunderstood.

When I'd done this kind of work before, one of the hardest things to find was a match. You'd be surprised how slapdash people's supply closets can be. But this time I didn't have to spend minutes scrambling around. The gasoline had been easy enough to discover. And those boys on the train had supplied me with a reliable heat source.

I pulled the butane lighter from my coat pocket just like King Arthur pulled that sword. Destiny. That's how all this felt.

I clicked the lighter, just once, and a tongue of flame peeked out. I brought the fire to the cloth and in an instant it lit up.

"Good-bye, my friend."

"I'll see you again." [Coke bottle; easy to understand, even with her mouth full; it was as if she said the words directly in my mind]

I flicked the bottle toward the pews. She erupted against the purple padding. She shattered and spread out her flames.

And then it happened.

I blinked once and felt the sudden *pull* of the red supergiant. UY Scuti. And there I was, at the viewing station, where we orbited at the nearest safe distance. From this close the star looked more orange than red. I wished I had a better understanding of the process the dying star underwent. But that wasn't my role. I was the Signalman. Clearing interference on the line.

[Excess background noise detected; you have work to do]

I had known the words were coming, but I still hated to hear them.

"When will I be finished?" I asked.

But I didn't get an answer. Instead, I found myself back in Queens.

I must've been gone far longer than I realized because the church was *blazing*. I mean, the pews had gone up as far back as the last row. And the fire had crawled up the curtains along the western edge of the room. I'd meant to go back and pick up the broken shards of the bottle, take them with me. I didn't like to leave evidence. But the fire was too damn big for me to risk wading in. I ran back into the office, hauled my bag and my ass out. I called the fire department from a payphone across the street.

4

I'm going to acknowledge the other reason people call me Grimace: I like McDonald's. Of all the fast food available in New York, it's my go-to. They also hire the kindest kids. At least that's been my experience. I've been to Burger King and Gray's Papaya, Church's Chicken and Wendy's, but no chain has been more consistent in letting me raid their garbage without chasing me off. Which is why I fled Queens and headed straight for the McDonald's down on West Third.

Now this is a famous block, even by New York City standards. The Blue Note sits across the street, and on the corner there's a basketball court called the Cage, second most famous ball court in the entire city. There's a club called the Fat Black Pussycat, used to be known as the Commons; I'd heard Bob Dylan wrote "Blowin' in the Wind" inside the place, but you know how some people like to tell tall tales. Anyway, all that history didn't mean shit to me. Not compared to the chance I might get inside the McDonald's and find half a Filet-O-Fish in the garbage.

I got inside. The place was crushed. But that wasn't new. Most tables had been commandeered by the usual crowds: teenagers here; basketball players on break there; a couple homeless dudes I knew as pure bad news in one corner; and, as always, a bunch of German tourists in another. Maybe, on top of the food, this was why I came. It was about the only place in New York where I went unnoticed. Compared to half the people in here, I counted as well-behaved.

But the trash proved unruly. Not empty, just so overfilled I couldn't fish out a morsel of food. And the only thing that would get me noticed—and ejected—was if I turned the trash area into a mess. There was a delicate dance between the workers and me. *Take what you want, but don't make more work for me.*

So that plan was a bust. I felt my adrenaline crash. I slumped against one of the wooden bins. I seriously considered that I might pass out. And then I saw it.

Actually, to be honest, I didn't see it.

"Hey, fool, look up." [Cherry Coke]

There, at a booth, right behind the garbage: an unattended cheeseburger and fries.

I felt like Indiana Jones when he sees that golden idol inside the temple. Approached with the same degree of reverence. A cheeseburger and fries, not a bite taken out of either. I crept closer. My mouth filled with spit. I eyed the path from the booth to the door. I wasn't known for my speed but figured I'd grab both and sprint.

I reached the edge of the table and then I heard the voice that changed my life.

"I will beat your ass if you touch my shit."

That's how I met Kim.

I didn't know her name yet, of course. She'd gone to the counter for ketchup packets, and now they were squeezed tight inside one balled fist. The lady stood ready to lay me out. I dropped my bag, put my hands up. But then I noticed something.

"You been crying."

She wasn't expecting that. Her right hand loosened, and the ketchup packets fell to the floor. I had a quick thought that even if I didn't get something to eat, maybe I could grab the ketchup, suck on the packets after I fled the scene. It's not food, but I'd survived on less.

After I said what I said—*You been crying*—Kim dropped the packets and then she dropped too. She didn't faint, but she fell into her seat. Then she looked up at me.

"How could you tell?" [Kim; her voice ragged, nearly whispering]

"Your mascara's run down to your top lip."

Any other day, a different night, and maybe Kim wouldn't have laughed. She would have chased me off or knocked me around. But how many different things need to go your way before you start believing there's a plan in the works?

"You were going to steal my food." [Kim; lifting a fry, eating it in one bite]

I couldn't even answer her for a moment because I'd been hypnotized by the fries.

Kim picked them up. Her nail polish had once matched her eyeshadow, a shade of purple the eye can't miss. She gestured with the box, and I held out my hand. She shook a few fries into my palm. They were still warm, and the heat felt like the flash of a red sun.

I didn't savor them; I stuffed my mouth. My legs sensed the salt. My knees shook. My two-day fast had come to an end. I had to sit down. I did and Kim reared back in her chair.

"I did not invite you to join me."

I waved a hand. "Just give me a minute."

She frowned. She tilted her head to look under the table.

"Did you just have an orgasm? Because I usually charge for that." [Kim; ready to run]

Kim noticed the ketchup packets she'd dropped and plucked them from the ground. She didn't like to leave a mess.

"You just saved my life," I told her.

She raised both eyebrows. "Is that good news or bad news?"

5

She told me her name only after we left McDonald's. She didn't have much of an appetite, so she gave me her cheeseburger as well. I walked alongside her, and as we headed toward Sixth Avenue, she didn't shoo me away.

Kim's face was covered in makeup. Her neck three shades darker than her cheeks in contrast. With some food in me, I slowed down. Her fingernails, while painted, were bitten down.

"Why not turn in the bottles and get some food money?" [Kim; the fine features of her profile emphasized by the streetlights above]

I had the bag over one shoulder, hobo-style. "It's not that simple."

"Nothing is."

Sixth Avenue is a romantic road. The high-rises and skyscrapers have receded. There's plenty uptown, and more down below; once you hit Canal, you'll know you're in New York City again. But it was a long way from here to there, and it seemed—whether by chance or some greater design—me and Kim were on a stroll.

"Will you tell me now?" I asked. "Why you were crying."

She looked at me quick, then straight ahead again.

"I lost someone tonight. A kid." [Kim; speaking so low it was hard to hear her, but I leaned in]

"Your kid?"

"Not like that. Not like . . . He was a kid I met out here." [Kim; waving one arm]

"And you took care of him."

She looked at me for longer this time. I did get it. Fast family, that's what these streets can create. Love and survival; the former helps with the latter. But the latter isn't ever guaranteed.

"I'm sorry," I told her. "I've lost loved ones too."

Does it make me seem stupid that I was thinking of Coke bottle in that moment? Can that compare to Kim, who had lost a kid? No. I guessed not. I wouldn't have told her. She might've thought I was trying to diminish her pain, or make a joke out of it. I wasn't.

We'd already made it down to Prince Street. The little wedge of a park there at the corner offered benches where I'd slept many times before. I waved to one so we could sit. It's not like we had a destination in mind. And to my pleasant surprise, she did sit, keeping about two feet between us.

"What was his name?" I asked.

She ignored the question. I figured that was more intimacy than she was ready to offer.

"I'll tell you the funny part. There's one thing I want to do for him, but I feel scared to do it." [Kim; right leg crossed over the left; right foot bouncing in the air]

"You don't seem like you're scared of anything."

She sighed. "I'm just a person, of course I get scared."

I realized, in that quiet moment, that none of my friends were interjecting; no comments from the aluminum gallery. This might've been the longest I'd ever gone without having at least one of them cutting in. It was like they were listening to her too.

"What are you too scared to do?"

She leaned forward so her chest nearly touched her knees. I thought she might cry again. My hand rose to console her, and I immediately pulled it back down. If anything would've made this lady flee, it would have been me grabbing at her just now.

"It's stupid. I mean, he wouldn't have cared. I don't know why I even care, but I do."

I didn't speak, just let her go on.

"I want to light a candle for him. I want to say a prayer in his name. I feel like I have to do it now, tonight, because I don't know what happened to him. There's not going to be a body to bury, you see what I mean? But I have it on good authority that he's gone. And I feel like, I feel like if I can't say a little prayer for him tonight, if I can't light a candle to show him the way home, he's just going to be out there, wandering. I won't be able to live with it. But none of these churches around here are open. And even if they were, they're not going to let someone like me stroll in. So I'm stuck, and I don't know what to do."

She'd gone quiet after all that, but I instantly got to my feet. I felt like I might've been levitating, to be honest. I turned away from her and opened the top of my bag and whispered my request. I'd been following their orders, so now they could do a solid for me.

"Kim," I said. "We can help you with that."

6

I waited for her outside.

She made me wait outside. She wanted to light a candle on her own, yes, but she also wanted someone to stand lookout. I tried to tell her that no one would see because no one ever saw me, but think about how *that* would have sounded. This lady met me about an hour earlier; I couldn't confess that I made a habit of invading houses of worship. She told me to stay outside, and she pressed one hand to my chest when she said it. I didn't realize how long it had been since I'd felt a human touch. She meant to stop me, but she only made my heart beat faster.

The second reason I let her go alone is because I wouldn't have set fire to the place anyway. It was a white church, and I'd never once been tasked with setting them alight.

She wasn't inside long. Might have been twenty minutes. And I stood across the street, on Washington Place, because I thought it would be too obvious if I parked my ass right at the church's gates.

When she came out—using the back alley path I'd revealed—I watched to see what she would do when it seemed I might have gone. Would she shrug and cross her arms against the cold and head back to whatever place she called home? Would she shout for me right there on the corner?

No. Instead she did something remarkable. She looked one way and the other, didn't see me, and leaned against the fence surrounding the church, casual as could be. It was like she knew I'd be back. And, of course, she was right.

7

This is a love story.

Right from the beginning, that's what this has been.

8

"What do you do at night?" [Kim; carrying two hot dogs in the sun; she bought them from a vendor on Fifth Avenue]

I imagine she and I stood out. We weren't far from Rockefeller Center. Fiftieth and Fifth, in the shadow of St. Patrick's Cathedral. A week since the night she lit a candle for her friend, whose name I still didn't know. She and I saw each other every day. We slept in separate places. She had a bed in a Hell's Kitchen rooming house; I had the streets of New York.

We'd started the habit of meeting at noon, around the corner from her place. No matter where I'd been the night before, I made it back. Then she and I would walk together until one of us had to be on the job. It may be obvious, but both of us worked nights.

"I have a different question," I said, mostly because I didn't want to answer hers. "Since you lit that candle, is your heart really at rest?"

Rockefeller Center, that general area, it tends to get busy. More crowded than even the McDonald's where we met. But me and her had plenty of room while we walked, headed uptown. The crowds parted for us. They were scared. Or disgusted. Who could say for sure?

No matter the reason, we strolled with the air of emperors. I made sure my posture matched such aspirations—and Kim had learned how to walk like a queen long ago—so, if you squinted, I think we looked the part.

"You make it sound like it was a silly thing to do." [Kim; looking down at me with one eyebrow raised]

"I'm not trying to insult you. I'm curious. I guess you could say I have a different perspective on the church."

We continued north. Past Cartier and the Polo Bar, Louis Vuitton and Bergdorf Goodman. None of them would get our money. If we had money, that is.

"It's where I was raised. Simple as that. Half my good memories happened in my church. A few of the bad ones too. But it's like first love, it always has a place in your heart."

Kim remained quiet and I did also. As we walked, I no longer experienced the old constriction around my ankle. When exactly had I stopped hiding my feelings in my sock? I looked at Kim. The answer stood right there.

"You going to make fun of me now?" [Kim; so vulnerable right then, I wanted to carry her in my softest pocket]

We'd reached Sixty-First Street. The entrance to Central Park. I waved her across the street with me, and we entered the grounds.

"This park is 133 years old. But before that, farther on the western perimeter, there used to be a town called Seneca Village. Two hundred twenty-five residents. Most of them were Black. Some Irish and German folks too. But it was a Black town. Started in 1825. It was safer to live together. White people in other parts of Manhattan were not kind. But then New York City decided they wanted to build a park right here, so what did they do? They snatched the land back. It was legal, but that doesn't mean it was right. By 1857, every resident of Seneca Village was gone. Scattered to the wind so people could go for a stroll or sunbathe on a rock."

Thank goodness for Mello Yello's lessons.

Kim and I walked alongside the pond, headed west.

"I didn't know any of that." [Kim; scanning the landscape as if she might still see evidence of those old homes]

"Sometimes, over by Eighty-First Street, where Seneca Village used to be, people will say they hear pigs snorting or the sound of a blacksmith hammering iron. But it's just for a second or two. Soon the sounds of the city, or the lights, they interrupt the transmission and it all goes back to static. The new thing gets in the way of the old thing. There's excess background noise."

I stopped and turned to her, set down my bag of cans. She looked at me, half smiling, half horrified.

"You look like you're about to propose to me." [Kim; kidding, but also not]

"You asked me what I do at night. I'll show you."

9

We found the mosque in Harlem. A small place, it was a 99 Cent store long ago, but went out of business. It had been repurposed to serve the faithful. I'd never made this kind of journey with anyone else before. No one would've been willing to travel by my side. What would Kim say or do? The closer we got to the destination, the more I understood how insane I might seem. For the first time ever, I doubted myself. It made me so nervous that I didn't speak the whole train ride uptown.

"Are we just going to stand on this corner all night?" [Kim; who, to my great surprise, took my hand]

I looked up at her—she stood six inches taller in flats—and then back at our joined hands. "We're going inside that mosque," I told her.

The streetlight on this block had blown out; she and I were shadows at this late hour.

"You don't understand why I'm a Christian, but you're going to try and get me to pray to Allah?" [Kim; pulling her hand away]

She walked off; I watched her go. She turned, came back. She pointed at the building.

"You know Allah *and* Jesus might not like a girl like me."

"You mean because you're a man."

I'd never heard New York City get so quiet.

Kim leaned as close to me as she'd ever come. She looked ready to bite off my nose.

"I am a woman. My name is Kim. If you hurt me right now, you will never see me again." [Kim; serious as a heart attack]

"I said the wrong thing. I'm sorry."

She watched me silently.

"And I want to see you every day for the rest of my life."

Kim took a deep breath. Finally she looked at the mosque.

"So what are we doing, robbing this place?"

"Just follow me."

As we walked, she patted my bag.

"Why not leave them somewhere else? They're noisy." [Kim; on the cusp of understanding]

I laughed a little. "Darlin', I wish you knew how loud they can be."

10

There was a back office with a window, and because it had been an old storefront, its security grate had rusted apart long ago. A single strong tug, and the grate gave way. The window was not locked. Kim said I was lucky. I didn't explain.

Inside there were reams of paper and stacks of neighborhood newspapers and supermarket circulars. A little TV sat on a bookshelf. The kind of stuff that finds a way to collect. I asked Kim to roll the newspapers and circulars into tubes. While she did that, I found the door that led down to a subbasement. They didn't have gasoline down here—no lawns to mow—but I found rubbing alcohol and turpentine.

When I got back to the office, Kim had turned on the television and I freaked the fuck out.

"What are you doing?" I growled.

"I couldn't see a damn thing in here. It was either this or turn on the light." [Kim; breathing heavy, shivering, she'd never done a B&E]

She had, at least, turned the volume down. It's funny, but when I saw the television light, I swore I heard the sound. Once I understood the reality, I did calm down.

She watched me as I opened the top of my garbage bag and set out Dr Pepper, Cherry Coke, and Mello Yello.

"Now I like kink, but this one is *elaborate*." [Kim; cracking jokes to hide her panic]

I took the rolls of newspaper she'd made for me and tossed them around the small office. I unscrewed the top of the rubbing alcohol and sprinkled it on the tubes. The same with the turpentine. Kim covered her nose from the strength of the smell.

"You remember what I said about Seneca Village and Central Park? Think of your church, this mosque, the same way. Before our people believed in these things, there was something else. Our gods, I guess. They made us. They miss us. They have been trying to reach us for five hundred years."

Had I ever said this out loud? No.

Before this, the idea lived only in my head.

And in the messages they sent, beamed across the universe, in the metal—and glass—that could carry their call.

"But most of us can't hear them. Not with all this background noise."

I waved to this space around us. A house of God. Yes. Definitely. But whose?

I pulled the butane lighter from the garbage bag, flicked the trigger once, twice.

That's when she punched me.

My feet left the floor; my soul left my body. Talk about contact.

Kim kicked the lighter away. She crouched above me.

"See, before this, I thought you was regular crazy, and I could work with that. But now I see you are the king of all flipped-out bums!" [Kim; rearing back to crack me again]

I did not want to get hit again, so I crawled across the floor, trying to make it to the door, a basic instinct to escape a whooping.

"You are wasting time!" [Dr Pepper; the voice coming through perfectly clear]

"This lady is about to beat your *ass*!" [Cherry Coke; enjoying the moment too much]

I couldn't move fast enough, so I curled into a ball, preparing myself for the blows to come. But they didn't. It took a minute, which felt like a month, but when I finally peeked behind me, Kim wasn't even looking at me.

She pointed at them.

The cans.

"How'd you do that?"

I sat up.

"I didn't do anything." I took a breath, rattled with understanding. "You heard them?"

Kim looked from the cans to me and back to the cans.

"She heard us!" [Cherry Coke, Dr Pepper, and Mello Yello; in three-part harmony]

Then Kim *really* screamed.

Shit, I might have screamed too.

Then we all remained still and silent. What now?

I heard my name. My real name. It had been so long since anyone used it that I didn't understand it referred to me.

"Give us a moment." [Mello Yello]

"To talk with her." [Cherry Coke]

I got to my feet. I looked at Kim. "I'll be right outside."

"Wait a second. Tell me the truth. Have I lost my mind?" [Kim; looking ready to crumble]

"Oh, you shouldn't ask me," I said, as I stepped out. "I lost mine a long time ago."

I shut the door and had to lean against the wall, shivering. I went down on my butt, looking back at the closed door. How much it would mean to do this work with a partner. And perhaps, together, we could work faster. How much longer before the signal could break through? At least I wouldn't be alone while trying to find out.

I stayed patient, gave it as long as I could, but finally I knocked once and opened the door. I don't think I'd smiled so wide in years.

But Kim was gone.

"I'm sorry." [Mello Yello; in her best consoling tone]

"Different people have different paths." [Dr Pepper; speaking as sweetly as I'd ever heard]

"We can cry and hold hands when you're done. Come on, my man. Finish the job." [Cherry Coke; urgent, no jokes now]

"What did you say to her?"

This time not one of them spoke. I looked at the open window. How far could she have gone in just a few minutes?

"What did you say?!"

"Come on. Don't lose sight of what's important." [Cherry Coke; working my last nerve]

"All right then, captain. I'll do my duty."

I picked up the lighter and set fire to one roll of newspaper after another. They lit quick. Then I picked up the bag of cans, upturned it, and spread them all over the carpet. Last I flicked Dr Pepper, Mello Yello, and Cherry Coke into the flames.

"Wait. You're not done." [Mello Yello; the only one whose destruction I regretted]

I walked to the window. "I'm done all right."

As bad as things were, they instantly became worse. The last thing I saw before I went out the window was my reflection in the little television on the bookshelf.

At least I thought it was my reflection. But the television had been left on. It wasn't my reflection, it was my face. A mug shot from years ago, but that was me all the same.

A muted newscaster spoke, but I didn't need to hear her words. A scroll ran across the bottom of the screen: "Fingerprints found on an incendiary device . . ."

Coke bottle had ratted me out!

I didn't climb out the window, I fell out the window. Landed in the cold hard alley, and the mosque had already started coughing up smoke. Then I shut my eyes, and when I opened them again, well, I wasn't in New York.

11

UY Scuti sits in the Scutum constellation. Scutum is Latin for shield.

"We're farther away from it now," I said. I stood at the viewing station, but I wasn't alone. Behind, beside me, there were others, but I couldn't turn away from the sight of the star. I had the impression the others wouldn't let me turn either. As if I wasn't prepared to see them yet. But if not now, when?

[It's collapsing.]

[When it becomes a supernova, we'll recharge the cells.]

"The cells in your bodies?" I asked.

[No. In our vessel.]

The viewing station appeared, to me, like a soap bubble, tethered by a walkway that seemed as fine as fishing line. We were inside the bubble, at a distance from a ship. Or no. Something too massive to be described as a *ship*. The bubble extended and floated at a distance so our readings would not be disturbed by the vessel's frequencies.

"I want to see it collapse," I said. "I want to stay. Let me stay," I begged.

[You aren't even here yet, Signalman. This isn't a trip your body can make on its own.]

"But I'm alone," I said.

I thought they would reassure me, maybe embrace me. But how could they? By the time I'd finished my last sentence, I was no longer *there*. I found myself at the subway station at One Hundred Twenty-Fifth Street. I found a payphone and called about the fire. Then I descended the stairs into the subway.

I didn't have Kim, I didn't have my cans, and on top of all that, apparently, I was now a wanted man.

12

Then I find Kim sitting in a fucking chicken wing joint down in Greenwich Village.

Chowing down like nothing was wrong.

This motherfucker.

I mean, how am I going to feel like I'm both Thelma *and* Louise, and you're ordering yourself a dozen buffalo wings?

This was at the Pluck U on Thompson Street. I'd fled Harlem but only made it this far before I ran out of ideas for where to hide. And then, there she was.

I entered the place and caused less of a fuss than I used to do. I mean, I took up less space. No bag full of cans, but that's not all it was. I shrank myself. Head down, no yelling. It was a small restaurant, a place where you order at the counter, so there was no hostess to stop my progress. Probably the only barrier between me and her was all the damn noise from the television hanging on a wall. Loud as hell, playing local news. Might only be a matter of minutes before they threw my face on the screen again. But I still had to ask Kim why she'd left me behind.

I walked in, sat down across from her, speechless.

Meanwhile she is *killing* those wings. Paying me no notice, not until the meal is complete. Then she looks up at me, so satisfied, and licks every one of her fingers clean. Then she leaned across the tabletop and wrapped her arms around my neck.

"I found you!" [Kim; smelling of hot sauce and something else, a scent I couldn't place]

I pulled away. "You left me."

Kim used a wet wipe on her fingers, almost like she hadn't heard me. But after a moment she leaned back, smacked by the revelation.

"They didn't tell you."

But before I could ask her anything more, the broadcaster on the screen cut in.

"New leads in a series of hate crimes across the city. Police have released information about a suspect wanted for arson."

The reporter continued to read, but I no longer heard the words. The same mug shot. How long before someone else in here realized that man was me? Kim turned her head, saw the news footage, and dropped her smile. She pushed her chair back so hard, it fell over. The customers in line, the cashier, they all looked our way.

"You can't be in here if you're not a customer!" [The cashier; waving for backup from the kitchen]

Kim grabbed my hand and leaned close.

"I've got a plan." [Kim; grinning with purpose]

We stepped onto Thompson Street and headed west. Sullivan. MacDougal. We got over to Bleecker Street and headed north. We passed pizza shops and bars, and I had the impression that I'd become the lead story in every one. My face flashed on every screen. For one day, or at least one hour, I had become the most famous man in New York.

"Where are we going? A bus out of the Port Authority? If they're showing my picture on TV, then they'll have the buses covered."

She didn't answer, just kept yanking me along.

"Same thing with the trains. I think I'll stand out on an Amtrak."

Bleecker led to Ninth Avenue, and still we kept going north. We were around Fourteenth by now. Were we going to walk all the way out of New York?

"Wait!" I shouted. "Wait."

Middle of the night, Ninth Avenue, and there were still a decent number of people around. More than enough to make a call to the cops. But I didn't care. Before I'd follow her one more step, I had to know. So I stopped walking, and when she tried to pull me forward, I wouldn't move.

"You have to tell me," I said. "Why did you go? Where did you go?"

Kim could see I wouldn't be moving again. Not without some kind of concession.

"Will you walk while I tell you?" [Kim; looking from me up to the skies]

"Yes," I said. "Tell me."

13

"UY Scuti is the largest star in our galaxy. A red supergiant. I know you've seen it, because they told me so. But you haven't been there. I mean, touching your feet down on a solid surface. But I've done that. I've been there. The Astral City. The place I now call home. The place *we* will now call home.

"I'm sorry I left without saying good-bye. I hope you can forgive me. But I came back for you. Though not only you. My job now wouldn't be possible if you hadn't reduced the background noise, the spiritual interference. I was standing in that office with you and for the first time in my life I heard their transmission. You are responsible for that, and I thank you. *They* thank you. They're proud of you. Do you know that?

"Lots of people would call them gods, but that's not what they call themselves. They are the Pathfinders. Twenty altogether. I have seen their true faces. I have heard their true voices. Wait until you hear them as they truly sound, not filtered through bottles and cans.

"They didn't understand how long it had been since they left. They saw their children, their land, broached from the west and the east. The continent we learned to call Africa, the place they knew only as the Center of the World, invaded by men who would enslave and indoctrinate. They decided to take us to the stars.

"I asked what took them so *long*. They said they'd just left! Gone ahead to prepare the Astral City, using as their models the great cities like Aksum, Lalibela, Djenne, Meroe. When I said it had been five hundred years since they left their children behind, they wept. It's strange to hear gods cry.

"Now look at you! Are you upset? About what part? Oh, I see. I see. Why did they pick me instead of you, that's what it is? Why did I receive the invitation? Well, I see human nature isn't going to change, whether down here or up in the stars. But cheer up, my love. Yes, I called you that. Cheer up.

"You can't travel to the Astral City without me. Each of us gets the job that suits us. You have been used to hearing the voices others can't hear. They called you crazy for it, but you were just more *aware*. That's why you're the Signalman.

"Well, traveling the path between Earth and the Astral City requires someone special too. Someone used to navigating between a world where they're understood and a world where they're misjudged. Someone like me. That's why I'm the Pilot.

"So come with me. Let's walk together in the Astral City. The Pathfinders want to touch your face, to embrace you. They've missed you. And so have I." [Kim; the love of my life]

14

We reached the piers, along the West Side. Chelsea Piers is where the *Titanic* had been destined to dock before it met that iceberg.

How can I explain the absolute certainty I felt that Kim had told me the truth? It helped that I'd been hearing the signal for so long, of course, but it was more than that. Her voice seemed to play three different notes at once, glorious chords that reminded me of the voices I'd been hearing all these years. Mello Yello,

Cherry Coke, Dr Pepper, Coke bottle. I couldn't wait to meet them in person and to speak their true names.

Out here there was only the sound of the waves slapping against the old wooden stumps jutting from the water. They hadn't been real piers in far too long.

Kim looked down the block, into the dark corners. "I went on more than a few trips around here, let me tell you." [Kim; laughing and speaking more to herself than to me]

"Bet you never guessed that at some point you'd be ferrying people to the stars," I said.

Now she looked at me. Grinning. "And this is only the beginning."

She leaned toward me, and I knew what she was going to do, but I still couldn't believe it was about to happen. It seemed even less likely than finding out you are loved by your gods.

"Is it going to hurt?" I asked, looking up to the night sky.

"Hurt? Why would it hurt? It's just a kiss."

Ruler of the Rear Guard

The cold stone of what remained of the ledge of a window of a slave dungeon chilled Sylvonne Butcher. The previous night she'd had a nightmare, having fallen asleep in the same clothes she'd traveled from the United States in and collapsed on the bed as soon as her host family showed her where it was. Only snippets of images from her nightmare remained. The leering faces. The claustrophobic swell of bodies pressing in on her, lost in a forest whose trees moved to block her way. By the morning, the only thing left behind was the lingering fear. Which she thought she had left behind in America.

The world of Ghana, however, was a dream. Endless skies dotted with patches of clouds stretched above her. A series of drones flew by in a patrol. One hovered overhead. She held up two fingers in a V to bid it "Deuces" and it departed. Sipping lamugin, the bite of lemony ginger soothed her while she listened to the birds. The breeze was a velvet finger caressing her face, though she was happy not to have to wear a rebreather mask like she did in Indianapolis. The oxygenators covered her entire face and she resented how it clutched to her mouth even though she needed its protection against the hazy quality of her hometown's air. Environmental collapse had taken a toll in a lot of western countries, but not here.

The Castelo de São Jorge da Mina was originally constructed

in 1481 and later rechristened Elmina Castle. There was a heavy spirit about the place. A powerful presence, the call of many souls crying out for home. Lost and searching. The sensation dogged her steps as she walked back to the house of the Pan-African Coordination Committee host family who sponsored her. The whole family had awoken to greet her when she first stirred from her rest before they scurried off to work, leaving her in the hands of the oldest son.

"Good morning." Kobla Annan bowed, the sleeves of his white tunic stamped with indigo Adinkra symbols. Taking her glass from her, he offered her a bowl of Hausa koko, a spicy millet porridge, and maasa, a pile of maize fritters. The family shared what they had with enthusiasm, rising to attend to her before she even knew what to ask for. "We're honored to have a student from the Thmei Academy with us."

"The honor is all mine, believe me. Thank you for hosting me. It's very generous of you." She waved him off. The idea of people going so far out of their way for her put her on edge. She couldn't help but feel like she was imposing.

"Aren't you hungry? If it's the food you don't like, we have a Burger King in the city." Though she also detected a mirthful sarcasm to his tone, he smiled enthusiastically, trying to be helpful. "And a KFC! To comfort a delicate palate that's attempting to acclimate."

The words still had a bit of a sting to them. Sylvonne turned off her reflex to not be her full self. That ingrained way of cutting off part of who she was to make another culture comfortable. Too often that wasn't reciprocated, with that culture never giving two thoughts about her comfort. Here, she was a repatriate, returning to her ancestral home, moving forward through—not just away from—her problems.

Relenting to his overwhelming hospitality, she scooted her chair to the table. She blew on the first bite of the porridge, an excuse to bring the food closer to her nose, before chancing a bit of it. She canted her head in approval. "You seem awfully young to be part of the PACC."

"Father always says, 'If you're old enough to form a sentence, you're old enough to speak out.'" Kobla straddled the chair across from her. "Besides, you're not much older."

"A few years makes all the difference at our age." She waved a fritter about, using it as a pointer between bites. "Your English is …elegant."

"We haven't employed our systems AI as universal translators. We're still, how do you say, old school in that way. In Wagadu, we speak English as a courtesy. I also speak Akan, Yoruba, and am working on Wolof." Kobla's generation kept referring to Ghana as Wagadu. "My father speaks Ewe, Swahili, and enough Kikongo to do business. What about you?"

"I speak American." Sylvonne tapped her chin in consideration. "And hood."

Kobla threw his head back in laughter. "So, Miss Sylvonne Butcher, I know you have only been here a day, but I was curious: What gift do you have to offer the community?"

"That's not exactly a small-talk question," Sylvonne said over a mouthful of fritter.

"I leave small talk for small people. I'm interested in you." Kobla leaned forward like a proctor taking keen interest in his test questions. "What brings you to us? What are your talents and passions?"

"I don't know." Wondering if the PACC onboarding family thought the screening interview might go easier with someone closer to her age, Sylvonne started to form a better follow-up response. Something along the lines of wanting to live a life in service to a cause, to make the world a better place, but all of that felt pat and almost being disingenuous. Taking stock of herself, she couldn't list any discernable talent or skill. She only knew that she would suffocate in America, literally and figuratively. But also that something called her here. None of which meant she necessarily had anything to offer. All she knew was that she needed time to figure out what she wanted to do and who she wanted to be. "There's a greater conversation going on between Alkebulan and the Diaspora and I'm trying to find my place in it. I guess all I have to offer is just me. Is that okay?"

"That's a great answer." Kobla directed the kitchen bots to clear the dishes.

"I need to get to my orientation." Sylvonne dabbed her mouth with her napkin, tossing it in the empty bowl before a bot skittered away with it. "Maybe I'll have a better answer later."

Kobla bit into the last fritter. "Maybe tomorrow."

Jammed full of people, the tro tro was a brightly colored maglev train which snaked its way from Elmina to Accra. Not too long ago, she'd have ridden in a rust bucket on wheels that had no business running, a minibus taxi that rattled to a halt at each bus stop along its route. Though even as it sped along, it wasn't like there were scheduled arrival and departure times, so Sylvonne was quickly adapting to no longer being married to her clock. As people held on to straps or overhead bars, the mate wove about and under musty armpits collecting fares. Sylvonne let him know she was heading to the Marcus Garvey Guest House. Glancing at her up and down, he already understood her story and smiled.

The trip would take a half hour, but a vague unease filled her at the thought of nodding off to pass the time. Sylvonne's mother was born in Jamaica. Watching the scenery roll by, the winding trip of the tro tro reminded her of her mother's stories of the bus rides through their hills. Whipping through traffic and pedestrians, skirting the cliffs' edge, moving at breakneck speeds. Her mother also told tales of the fierce Maroon tribe who fought off the British and kept their cities out of the hands of colonizers.

Theirs was a storied history, a proud past. Meeting the man who would become her father, her mom left her home for love. Sylvonne fled hers for freedom.

The tro tro crawled into its station. Hawkers passed by with water and juice for sale, the exchanges happening through the open window. The mate called out, "W.E.B. Du Bois Memorial Centre for Pan African Culture."

"Bus stop!" Sylvonne yelled in response. She was picking up the customs quickly.

Accra was different than she imagined. She tired of the constant stress of LWB in America. Living While Black. The threat—that horror of existential ache—of the endless monochromatic aggression. So she set out to find something new. Stalls filled the open-air market, with red, yellow, or green disks spinning above each one, both fan and canopy. The smells of cooked meat or grilled vegetables caused her belly to rumble despite her breakfast. Musicians played while spontaneous dancing broke out if the spirit moved the people. The crowd pressed in all about her without them producing the sense of dread which had been coloring her feelings lately. Sylvonne loved seeing the black people on billboards, families, couples, just vibing and being. The smiling faces of random people passing her. In her mind, any place in the continent meant safaris, beaches, and potbellied children. All tribal clothes and no modern buildings. No air conditioning, just endless hot. She'd been made to think, conditioned to be ashamed of the African part of her.

Even as she walked about, her hair was done in a twist out with a flat twist in the front, yet no one wanted her to straighten it, make it more professional, or tried to touch it. A gold disc with a matching hoop drop dangled from her ear. Sunglasses covered most of her face, the tint filtering the world through her already unrealistic lens. She was surrounded by people who looked like her. Who didn't want her to become part of their assimilation construct. Who could provide her with a sense of authentic, black belonging.

As she milled about the market, she had a feeling she was being followed. Ghana wasn't perfect. Among the milling folks were Sons of Br'er Nansi, ready to "chop your money" and separate wallets from tourists. But she wasn't a tourist. She was a student of the Thmei Academy on a pilgrimage. She activated her wristband to display her orientation message; the letters scrolled by, a reassurance to occupy her as she walked.

PACC Wants You!

- *In 2019, Ghana called for the return of the African Diaspora.*
- *The year marked the 400th anniversary of the Dutch ship White Lion arriving in Jamestown in what would become Virginia.*
- *The beginning of the holocaust known as the Maafa.*
- *The delegates from the Pan-African Coordination Committee (PACC) have called to continue that homecoming conversation.*
- *PACC wants further collaboration between the countries on the African continent as well as the communities of the Diaspora.*

PACC rolled out a pathway to citizenship and a "Right to Abode Law" which allowed the Diaspora to settle, all towards building a strong, unified Alkebulan. What the brochures never explained was how the political winds fomented by the militias of ARM, the American Renaissance Movement—which sprang up like weeds in the United States—complicated such journeys. Listening to their rhetoric, they said the wrong parts out loud: They didn't want black people, but they didn't want to lose them either. Their compromise was to make it harder and harder for them to leave. However, Sylvonne was determined to claim her birthright, her heritage.

The W.E.B. Du Bois Memorial Centre for Pan African Culture consisted of four buildings: his home, an administrative building, the Marcus Garvey Guest House, and his tomb. Hard light constructs allowed her to interact with him, like a movie projection she could walk into. Snippets of him and Marcus Garvey, AI recreating them as holograms. She stopped at the statue, a bust the size of W.E.B. Du Bois.

"Pan-Africanism equals community. A shared story against the negativity of racial caste supremacy. We were once fierce and noble warriors. Now too many don't like to rock the boat. Too many stand ready to run home and hide in a cupboard rather than fight for their rights." Wrapped in black-and-gold kente cloth—with a matching stole—a tall man whose belly jiggled as he moved sidled up to her. He had the regal waft of privilege about him. A carefully trimmed close beard—his edges were clean and tight—though his face had the doughy quality of having been pampered for decades. "I'm Safo Atakora Asantehene, a board chief of the Bureau of State Acquisitions."

"I'm Sylvonne Butcher." She hated her name, finding the portmanteau of Sylvia and Yvonne—her grandmothers—more than a little cheesy. She also loved her name, with it being both unique and tying her to the family she knew. "I'm a black woman on sabbatical."

"There are no black people here." His lips peeled back to reveal rows of bleached white teeth, an affectation of his wealth. "We know who we are. Igbo. Akan. Ewe. And so on."

"If I'm not black, what am I?" She bristled. Too often she ran into those who questioned her blackness, her commitment to The Cause, because she didn't talk, act, or dress the way others defined blackness.

"You have had a lifetime being taught the illogic of race. You may spend a lifetime unlearning it. There was no such thing as Africa until Europeans showed up, either. Just imperial powers using the cover of wars for their land grabs, assuming control of Alkebulan history."

"Yes." Sylvonne stopped him before he asked. She was equally used to these kinds of insulting "black quizzes" to prove she was authentic. "What we named our continent. 'The Mother of Mankind.'"

"Exactly. Those powers not only changed our names, but they carved up the motherland according to a geography which matched their interests. Whenever they need to rebuild their economy, they do what they have always done: turn to us. Our mineral and agricultural wealth. Removing our chieftains and kings in favor of more . . . progressive forms of government under their control."

"Seriously, y'all need to work on your small talk. Maybe ease a sister into this." She took a step back in case he erupted in a case of full-blown Hotep. Or whatever the Alkebulan equivalent was.

"We don't have time to ease. We dare to dream. Big. If we are to forge a new African community, a United Empires of Africa—if we want to build a new world—we have to have a new way of doing things. We need to promote unity, cooperation, and action. Getting people to want to do what must be done. We must be prepared to defend ourselves because imperialism always finds its way to us."

"What would you have me do?"

"Relationships and time are critical to the work moving forward. It's important to know yourself. It's important to know your identity." A masked woman appeared, her robes fluttering with each step. Her wood headdress was carved into the image of a face, the nostrils pierced for her to see out of, though the nose shadowed her eyes. Bird's wings—an African gray parrot—formed the superstructure of the mask rising across either side of it to create a perch for the bowl cradled in it. Her hair a crown of long, gray braids. "Quit bending the poor child's ear, Safo."

"I was just making, uh, small talk until you arrived." Safo bowed, a stiff, awkward thing, stepping away from Sylvonne in the same movement. "How went your survey of the United States, Elder of the Night?"

"As always, the West views us with a mix of horror and disdain," she sniffed.

"And sympathy. Never forget they are always sympathetic."

"It's easier to do that than wrestle with this being a problem they are responsible for. Allow me to introduce myself to the girl." The mask turned away from him.

Dismissed, Safo scuttled toward the administrative building without another word.

"Men. Always so transactional. They see everyone as opportunities for weapons or wealth. The ways of our oppressors so deeply ingrained in them." The woman extended her hand. "You must forgive our security chief."

Sylvonne hesitated, but accepted her proffered hand. "Who are you?"

"That is the question you are asking yourself."

The woman brought her hands together. The dangling sleeves of her robe formed a curtain when they met. "I am the Ban mu Kyidomhene."

"That sounds more like a title than a name."

"It means 'Ruler of the Rear Guard.' It has become my name. The name I have chosen."

"What's with the mask?"

"We all wear masks. At least mine is visible."

"Are you my mentor?"

"That is the question before us both. I answered your call. Come, walk with me." Her arm swept in a direction for Sylvonne to lead.

The maze-like structure reminded her of a labyrinth. A winding path through a garden gilded with bright flowers; their placement had the intentionality of design behind it, a sculpture of petals. As they strolled, they passed through several gates. A calm settled into her, pieces of her slipping into place, but she still knew that something was missing. A fragment that her mind, her body, her soul, whatever that part of her was, didn't have the tools to recognize what was absent. Her mother often regaled her—mostly unwanted intrusions on early Saturday mornings as Sylvonne was trying to sleep—with stories of rising before sunrise to walk to the caves a few miles from her house to collect the water they would need for the day. She hung clothes on the line to dry long after the family could afford a washer and dryer simply because those were the old ways her mother knew. Sylvonne didn't know why that memory sprang so fully to mind right then.

"Where are we going?" Sylvonne slowed to make sure her pace matched the woman's.

"You can't know until you get there."

"It's not where you're from, it's where you're at."

"What?" The Ban mu Kyidomhene faced her.

"I was quoting Eric B. and Rakim. It sounded just as vaguely deep without meaning anything. I figured that was what we were doing."

"You're so . . . American." She said the word without heat of insult.

The path forked. The Ban mu Kyidomhene paused, waiting for Sylvonne to choose the direction. She went left. Loud birds chirred from the bushes. Sylvonne felt it again: the palpable sensation of authentic, black belonging. She didn't know how else to describe it. Give her that feeling that she was important. That she mattered. This was how it felt to be among her own people. Welcomed. She had come home. She knew it in her bones, the deep ancestral call in her soul. It hadn't always been this way. Her people fought and survived for her to return here. She wanted to keep it safe.

"Safo called you an Elder of the Night. That have anything to do with the mask?"

"I am of the order of the Iyami Aje. Both are titles of respect for a woman considered to be Aje, one who wields the power of womanhood. The Gelede mask symbolizes our society. Some even hold festivals to honor us, thankful for our protection and support."

"What power of womanhood?"

"To understand that you have to know our story. It is old, starting with Odu, the creator of the Universe and all that thrives in it. The only female among the three other male divinities. The other gods tried to create the world but failed. Only when they included her could the world be formed, since creation, childbirth, and protection was mostly the domain of women. From her, the womb of all origins, the life force breathed into all things and with a single oracular utterance—'Ase' the power to command, 'So be it'—created existence. 'Aje' became the word for us. A feared and revered term which our oppressors translated as 'witch' to demonize us. We are the creators and sustainers of life. Sometimes the destroyers."

"Destruction sounds like people ought to be scared of you."

"Destruction isn't always bad. Some things must be destroyed to be birthed on higher ground. That said, a mother is the guardian and protector of earth."

"So you have real . . ." Sylvonne's voice trailed off as her mind scrambled for the right word.

". . . magic?"

"No." She settled on a different one. "Power."

"Power is easy." The Ban mu Kyidomhene unclasped her hands. She waggled her fingers in a complex pattern. Light without heat trailed her fingers in a rainbow afterimage. When she closed her fingers into a fist, the light became a ball. She shoved it into the air. It dissipated in the sunlight above them. "I draw my power from the spirit of Nehanda, a mhondoro. A powerful and revered ancestral spirit. Her name means 'The beautiful one has arrived.' Mhondoro are particularly revered because they help people interpret the wishes and desire of our creator."

"What was that, a hologram? Activated by gestures, like keying in a program using sign language?"

"Our technology has come far. However, science is but diluted magic."

"Magic, huh?" Sylvonne rolled her eyes.

"You cannot give what you do not have. You cannot speak on what you do not know and have never been taught. According to our elders, the Iyami are neutral forces. They can work for the positive or the negative."

"Is this what I'm to become? Is there some sort of initiation?"

"No, my little, lost tourist."

"I'm not a tourist." Sylvonne spat the words out like a curse. "It's just . . ."

". . . a story."

"What?"

"Tell me the story. Of what made you uproot your life and come halfway across the planet in search of . . ."

"Home." Sylvonne slowed down. "My father born and raised on the east side of Indianapolis, where not even an ARM militia member was bold enough to set foot. But gentrification is the new colonization. ARM-backed politicians talked about his neighborhood like it was some savage wasteland, the streets turned over to animals. Neglecting the part of the story about the local government allowing the militia to cordon it off, set up checkpoints to detain citizens. It was easier to call us lazy and declare 'This is bad neighborhood.'"

The Ban mu Kyidomhene swayed back and forth, a reed caught up in an unfelt breeze. Though she produced no sound, Sylvonne had the distinct impression that she was humming. Or perhaps chanting.

"One day the sun set earlier than I expected. It was sometimes hard to tell what was encroaching night and what was pollution choking out light. These days we treated every town like it was a sundown town. Despite the empty storefronts, residents who took flight to suburbs, and the businesses who followed them and police and militia left behind them, everyone sang the same song. Spreading the myth of how well everyone got along. But we knew. We understood that we could pass through the streets by day—work and shop, certainly hand them our dollars—but had to be off them by nightfall. Otherwise, we risked being detained, arrested, beat, or . . . worse."

The Ban mu Kyidomhene wriggled her fingers. The surrounding bushes faded to black. Sylvonne was no longer sure she was on the path, but she kept walking, taking each step in faith.

"They caught me slipping. Only a few blocks from my house, my porch literally in sight, an ARM militia rolled up on me without warning. The men hopped down from their truck. An American flag, frayed from how it whipped about in the wind when they drove, dangled from the back. The men surrounded me."

With a fluid movement, the Ban mu Kyidomhene gestured. The drape of her sleeves a curtain drawing back. Sylvonne found herself surrounded by the men of ARM. A man in a baseball cap whose message she couldn't make out extinguished a cigarette under his heel before approaching her. His eyes full of anger and resentment.

"Their leader asked me if I was lost. When I told him 'no,' he demanded my identification, proof that I belonged there. They closed in on me, their bodies pressing so close I could smell the beer on their breath, the aroma of cigarette smoke bleaching their clothing. And the rush of authority they were drunk on. All eyes leering at me. No safety in any of them to ask for help. To trust that they had my best interest in mind, if I was a person in their minds at all. They could stop me on a whim. Corrupt police, judge, and law could remove me from my family. Their leader snapped my wallet shut and handed it back to me. Letting me know that they knew where I lived and I'd best make my way there directly if I knew what was good for me. That I'd do well to remember my place."

The Ban mu Kyidomhene raised her arm and lowered it again. When her improvised curtain fell, Sylvonne as a little girl stood there. Alone. Scared. Clutching a blanket desperately wrapped about her like a totemic shield against the harsh cold of night. Lost, unable to find her father. Unable to hear the stories of her mother. Untethered in the world.

"And I broke. I was tired of my body being weaponized against me. I didn't want my children to have to worry about looking over their shoulder worrying about the police or militias. I never wanted to be powerless again. So I quit."

The Ban mu Kyidomhene dropped her arms. Daylight chased away the darkness. "Your job?"

"No, the US."

"You quit the country? Can you do that?"

"I'm not sure. But I did."

"If you do not listen, you will feel! If you don't listen, life will teach you." The Ban mu Kyidomhene laughed, a sad, rueful thing. But she had stopped walking. Sylvonne studied the surrounding topiary. They were at the center of the labyrinth. A stone waterfall bubbled at the crossroads of several paths. "What would you do, what would you have done, if you'd had the power?"

"I would keep them from us." Sylvonne tapped her chin. "I

don't know, been a shield somehow. Keeping them away from our neighborhood. Us."

"They are always coming after us."

"That's why I left."

"What makes you think coming here will help?"

"They can't reach me here."

"Really? How did you and your people get 'there' in the first place? They'll always come for us. The question is what are you going to do about it?"

"I need to . . ."

The Ban mu Kyidomhene held up her hand to stop her. "There's the flaw in your strategy already."

Sylvonne reflected on her choice of the words. "We?"

The Ban mu Kyidomhene nodded.

"*We* need to become strong."

"*We* cannot compete with the West on their terms. They have a devouring serpent at their hands. A long, writhing army with nuclear missiles for fangs. So how do we do that?"

"I don't know." In her heart, Sylvonne just wanted to be able to laugh, dap folks up, and simply . . . exist. Without being seen as a threat. It was why she wished to return to where her people originated. "It's just, it's important to know where we came from. Find our roots. Find our history. Gain the sense of confidence that comes from being with those who share your story. That's what I want to join in on."

"Iyami choose who they want."

The Ban mu Kyidomhene filled a pot with water from the fountain crèche. "Not all women are prepared for such a journey. Few have the discipline or moral aptitude to walk the path. We Iyami Aje each have our own approach. These healing waters symbolize the primordial waters that protected every child in the womb. A mother is the first teacher. The first person you look upon when you are born." The Ban mu Kyidomhene poured a bowlful of water over Sylvonne. As the girl shivered, the Ban mu Kyidomhene refilled the bowl again, reciting words like an oath. "A mother experienced pain and a near-death experience in order to give us life. This is your inheritance. You are worth everything. Take the first step into being your full self."

A subtle agitation fluttered in Sylvonne's spirit. She felt whole, herself for the first time in a long time. "I need here. And here needs me."

"You have spoken a deeper truth. You have earned my face." With that, the Ban mu Kyidomhene lifted her mask. The woman's high cheekbones and wide nose gave her a regal bearing. Markings had been painted under her eye, almost like it could see into many realms and hearts. "One of the first things those on such a path often do is choose a new name for yourself. It is a promise you make to the creator, the story of yourself you present to the world."

Stories began, but they never truly ended. They simply went on, passed down from one generation to the next. Sometimes they wound back to their beginnings. Sylvonne studied the sky. The bright sun removed the chill from her bones. "Maybe tomorrow."

Biographical Notes

NANA KWAME ADJEI-BRENYAH, a New York native, won the PEN/Jean Stein Book Award for his first story collection, *Friday Black* (2018), and was named a National Book Award finalist for his first novel, the best-selling *Chain-Gang All-Stars* (2023). He is currently pursuing a "secret rap project," *The Pisces Sciatica*, while working on new fiction.

VIOLET ALLEN was born in Covington, Georgia, and lives in Chicago. She majored in classics at Princeton, where she also studied with Jeffrey Eugenides and Joyce Carol Oates. Since 2015, when her first story was published, her work has appeared in anthologies including *The Best American Science Fiction and Fantasy* (2017), *A People's Future of the United States* (2019), and *Out There Screaming: An Anthology of New Black Horror* (2023). She is currently at work on her first novel.

DAWOLU JABARI ANDERSON is more widely known as a painter than as a writer and has had work exhibited at the Whitney Museum, the High Museum (Atlanta), and, in his Houston hometown, at the Museum of Fine Arts, the Menil Collection, and the Art League. His experimental story-in-dialogue "Sanford and Sun" was first published in the influential anthology *Octavia's Brood: Science Fiction from Social Justice Movements* (2015).

JENNIFER MARIE BRISSETT was once an independent bookseller, the owner of Indigo Café and Books in Brooklyn, but began writing fiction after her store went out of business. Along with her short stories, she has published two acclaimed novels, *Elysium* (2014) and *Destroyer of Light* (2021), and is at work on a third, *Daughters of the Night*. She was born in London and now lives in New York City.

MAURICE BROADDUS, a teacher and librarian, has published the story collection *Voices of Martyrs* (2016); the novels *King Maker* (2010), *King's Justice* (2011), *King's War* (2011), *Pimp My Airship* (2019), and *Sweep of Stars* (2022); the novella *Sorcerers* (2020), currently being adapted for television by AMC Networks; and much more. He also edited and coedited several fiction anthologies, including the lauded *Dark Faith* series (2010–12), which explores the intersections of horror and religious faith. He is a longtime resident of Indianapolis.

TARA CAMPBELL, a graduate of the MFA program at American University and a former university admissions director, has published two ecofiction novels, *TreeVolution* (2016) and *City of Dancing Gargoyles* (2024); two hybrid collections of poetry and prose; and the story collections *Midnight at the Organporium* (2019) and *Cabinet of Wrath: A Doll Collection* (2021). She lives in Seattle and is fiction coeditor at *Barrelhouse*.

PHENDERSON DJÈLÍ CLARK, Dexter Gabriel by day, is a history professor at the University of Connecticut, author of *Jubilee's Experiment: The British West Indies and American Abolitionism* (2023). As Clark, Gabriel has published Nebula and Locus Award–winning stories and novellas, including "The Secret Lives of the Nine Negro Teeth of George Washington" (2018), *Ring Shout or, Hunting Ku Kluxes in the End Times* (2020), and "How to Raise a Kraken in Your Bathtub" (2023). His 2021 novel, *A Master of Djinn*, won Ignyte, Nebula, and Locus Awards.

CRAIG LAURANCE GIDNEY, a native of Washington, D.C., studied with Samuel R. Delany in college and has published three collections—*Sea, Swallow Me & Other Stories* (2008), *Skin Deep Magic* (2014), and *The Nectar of Nightmares* (2022)—as well as a young adult novel, *Bereft* (2013), and the horror/fantasy novel *A Spectral Hue* (2019). He is currently at work on a new novel, *Hairsbreadth*, and coedits *Baffling Magazine*, which specializes in queer speculative flash fiction.

NALO HOPKINSON blends science fiction, fantasy, and Afro-Caribbean folklore in her works, which include the Locus Award–winning novel *Brown Girl in the Ring* (1998) and World Fantasy Award–winning story collection *Skin Folk* (2001). In 2021, she was named a Nebula "Grand Master." She teaches creative writing at the University of British Columbia.

THADDEUS HOWZE is a U.S. Navy veteran and a founding member of the Oakland-based AfroSurreal Writers Workshop. He is the author of *Hayward's Reach: Tales of the Twilight Continuum* (2011) and the novella *Broken Glass* (2013). A new story collection, *Visiting Hours*, is currently in the works.

JUSTINA IRELAND, who cofounded the Black speculative fiction magazine *FIYAH* and served as its executive editor in 2017–18, won a Locus Award for her YA novel, *Dread Nation*, which reimagines the Civil War in a zombie-infested America. She followed it with *Deathless Divide* in 2020 and several novels contributing to the Star Wars universe. A former U.S. Army Arabic language specialist, she lives with her "husband, kid, and dog" in York, Pennsylvania.

N. K. JEMISIN is the winner of a Locus Award for her debut novel, *The Hundred Thousand Kingdoms* (2010), and in 2018 became the first writer to receive the Hugo Award for Best Novel three years in a row, for her Broken Earth trilogy (*The Fifth Season*, 2015; *The Obelisk Gate*, 2016; and *The Stone Sky*, 2017). She collected her stories in 2018 as *How Long 'Til Black Future Month*. Her most recent book is the Great Cities novel *The World We Make* (2022). She was born in Iowa City and is now based in Brooklyn.

ALAYA DAWN JOHNSON was born in Washington, D.C., and educated at Columbia University and the Universidad Nacional Autónoma de México. She has published four novels, including *Love Is the Drug* (2014), winner of the Andre Norton Award, and *Trouble the Saints* (2020), winner of a World Fantasy Award, as well as the short story collection *Reconstruction* (2020), which includes "A Guide to the Fruits of Hawai'i," winner of a 2015 Nebula Award. In 2022, she collaborated with Janelle Monáe on the title story in *The Memory Librarian, and Other Stories of Dirty Computer*. She now lives in Oaxaca, Mexico, with her partner, six dogs, and a horse.

VICTOR LAVALLE is the author, among other works, of the novels *The Ecstatic* (2002), *Big Machine* (2009), *The Devil in Silver* (2017), *The Changeling* (2017), and *Lone Women* (2023), and the novella *The Ballad of Black Tom* (2016), which reimagines H. P. Lovecraft's "Horror at Red Hook" from the perspective of a young Black man in Harlem. He has won the Shirley Jackson, British Fantasy, Stoker, World Fantasy, and American Book Awards. An adaptation of his novel *The Changeling* premiered on Apple TV+ in 2023. Raised in Queens, he now lives in the Bronx and teaches at Columbia University.

TOCHI ONYEBUCHI, the son of Nigerian immigrants, attended Yale, earned an MFA in screenwriting from NYU, and then graduated from Columbia Law School. In 2019, after a brief career in civil rights and corporate law, he turned to writing full-time. Along with the YA novels *Beasts Made of Night* (2017), *Crown of Thunder* (2018), *War Girls* (2019), and *Rebel Sisters* (2020), he has published the World Fantasy Award–winning novella *Riot Baby* (2020), the novel *Goliath* (2022), and a book of autobiographical criticism, *(S)kinfolk* (2021), as well as many short stories. He has also worked on Black Panther and Captain America comics projects. He lives in Connecticut.

An Owomoyela has published stories in *Apex*, *Asimov's Science Fiction*, *Clarkesworld*, and *Lightspeed*, and often appears in *The Year's Best Science Fiction & Fantasy* collections. A former fiction editor for *Strange Horizons*, they are a software engineer living in the San Francisco Bay Area.

Sofia Samatar is a poet, critic, multilingual scholar, and writer of speculative fiction. She has published two novels, *A Stranger in Olondria* (2013), winner of a World Fantasy Award, and *The Winged Histories* (2016); the story collection *Tender* (2017); a travel memoir, *The White Mosque* (2022); and most recently *Opacities*, a book about writing, publishing, and friendship. She currently teaches at James Madison University and lives in Virginia.

Kiini Ibura Salaam won the James Tiptree Jr./Otherwise Award for her debut story collection, *Ancient, Ancient* (2012). She followed it with *When the World Wounds* (2016) and the YA novel *When the World Turned Upside Down* (2021). In 2023, with Khadijah Queen, she coedited *Infinite Constellations: An Anthology of Identity, Culture, and Speculative Conjunctions*. She works as a book editor and lives in Brooklyn.

Rion Amilcar Scott has published two award-winning story collections, *Insurrections* (2016) and *The World Doesn't Require*

You (2019), both set in the fictional town of Cross River, Maryland, which was founded after a successful slave revolt in 1807. His story "Shape-ups at Delilah's" originally appeared in *The New Yorker.* He teaches English at the University of Maryland and lives in Annapolis.

ALEX SMITH is a cofounder of the Philadelphia science fiction collective Metropolarity and a vocalist and lyricist for the punk bands Rainbow Crimes and Solarized. He is the author of *Arkdust* (2018), a story collection that combines fantasy, horror, and sci-fi. He has also recently collaborated with artist James Dillenbeck on the comic book series *Black Vans* (2021–) and has published new work in the anthology *Black Punk Now* (2023). He lives in Philadelphia.

Notes

In the notes below, the reference numbers denote the page and line of this volume (the line count includes headings but no blank lines).

5.2   "Herbal"] When she included this story in her 2015 collection, *Falling in Love with Hominids*, Hopkinson introduced it as follows: "I was once talking online with a group of writers and writing students about tactics for suspending the reader's disbelief in the fantastical elements of a story. I found myself typing something to the effect that one possible strategy was to never give the reader the time to disbelieve. Start the story with a bang, I wrote. Have an elephant . . . then I realized I had a story. I got off the Internet and wrote 'Herbal.'"

50.15   Honouliuli] A World War II internment camp on Oahu, open from 1943 to 1946. It held more than 300 Japanese and Japanese American civilian internees, and more than 4,000 prisoners of war.

81.2   Sanford and Sun] This story imagines an appearance, on the TV sitcom *Sanford and Son* (1972–77), of the avant-garde Afrofuturist bandleader and composer Sun Ra (Herman Poole Blount, 1914–1993), who led the Sun Ra Arkestra from the mid-1950s until his death. Junk dealer Fred G. Sanford was the show's title character, Grady Wilson one of his friends, Lamont his son, and Rollo Lawson his son's friend.

84.18–19   Dock Ellis] Ellis (1945–2008) played baseball for the Pittsburgh Pirates and other major league teams.

88.1–4   *If I didn't . . . this way*] From "If I Didn't Care," a 1939 song written by Jack Lawrence and first recorded by The Ink Spots.

88.16–19   *The five o'clock . . . all night long*] From "Five O'Clock Whistle," a 1941 Ella Fitzgerald song.

97.8   Monty Hall] Hall hosted the TV game show *Let's Make a Deal* from 1963 to 1986.

98.13–16   *Hereby . . . space world.*] From Sun Ra and His Arkestra's "Enlightenment," first released on *Jazz in Silhouette* (1959).

105.1–2   my leader . . . some tapes] The existence of tapes of President Nixon in conversation with members of his administration and staff was revealed during the Watergate scandal of 1973–74 and led to his resignation.

123.14   Attar's *Conference of the Birds*] A Persian poem (1177 CE) by the Sufi mystic Attar of Nishapur (Farid ud-Din Attar, c. 1145–c. 1221).

125.4–5   Rabi . . . into you."] From a speech Rabi gave at the Boston Institute for Religion and Social Studies on January 3, 1946.

126.1–2   J. Robert Oppenheimer . . . cannot lose."] From "Physics and the Contemporary World," a lecture Oppenheimer presented at the Massachusetts Institute of Technology on November 25, 1947.

126.11   Abba Moses . . . teach you."] Abba Moses (330–405 CE), an ascetic priest of Roman Egypt also known as Moses the Black or Moses the Ethiopian, is quoted in the fifth-century *Apophthegmata Patrum* (*Sayings of the Desert Fathers*).

131.8   Maenad Sicagi] In Greek mythology, the Maenads (literally, "raving ones") were followers of Dionysus, often seen dancing and intoxicated; *Sicagi* is Latin for "of Chicago."

132.8–10   *We know that the tail . . . Art?*] See Rudyard Kipling's poem "The Conundrum of the Workshops," first collected in *Barrack-Room Ballads and Other Verses* (1892).

133.6   The center . . . fall apart.] From William Butler Yeats's poem "The Second Coming," first published in 1920.

143.30   "Lost in the Funhouse"] The title story of a 1968 collection by John Barth (1930–2024).

148.18   Barth . . . exhausting.] Barth's essay "The Literature of Exhaustion" appeared in the April 1967 issue of *The Atlantic.*

158.30   full Morrison] In the style of Toni Morrison (1931–2019).

162.8–9   Ibani . . . Bonny Land] A traditional sovereign state in the Niger delta, centered on what is now Bonny, Nigeria.

164.31   obeah] Sorcery, witchcraft, or folk medicine as practiced in the British Caribbean.

166.14   gris-gris] An amulet consisting of a piece of paper inscribed with text and placed in a cloth bag.

193.15   Omelas] See Ursula K. Le Guin's story "The Ones Who Walk Away from Omelas," first published in 1973.

248.10   George Jefferson] Protagonist of the TV sitcom *The Jeffersons* (1975–85), played by Sherman Helmsley.

252.2   brolic] Having an extremely muscular physique.

256.2   kanafeh] A popular Middle Eastern dessert made of cheese and spun phyllo pastry, soaked in sweet syrup.

261.24   George Zimmerman] In February 2012, Zimmerman (b. 1983) shot and killed an unarmed Black teenager, Trayvon Martin (1995–2012), in Sanford, Florida; at his trial, he claimed to have been acting in self-defense, and was acquitted of second-degree murder and manslaughter charges.

280.23   *Mahogany*] 1975 film directed by Berry Gordy, Tony Richardson, and Jack Wormser and starring Diana Ross, Billy Dee Williams, and Anthony Perkins.

290.11–12   HeLa cells] Cells from a line cultivated in vitro, for use in medical research, since 1951, when they were taken from an African American cancer patient, Henrietta Lacks, without her knowledge or consent.

331.5   Aksum, Lalibela, Djenne, Meroe] Ancient African cities, Aksum and Lalibela in what is now Ethiopia, Djenne in Mali, and Meroe in Sudan.

334.10   Adinkra symbols] Traditional Ghanaian symbols, often signifying particular concepts or proverbs and commonly seen on clothing or in architecture.

340.19   Hotep] An African American subculture inspired by visions of ancient Egypt as a wellspring of Black culture.

342.22–24   *"It's not where . . . Rakim.*] From "In the Ghetto," a song on the Eric B. & Rakim album *Let the Rhythm Hit 'Em* (1990).

Sources & Acknowledgements

The stories in this book have been arranged in chronological order of first publication. They have been reprinted from these first publications, except where their authors later collected them in books of their own, with an opportunity to correct and revise.

Nana Kwame Adjei-Brenyah. The Hospital Where. *Friday Black* (Houghton Mifflin, 2018), 67–84. Copyright © 2018 by Nana Kwame Adjei-Brenyah. Used by permission of HarperCollins Publishers and Quercus UK.

Violet Allen. The Venus Effect. *Lightspeed*, December 2016. https://www.lightspeedmagazine.com/fiction/the-venus-effect/. Copyright © 2016 by Violet Allen. Reprinted with permission of author.

Dawolu Jabari Anderson. Sanford and Sun. *Octavia's Brood: Science Fiction Stories from Social Justice Movements*, Walidah Imarisha and Adrienne Maree Brown, eds. (AK Press, 2015), 145–66. Copyright © 2015 by Dawolu Jabari Anderson. Reprinted with permission of AK Press.

Jennifer Marie Brissett. A Song for You. *Terraform*, May 11, 2015. https://www.vice.com/en/article/a-song-for-you/. Copyright © 2015 by Jennifer Marie Brissett. Reprinted with permission of the author.

Maurice Broaddus. Ruler of the Rear Guard. *Africa Risen: A New Era of Speculative Fiction*, Sheree Renée Thomas, Oghenechovwe Donald Ekpeki, and Zelda Knight, eds. (Tor, 2022), 205–20. Copyright © 2022 by Broad Futures LLC. Reprinted with permission of the author.

Tara Campbell. The Orb. *Black Sci-Fi Short Stories*, Tia Ross, ed. (Flame Tree, 2021), 38–47. Copyright © 2021 by Tara Campbell. Reprinted with permission of the author.

Phenderson Djèlí Clark. The Secret Lives of the Nine Negro Teeth of George Washington. *Fireside Magazine*, February 2018. https://fire-sidefiction.com/the-secret-lives-of-the-nine-negro-teeth-of-george-washington. Copyright © 2018 by Phenderson Djèlí Clark. Reprinted with permission of Fireside Magazine and the author.

Nalo Hopkinson. Herbal. *Falling in Love with Hominids* (Tachyon, 2015), 111–14. First published in *The Bakka Anthology*, Kristen Pederson Chew, ed. (Bakka Books, 2002). Copyright © 2002 by Nalo Hopkinson. Reprinted with permission of the author.

Thaddeus Howze. Bludgeon. *Mothership: Tales from Afrofuturism and Beyond*, Bill Campbell and Edward Austin Hall, eds. (Rosarium, 2013), 41–50. Copyright © 2013 by Thaddeus Howze. Reprinted with permission of the author.

Craig Laurance Gidney. Spyder Threads. *The Nectar of Nightmares: Stories* (Underland Press, 2022), 106–15. First published as *Spyder Threads* (Tor Nightfire, 2021). Copyright © 2022 by Craig Laurance Gidney. Reprinted with permission of Underland Press and the author.

Justina Ireland. Calendar Girls. *A People's Future of the United States*, Victor LaValle and John Joseph Adams, eds. (One World, 2019), 191–204. Copyright © 2019. Reprinted with permission of the author.

N. K. Jemisin. The Ones Who Stay and Fight. *How Long 'Til Black Future Month* (Orbit, 2018), 1–13. Copyright © 2018 by N. K. Jemisin. Reprinted with permission of Orbit, an imprint of Hachette Book Group, Inc. and Little Brown Book Group Limited.

Alaya Dawn Johnson. A Guide to the Fruits of Hawai'i. *Reconstruction* (Small Beer, 2020), 1–35. First published in *Magazine of Fantasy & Science Fiction*, July–August 2014. Copyright © 2014. Reprinted with permission of the author.

Victor LaValle. *We Travel the Spaceways. We Travel the Spaceways* (Amazon Original Stories, 2021). First published in *Black Stars*, Amazon Original Stories, in coordination with Plympton. Copyright © 2021 by Victor LaValle. Reprinted with permission of the author.

Tochi Onyebuchi. Habibi. *A Universe of Wishes*, Dhonielle Clayton, ed. (Crown, 2020), 361–92. Copyright © 2020 by Tochi Onyebuchi. Reprinted with permission of the author.

An Owomoyela. All That Touches the Air. *Lightspeed*, April 2011. https://www.lightspeedmagazine.com/fiction/all-that-touches-the-air/. Copyright © 2011 by An Owomoyela. Reprinted with permission of the author.

Kiini Ibura Salaam. The Malady of Need. *When the World Wounds* (Third Man Books, 2016), 1–6. Copyright © 2016 by Kiini Ibura Salaam. Reprinted with permission of Third Man Books.

Sofia Samatar. Tender. *Tender: Stories* (Small Beer, 2017), 115–24. First published in *OmniVerse*, August 2015. Copyright © 2015 by Sofia Samatar. Reprinted with permission of Small Beer Press.

Rion Amilcar Scott. Shape-ups at Delilah's. *The New Yorker*, October 7, 2019, 56–64. Copyright © 2019 by Rion Amilcar Scott. Reprinted with permission of the author.

Alex Smith. The Final Flight of Unicorn Girl. *Arkdust* (Rosarium, 2018), 9–21. Copyright © 2018 by Alexander Smith. Reprinted with permission of the author.

The text in this book is set in 11 point Kepler, one of the many popular fonts designed by Robert Slimbach in his more than thirty years at Adobe Inc. Named after the German Renaissance astronomer Johannes Kepler and first released in 1996, the typeface family now includes 168 variations of differing weight and width; this book uses Standard Light for the text and two Extended options for the display type. Inspired by various classic fonts of the eighteenth century, Slimbach attempted to capture their "modern style in a humanistic manner . . . with a hint of old-style proportion and calligraphic detailing."

The paper is an acid-free Forest Stewardship Council–certified stock that exceeds the requirements for permanence of the American National Standards Institute. Text design and composition by Gopa & Ted2, Inc., Albuquerque, New Mexico. Printing and binding by Versa Press, Inc., Peoria, IL.